PRAISE FOR DEE HENDERSON'S
TRUE DEVOTION

"Dee Henderson has done a splendid job mixing romance with the fast-paced action of a Navy SEAL platoon."

STEVE WATKINS, FORMER NAVY SEAL

"Action, adventure, and romance! *True Devotion* has everything a reader could want!"

ANGELA ELWELL HUNT, BESTSELLING AUTHOR OF *THE NOTE*

"[Dee Henderson] has created a truly stunning tale of love and devotion to God, country, and to those left behind when the missions are done."

COMPUSERVE REVIEWS

"A wonderful story with real and entertaining characters. Ms. Henderson's gift with words makes this book impossible to put down."

WRITER'S CLUB ROMANCE GROUP ON AOL

"Definitely a must read for all lovers of suspense and military heroes!"

ROMANCE COMMUNICATIONS ONLINE

"Dee Henderson and *True Devotion* earn my first platinum medal for excellence."

BRIDGES MAGAZINE

"Dee Henderson delivers an uncommonly good story with grace and style."

ROMANCEJOURNAL.COM

READERS' PRAISE

"I served in the U.S. Navy during Desert Storm, and your book is one of the best books I have read in a long time! Can't wait for the next Uncommon Heroes book!"—M. M.

"My husband is in the Air Force so it is nice to read military stories that are based in reality!"—R. G.

"You have an amazing ability to weave a tale about Christians struggling to make sense out of their lives and the curve balls they're thrown. The Scripture verses used throughout the story are well placed and fit the story masterfully."—K. R.

"I have just finished reading your book *True Devotion*. I thought it was one of the best Christian romance adventure books I have ever read. I look forward to reading more of your books."

"I couldn't put down *True Devotion*. I've read it twice already and I have only had it a week. My husband was in the Navy for six years, and this book just touched my heart. I can't wait for the next one."—M. K.

"Thank you for sharing your gift and love of God!"—S. H.

TRUE

VALOR

DEE HENDERSON

Multnomah®Publishers *Sisters, Oregon*

TRUE VALOR
published by Multnomah Publishers, Inc.
© 2002 by Dee Henderson

International Standard Book Number: 0-7394-2370-3

Cover design by Chris Gilbert/UDG DesignWorks
Cover images by Aleta Rafton
Illustration of seal © 2001 by Dawson 3D, Inc.

Scripture quotations are from: *The Holy Bible,* Revised Standard Version (RSV)
© 1946, 1952 by the Division of Christian Education
of the National Council of the Churches of Christ
in the United States of America

Multnomah is a trademark of Multnomah Publishers, Inc., and is registered in the U.S. Patent and Trademark Office.
The colophon is a trademark of Multnomah Publishers, Inc.

Printed in the United States of America

GLOSSARY

AAA: AntiAircraft Artillery.

Afterburner: Extra fuel injected into the hot exhaust gas of an aircraft for added thrust.

Angels: Altitude in thousands of feet. "Angels 10" indicates 10,000 feet of altitude.

AWACS: Airborne Warning And Control System. Aircraft fitted with long-range radar that provides tactical and target information to air and ground control units.

Bingo fuel: Not enough fuel to return to a location.

C-130: Air Force transporter for a long haul.

Chaff: A small cloud of thin pieces of metal, such as tinsel used to confuse enemy radar and divert a radar-guided missile away from the plane.

CO: Commanding Officer.

F/A-18 Hornet: Navy fighter aircraft used for air and ground offensive strikes.

FOD: Foreign Objects on the Deck of an aircraft carrier that can damage planes.

G: Gravitational force through acceleration.

GPS: Global Positioning System. Satellite guidance around earth used to precisely pinpoint aircraft, ships, vehicles, and ground troops.

HARM: High-speed, Anti-Radiation Missile. Missile whose seeker head homes in on radar-emitting sources.

IFF: Identification Friend or Foe. A coded message sent to a target's IFF transponder.

Jink: Erratic flight maneuver(s), dodge, slip, etc.

LSO: Landing Signal Officer.

MiGs: Russian-built fighter jet, used in many nations around the world.

Nugget: A new pilot in the air wing on his first sea cruise.

PJ: Pararescue Jumper.

PT: Physical Training.

EA-6B Prowler: Navy aircraft used to map enemy radar and suppress them.

Roger: A yes, an affirmative, a go answer to a command or statement.

SAM: Surface-to-Air Missile.

SEAL: One of the elite branches of the U.S. Special Forces operating from the sea, air, or land.

Sidewinder: Heat-seeking (infrared) missile.

TDY: Temporary DutY assigned outside of normal job designation.

XO: eXecutive Officer.

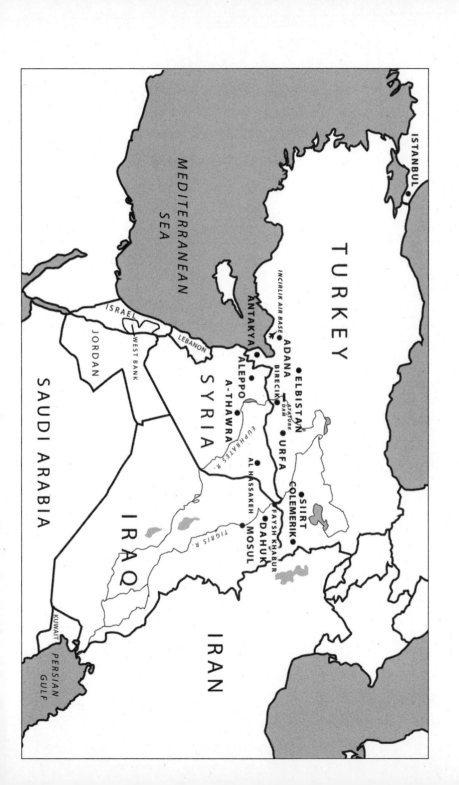

Peace I leave with you; my peace I give to you;

not as the world gives do I give to you.

Let not your hearts be troubled, neither let them be afraid.

JOHN 14:27

PROLOGUE

★ ★ ★

"I t won't fly."

Grace rescued the airplane for her younger cousin from where it had crashed into the tile around the backyard pool, smoothing out the smashed nose of the plane. "It didn't have enough lift under its wings," she encouraged, seeing the problem. She carefully folded stabilizers on the wingtips. "Try again."

Tom took the plane. She bit her lip as he swung himself up into the old oak tree. Spring leaves hid him from sight. He reappeared straddling the big limb that held the rope swing. He was determined to get his plane to fly farther than hers. He tossed the plane with so much force it hurdled toward the ground until the aerodynamics took over and the plane lifted and suddenly soared. "Yes!"

Grace smiled as she turned on her heels to watch it fly. He'd been smart to launch it from high up. Hers had skimmed the swimming pool, just about landing in the shallows, and finally settled under the potted planter beside the patio table. Tom's plane rolled to the right as it neared the backyard fence. She frowned. She must have made one stabilizer longer than the other.

"Did your mom say yes to the lesson?"

Grace turned to look up at her cousin and tilted her head, as he was now hanging upside down like a monkey. "She said maybe."

He stopped his swinging and looked at her for a moment. "Better than a no."

It was better than a no. But it was still frustrating. She'd been trying to talk her mom into letting her have pilot lessons this summer. She was almost fourteen; she was eligible for the lessons. Her dad had said yes. But her mom was holding out.

Dad. Her favorite man. She had buried her nose in his burly chest in thanks when he said yes and she embarrassed him. He talked so often about flying, telling his war stories about his days in Vietnam flying off a carrier. He talked about the dogfights and nursing his plane back to the base with bullet holes in the wings, and he laughed at the risks and the belief he had been invincible.

She wanted to be like her dad. The Navy wouldn't let her fly the jets like she dreamed of doing, but they would let her fly the big cargo planes, the fortresses in the sky that would mean landing at interesting airfields—short, rough surfaces in Third World countries—giving her a chance to fly to where the action was happening in the world. She really wanted to learn to fly. And while she couldn't solo until she was sixteen, she had several friends who had already started lessons. She just had to convince her mom.

"You can have my allowance to pay for the lessons."

"You give away your allowance too easily."

Tom climbed down from the tree. "You'd enjoy them. Want to go watch the planes at the airport?"

"Sure."

"I'll get us sandwiches. You tell your mom where we're going."

Tom would probably make them peanut butter and banana sandwiches, but she liked him enough she'd eat hers without comment. Her cousin was the brother she didn't have.

She went to find her mom. On Friday afternoon the current class of pilots in training often practiced their landings. If she watched closely, she could figure out what the pilots did right and wrong as they landed. If she couldn't take lessons, she was still determined to learn what she could through careful observation.

Tom was lucky he had been born a boy. He constantly got himself in and out of scrapes as he tried anything that sounded fun. She longed to have that same freedom. He'd probably grow up to be a baseball player or a coach or a sky diver, something outdoors and fun. Even though he was two years younger, she was trying to be more like him. Tom had figured out how to enjoy life. She wanted a big bite of life too, even if she was a girl.

"Are you coming?" Tom shouted at her.

"Coming!"

"I dare you to try."

Bruce looked at his friend and then back at the water around the end of the pier. It was murky. The storm in the gulf last night had churned up the silt. To find the tackle box washed off the pier during the storm would mean holding his breath and searching by feel while the waves tried to knock him into the posts. "Why don't you try?"

Scott dropped a pebble into the water and watched it disappear. "The PJs do it all the time."

"Not all the time," Bruce muttered, wishing Scott would leave his heroes out of it. Living next to a military base had given him a chance to meet over eighteen of the men he admired. They trained to rescue shot down pilots. He wanted to be a Pararescueman someday, but he didn't have to love water. He just had to figure out how not to be afraid of it.

The tackle box had probably popped open as it hit the bottom and spilled all their favorite lures across the seabed. The tides would have swept them around and the hooks would catch at his hands if he just felt around. Several years' worth of handmade lures had been in that tackle box. Recovering them mattered.

"I need a waterproof light," he decided. PJs went in prepared.

He wasn't going into that swirling water without being prepared. His friend looked disappointed. "I didn't say I wouldn't get it; I said I need a light." Their bikes were balanced at the end of the pier. "Come on. My dad will have one."

Scott turned back toward their bikes. Bruce paused to look one more time at the churning water. Scott was always pushing him to do hard things. He wanted to be able to do anything that had to be done, just like the PJs did. It just wasn't easy to be brave.

ONE

★ ★ ★

MARCH 4

NORFOLK, VIRGINIA

He stood out in his flannel shirt and jeans, but so far none of the sailors had made the mistake of assuming he was a civilian. Air Force Major Bruce "Striker" Stanton warily watched them continue to arrive and crowd into his sister's backyard, and he wondered how many sailors Jill had invited from the aircraft carrier USS *George Washington* to come to the predeployment party. It would be like her to invite them all so as not to leave anyone out. All five thousand plus of them.

He felt like he had invaded enemy country. The sailors, the average age of which was twenty-one, looked like children. They got younger every year. And those for whom this was their first six-month sea tour tended to travel together in clusters like penguins. A few of his friends cut from Air Force cloth were here but had long ago been swallowed up in the sea of white.

Striker maneuvered through guests to the chair he had staked out on the patio, doing his best to ignore the stab of pain from his right knee at every step. His dog was curled up asleep under the chair. Bruce used his left foot to push the dog's tail farther under the chair to protect it from being stepped on. A party, food, and many willing hands to offer treats, and what did his dog do? Sleep. He had yet to figure out this yellow Labrador he had acquired two months ago from the pound.

Bruce nodded a greeting to one of the Navy SEALs he knew

15

as he settled into the chair and prepared to stay put for a while. Sprinkled in the mix among the young sailors there were a few grown-ups. The ship's officers, SEALs, and naval aviators stood out by the self-assured way they staked out their space.

As far as parties went this one was living up to past history. The soda was cold to the point ice crystals formed when he opened the can, while the hot dogs were burnt because his sister had insisted on working the grill. People came for the tradition of it, not for the food.

He'd driven up from Pensacola, Florida, where he was based, to Norfolk, center of gravity for military operations in the state with nine military bases for Air Force, Navy, and Marines clustered within the Hampton Roads area. He'd come for the weekend because his sister had invited him. He had news to share that was best done in person. And he'd come to see Grace.

He didn't have to search to find her; he'd kept track of her in his peripheral vision throughout the afternoon, anchoring her as part of his frame of reference. Grace stood out in red. The sweater over jeans was a simple bold splash of color in a sea of white. His sister's best friend, the cohost of this party, had been in his sights for years. Jill had introduced them. Lieutenant Grace Yates was one of the self-assured naval aviators. She was going to spend the next six months hurling off the deck of the USS *George Washington* in an F/A-18 Hornet.

He watched her mingle and chat with the other squadron pilots; she'd long ago been accepted into their exclusive ranks. Ever since the combat exclusion rules had eased in 1993 to allow women to fill combat flight roles, she'd been showing she had the right stuff. Not flashy, not pushy, just one of the best pilots he'd ever met. She exemplified grace under pressure.

He admired what she'd done and how she'd accomplished it. She loved to fly and she turned that passion into a single-minded focus to be the best. She'd picked up Gracie as her call sign. She rarely commented on the ground she broke in her profession but she'd done so about the handle. Grace thought it was too soft a call sign. Bruce thought it summed her up in one word. It suited her.

Grace was the deep waters while Jill was the clear shallows. Grace rarely talked about herself. How many layers were there to the mystery that made her who she was? He was determined to find out. He was on a mission. Grace was the objective. And his profession had taught him well the value of good reconnaissance. He had known her for years, but only in the last few months had he decided to do that digging.

He liked what he had found. She was loyal to her friends, was close to her family. She sang with her church choir, rather badly he thought. She liked vanilla ice cream, scary movies, skiing, and anything related to flying. Competitive in sports, tall, slender, fast on her feet, she had the arm and wrist strength to play a tennis game that decimated opponents. She'd broken her arm skydiving, had crashed her car at age seventeen and had to be talked into driving again, and never had more than a goldfish as a pet. There was a tightness to her mouth when she was mad and a smile that came easy around friends. He'd enjoyed the reconnaissance.

She'd dated Ben Grossel for many years. Bruce had met Ben a couple times and he'd found the former Navy pilot turned astronaut an exceptionally nice guy. Ben had been killed in a car accident two years ago while Grace was on her second sea tour. Bruce suspected that had rocked her life pretty hard although she had never said much.

A young boy in a blue sweatshirt slammed into the back of Grace's knees, enveloping her in hug. She turned with a laugh to rescue him and haul him up to perch on her hip. She was often being tailed by her own fan club at parties such as this one. She'd started a kids' flying club last year with some help from his sister and had become a bit of a hero to the kids. She had the rare touch of not only being a good pilot but also a good teacher.

His dog moved and Bruce reached under the chair to ruffle the dog's ears. Today was going to be his last chance to see Grace for six months. He was a patient man. This gathering was scheduled to go until seven. His plan was simple, and he needed to accomplish only one thing with her today. He had the luxury to choose the right moment.

"Have you told Jill the news?"

Bruce looked over at the Navy SEAL trying to relax beside him in a patio chair too small for his frame. Life itself often seemed too small for Grace's cousin, Tom "Wolf" Yates. They were rivals and competitors in the best Air Force versus Navy tradition. The women in their lives had been best friends for years, and on that common ground they had long ago forged an amicable friendship. "Coward that I am, I was hoping you would mention it first."

Wolf grimaced. "We're a sorry lot."

"Have you heard how long you're going to be gone?"

"Twelve weeks. You?"

"Sixteen."

Silence stretched as the implications set in. They were both going to miss Jilly's birthday on May 19. And not just any birthday—her thirtieth birthday. Bruce watched his sister turn hamburgers on the grill and laugh with the sailor keeping her company. The young man stood at relaxed attention, hands behind his back, being friendly in a very polite way. He wasn't a fool. Jill was dating Wolf. It was dangerous territory to tread on.

"We need to do something special." Bruce had planned to

arrange another weekend like this one, come up and take Jill out for dinner, probably buy her a nice necklace since she loved jewelry. Rushing to do that before he deployed would just not be the same. Jill would be having her birthday without family, without her best friend Grace, without her boyfriend Wolf. She was getting a raw deal.

"I got her that inlaid jewelry box she fell in love with, but I'm doomed before I even wrap it. She's going to feel like the gift is compensation."

"She'll cry," Bruce predicted, knowing his sister. She'd cry, get over the disappointment, then put on a smile to tell them good-bye. But the initial news would hurt. Big days mattered, and through the years she'd been asked to spend so many of them alone.

Jill had a love-hate relationship with dating someone who put her third in his life behind God and the Navy. Bruce understood where she was coming from. It was one thing to pay that price of separation when you held up your hand and volunteered to take the oath of service; it was another when you had no choice but to accept it.

"To top it off, I'll probably be somewhere that doesn't have a phone."

"She likes you too much to dump you over this."

Wolf growled at him for suggesting it. Bruce laughed and wondered not for the first time how he'd handle having Wolf for a brother-in-law. Wolf was good for his sister. He was a solid man with a strong faith who didn't get troubled by events; he simply solved the problem. Like most SEALs he was addicted to adrenaline rushes and was intensely competitive. But he also had a maturity well beyond his years, and Bruce knew the man's heart. He could trust the man to be gentle with his sister. Jill was high energy and laughter, a lady who loved making sure people had a

great time and who would go the second and third miles to help a
friend.

He hoped it worked out for the two of them. Jill dated Wolf
because she admired him and what he did; she just hadn't escaped
the hurt that went back to childhood with their dad always
putting the Air Force before family.

It was hard being a big brother. It wasn't until their parents
died three years ago that he realized it had been four months since
he'd last seen his sister, and a month since he had talked with her.
He'd been ashamed of that. He wasn't going to miss events in Jill's
life unless it was truly unavoidable. His focus had changed, but
this deployment was coming at a vulnerable time. He wished he
had another six months stateside before he had to do another
TDY.

Her birthday party would be disrupted, her vacation plans
forced to change as she had been planning to come down to see
the house he was remodeling. And he'd have to reschedule the
date he could come up and help her fix up the new offices she
was in the process of leasing. *Lord, how do I tell her?* He wished he
had the right words. She didn't adjust too well to the long
absences. And Bruce knew part of that was his fault for how he'd
handled the past ones.

She'd be busy while he was gone. Her business was thriving—
Stateside Support, Inc. had over a hundred clients. While the
sailors were deployed overseas defending U.S. interests, Jill would
be doing everything that needed to be done back on the home
front from watering plants and caring for pets to paying bills and
supervising yard work. Those lucky enough to be a Stateside, Inc.
client got gold-plated care. Grace and Wolf were both clients.
He'd be one just as soon as his sister opened an office in
Pensacola.

Bruce could send Jill roses for her birthday, tickets to a concert, something he could arrange before he left. For Jill, being remembered on the correct date mattered as much as the gift. The options were depressing. He needed to have the day with Jill as much as she did.

Bruce jolted as a hand slid across the top of his right shoulder. Grace moved past him and leaned over the back of Wolf's chair. "We need more ice."

Tom tipped his head back to look up at her. "I brought four bags."

She smiled down at him. "Cougar wants to make homemade ice cream. He's found the hand turn freezer and the rock salt, and he's got some concoction on the stove. Go corral your partner before he gets in over his head."

"Yes, ma'am."

Wolf got to his feet and towered above her. They were cousins but closer than most.

Gracie handed him her empty glass. "And Jill is getting lonely."

"Is she?"

"Shoo."

"You want your favorite chair back."

"And you normally catch on faster. My feet are killing me. We've got too many friends."

Wolf laughed. "I'll bring you some ice cream if it turns out to be edible."

"Appreciate it." Grace settled with a comfortable sigh in the chair Wolf had vacated. "I'm glad you could make it, Bruce."

An odd tension settled in his gut to replace the relaxation of moments before. Early thirties, brunette, a smile that flirted with the camera, and blue eyes that were alive—she was a photogenic dream. He'd borrowed one of Wolf's wallet pictures months ago. "Good party."

"Enjoying yourself?" She held down her hand and his dog emerged to say hello.

"I always do," he replied truthfully.

"Jill mentioned you had acquired a pet. She's beautiful."

"Timid."

"She's old," Grace corrected, smiling at the animal.

Bruce watched her focus on his dog, her voice softening as she murmured a welcome. It shouldn't be so hard to get to know her. He'd worked around pilots for over a decade. Everything he knew about her suggested he was talking with the person likely to become the first female squadron commander. The problem was basic—just under that smile and friendly welcome was an impenetrable wall guarding her thoughts. What went on behind those blue eyes? Was she content with her life? Lonely? Having a good year? A hard one? She tended to deflect questions and it suggested a deep reservoir inside. Finding answers was a challenge, but he liked a challenge.

"So where are you going?" she asked as she scanned the crowd.

She'd kept her ear to the ground, or else she cornered his partner Rich who was wandering around this party somewhere. "Turkey." Operation Northern Watch over northern Iraq had its headquarters at Incirlik Air Base, Turkey, and the no-fly zone had been a low-grade constant conflict for years. The Twenty-third Special Tactics Squadron would be replacing PJs who were stationed there for the last three months.

She turned to give him her full attention. "The *GW* is heading to the Med for part of this deployment."

"I know." The USS *George Washington* would be handling some of Operation Northern Watch's flight assignments. "I'll be playing catch on the ground if you get in trouble," he teased her. He had been pulling pilots and Special Forces soldiers from behind enemy lines for twelve years. If she got in trouble, his unit would be the one getting the call.

"It's interesting flying, but please," she teased back, "antiaircraft artillery and surface-to-air missiles? I can fly my way through that clutter in my sleep. I'm more curious about what Wolf will be doing over there."

There were only 313 PJs and a few thousand SEALs on active duty. They trained in similar ways: to fight behind enemy lines, to be experts in night insertions by air or water, to be the best at unconventional warfare. But in roles they were very different. The SEALs went out to accomplish their mission at all costs, were often sent into situations where military muscle had to be exercised just short of war. The PJs deployed for only one mission: rescue. Bruce knew his friend. Wolf would downplay the assignment, but a rotation to Turkey meant the SEALs would probably be doing some work inside Iraq.

"Getting into trouble," he predicted.

"I think he was just born to do difficult things," she agreed. "I saw you on the news." The lightness in her voice had turned to subtle concern.

Bruce didn't have to ask what the clip had shown; it had been running in the national news spot. The rescue in the Gulf last week had been interesting but not as much of a crisis as the media made it out to be. A sudden storm had floundered more than a few boats; the PJs routinely helped out the Coast Guard in such situations. Bruce reached over and patted Grace's arm. If he let her worry about him, it would change the entire tenor of their relationship. He was the one who got to worry about her. The Air Force paid him to do so. "It wasn't that big a deal."

"You were limping. And you've been keeping station in that chair all day."

Trust her to notice. He had a bruise on his thigh the size of a melon where the sailboat mast had struck him. "I'm old. I get tired now," he replied with a slight laugh.

"I should have told Wolf to get you the ice."

"Let it be, Grace. Jill will just hover."

"How's the boy you rescued?"

"They sent him home from the hospital this morning."

"I'm glad to hear it."

Silence settled between them. Bruce didn't try to break it. Words were at times overrated. Life was a gift and he was done rushing through it. Shoot at him a few times, make him realize still being alive was a blessing, and his perspective changed. There was no hurry. Besides, he liked looking at her. She was easy on the eyes.

This party had been a lot of work, and behind the smile were signs of her tiredness. The wind had been blowing her hair. The short haircut was new, a practical step given fresh water on an aircraft carrier was one of the most carefully conserved resources: Showers were short. He recognized the necklace; he'd bought the gold pendant of an opening rosebud when he'd been in France. Grace and Jill had been sharing jewelry again. It looked good on her.

"I just realized I set the Bear Cubs loose in the kitchen. I suppose I should go supervise," Grace remarked, but made no move to do so.

"I can't believe they let you get away with that handle." Wolf's boss was Navy SEAL Joe "Bear" Baker. Grace had long ago tagged Wolf and his partner as the Bear Cubs.

"Joe thinks it's cute. He's taken to calling them that."

Cute. Bruce winced. The call sign had stuck. He sympathized with Wolf, but it was a pretty good tag to have considering what it implied. Bear was a legend among the SEALs.

Grace shifted and ran her hand through her hair. "I got your letter."

He stilled.

"Did you think it had been lost?"

He forced himself to breathe. "Hoped it."

"It trailed me around the world for eight months and showed up two weeks ago."

Two weeks ago. It coincided with his weekend remodeling his house and his long talk with the Lord about his future. He was a man who made plans and executed them. It was hard to wait indefinitely for open doors and new directions. He'd been hurting because the answer to his prayer had been silence, but the resurrection of the letter written when he expected to be dead by nightfall— *Lord, this is not the answer I had in mind.*

He'd sent it from the jungle of Ecuador, handing it to a fellow PJ leaving the area. "The helicopter went down. I didn't realize the letter had been recovered and sent on." He'd buried a friend when he thought he would be the one in that coffin.

"The letter for Jill is still sealed."

Left unsaid was that the letter to her wasn't. "I didn't have anyone else to deliver it since Wolf was with me, and I wasn't in a position to call up and ask if you would be willing to handle it."

"Bruce. I understand."

Letters were words that could haunt a man when written under stress. Had those fatal two words been in it or had he marked them out? He'd changed his mind so many times on what to say, grabbing moments to write the letter under utterly chaotic circumstances. He felt a bone deep weariness settle inside as he looked at her. "Do you?"

She just looked at him. Wise eyes. He'd started to think of them as that ages ago. "You write a nice letter. It's a lost art."

"Grace—"

"You had few regrets when you looked back on your life. If I ever tried to write that letter, I couldn't say the same."

His eyes narrowed. When she swung open a door, she swung open a big one. "What regrets?"

She shook her head and focused her attention on his dog, stroking the warm fur. "It looks like you've been correcting the few regrets you had. You got your dog; Jill said you were remodeling a house."

She didn't mention the third item in the list. He wondered if he'd crossed the words out or if she was just being kind. "I'm trying to." His life had reoriented itself since Ecuador. There had been only one focus in his life before then; now there were four priorities.

"The letter to your sister is at my place. I'll get it back to you."

"Thanks."

"Gracie, we need an opinion." She turned around in her chair at Wolf's call.

"Coming!"

Bruce touched her hand as she rose, pausing her. "If I don't see you again before I have to head out—be sure to catch the third wire."

She turned her hand around and tightened it on his. "I will." Her smile was kind. "I'll pray you have a boring deployment." She slipped her hand from his and turned toward the house.

"Hey, Grace."

She glanced over her shoulder.

"You like getting letters?"

She turned to walk backward toward the house. "Wolf writes me what turns out to be dated weather reports—faithfully—every Monday, Wednesday, and Friday."

"Maybe I'll write you sometime."

"Maybe the military mail will find me."

"Can you read my handwriting?"

She laughed. "It's awful. But mine is worse." She disappeared into the house.

Bruce pulled a peppermint from his pocket and unwrapped it.

Six months. He was going to miss her. A six-month deployment was 27 weeks, 182 days, an exhausting 4,368 hours. He'd figured it up on the back of an envelope during the trip here. He closed his eyes and every bruise from the recent rescue was suddenly and forcibly felt.

Grace was the first lady he had met who he thought could handle his profession. She just kept heading halfway around the world. Service came first. Duty. Honor. Country. He watched Jill and Wolf struggle to make a civilian and military relationship work. A relationship where both were military— He'd been doing hard things all his life, but this one was definitely going to be a challenge.

The Ecuador letter was a serious problem. He couldn't change that first impression; he could only try to recover from it. She'd had the letter for two weeks. His profession taught him to know the terrain, to eliminate variables, to minimize surprises. Bruce sighed, feeling his emotions that had knotted at the news unwrap.

Lord, was it really necessary to hand her that letter first? It was raw emotion from a foxhole, meant to be read only if I died there. If I died it meant Wolf would likely also die there, and Grace needed to hear what Wolf had done. He was a hero that day. Now—the letter just confuses the situation and enormously complicates it.

But the letter had been delivered. It was going to take some time to figure out how to adjust his plan. It established a first impression far different than the one he had desired to convey.

Bruce reached for his empty glass and got up. It was time to find his sister, time to break his bad news. He owed it to Wolf to be the one to do it. The way things stood, he was going to need Wolf's help with Grace.

ECUADOR

Grace –

Wolf's with me. We've been pinned down about six hours and ammo is low. We came in after a downed helicopter only to get caught by weather and rebels. Only one more rescue flight can be attempted before nightfall. I've watched Wolf save three Marines. He's a hero. It's going to come down to one of us going out with the injured while the other covers in order for any of us to make it out alive. I'm sending out Wolf. Force him to get over the grief.

I apologize for asking this of you. Jill's letter is enclosed. Tell her I love her. She needs words in person, not writing. It hurts to think of leaving her with no family left. But there's not much I can change about that now. On the whole, I've got few regrets. Not having a dog. A house. A wife.

I want to live.

I may not get what I want.

God bless, Gracie. I'll see you in heaven.

TWO

★ ★ ★

The party cleanup was just about done. Grace dropped the dishrag into the sink and walked back to the kitchen table she was working to clear, wedging her cellular phone against her shoulder while she dried her hands. The handmade mahogany display case she'd ordered for Jill's birthday was in. Grace listened to the message as she pulled out a chair, found a pen, and turned pages in her day planner.

How was she going to fit a trip into her schedule before she left without Jill hearing about it? It was perfect for the blown glass figurines Jill collected and too important a gift to risk getting damaged in shipping. The next week was already packed with notes; she turned the page and bright red boxes met her. The deployment date wasn't moving.

"Okay if I join you?"

Grace waved her cousin into the kitchen. She saved the message and closed her phone. "As long as you don't expect much. I'm talked out," she whispered, fighting the hoarseness that had messed up the end of her day. She bit her lip to stop the laughter—someone, probably Jill, had given Wolf one of the white paper sailor hats. It had been autographed by a number of people, and he had one of the party toothpicks stuck in the crown.

Wolf settled beside her at the table as she refilled her glass of ice water from the pitcher. Grace rested her cheek against her palm and felt the ring she wore cut into her cheek. She turned it back around with her thumb. The party had been a smashing success. If she gained the energy, she would go home and take advantage of having a real bed. Of everything she knew she would crave while on deployment, topping the list was a real bed and a soft pillow.

"Good party."

"Thanks. I knew you'd enjoy it." His definition of a good party was quite broad: the general denominator being "unstuffy" people and edible food. "How did Jill take the deployment news?"

"Got quiet. Said oh."

Grace read between the lines. The news had stung. "It's a long time."

Wolf just nodded. He returned the salt and pepper shakers to the center holder, then tugged out a napkin and shook it out. She slid him her glass of ice water. He wet the napkin and scrubbed at a spot of drying chocolate topping she had missed. Emotion swelled up inside as she watched him. She loved this man, and there was something so endearing about the boy still inside. She was two years older than he was; he'd been the brother she never had. "Going to tell me what else she said?"

"Nope."

"I can get you a dishrag."

He wadded up the napkin.

Grace knew the problem. For the first time her cousin was letting his heart get deeply involved. He was scared to leave. He couldn't control what would happen to his relationship with Jill while he was gone. Grace had been there; she knew exactly what it felt like to be heading for a deployment with uncertainty on the home front. The pressure of her first deployment had been complicated by Ben's reaction to her being gone.

She could count on one hand the best friends in her life. Jill was at the top of the list. They'd met when she had flown into Norfolk and over one weekend had to find an apartment near the base, get her car tags for the base, and make arrangements to ship furniture. Jill had become a friend in those twenty-four hours of whirlwind decisions. Wolf had his work cut out for him to make the relationship with Jill work, but Grace had never counseled against it. She'd been the one to introduce them three years ago. The man deserved to be happy. And she knew they were both too stubborn to give up. "Why don't you take her to a movie?"

"Tonight?"

"Take advantage of the time you have left stateside. Trust me, she'll say yes." He had no idea. For the last decade, Jill had been talking about being married by the time she was thirty. Wolf dragging his heels was making her best friend miserable. Grace was afraid Jill was going to get tired of waiting for him to reach the point he wanted to settle down.

She had never been a civilian, never been the one left stateside, so it was hard to offer much practical advice. It wasn't that she didn't understand; she just didn't know what to suggest. Wolf was not leaving the Navy, and at times that was the only solution Jill could see to the separations. Silence was hard on a relationship, and Wolf deployed places where no mail or phone for weeks at a time was common.

"She's still talking with Bruce, saying her normal very long good-bye."

"She doesn't see him often enough."

"I'm not complaining. I know the feeling. I haven't been able to see you nearly enough either."

"You mean you're not tired of me yet?" she teased and he laughed as she had known he would. She knew being around to see her was one of the reasons he'd accepted a transfer from the West Coast back to the East, though Jill had been the main reason. He normally worked Pacific assignments, but the increase in military deployments over the last two years had led to the shifting around of SEAL teams to help cover the demands in Europe.

But even living in the same area, they still had to coordinate schedules to see each other.

"Are you ready for the next six months?"

That she should have given him reason to wonder made her sad. "I'm ready. It's too quiet here. I want to get back to sea." She was ready to get away from the low-grade grief she felt stateside. There was peace to be found in work and she needed it. Too many places stateside had been shared with Ben, and she kept encountering reminders of what she had lost.

"I've got few regrets." The words from Bruce's letter echoed in her memory. His letter had arrived at a vulnerable moment, catching her off guard. She'd read it many times during the last two weeks. She had regrets, so many they haunted her. *If only...* She'd been living with the words during this shore leave and they were wearing her down. She envied Bruce that peace he had about life. She had made one decision. No more regrets. It was time for better decisions. Wiser ones.

"You can't hide in work forever."

She smiled at Wolf, appreciating the fact he cared enough to push. "Another six months. You can give me the moving on speech after this tour."

Wolf crossed his arms, the fabric of his shirt pulling taut against well-defined muscles, and he rocked back in the chair as he considered her. "Promise me you'll be extra careful while you're gone. I don't want to have to open that letter you insisted on handing me."

"It's the grown-up thing to do, writing that letter."

"I'm not writing you one."

She reached over and squeezed the back of his neck. He wouldn't need to write one. She knew he loved her. "Write one for Jill. Just in case."

"Grace—"

"Sweetheart is a good way to start it."

"Mushy."

"Relationships are designed to embarrass guys with mushy words. Go find Jill."

"Want to come along to the movie?"

"Thanks but no. My feather pillow is calling my name." Had Ben been here, she would have found the energy, but tagging along as a third wasn't worth it. She could feel herself growing old in the little changes to her priorities. "Same plan for phone calls as last time?"

"Yes. I'll track you down."

"Good. Finding you is hard. Your platoon tends to hide."

"Just look where the shooting is going on."

She laughed. "You *will* come back in one piece—you owe me after Ecuador."

He got to his feet and ruffled her hair. "Promise. Have a good deployment, Grace."

"You too, Wolf."

"You're sure you don't mind watching the mutt?" Bruce asked.

Jill leaned through the car window to reach in and pet the dog curled up in the passenger seat. "You're going to hurt her feelings. I'll be glad to have Emily while you're gone."

"I'll bring her bed and food and chew toy with me. Extra keys to the car. My checkbook. What else?"

Jill chuckled. "I like the list so far. Don't worry about it. If I need anything else, Beth has your house keys and can forward it to me." She stepped back from the car as the porch lights came on and Wolf stepped outside. "Give me a call when you reach Charlotte."

"Will do."

Jill waved as Bruce pulled out of the drive. He'd had a good time today; she took comfort in that as she asked him to make yet another round-trip from Florida to Virginia. He sometimes could catch a flight into Naval Air Station, Oceana, but he'd driven this time in order to bring her the old hutch that had been in their parents' home. She'd seen him talking with Grace. This deployment was putting so many things on hold, not the least of which was a budding friendship between her brother and Grace. It was hard to play matchmaker when they were leaving for four and six months respectively.

Wolf wrapped her in a hug from behind and she leaned against him, enjoying his strength.

"Good party."

"Great party," she corrected, wrapping her hands around his.

"Grace suggested I take you to a movie."

She giggled. "You didn't tell her?"

"Honey, I know better than to tell my cousin I'm taking you to look at rings."

"I said we could look, not that I'd accept one."

"I'll convince you."

"You've been trying." She knew how miserable she would be while he was gone. She was still trying to adjust to a relationship where bad news was inevitable, but it wasn't easy.

"We'll make it through this separation. I'll write at least every other day."

"I know you will." She turned. Wolf would do everything he could to make it work. She reached up to tap his square jaw. The man was a SEAL, had the build of a boxer and a great smile in a face that was far from symmetrical. She looked into his deep brown eyes and found steadiness. She loved him. "Let's go look at rings." She'd know by the end of the summer if she could deal with what it meant to accept one.

THREE

★ ★ ★

MAY 10

USS *GEORGE WASHINGTON* (CVN 73)

MEDITERRANEAN SEA OFF WEST COAST OF TURKEY

Her flight boots had salt whitened from months at sea, and her flight suit under the white life vest had picked up a long day's worth of grime inherent with working on an aircraft carrier flight deck. Grace narrowed her eyes against the sun as she tracked the plane in the landing pattern.

She wore wraparound sunglasses, ample ChapStick, and had brought thick foam earplugs to cope with the noise of jets landing a few feet away. In her left hand she held the handset putting her in open radio contact with the approaching plane. At this moment she was the most important person in that pilot's life.

The aircraft carrier had turned into the wind to allow for recovery of planes from the second op of the day. Grace had been flying during the first op, doing a mirror-image training flight for what she would be doing for real tonight. After the debrief, she had come up to take a rotation as the landing signal officer. This was the eleventh plane landing in this cycle. They were arriving in sixty-second intervals, and she was handling the pressure with a cool precision.

Grace kept her right hand over her head holding up the pickle switch controlling the Fresnel landing lights, reminding all the other LSOs on the platform with her that they had a foul deck. The F/A-18 Hornet that had just landed had not yet cleared the deck. Grace resisted the impulse to turn and look over her shoulder to see what the holdup was. She had a bigger problem coming toward her. The EA-6B Prowler on approach was flown by a nugget—a new pilot in the air wing on his first sea cruise.

The USS *George Washington* had been at sea two months now of this six-month deployment, and Grace worried that Lieutenant Junior Grade Ellis "Patrick" Jones was losing confidence in his flying skills, not gaining it.

She'd mentally nicknamed him "Jittery" because he got excited easily, and from the very first meeting it was apparent he was overwhelmed with the transition to carrier operations. Unlike shore deployments, life aboard an aircraft carrier ran at high speed with only rare pauses. Every nugget had to learn to cope and there was precious little time to learn how. He was task saturated. It was showing in his landings, and she knew that would sink his career if he didn't improve soon. The Navy didn't have much use for a pilot who couldn't safely land a plane on a ship.

If he came in high as he tried to land, the Prowler's tailhook would miss the wires, and he'd be forced to go full throttle to fly off the deck before he careened into the sea. If he drifted right, he'd take out a row of parked jets at millions a pop. If he drifted left, he'd slide off the ship. And if he came in low... The Navy called them ramp strikes when a pilot literally flew his plane into the back of the ship. At a hundred plus knots, the resulting fireball was spectacular. Grace was standing a few feet away from the point he would impact.

It was her role to talk him safely down onto the deck. She would get him down alive. It was her job. And she was good at her job.

"Clear deck!"

"Roger, clear deck. Lights and gear set for a Prowler," Grace shouted back to the LSO to her far right. She lowered the pickle switch back to her side. She had a radio handset and the large bank of signaling lights behind her. With them she had to work a minor miracle. She was earning her pay today. Patrick was plane number 774, and Grace listened to the radio traffic bringing him in.

"774, three quarters of a mile, call the ball," the air controller said.

"774, Prowler ball, 4.5," Patrick tersely replied.

Patrick could see the massive glowing "meatball" light behind her. The plane was now hers.

The big meatball light moved up and down, tracking with his plane. As long as his light intersected the horizontal line of green lights, he was on a perfect approach. If Patrick came in high, he would see the big yellow meatball light that tracked with his plane move above that line of green lights. If the light drifted below the green lights, his approach was low. If it went red, he was about to plow into the back of the ramp. He was trained to fly the meatball. She was there to remind him of that.

A good landing wasn't complicated. Watch the centerline, the glide slope of the approach, and the speed. Then land the plane on the centerline, catch an arresting wire with the tailhook, and be jerked to a stop. It was the same process day or night. Rather heart stopping at night but still a routine part of a naval aviator's job.

"Right for center," Grace corrected, seeing his plane drift left. The white centerline had nearly worn off the carrier deck after the months of heavy flight operations. Patrick either couldn't see it or couldn't get aligned.

His wings dipped and he overcorrected. She waited two heartbeats for him to realize the error. "Left a little," she cautioned.

The Prowler nosed down. Her muscles tensed. "Power. You're settling." He was fighting left and right drifts while forgetting he was falling out of the sky. He was below the glide slope and rapidly closing distance with the ship.

Come on, correct. "Power. Power."

He aggressively added power so as not to slam into the ramp and he drifted left.

She hit the pickle. "Wave off. Wave off!" The bank of lights burst into flashing red as she ordered an abort.

She ducked as the jet roared overhead.

The windshield on the LSO platform rocked at the fury. Gracie forced her hand to relax its white-knuckle grip. No one in the LSO group had jumped into the safety basket, diving off the edge of the ship to avoid being engulfed in a ramp strike. If she hadn't been holding the stick, she would have jumped.

Never, ever, be low. Suffering the emotions of being an LSO taught her more about landings than she learned at the controls of the plane when she was the one flying the pattern.

"Good call." The senior carrier air group LSO said. He stood behind her with a second handset and a pickle switch backing her up. She wanted his job someday but for now was relieved to know she had him around to back her up. Grace nodded her appreciation of the quiet words as she pivoted and watched Patrick climb back into the sky. Air control gave him vectors to come around and try again. He had about two minutes to mentally get ready. She was going to need more than that. He'd been flying at her face that last hundred feet.

She shook off the adrenaline as she wondered what Patrick's three-man crew was thinking about now. She was grateful she flew the single seat F/A-18 Hornet and didn't have to worry about killing her flight crew in a landing mistake.

Turning to the LSO acting as secretary for this recover, she graded the landing. "Wave off. Left drift on approach, overcorrect and settle in the middle, not enough power at the ramp." The no grade would sting. Patrick's landing grades for this deployment were still average "fairs" with all too frequent below average "no grades." He was heading toward a flight review board.

The phone beside them on the LSO platform rang.

The senior LSO picked it up. From the "Yes, sirs" she knew it was probably the air boss watching events from his perch in the tower high above the flight deck.

The senior LSO hung up the phone. "One more try, and then he gets diverted to Incirlik. There's no slack in the timeline for tonight."

Grace nodded.

She raised her right hand with the pickle stick over her head to signal a foul deck as one of the many plane handlers used the free minute to maneuver and park an F-14 Tomcat at the edge of the flight deck. The red shirts had already begun loading live ordnance for the missions tonight. It would be a big strike. An entire air wing could only pause for one pilot so long.

"Clear deck."

She lowered her hand. "Clear deck. Roger. Lights and boards set for a Prowler." Patrick's plane would be at a lighter weight on this approach, having burned fuel in the abort and circle. It would likely cause him to be high and fast. And given the near ramp strike, he'd already want to overcorrect high.

"774, three quarters of a mile, call the ball," the air controller called.

"774, Prowler ball, 3.7," Patrick replied. His voice sounded shaky.

"Wind at twenty-nine knots, even keel," she said, relieved not to have a pitching deck adding another element of complexity.

Patrick was focusing better this time. He was above the glide path as she had suspected. "You're long."

She saw him inch a little steeper angle of attack. It was a decent approach. She let the minor errors that weren't going to kill him go without comment.

She pivoted and followed him into the wires. The Prowler hit the deck hard, the tailhook missing the third wire and sending sparks flying as it rubbed metal on metal until it caught the fourth wire.

The fourth wire spooled out with a vicious slap and jerked the plane to a stop. As soon as the engines were throttled back to idle, Patrick raised the tailhook and a yellow shirt plane director waved him to taxi from the landing lane. Life on the carrier deck returned to normal.

"Fair pass. High in the middle. Long on lineup. Taxi into the wires." Grace set down the pickle switch and handset. "That's the last plane for this cycle. Secure stations and let's go deliver grades." Every pilot would hear directly from her their landing grade and a detailed description of what they did wrong. It was learning at the most intense level.

There was a camera on that centerline broadcasting live every landing aboard the carrier to the ready rooms and staterooms. Peer reviews were intense. Add the formal LSO's review and posted landing grades in each squadron ready room and pilots worked on improving their landings with an intensity that had no comparison. Every pilot wanted to walk away with the Best Hook Award for the deployment.

Grace reapplied her ChapStick. JP-5 jet fuel, oil, hydraulic fluid, and salty sea air mixed with the strong wind across the flight deck assaulted everyone exposed. Small pieces of the non-skid deck surface tossed up by the landing Prowler peppered her flight suit. The surface was being pounded into dust by the constant landing assaults. Before long the ship would have to suspend flight ops for several days to allow a new surface to be applied. The daily patches weren't keeping up with the damage.

Grace was ready for a break. Being responsible for other pilots was more exhausting than being at the controls of the landing jet.

"Lieutenant Yates."

She turned to find the squadron executive officer had joined her on the platform. "Yes, sir."

"We're adding Zulu-7 to tonight's flight. Brief at 1700."

The message was simple, the implications complex. "Yes, sir." One of the many options they had practiced and put on the shelf for tonight's Operation Northern Watch flight was being activated. The last minute nature of the change suggested a target of opportunity. And for her, a very long night.

FOUR

★ ★ ★

NATO FORWARD OPERATING LOCATION
TURKEY/IRAQ BORDER

ruce zipped the duffel bag of medical supplies closed as he studied the latest maps of northern Iraq spread out under the Plexiglas cover on the worktable. Several EA-6B Prowlers had been up during the day gathering the latest signals. The threat areas looked like rings of Swiss cheese. Already he saw the subtle shifts of Iraqi military during the day. They knew something was coming.

Over the last several months, the Iraqi military had been doing their best to shoot down a plane taking part in Operation Northern Watch. The Iraqis had come close to succeeding yesterday. The F-15E Strike Eagle hit by antiaircraft artillery had barely made it back to Incirlik Air Base, Turkey. Tonight the gloves were coming off.

The air tasking orders put thirty-eight pilots in the air to knock out ground control radar facilities, AAA sites, and radio relay sites around the town of Mosul and south of Saddam Lake. Those were the distributed orders; he'd been briefed on other classified missions.

They weren't going to launch this mission from Turkey air bases and risk the fallout should something go wrong. Turkey had to live with not only Iraq but Syria as a neighbor. Eighty percent of the planes in the tasking order were launching from the USS *George Washington.*

He thought of Grace many times in the last weeks, wondering how her deployment was going, but he'd never had this kind of tension in his gut. What assignment had she drawn? She'd be flying. She was too good a pilot not to draw one of the tougher strike assignments. *Lord, please, keep her safe during tonight's flight.* He hated the sense of worry, hated worse the lack of information.

Bruce hoisted the heavy medical bag off the improvised table built from plywood resting across two sawhorses. The odds were good he would be flying tonight.

He exited the tent carrying the gear and walked across the field to the flight line. Eight weeks ago sheep had been grazing in this plateau. The Twenty-third Special Tactics Squadron out of Hurlbert Field, Florida, had made it home.

Bruce hadn't seen much of Turkey proper. The PJs had flown over on a commercial flight to Istanbul, then shuttled down to the Incirlik Air Base and been flown out to this forward operating location within days of coming in-country.

The coalition pilots in the area—British and American—were counting on him. They could be aggressive in the air because the PJs guaranteed if a pilot got in trouble, they would get him out.

Inside his uniform, dog tags clicked. Bruce wore his own plus three others. He'd pulled a helicopter crew out of danger two weeks ago when a training mission through the tight passes of northern Turkey had ended in near tragedy. The rescue had cost the crew the price of their dog tags, a tradition that went back more PJ generations than he had been alive.

Before this deployment was over he'd likely be wearing more.

Bruce stored his gear in the first of the Pave Low III helicopters on the flight line, the black menacing machine one of the reasons he could deliver on that rescue promise. Life in the PJs was all about preparation. If they went out tonight they would be ready to hit hard.

It was 1410 local time. It would be 0200 before he got clearance to stand down. Bruce thought about it and decided he had time for a late lunch and a nap before the evening watch began.

"Striker."

He turned to see Wolf coming toward him from the mess tent. The Bear Cubs had shown up three weeks ago. Navy SEAL Joe "Bear" Baker and his team were operating throughout this region, and Bear had assigned the Cubs to handle the briefings.

"Got a minute?"

"Sure."

Wolf offered one of the sandwiches he held and Bruce took it with a quiet thanks. It was another of Tom's infamous peanut butter and banana sandwiches. Striker had long ago figured out it was his premission ritual. "Any word on tonight?" Bruce asked.

"They've moved us up to standby."

What the SEALs would be doing tonight if they got a go-ahead Bruce wasn't fully briefed on yet; that would happen after there was a green light. But he knew one fact: On the map the Iraqi-Syrian border was a bright red line. The SEALs would be crossing it.

"Did you get through to Jill?" Bruce asked. Wolf had been down at Incirlik early this morning where there were phones available. Communication from here was restricted to mail.

"I got her answering machine. I wanted to strangle the cord."

"I thought she said four o'clock her time."

"She did. I don't know if that means she got my last letter and doesn't want to speak with me or if something happened."

"And it's going to be a couple days before you get a chance to call again."

"Exactly."

"I pity you."

"You're supposed to sympathize and offer to help."

Bruce laughed. "I'm letting my sister date a Navy guy. Don't push your luck." He knew all about the dilemmas of missed phone calls and the uncertainty about mail. He'd worked to get just the right tone for his first letter to Grace written since he had deployed, and he still hadn't heard back from her. Had she received the letter? It was tough, the silence, tougher than just about anything he might hear back as a reaction.

"Ready for tonight?"

Wolf, worried? Bruce narrowed his eyes as he searched his friend's face, then smiled as he caught the dig. "Being brave is hard work. But I'll live up to my reputation. Going to live up to yours?"

"What's life without a little danger?"

"Peaceful." Bruce replied, amused. "And peanut butter and banana sandwiches do not make you bulletproof."

Wolf shrugged. "Somebody's got to cover Bear's back."

And Bruce knew that simple statement said it all. For the SEALs as well as for PJs—friendship was more than just a personal loyalty, it was a tactical advantage. The enemy wasn't fighting one man; it was fighting a team. And when dying for a friend was the price every man was willing to pay without a second thought, the teams could do what individuals could not—bring everyone home. Bruce knew that truth from personal experience. He had his partner Rich to thank for surviving more close calls than he cared to put into words. "Got enough ammo?"

"Quit nagging. We learned the lesson of Ecuador. We're ready."

STATESIDE SUPPORT, INC.
NORFOLK, VIRGINIA

"What do you think, Scott?" Jill Stanton tried to sound calm as she stood in the mess that was Seaman Tyler Jones's living room.

The stereo speakers he had considered his pride and joy were gone. Half the CDs. A video camera. The burglar had been thorough, taking things he could carry and easily resell. The shock she'd gotten hit with on walking into this crime scene was wearing off. She was still feeling shaky, but it was being replaced with a growing sense of anger.

Detective Scott Reece walked down the hall to look at the bedroom. Her brother's friend from childhood was a police officer for the Hampton Roads communities, and he'd been prompt in answering her page. "Five burglaries in the last two months, three of them your clients. Not so unusual when you consider your clients are primarily single, collect expensive stereo equipment, and the news of their deployment is advertised in the local newspaper. When was the last time you were here?"

She followed him into the bedroom where the dresser drawers remained half open, pulled off their tracks and shoved back at odd angles. "Two days ago, midafternoon. I watered the plants and fed his turtle." The burglar hadn't bothered to take the turtle.

"Do you have the list of belongings and photographs of the apartment?"

"Terri is bringing the file from the office." Jill prepared for this kind of crisis with every client—burglary, fire, and storm damage. Making sure possessions were inventoried and that there was adequate insurance coverage was part of the process of taking on a new client.

Tyler had elected not to be told about something like this, but rather have her simply deal with it for him. She couldn't blame him. He was working on the *GW* flight deck, and he didn't need to be distracted from his job by something stateside that he could do nothing about. Tyler's insurance was up-to-date. As soon as the settlement amount was known, she'd get started replacing and repairing the damage to give him the best possible news on return. Where was she going to find replacement speakers?

"It will be the same routine as last time. We'll dust for prints, talk to neighbors, inventory what's missing." Outside the apartment, two officers had already begun the canvas of the building residents to see if anyone had observed something unusual. "We'll get him, Jill," Scott said. "Something stolen will turn up and give us a lead. It doesn't make sense that he's keeping everything he's taken. He's selling it somewhere."

Jill wished she believed him. He'd said the same thing after the last two break-ins at clients' homes. She knew he was working the cases hard, but she had clients to protect and she needed the man stopped today, not tomorrow.

Scott led the way back to the living room. The burglar had run something sharp along the hallway wall, scraping the paint. Car keys probably; the same senseless damage someone would do in a parking lot out of boredom. "Same man?" she asked.

"It looks like it." He walked over to check the timer being used to control the room lights. "Six P.M. on, 10 P.M. off?"

"A few minutes off the hour, and the radio in the bedroom comes on about ten-thirty."

"All your clients have something similar?"

"Yes. I've double-checked locks, set lights on timers, made sure drapes were drawn." She paced over to the window. When she had first arrived, she had pushed open the doorway, juggling her briefcase and the mail she picked up for Tyler. She had glanced in the living room and felt like someone had punched her. "Are you sure it's not related to my clients?"

"I've run all your clients' addresses and didn't find a pattern. This looks like another target of opportunity. Have you called the insurance agent yet?"

"He's coming."

"Then go get yourself a cup of coffee at the corner deli, take a walk, and blow off the stress while you let me do my job. There was nothing you could have done to prevent this."

She turned from the window. "I suppose."

"Why don't you tell Bruce?"

She'd tell Wolf before she'd tell Bruce; her brother would just overreact. "No."

"He has a right to know this is going on."

"He's overseas. He can't do anything about it from there, and I don't want to add this kind of worry."

"Brothers are supposed to worry." Scott pulled out his notebook and a pen. "It would be good for you to start taking a few precautions. Bring Bruce's Labrador to work with you when you visit clients' homes."

"Is that necessary?"

"Dogs sense trouble. Do it for a few weeks while we figure out who this guy is."

She nodded, accepting she needed to do something. Three burglaries were three too many when she was the one discovering them. She missed Bruce; she missed Grace. And Wolf—she'd never realized how big a hole his absence would make in her life until he wasn't around.

FIVE

★ ★ ★

USS *GEORGE WASHINGTON* (CVN 73)
MEDITERRANEAN SEA OFF THE COAST OF TURKEY

The stateroom was hot. Grace shed her flight suit and pulled on a T-shirt and shorts. It was a small room for six women to share, three bunk beds on one wall, lockers and small desks on the other. Her roommates were two pilots and three electronic countermeasure specialists who flew in the Prowler's backseats to handle the intricacies of navigation and electronic jamming. By combining personal effects, the six of them had been able to squeeze in a semblance of a bookshelf and a music collection.

Grace stretched out on the lower, middle bunk, her one spot of personal space for this six-month deployment. She had two feet of clearance to the bunk above, enough to turn over without hitting her head if she was careful and a width that meant she would tumble onto the floor if she woke and turned without realizing where she was. The mattress could hardly be called comfortable, but exhaustion changed her definition of acceptable. Whenever possible she tried to catch a few minutes of quiet time before a mission in order to separate everything that had gone before during the day from the reality of what was coming.

Out of long habit she set her watch alarm for twenty minutes before she settled her head back. At this point in a sea tour, making the assumption she wouldn't fall asleep the moment her body relaxed was a mistake. The pillow had a new pillowcase and it still

49

smelled faintly of Downy. She had brought six pillowcases, folded and sealed in plastic bags, so that she would have a new one not washed in shipboard laundry available for each month.

There was an inch-wide red ribbon stretched taut under the frame of the bunk above her. A letter she was writing to Jill was tucked under the ribbon on the left side. A white envelope addressed to her with a scripted *B* in the return address corner was tucked on the right. It was from Bruce. It had taken three weeks for the letter to get from wherever he was stationed back to the U.S. and then through channels to catch up with the carrier group to her. She had read the letter so many times it was close to falling apart. She fingered the envelope and tugged it down to read again.

Gracie ~

Wolf tells me you prefer Gracie and that you're afraid of heights. Instinct tells me he's probably exaggerating a bit over the heights and stating his preference for your name. Feel free to correct both.

This note is to tell you that Wolf is fine. I don't want you to worry when you hear what happened. I've noticed the way you bite your lip when watching Wolf do his I'm-invincible imitation.

He's not invincible.

Some idiot (me) made the mistake of assuming Wolf would weave left like a smart man instead of right. We were playing some basketball and—long story. He's got an interesting looking eye. The swelling isn't bad and his sight is fine; it's just colorful. Two SEALs against two PJs—okay, it wasn't the smartest decision we've ever made to kill some time, but at least it was basketball and not something more interesting.

Did you know Wolf carries your picture? He used to pull it out when he needed cover to say he already had a lady in his life. I personally think it's just because he likes to let it be known he's got good taste. He loves you, Grace. A lot. (Lately he's been pulling out Jill's picture to make his point. That's not as easy to take as yours, but I'm working on it.)

The SEALs won the game. Wolf is gloating and crowing and making me miserable. What do you have on him that I could use to level the accounts a bit? I'd owe you one.

Yours, Bruce

Bruce wrote a nice letter; it made her smile. In prior tours she had been so busy just figuring out carrier life that homesickness never had a chance to settle in. Now she was older, tired, and sea life had a sense of routine to it. When she stopped and caught her breath, there was a new sense of loneliness. She wondered about what was going on in Jill's life, and she worried about Wolf. Lately she'd been thinking about Bruce too. The letter was a blessing.

Had he received her reply? She hadn't been sure how to answer it and in the end had just picked up a pen and written her first impressions.

Her watch alarm sounded. Grace checked the time. She had a mission briefing in fifteen minutes. It was just as well. She'd lay here in her bunk and puzzle about Bruce. He had the same dilemma she did of juggling a stateside life while being gone for long periods of time, and yet it appeared he'd figured out how to be comfortable with his life. He'd come to the deployment party, sat by the pool, content and in no hurry. She envied him that.

Lord, I decided no more regrets, just wise decisions. Bruce—he's a nice guy. Watching him with Jill over the years sealed that conclusion.

I made the decision to answer his note with more openness than I normally would have. Did I make a mistake in my reply?

NATO FORWARD OPERATING LOCATION
TURKEY/IRAQ BORDER

Someone had mailed him chocolates. Bruce looked with regret at the mess of melted chocolate with bumps of nuts and square-cut caramels. The sugar hadn't crystallized; it was new chocolate. It had pooled at the left edge of the candy box and hardened there. A swirl of green from a mint-flavored chocolate ran through it.

He looked at the packing. The box was from a candy shop in Indiana. It had traveled halfway around the world to find him.

"Another one?"

Bruce moved so his partner could get past him in the small tent. "I told you there was a reason Alaska would make a better deployment." He cracked the chocolate mass to pull free the envelope that had been inside the candy box tucked in a plastic bag. He handed the candy to Rich.

Striker opened the letter. The handwriting was shaky and had the elegance of someone from a former generation who had learned to write in beautiful script. Since it didn't look like a letter from a twenty-something, bubbly, blue-eyed blonde who couldn't write in paragraphs, he set the note aside to read and answer later. He'd made a rule about the bubbly blondes who lately sent the bulk of his mail—he didn't answer them. Writing back just encouraged them.

Rich took out his pocketknife. "We can shave it into edible chunks."

"Sanitize that thing first."

Rich tugged open the pocket of his cammies and retrieved his lighter. He sterilized the blade.

Mail for most military men was their lifeline. For Bruce it had become something of a problem. "I wish they would start writing you." Rich was wealthy, good looking, a first generation American born of European immigrants. His partner should be the one getting this deluge of mail, not him.

Rich used his hot knife to melt through the chocolate and break off a chunk. "You're the legend."

"You were at that rescue too." That rescue in the gulf was beginning to haunt him. Yes, he'd rescued the boy and it had been pretty dramatic footage. But while he'd spun in the air hoisting out the boy, his partner had been on the deck securing the captain.

"I'm smart. You're dumb. You got your picture taken," Rich replied, reaching down to see how much mail was in the burlap sack emblazoned with the warning *Property of the Air Force Postmaster*. "You'd think they were writing Santa Claus."

"I wish I could find that reporter and make him eat his dictionary for calling me an eligible bachelor." Bruce nudged the sack with his boot. "Quit laughing at me and help."

The picture of him dangling in the air under the massive Seahawk helicopter with the kid swallowed against his uniform had shown up not only in the newspapers but now in the popular entertainment magazines. The story of the rescue grew with every retelling the reporters did.

The least the postmaster could do was lose his forwarding location for a few weeks to stop this deluge. "You ducked the AP reporter and left me like a sitting duck. I thought you were my partner."

"I am in things that count. Your life was boring. I helped you out."

"Your definition of help is interesting."

Rich waved a letter. "This one is good. You're to come to dinner next month." Rich moved the page closer to his face to make out the writing. "I think this is her e-mail address. It's smudged with lipstick."

"Trash." He had long ago gotten over the disquiet of tossing mail without a reply.

The tent flap was pushed back. "So this is where you two disappeared. I thought you were coming to watch CNN."

"Wolf, get in here. You're recruited to open mail."

"I might get a paper cut."

"Sit."

The Navy SEAL awkwardly folded himself into a chair not designed for a man his size. The boredom of afternoons on deployment never changed. There might be action coming tonight, but all the preparations were over and they had a few hours to kill.

Wolf picked up a letter and tore open the end. He dumped the contents out. "This one is kind of cute." Wolf turned the picture for his consideration.

Bruce tugged out a shoebox from under his cot. "Add it to the gallery."

"How many pictures have you been sent?"

"I stopped counting."

"I guess you don't need Gracie's picture anymore."

"Don't you dare tell her about this mail." Bruce saved the stamp to add to his collection. "Any word yet on tonight?"

"Bear is checking." Wolf picked up another letter from the bag. "I was able to snag a lift to Incirlik this weekend so I can try Jill again. You two want to come?"

"And be confined to another base? Boring," Rich replied. The recent earthquake had damaged roads and bridges in the Incirlik area so traffic off the base had been limited to essential travel.

"A real shower with hot water."

"True. Is Cougar going with you?" Rich asked.

"Yes."

Rich looked over at Bruce. "I still don't know. Tagging along with the Bear Cubs would be bad for our image."

Wolf flicked his wrist and sent a letter spinning into Rich's chest.

"We'll come along to keep you out of trouble," Bruce agreed.

"We'll teach you how to get into some." Wolf offered as he picked up another letter. "Well what do we have here—" He wagged the envelope. "Gracie's handwriting. What's it worth to you?"

Bruce dropped the stack he was sorting. "You don't want me to answer that."

Wolf held it up. "I find it interesting she wrote you and not me."

"Your letter got lost."

"Nope. I just got knocked down in her priorities. You know on a carrier it's letters or sleep, rarely time for both." He relented and handed over the letter.

Rich and Wolf were both watching him. Bruce tucked Gracie's letter in his pocket. "I think I'm going to take a walk and stretch my legs."

Wolf laughed. "The ducking out is noted."

"I'm a smart man." The few letters he would answer, including the one that had come with the chocolates, Bruce put with his personal papers. He found a notebook. "Come find me if there's news."

"Sure. Rich, where's that sports magazine?"

Bruce retreated to the bench set up at the end of the flight line, sat down, and propped his feet up on an empty packing crate. It had been ages since he felt this kind of anticipation. The envelope was white, creased, and it showed postmarks over postmarks from the various military stops. He took out his pocketknife and neatly opened the envelope. He was delighted to see the thick contents. He pulled out the pages.

Bruce –

You're hearing laughter. I know Wolf. It's a safe assumption that he was the one who suggested the basketball game. Sorry for a less-than-coherent note. I'm trying to wedge this pad of paper on my bunk since my desk has a super-glue experiment drying on it at the moment (don't ask). I forgot how noisy it is to sleep one level below the flight deck. The squadron is landing literally over my head. I drew a stateroom on the 03 Gallery deck near the dirty-shirt wardroom. I can have lunch in my flight suit and come back to the stateroom for a nap before evening briefings. (That hasn't happened yet since deployment, but I dream about doing it.)

We've been having moderate seas and good weather. I'm loving the flying time and often getting two hops a day. Tell Wolf my landing streak is growing; the recent streak is eight of ten okays. He's going to owe me a nice dinner next time we meet up. *GW* had a pitching deck during a night landing and it sent me into the second wire, and I got a fluke bolter last Friday when the hook bounced. I'd already kicked in the afterburners just in case, but there was a heart-stopping moment as I ran out of ship before aerodynamics kicked in. I hate the water, big time. And the ship just about slammed into the rear of my jet.

I'm tired. It is very late. I just wanted to say thanks for your note. I appreciate it. I'm sorry this reply is all about work.

I'm fine with being called Gracie, and I'm only scared of heights when I'm watching Wolf do something foolish. Someone forgot to tell him about gravity.

He likes to jump out of planes. Mr. Parachute Jumper— would you care to explain that fascination? I've never understood it. The dread of my life is pulling that ejection handle.

You asked for something on Wolf. That's easy. Just ask him what he did when he was fourteen that got him grounded for a month. Think fireworks, a magnifying glass, and a microphone. You'll get the picture. It was quite an experiment. He did shatter the crystal glass on the stoop…and the car windows.

I'm listening to The Fly, our very own FM radio station. Navy Seaman Jules Porter just began a trio of fifties' hits. I do love the old music.

News of the world comes in bits and pieces. I've heard the drought is getting worse across Syria and that the Turkish currency is going through another upheaval. Jill sent me copies of the NASA newspapers. There was a write-up on the cancellation of the X-33 space plane. In a way I'm glad Ben isn't around to see the failure. He always hoped to see the replacement to the shuttle during his lifetime. He wanted to someday fly that vehicle. Riding a rocket—he had more confidence in technology than I do.

It's late. I'm rambling. Whether mail gets off this ship anytime soon is anyone's guess. I hope this finds you having a boring deployment.

Good night, Bruce.

Grace

He read the letter twice. It was a good note; it sounded like her. The handwriting had begun to wander on the last page and he could see her fighting sleep. There wasn't much personal but he hadn't expected much. She'd gone well beyond what he thought she would write. She sounded focused on the job at hand.

Bruce smiled as he tugged out his pen. He'd been thinking about letter number two.

Gracie ~

It was good to get your note. There's a mission tonight and I'm wondering what you'll be doing. I don't question your flying skills; it's all those people on the ground trying to shoot you out of the sky that I'm a little concerned with. My deployment has been boring—only one set of dog tags so far—and I hope tonight continues that streak.

Congratulations on the landings. I hope the bolter represents your one and only close call for this tour. I bet you could will that plane to fly if it came down to it.

I understand Wolf's love of jumping. It's skill versus the elements. Jumping at night from high altitude with oxygen—it's not a civilian thing to do. It's falling through a cloud and getting stung with water drops. (By the way, they are pointy at the top.) It's trying to navigate when there is no sense of falling. Once you reach equilibrium you are essentially floating and it's serenely quiet.

Jumping is all about watching your altimeter and GPS and trying to figure out how to land on exact coordinates that may be twenty miles away from where you stepped out of the plane. It's a challenge, Gracie. And for that reason, you might as well have written Wolf's name on it.

I've lived long enough to learn all of the "oh, by the ways" that come with combat jumping. I've only had a canopy fail twice and a guy crash into my canopy once. There was that one time I accidentally dropped through a thunderstorm—don't ever do that, Gracie. It scares the daylights out of a sane person.

The news about Wolf and fireworks will be useful; thanks.

I've stood watch for some of the shuttle flights. Ben was one of the pilots who knew the nuances, and when he briefed he did it with a practical style. Ben trusted the technology, but even more he trusted the people who made up the NASA team backing him up.

NASA lost a good man when he died. I know how painful it had to have been to get news of his accident while on deployment. Jill called me the day Ben was killed; I was stateside that day. She wanted so badly not to have to call you with the news, but she also didn't want the news coming from someone else. Thank you for the gracious way you handled that moment of grief.

Not taking relationships for granted is part of what life teaches everyone. When you're in the military, you just learn that lesson sooner. I think of it as the life squeeze, the pressure deployments put on decisions about priorities. Most people in the civilian world can become workaholics and ignore family because they come home every night and think it's enough. Only when you're gone for months at a time do you learn how strong the relationships you have really are.

Civilians lose out on so much: doing something that benefits a nation, being in a job that requires excellence every day, getting reminded regularly why you should pay attention to the real priorities in life. The military teaches you not to get attached to the place or the thing but the people.

Ben carried your picture. I mentioned I knew you through Wolf, and the man lit up and tugged out your picture and talked about the trip you two were planning to the Dallas air show. Remember those good times. God can fill those holes I'm sure you feel when life gets quiet.

I've been thinking, Gracie—since I spend the majority of my time waiting for something to happen and you run an eighteen-hour-a-day schedule, my next letter might just be reflections on Ecuador, on dogs, and remodeling a house. I owe you a better explanation for that first letter you got out of the blue. I heard from Wolf that after you got my letter you grilled him about Ecuador because he had never mentioned how close to the edge it was.

Knowing what happened, I'm not surprised Wolf decided to remain silent. The man saved a lot of lives that day. I could patch them up and keep them alive, but Wolf was the one holding back the onslaught so I could work. My partner Rich had been hit in the initial rescue attempt and Wolf became my second. He jokes, he loves adrenaline, but when you need him, Grace, Wolf is the steady man who is there to do what needs to be done.

You'll probably be on the way from the Med to the Persian Gulf by the time you get this note. I'm sorry mail is so slow. When I'm stateside I'll try e-mail and see if I can get a message through, although shipboard e-mail has its own problems. I know, however, how nice it is to get real letters that can wear out from being read many times. I'll let you go. Good night, Gracie.

God bless, Bruce

John 14:27

Peace I leave with you; my peace I give to you; not as the world gives do I give to you. Let not your hearts be troubled, neither let them be afraid.

SIX

★ ★ ★

USS *GEORGE WASHINGTON* (CVN 73)
MEDITERRANEAN SEA OFF THE COAST OF TURKEY

Grace tugged open the steel door to the squadron ready room. It was painted a deep blue with the VFA-83 RAMPAGERS emblem emblazoned at eye level. It wasn't a large room, space on an aircraft carrier was measured out in inches, but it was a great home. It was aviator country not sailor territory.

On the nearest leather chair—designed with a swivel writing board to become a desk and to recline to become a comfortable place to sleep—she dumped her gloves and her kneeboard. The briefing was over and the final weather report was due in forty minutes by closed-circuit TV. Gracie checked the mail slots tucked along the wall. "Dragon, no mail? I saw the prop flight arrive."

She was disappointed at the empty cubbyhole. Wolf's letters were stacking up somewhere; she knew he was writing one every Monday, Wednesday, and Friday. They would eventually arrive in a big stack. Jill was great about writing every week and sending notes in her signature Stateside Support blue envelopes, but this week's letter had not yet come through. Grace normally didn't let herself get up for mail call to avoid the inevitable disappointment when nothing came for her. But today was different. She was also hoping to hear from Bruce.

The junior officer assigned to housekeep for the squadron for the day reached in the bottom drawer of his desk and pulled out a white box. "Are you going to share the loot? It wouldn't fit in your box."

Gracie tugged open the card, delighted when she saw the scrawl. "Wolf." She was going to have to hug that man next time she saw him. His packages were the best. She split open the tape and opened the box. "Licorice." Red. Her favorite. She laughed at a second note inside stuck to a cartoon of a penguin trying to fly.

"You are lucky in your relatives."

"Absolutely."

Grace offered Dragon a piece and then took the package over to leave by the coffeepot. She loved to be able to treat the squadron.

She took a licorice whip back with her to the recliner and pulled up the writing board that swiveled and locked over the right chair arm. She sorted out the kneeboard cards and maps that would fly with her tonight.

She'd helped plan the mission over the last week so the times, altitudes, flight lanes, and fuel numbers for the six-hour flight were already neatly written down and color coded. She was flying the Syrian border with the squadron executive officer while others in the squadron diverted to strike assignments. The last minute change had been to the duration and altitude profiles they maintained as they lingered on that border.

Peter had assigned himself to the lead of her element for one simple reason: They were the west flank of this strike mission. Syrian airspace would be less than a mile away. If Syria decided to intrude, they'd be on the front line with MiGs coming at them. She'd been flying an F/A-18 Hornet for six years. As a team they could mount a hard fight if required to protect the others in the squadron. Tonight would be an intense flight.

She scanned the gray security card. It was generated each day by carrier intelligence. The card listed code words for locations and planes so that the daily radio traffic made sense only to someone else working off the same sheet. She was a Viper tonight.

From the drawer under the footrest she pulled out her small tape player and earphones. She slipped on the earphones and clicked on the music. Settling back in the recliner, she closed her eyes and started visualizing the mission from launch to trap recovery back on the deck. In her profession, danger was tucked far down the checklists. Point and counterpoint. In the time it took a bullet to fly she could launch a missile and move her plane a thousand feet in the air. Shooting her out of the sky would take a golden bullet and a lucky shot.

"I want to live." She shook her head to dislodge the words Bruce had written her all those months ago while in Ecuador. The letter had been eloquent. And it was still haunting her.

NATO FORWARD OPERATING LOCATION
TURKEY/IRAQ BORDER

The headquarters building was cramped as communications, weather, weapons, and logistics all vied for space. Bruce followed Wolf to the secure room. Action for the night was beginning to pick up. The SEAL mission was a go. The map on the wall overlaid the classified missions with the air tasking orders. It was a complex mosaic.

"Do you really think he's going to defect?" Bruce asked, getting to the heart of the question that would be answered tonight.

"Fifty-fifty. He stood us up last time. He'll likely do it again."

"Quite a risk just to go see."

Wolf nodded. "The official orders came down as 'at all cost.' If he wants to come out, we'll go get him."

The Syrian deputy intelligence minister had grown up a friend of the royal family, attended Western universities, and had a master's degree in English history of all things. He'd been a hawk at the Israeli-Syrian peace negotiations, and yet from the classified intercepts appeared to be a dove within the government. It would be the highest-level defection since the death of President Hafez al-Assad and the ascension of his son to lead the country.

Wolf leaned against the wall beside the map, crossing his arms. "He was involved in the quiet trade that happened to get the CIA station chief kidnapped in Lebanon out safe and fast. He's plugged in, and if he wants out—the risk is worth it. The meeting has been set up for west of Al Hasakah."

Bruce looked at the location and winced. Twenty-two miles inside Syria. A desert approach, but still one that would expose the SEALs to enormous risks. "What can you tell me about the area? I know you've been there before."

Wolf just smiled. "There's a Bedouin oasis around the deep well that is one of the few watering places in this area. It's a small place, a couple tents, more camels than cars. Desert all around. It's normally not inhabited during the night as it's open to the desert winds. It is more a passing point to the rock ridge to the south where there is decent shelter and some vegetation for livestock. We'll come in from the north, scope it out, and if we see the signal, one team will go in while the gunship chopper circles." Wolf opened the flap of his jacket pocket. "I'll save you some time. My updated security info."

"Not very confident, are you?"

"Defectors have a habit of changing their minds."

The information used to identify a man behind enemy lines as a friendly—unique number, unique facts—had been written for convenience on the back of a pocket-sized photo. Bruce glanced at the photo. This one of Gracie was new. Wolf had snapped her picture while she was playing volleyball, and that gleam in her eye as she got ready to spike the ball made Bruce smile. He missed her enormously. "Thanks for the picture."

"My pleasure."

Bruce slipped it into his pocket, not missing the fact Wolf had sacrificed a picture of Grace rather than Jill when he needed something small and lasting on which to write down the information. "Grace is going to be mad if you get hurt tonight." Not to mention Jill's reaction. That was one call Bruce did not ever want to have to make.

"Tell me about it." Wolf ran his finger along the map. "New tasking orders were issued to extend the air cover on the border."

Bruce noted the transit times and mentally shifted his own watch schedule for the night out to 0300. "You'll have all the air cover you need." The planes covering the Syrian border were launching as part of the strike package. "*GW* has already launched the first planes."

SEVEN

★ ★ ★

The flight deck of the USS *George Washington* was deafening, and the thirty-one knot wind over the deck drove the dissipating steam and engine exhaust in eddies. Planes were wedged together with their wings folded up to squeeze the maximum out of every inch of precious space. Catapult 1 hurled a Prowler into the air. It was not a place for pilots to linger.

"Have a good flight, Gracie."

"Thanks, Henry." The plane boss had the jet ready to fly, and her preflight had found nothing amiss. Grace slid on the fire retardant flight gloves and tightened the flight suit wristbands, then grasped the handholds and swung her legs over and slid down to the seat of the F/A-18 Hornet.

Leaning down, she removed the safety pins on the ejection seat and stored them away, then fastened the multiple-point safety harness. She secured the ankle restraints and tested them by pulling hard against the seat. If she had to eject, firing the explosive bolts would propel the seat from the plane. The last thing she wanted was two broken legs in the process.

The ties between her and the plane increased as she plugged in communication and the oxygen necessary for high altitude flights. She secured her kneeboard. Even as she did the routine she was aware of the need for speed. Twenty-three planes had to launch in eighteen minutes. Making that happen without killing someone took a miracle of coordination.

Men and women in different colored shirts to make very clear their assignments ran the flight deck, and there wasn't a pilot aboard who didn't know at the moment they were at the bottom of the totem pole. The purple shirt "grapes" were handling fuel, tons of it, and the red shirts were handling live ordnance. They were sweating every detail. Grace tried not to think about the dangers she could do nothing about as she sat in her plane and finished the internal preflight checklist. The sooner she got off this flight deck the better.

She signaled the yellow shirt plane director she was ready to start the engines. After a check around the plane he cleared her to do so. She started first the left and then the right. They came alive with a muted roar. She ran them up to check fuel and power flow and found all systems were nominal.

The plane director motioned her to taxi. Grace kept a sharp eye on him as she eased the throttle forward with her left hand to move the Hornet from its deck-edge parking place. Her jet wash could kill someone or explode another aircraft, and she couldn't see the carrier deck around her plane.

He motioned her to hold and she eased back on the throttle, bringing the jet to a stop with the nose nearly touching the massive blast deflector protecting her plane from the jet wash of the plane being launched. The F/A-18 Hornet was a heavy, stubborn plane when fully fueled and armed. As graceful as it was in the air, it was unresponsive on land, or in this case steel, due to its back-weighted center of gravity. It took throttle on both engines to move its bulk.

She would be launching into the twilight. She took a deep breath as the plane ahead went to maximum burners. She hoped his launch was smooth so she could get away before that moment where the horizon shimmered in the fading light and her eyes lied about what was water and sky.

She punched a button and the takeoff checklist appeared in her left display. She was fighting the clock now and there was no time to waste. She ran the list, slamming the control surfaces around to check maximum movement, pushing the rudders, scanning the internal panels checking oil pressure, hydraulics, fuel flow—looking for anything with even a hint of a problem before it became too late to address it.

The safety officer gave final approval, the deflector shield lowered, and the plane director signaled her forward onto the catapult track. Steam was still swirling from the catapult shot of the EA-6B Prowler just launched. Dread began to build deep at the base of Gracie's spine as she eased the throttle forward and rolled the Hornet across the catapult hook. The nose wheels locked and the green shirt catapult crewman hurried to attach a holdback bar to keep her plane in place until the catapult fired.

Two ordnance men moved beneath the wings of her plane, pulling safety pins to arm the weapons. One of the catapult officers held up a weight board, 41,300 pounds, and Gracie confirmed it with her own readouts and signaled her agreement.

Underneath her, in the interior of the carrier, pressure was building to the point at the touch of a button, the steam-driven catapult would hurl her from the carrier deck, taking her from a dead stop to 125 knots in under 2 seconds.

She rested her hands on her thighs and deliberately tightened then loosened each muscle group in her arms and back to help her settle more deeply into the seat while she waited for the catapult officer to signal full burners.

On the next catapult the executive officer, Peter "Thunder" Stanford, was also getting ready to launch. She'd be off first. She felt an overwhelming sense of dependency on God during these moments. She knew if the catapult failed she was dead. She would hit the water doing anywhere from sixty to a hundred knots, and the impact would shear the plane into pieces.

If she did manage to eject in the two seconds before impact, she would either land on the carrier deck like a pancake and have her ejection seat chute get sucked into the roaring jet engines of another F/A-18 Hornet or she would land in the water and literally get run over by the carrier steaming ahead to maintain the thirty-knot minimum wind across the flight deck.

She prayed for safety but she didn't dwell on it. She had decided years ago when she chose this profession that she would accept the training rigors, the risks, the dangers, and not ask God to remove the consequences of her choices. She was a Navy pilot. She loved it. And she accepted everything that meant.

The catapult officer signaled for full burners. Gracie tightened her left hand, took a deep breath, and shoved the throttle full open. The engines roared as the afterburners kicked in, the sound deafening even inside the cockpit with the helmet on, and the plane began to quiver around her.

The status screens were still green. She was good to go.

God, don't let me die in the next twenty seconds.

She took her right hand from the stick and saluted the catapult officer, signaling all systems were good for launch.

She braced her head against the seat rest as the catapult officer reached down and touched the deck, getting himself down to survive the wash of air as he visually told the operator just off the flight deck to launch the plane. The operator depressed the launch button.

The hold bar released. The steam-driven catapult fired.

The F/A-18 shot forward.

Her head was driven back, her chest felt like it was being crushed, and her eyes watered.

Aerodynamics. Lift. Propulsion. *Come on, beat gravity; you can do it....*

The ship was gone from beneath her; she was looking at the sky. Her hand crept toward the yellow-and-black striped ejection handle as the plane dipped and the airspeed slowed approaching 110 knots. She had to reach 120 knots or she died. Had they set the catapult weight wrong? Was she going to suffer a cold shot?

The plane's speed crept past the safety of 120 knots and her hands returned to the stick and throttle. The thirty-degree climb was grabbing air now, beating it into submission—she could feel the plane taking control of the aerodynamic battle.

"Viper 02, airborne." Her calm words reflected none of the surging adrenaline. She'd survived.

A launch was almost as harrowing as a landing, a moment in time where everything she had ever feared dumped its emotions into her system and left her with wet palms and exhausted muscles when it was over.

The ship and its carrier deck were half a mile behind her. She had the sky, the plane, and the beat of her own heart. Six years flying an F/A-18 Hornet and every time up was like the first time. This moment of joy could never be described.

There wasn't time to savor it. She switched from talking to the carrier air traffic control center to the combat control center, cleared her panels to flight status, and scanned for weapons or navigation failures. The last thing she needed was for live ordnance to jam during the jolt of takeoff and be stuck a few feet away under her wing.

"Viper 01, airborne."

She couldn't see Thunder, but he was now in the climb-out pattern somewhere to her right. They would be flying a mile apart in a combat spread, protecting each other from a plane getting in their dangerous six o'clock blind spot. The full squadron would be in similar formations assigned to a half-mile wide lane of airspace.

A touch of a button brought up the navigation markers she had preprogrammed into the system. They would enter Turkish airspace, fly the length of the country, and pass over the massive dams on the Euphrates. They would enter Iraq along the Tigris River valley.

Gracie arched her back and settled deep in the seat, getting comfortable; they would be flying over international waters, and then it would be land beneath them. Another long mission had begun.

EIGHT

★ ★ ★

FORWARD OPERATING LOCATION
TURKEY/IRAQ BORDER

M ission underway."
The communications officer didn't have to raise his voice to be heard. He was giving play-by-play and there was not a PJ in the room who wasn't hanging on those words. The planes had just crossed into Iraqi airspace. Wolf and the other SEALs led by Bear Baker would soon be crossing the Syrian border to race for their pickup.

Striker glanced at the clock. Right on time. It was going to be a very long night. He got to his feet and stepped around Rich who was spreading out his first of hundreds of games of solitaire. Bruce stepped outside. The sun had set over the Taurus Mountains and stars covered the sky. To the west the first clouds of the incoming cold front darkened the horizon. The temperature had dropped noticeably.

As soon as Iraq realized the extent of the strike, they would throw everything they had at the planes. Surface-to-air missiles, antiaircraft artillery—as good as the coalition pilots were, there were still serious threats that could bring down a plane.

Bruce didn't wear a maroon beret because the military thought it was a nice color. It spoke for all the blood PJs had spilled over the years doing this job. The motto they promised came from the heart. They went out that others might live.

Lord, don't let me need to rescue a pilot. Please keep Grace and

Wolf safe. He could do what needed to be done. He could be brave. He just couldn't always be there in time. He wanted no family to face devastating news tonight hearing a plane had gone down.

CNN would be going live as soon as it became apparent a strike of this scale was being executed. Jill would be watching, locked on every word of news. Bruce wished she had been able to talk with Wolf today.

Bruce had chosen the right profession. Nights like this confirmed it. No matter what the personal cost, he was the man on the front line to keep danger from touching those at home. He walked down to the flight line. Friends were risking their lives tonight. It was going to be a very long night.

NINE

★ ★ ★

TWENTY-TWO MILES INSIDE SYRIA
WEST OF THE TOWN OF AL HASSAKEH

Wolf felt the sweat under his flak jacket freeze as the air rushed in the open door of the helicopter. He had the forward gun trained at the racing sand and the occasional break of scrub bushes that struggled to hold on to what soil there was in the rocky terrain at the edge of the desert. In the night vision goggles, the plants stood out as obstacles in the smooth backdrop, spots of accumulated heat cooling in the night air.

Most of Syria was desert, and while there was safety in the vast distances, there was also danger as sounds echoed and visibility stretched for miles.

Ahead of them, the lead helicopter raced toward the pickup with its engines red-lined for all the speed that could be pulled from them, taking the most risk by leading the way.

If the man had stood them up again, if he had set a trap... They were ready to hit hard in order to get out of the area. But if he did defect... It was a constant effort to avert war, Syria and Israel over the Golan Heights, Syria and Turkey over the simmering crisis of water as drought took hold in the region and dams along the Euphrates robbed Syria of critical water. Intelligence was everything in this conflict.

Wolf glanced over at his partner. Cougar was scanning the frequencies listening for anything out of the ordinary on the Syrian defense network. "Anything?"

Cougar gave a thumbs-up.

"Thirty seconds."

Wolf shifted around as the warning came from the pilot. Bear in the lead helicopter would be taking the most risk, scoping out the area. Only then would they go in to bring the man out.

The helicopter ahead flashed red infrared strobes and moments later it flared, dropped speed, and began to circle. "Clear!"

Wolf braced his weight as the helicopter went nose down and spurted forward toward the pickup point. The lead gunship swerved left and took a defensive higher circle.

"Setting down."

Sand rushed up as Wolf strained to see the man they had come to meet. A desert animal the size of a rabbit jumped and Wolf had to check the instinct to fire. He wanted to be the one racing out to grab the man, but that task had been given to Cougar and Pup. The arrangement had been precise. The man would be at the well, alone.

There!

Cougar and Pup jumped out and took off at a sprint.

It was an agonizing minute.

"Do you have him?" The terse request from the pilot in the chopper above broke the silence and put into words the growing unease with sitting exposed. *Come on. Come on.* Wolf willed his partner back.

Pup appeared from the whirling sand. Then their guest. Then Cougar.

Wolf snagged the man's arm as Cougar literally threw him aboard. He tugged Pup aboard and then grabbed his partner. "We've got him. Go!"

The helicopter went airborne and a wall of sand rose to swallow them. They turned on a track to the north in order to exit the country along a different vector.

Time began to crawl by. Twenty-two miles was a lifetime of flight.

"We've got trouble coming," Cougar said over the internal comm. "Fighters to the south are hearing orders. Push it to the border, gentlemen."

Their pilot didn't wait to see radar tracks to confirm what Cougar was overhearing on the burgeoning radio traffic. He angled the blades to maximum tolerance.

Wolf watched the night sky for moving points of light on the horizon. He could fight a man. He couldn't fight a plane.

OPERATION NORTHERN WATCH

NORTHERN IRAQ, THIRTY-SIXTH PARALLEL

"Viper 02, radar check."

Grace scanned the displays. Long-range radar showed the friendly signatures of their own strike fighters at twenty-eight miles west. She toggled a switch. Threat radar was seeking to the south and one far to the west was reflecting their direction. Syria was still quiet. "We're clear."

She felt for the others in the strike package who were getting the brunt of the Iraqi reaction. In the distance the barrage of exploding AAA was bright in her nightscope.

Flying two feet off Thunder's wing in formation was an experience. Peter began the curl to reverse their track and smoothly took them to the lower altitude in the tasking orders. She matched his moves. So far this mission had ticked off like clockwork. Syria was now on her left. They were at the halfway point.

Her radar showed a response from an IFF transponder far inside Syria. Gracie looked twice and went to a targeted search. "Sixteen miles, ten o'clock, low."

"Cowboys," Peter replied after he took a look.

The radar tracks were lifting out of the background clutter

moving on a vector north. They were distinctive blips now. A Pave Hawk and a Pave Low III, the helicopters were flying close to the ground. Some sort of special op was underway deep inside Syria. It explained the change to their tasking orders.

Wolf? It would fit a SEAL op.

A bright flash lit up the skyline over Mosul. Gracie glanced at the time. The power station should have just been hit. It was the key node for Iraqi's entire air defense grid. It was also the last strike point for the mission. The fighters should be racing back north to the Turkish border.

Peter led them in a change of altitude again.

Warning tones burst on around the cockpit. "Break!" Peter ordered. Gracie rolled hard right away from Peter as he broke high. A tracking radar had painted them. She flipped a switch with her thumb to change from air-to-air to air-to-ground.

Warble tones sounded as a surface-to-air missile cone of energy searched the sky.

She slammed the stick back to get altitude.

A SAM raced up from the ground, a white heat trail blazing in the night.

A low shot. The helicopters were being targeted. It was cold comfort. She had a reasonable probability of breaking lock whereas the helicopters were practically stationary targets for a missile.

The helicopter pilots reacted and were already racing apart in ninety-degree angles, firing chaff as they jinked directions. The trailing helicopter didn't have a chance. The SAM exploded in a bright fireball. The helicopter showed briefly on the other side of the fireball and then disappeared from view.

Wolf.

Lord, don't let it be Wolf.

"He's down," Peter said, his voice cold. He immediately passed the vectors to the circling AWACs.

Come on, lock on. Gracie listened to the HARM missile search for a lock on the radar that had directed that SAM. The seeker warbled in her ear but never pitched high. They'd fired point-blank and the radar was already off. "No lock."

"Close to half a mile."

She was relieved at the order. Whoever was down below was a friend. She moved closer to the Syrian border to tighten the air cover even while she tensed for another SAM to suddenly come up at them.

"Bandits at 38 south, climbing," Peter warned. She went to long radar. Syrian fighters were taking off.

She prayed they stayed on their side of the border.

SYRIA/IRAQ BORDER

The ground exploded under them in an upshoot of sand. Wolf had crashed before but nothing like this. He saw the falling tail rudder hit the ground and explode. "Don't," he yelled at Cougar as he reached out and yanked his partner back inside. "We landed in a mine field!"

He strained to look forward. The pilot was moving but the copilot was slumped. The noise was deafening as the pilot struggled to kill engines still turning. The hardened undercarriage had saved their lives but the probability of fire was high if the fuel tanks leaked.

He shoved their guest back into the center seat. "Pup, cover him." The youngest SEAL in the squadron already had his sidearm out. Defector or not, the man would turn them in to try to save his own hide.

"Get on the door gun and hit anything that moves," Wolf yelled to Cougar. He struggled forward to help with the copilot. Grace nagged at him about getting into trouble. This was beyond trouble.

A minefield, but which side of the border? Syria or Iraq?

A bullet slapped at the inside roof of the chopper. And Wolf started praying. A sniper had already found them.

TEN

★ ★ ★

SYRIA/IRAQ BORDER

A minefield. Striker braced against the restraint harness as the Pave Low helicopter raced south. He'd gone into tough places before, but this had him wishing he'd finished writing Grace a very special letter. One that began *Dear Darling...*

He secured another clip for his weapon. There were times he appreciated being a soldier first. They would have to hover high and hoist the SEALs out so as not to set off more mines with the change in air pressure. The lead SEAL helicopter could provide cover but it couldn't get to the men on the ground without help.

Sand was swirling behind the Pave Low as Dasher hugged the ground. His friend was one of the best pilots in the 720th Special Tactics Group, but that didn't eliminate the nerves tightening Striker's gut. He hated being this distance from the ground. He preferred a height he could parachute from, not one that threatened to slam him into the ground if they breathed the wrong direction.

Striker braced his hands on the crash bar as the helicopter flared and abruptly dropped speed. The gunship providing their escort continued at maximum speed to join up with the circling helicopter. His night vision goggles picked up the radiating heat of the shot down helicopter in the distance. A surface-to-air missile had brought it down. Another one would likely be waiting with their name on it. Over his headset he could hear the SEALs talking about a sniper.

"Air cover?"

His partner Rich was searching for it. "There! Seven o'clock low."

Bruce found the blur in the sky and realized as the image clarified that the planes were racing directly at them. There were two of them but they looked like one dot in the sky they were hugging so close together. "Do they know we're the good guys?"

"AWACs is relaying."

"I bet they're a little edgy right now."

"MiGs. SAMs. Downed men. I wouldn't trade places," Rich agreed.

A burst of automated gunfire erupted, tracers sweeping out before the lead gunship. "Let's hope that sniper decides to slink away."

"Don't burn the leather off your gloves," Rich warned. They had flipped to see who would go down. They both wanted it, but Bruce had won the toss.

"A fast drop and an abrupt stop. The first man will be coming immediately up."

"The hoist will be ready to spin."

Bruce picked up the rope that was going out the door as soon as they hovered. They would buddy hug the injured copilot out rather than slow for the basket.

The intercom crackled. "Twenty seconds."

OPERATION NORTHERN WATCH

How did you not aggravate Syrian fighters? Gracie had no answer. The rescue flights were coming from the north, the Syrian fighters from the southwest. It was a standoff happening at blistering speeds over airspace divided by a thread.

She was tucked in tight beside Peter ready to act, but how to act was not at all clear. If the chopper was down in Iraq, they could be offensive to protect it; if it was down inside Syria, all they could do was argue over the airspace. No one had figured out that critical answer.

"Warn them."

She lit up the oncoming Syrian fighters at Peter's order and got hard tone in her ear signaling missile lock.

SYRIA/IRAQ BORDER

Sand stung everything it touched. Bruce could feel it finding ways into his clothing. The helicopter had pancaked, the side door tilted toward the ground. No entry was visible. He would have to swing in from the side as the hovering chopper struggled to hold stationary while the sniper shot at him. *Lord, I'm trying to be brave. Give me Your courage.*

Bruce moved onto the skid and stepped off, falling, letting the rope race through his hands. The task was simple. Just get down before he got shot. Striker twisted his hands at the last moment and felt heat burn at the friction; the jerk tore into his muscles as he yanked himself to a stop. He swung like a pendulum into the black opening, hoping the SEALs had a place cleared for him to land inside.

Hands grabbed him.

He landed on his back on the sloped deck of the crashed chopper.

He shook his head and cleared the disorientation. "Wolf, I rarely do house calls."

The black-and-green face looking down at him grinned. "Nice entrance." Not Wolf. Cougar.

Another sniper round slapped against metal, and Cougar swung around to grab the door gun and fire back. Bruce had a feeling there would be holes in his body armor before this mission was done. He pulled himself up and looked forward to see the pilot and Wolf moving the injured copilot toward him. "Let's go, gentlemen."

"He goes first." Wolf replied with a jerked nod to the guest Pup was guarding.

The SEAL already had him in body armor and a harness. "Pup, you'll have to buddy hug him up." Bruce pulled the man toward the door and fought the jerking line from the hovering helicopter to get the clasps locked. In the same fashion two parachute jumpers would link together and jump under one canopy, Bruce securely locked the two men for the lift. The defector was smart enough not to try to help. "Are you worth this?" Bruce asked tersely.

"I can stop a war."

Stop a war or start one. Striker wasn't sure which was more likely. The last clamp clicked metal on metal. He slapped Pup's shoulder. "Swing out as far as you can and keep your head down!"

Cougar opened up a burst of fire from the door gun, he paused, and Pup swung out with the man. As soon as the men disappeared with a jerk upward, Cougar opened fire again.

"Cougar, you and the pilot out next," Bruce ordered as he moved to do what he could for the copilot. He dealt with men and war and bullets. A pulse meant something could be done. The man had a pulse. There was blood, a lot of it, and fixed eyes. He was deeply unconscious. Bruce knew the odds against the copilot making it, and he prayed for a miracle as he worked. He used duct tape to strap the man's arms and hands against his chest.

Cougar and the pilot hurried to secure the rope as soon as it came back down.

"Tell Rich the injured man is coming next. I'll need a slow winch."

"Got it."

The two men swung out.

A sniper round hit and hydraulic fluid spewed like rain finding its way inside, making the floors slick. Wolf struggled to reach him.

"How do we do this?"

Bruce didn't like either option. If Wolf went up with the injured man, he would be a sitting duck on a slow-rising line. If Bruce took the injured man up, it left Wolf coming last with no cover. Bruce owed Gracie, owed Jill. The situation reminded him too much of Ecuador. "I'll go up with him. Give me all the suppression cover you can, no use leaving bullets behind. When the rope comes back for you, make sure you don't signal a lift until you're absolutely ready because Dasher will break hover and hoist as he flies."

"Piece of cake."

Striker smiled at the prompt reply; he had to give Wolf points for handling the pressure. He eased the injured man up. Wolf helped him as they fought the rope and the locking rings. He leaned back against the rope and found it taking his weight.

"Don't get shot."

"Now you tell me," Striker yelled back. He pushed himself and the injured man out into the night.

It was a thousand times worse than he had braced himself for.

The wind started them spinning. He was going to get shot. He knew it as the hoist began to pull them to the black hovering beast. *Jesus, please. Get us safely up.* For the moment, he was totally helpless. The noise became deafening as they drew near the helicopter. The wind spun them underneath, threatening to slam them into its belly. The winch slowed even more until they were clear and could come up the last few feet.

Rich grabbed the back of his flight suit, and Striker forced himself not to try to help but to let his partner pull them back into safety. Pup and Cougar reached for the injured man. Once freed they eased him onto a stretcher. The waiting medics started stabilizing his breathing. Bruce fought with his gloves to free the locks and get the rope back down to Wolf. Rich was a step ahead of him. The rope came free and Rich locked on the counterweight. "Let it down!"

The rope dropped with a fast whine.

They waited.

"Come on, come on."

Striker tightened his hand on Cougar's shoulder, understanding perfectly. Rich was leaning out the door on his belly, night vision goggles peering down.

"Bring him up." The winch began to turn. "Dasher, go!"

They began a runaway from the danger, Wolf swinging out on the rope behind the moving helicopter.

It took forever.

Striker locked his safety harness to the door frame, ignored common sense, and reached out and down. "Get up here." He hauled Wolf aboard.

Wolf landed on his back, hands grabbing the safety bar to keep from pitching back out.

"Wow. Was that ever an interesting ride."

Striker searched for holes in the man and blood, then slapped his chest. Wolf had used up a life or two but he was in one piece. "Stay out of minefields! You're giving me gray hair."

"Once was more than enough." Wolf raised his hand to wipe away the bath of hydraulic fluid he'd taken and in doing so smeared his face paint. He leaned his head back against the metal floor, trying to get his breath back. "Don't you dare tell Grace. She'll never let me live it down."

"Remember that next time." Striker looked at the man who

was responsible for this close call, then forward into the cockpit. "Incirlik, Dasher, and don't stop to admire the scenery. Our guest has a direct flight to Washington waiting for him."

ELEVEN

★ ★ ★

Providing cover for helicopters was difficult given the disparate speed. Grace watched the two rescue helicopters and the one that had been circling form a *V* and head north.

What had they gone into Syria to do?

Was Bruce part of that rescue flight?

An aircap of eight Tomcats had formed to the east, and the Syrian MiGs had turned parallel to the border. Neither side wanted to stand down from the fight. The crash was four hundred yards inside Iraq, and this had become an aggressive show of force as they jockeyed for airspace.

Grace scanned radar, altitude, and fuel, all three generating equal concern. Getting shot out of the sky or crashing from lack of gas had the same end point. She had already crossed bingo level for the return flight and would have to tank on the way back. Her worst-case scenario was going bingo fuel for Incirlik and it was now at least a theoretical problem.

"Viper flight, Birddog. Vector rainbow plus 10, angels 9. Sharpshooters lead, Birddog. Four bandits at rainbow plus 60, vector 40, angels 15. Hold Boxer," the AWACs controller ordered with terse dispatch.

"Birddog, Vipers flight. Roger," Thunder acknowledged for them. Grace closed formation with his Hornet, moving to just feet off his right wing. Their flight had just been vectored to a route that would pass over the helicopters and send them ahead to clear the egress route. The Tomcats had the more interesting orders that put them on direct vector to the MiGs with orders to set up a box rotation at the border.

Grace would leave the MiGs for the Tomcats. She wanted to see those helicopters back on friendly territory and get herself to a tanker.

Peter led them down to nine thousand feet. Within moments their flight crossed over the helicopters and raced ahead.

Antiaircraft artillery started to come up ahead of them. There was no radar to guide it onto the planes; that had been knocked out earlier in the evening. It was cold comfort. Without direction for the guns the Iraqis were sending up the AAA in a blanket. It began exploding in white flashes between eight and twelve thousand feet, the concussions hollow, sharp echoes heard through the cockpit canopy and helmet.

"Viper 01, Fox one." Peter sent a missile racing toward the ground at one of the AAA batteries. "Viper 01, Fox two." He sent another missile right behind it.

Half the antiaircraft artillery ceased.

They banked ninety degrees to slice through the remaining AAA with a minimal profile.

A bright explosion nearly blinded her and something loud smacked into her canopy. The concussion shoved her plane right.

"Viper 02?"

She had her hands full. The g's were intense. She fought the many times force of gravity to move her hands and her head. Her panels were lit like a Christmas tree. The checklist to follow was red, short, and immediate in her mind's eye. Do this and if it doesn't work, pull the ejection handle.

She had engines; she didn't have flight controls. The left wing flaps had been shoved upward by the explosion, and aerodynamics was trying to roll the jet and put her into the sand. Grace fought it back. The altimeter raced down. *Lord, pull with me.* She was going to be eating sand in a few seconds. If she rolled she had no altitude to recover.

Something more than flaps was wrong.

She cut free the missile under the left wing, praying the sway-bracing had not been damaged. It dropped away with a deep thunk. The severe pitch to the roll stopped and she got the nose up. She started to regain altitude.

"Viper 02?"

Besides fighting a constant pressure for a left roll, she was going to be able to hold the climb. "I can make it. Mushy, but there." She was not ejecting inside Iraq when her plane was still airborne and Turkey was within reach.

She looked out into the darkness wishing she could see what it was she was fighting. Night vision goggles couldn't help her see the back of the wing. She didn't need to see it to know the back of the wing probably looked like someone had hurled baseballs through the metal. Landing would be interesting.

"Viper 02, angels 15." Peter brought his Hornet alongside. She admired his nerve. He was staying a few feet above her so if she did roll, he'd have an instant to get himself high and out of the way.

She climbed slowly to fifteen thousand feet, feeling relief at every foot of altitude that gave her that much more recovery time. She started checking systems. She had gas, not a lot of it, good hydraulics, minimal flight controls, and avionics were a mess. According to the readout she was now flying over Oklahoma. She reset the system.

"Viper 01. I'll have to hold hands." She'd fly with him like a chick with a mother and let his navigation control.

"Viper 01. Roger. Mandus in eighteen."

The code name for Incirlik was a welcome word. It had the runway distance she would need and the best emergency landing crews. She scanned radar for the helicopters. The triangle of blips was to the northeast. While she'd been fighting to stay aloft they had crossed into Turkey.

"Viper 02, say your state." Whatever her XO was thinking about her flying, his voice was matter-of-fact.

"Viper 02, angels 14, 3.1," she replied, giving altitude and gas.

There were problems to solve. She had flown birds that were beat up before, but this was the first time she was doing it in the middle of the night with no good sense of the damage. She'd lost an engine last time and it had not been nearly this difficult to fly.

The AAA had taken out the slotted flaps; it felt like the aileron had taken secondary damage. She asked her plane to do something and it wasn't able to deliver. Simulators had failed to convey how much she would be 110 percent tuned in to her plane. She could feel it hurting with every gentle move of her hands on the throttle and stick. Could she get the landing gear down and locked?

"Viper 02, mark home base."

They were over Turkish airspace. "Viper 02. Roger."

"Viper 02, watch your speed."

Her eyes jerked to the airspeed. She was on the edge of a stall. She'd been fighting the roll and had let herself become dangerously slow. She was task saturating and had not even noticed it. She eased the throttle open and felt the plane shudder as it responded.

Below her there were now town lights shimmering and an occasional road.

"Viper 02, say your state."

Grace looked at her panels. "Viper 02, angels 14, 2.8."

"Viper 02, try dirty."

"Viper 02. Roger. Going dirty." She began working the landing checklist, bypassing what she could not predict, turning her plane from graceful aerodynamics into one that gave a rough air profile configured for landing. The landing gear lights turned green, showing they were locked. "Viper 02. Configured."

"Viper 02. Roger. Viper 01, Mandus." Thunder called the Incirlik Air Base controller.

"Viper 01, Mandus. Standing by."

"Viper 01, 3.1, holding hands with Viper 02, 2.8. Crossing 1.2."

"Roger, Viper 01. Winds 12 NW, runway 144 clear for approach, crews standing by."

Grace wished she was leading Peter in and not the other way around.

"Viper 02, lights." Grace relayed, able for the first time to see the base runway. It looked huge compared to a ship but not nearly long enough given there wasn't a wire to catch and stop her, and she had uncertain brakes. If she had problems, she wouldn't be able to abort a landing and climb again without flaps. She eased right to line up with the runway. It was like wresting a heavy hunk of metal falling through the sky.

Peter broke off as she passed below five hundred feet.

She was committed to the glide down. She eased back on the speed. The ground rushed up. She fought the desire to close her eyes.

Rear wheels touched down. Smooth air became rough concrete. She eased the nose forward. Front wheel touched. Lights on either side of the runway streaked by. She fought to keep the plane on the runway.

She carefully applied brakes. Without flaps she was fighting to slow before she ran out of distance. Runway careened by.

The plane slowed its rollout and fell to taxi speed. Grace took her first deep breath since landing. Her muscles unlocked enough

for her to move the stick, and using the rudders she turned the jet
toward the ramp and the taxiway. The emergency vehicles racing
along were now distinguishable as fire, rescue, and ambulance.
"Thanks, Viper 01."

"Good flight, Viper 02. Check-in 0800 *Crawler*."

She chuckled and queued her mike. "0800 prop flight. Roger.
I can walk faster."

"Viper 01, approved to try," Peter replied with his signature
dry humor.

She clicked her mike twice, sharing her laughter.

Her jet would be down for repairs for more than a day. She
was going to be catching the mail run flight out to the carrier in
the morning. The thought of the paperwork for this flight was
enough to make her headache intensify. She'd spend the first day
doing the debriefing of this mission, and the time after that bor-
rowing a jet and covering all the odd jobs that fell to the poor
pilot without a plane.

Yellow light sticks directed her to the far end of the runway
away from buildings and waved her to a stop. She shut down her
engines. She was so tired it took a great effort to lift her hands
from the stick and throttle to retrieve the pins to secure the ejection seat. Men in silver fire suits surrounded her plane ready to
deal with the possibility of fire.

In the spotlights from the recovery equipment she could see
the crack and smear of black that marred the canopy. It had been
a vicious hit. The AAA canister had tried to come into her lap.

As the cockpit canopy came up, fresh air swirled around her.
It was delicious, in the upper sixties and moderate humidity. She
eased off her helmet and found her hair wet with sweat. The
maintenance crews scrambled up on ladders to help her out. She
saw the surprised look on the maintenance chief's face as he realized it was a woman in the cockpit. She glanced at his uniform.

"Dakota, give me a hand out of here. I feel like I rode a roller coaster a few too many loops."

The older man smiled and reached out a meaty hand and grasped hers. She wrestled herself up out of the seat. She handed him the flight pouch with her maps and kneeboard and her helmet. She carefully climbed down to the runway. Her legs felt like rubber. She deflated the g-pressure puff suit she wore around her legs to keep blood forced to her head. She took her first steps and found her boots felt like lead.

She ducked around the wing to get her first look at the damage. "What a mess."

"At least two shells exploded close, and one tried to knock you out of the cockpit," Dakota assessed.

"Golden BBs."

"Lieutenant, hold still." She'd been doing her best to avoid the doctor in the wave of men that had surrounded the plane, but he stepped in her way. Grace reluctantly stopped. She looked over the doctor's shoulder to Dakota. "Take good care of her. She was kind to me tonight."

"We'll fix her up good as new," the maintenance chief promised. "We'll haul her under lights. Give me till morning, then we'll talk about what you felt and what I found."

"Thanks, Chief."

A firm hand tipped up her chin and a light flicked across her eyes. "Your plane will be fine. How many g's did you pull?"

She knew the drill, and the last thing she wanted was to spend an hour at the clinic. From the jacket the man was top doc at the flight medicine clinic. The Navy docs on the *GW* were going to repeat it all anyway before they'd put her back in the cockpit. "Four, maybe five."

"Double vision?"

"No."

"How's the headache?"

She wanted to lie but didn't. "Bad."

He pointed her to the back of the red-and-white rescue squad. "Sit."

She bit back a sigh and reluctantly followed orders. It was a fully equipped medical squad, better equipped than most ambulances in the States. She took a seat on the tailgate. The fatigue was enough she put her elbows on her knees and lowered her head. She was so tired she was ready to stretch out on the ground.

Lord, when it starts to sink in just how close it was, this prayer will have even more emotion under it. Suffice it to say—I owe You one. A big one.

She wanted to ask if the helicopters had made it in, but she knew there would be no answer even if the men around her knew. Ops into Syria would be classified. The lack of other visible signs of rescue squads anywhere on this side of the base suggested she was the only flight to have trouble.

The doc handed her two aspirins and a bottle of ice water. Her opinion of him came up a notch.

"Ears ringing?"

"No."

"Nausea?"

"No."

"Finish the bottle of water. I want to see how you're doing after the adrenaline fades. If you can still walk a straight line I'll send you to billeting, otherwise you're my guest for a while."

She raised the bottle of water and gave the man a smile. "Deal."

The maintenance men were draining fuel and waiting for the engines to cool down before they moved the jet. Dakota was already tinkering.

"Lieutenant Yates."

She took the flight pouch and helmet from the airman. "Thanks."

She looked at her watch. Planes would be starting to land on the *GW* soon. She would miss out on the gathering in the ready room to debrief; she'd miss watching the strike tapes; she'd miss the hour in the dirty-shirt wardroom eating sliders (cheeseburgers) and sharing flight experiences. They'd be talking about her, the one plane that didn't come back. By morning the story Thunder told in his calm manner would have traveled and gained a few embellishments. She missed that routine at the end of a flight.

Grace pushed it aside and finished the water. She'd grown accustomed to the tight quarters of the *GW,* and this base was huge. On the other side of the runways she could see the large open hangars and the big cargo planes. She had grown up expecting to fly one of those C-17s. The building was open and bright with lights. The graveyard shift was at full staff, for most of the cargo in and out of the base was loaded at night in the cooler temperature and at the low point of flight ops. She felt very small; she was once again low man on the totem pole, a pilot without a plane.

The doctor finally released her when he was comfortable she wasn't suffering anything more than adrenaline wipeout. He held out a release approval. "If you need me, page. My numbers are on the card."

She tucked it in her flight pocket. "I'll do that. Where can I find the billeting office?"

He waved over one of the men. "Airman First Class Andy Walsh. He'll give you a lift to the Hodja Inn-Billeting. Make sure you ask for a room far from the Teen Can. It's the youth movie and popcorn night, and they chose a *Back to the Future* movie marathon. It's just breaking up."

"Thanks for the warning." Incirlik had several housing complexes, a swimming pool complex, a bowling alley, a community center, and even had both an elementary and a high school for the kids of the servicemen living on base. "Is there a gathering spot for the graveyard shift where I can get a meal?" She needed a place to unwind.

"Try a place called the Air Wing Flag on the east side of the quad. It has the best food on base."

She nodded her thanks. Billeting to get a place to sleep, then something to eat. There were worse ways to end a night of flying. "Dakota, I'll see you in a few hours."

"Your bird will be here."

TWELVE

★ ★ ★

INCIRLIK AIR BASE, TURKEY
AIR WING FLAG COMMUNITY CENTER

You owe me your dog tags." Bruce leaned his elbows on the table and pointed the neck of his cold soda bottle at Wolf. The round table was crowded with men as Bear, Cougar, Wolf, and Pup from the SEALs and Rich, Dasher, and himself from the PJs fit themselves around it. The center of the table was crowded with empty glass bottles because the military had taken the unusual step of importing water into the country because of the drought. The remains of two large pizzas crowded the remaining space.

"Never let it be said a SEAL welched." Wolf ducked his head and slipped off his dog tags. Bruce accepted them amongst a chorus of laughter.

They hadn't talked much about the mission since the debriefing. The defector had been hustled from their helicopter to a military transport, spending no more than three minutes on the ground in Turkey. It was likely they would never know if getting him out had been worth the risk, would never hear about him again, but they'd celebrate the successful mission just the same.

Bruce knew either Iraq or Syria would be exploiting the wreckage of the downed helicopter by morning. He figured it would be revealing as to whether Syria officially said anything. Silence would be the most interesting reaction. It would show the defection had stung.

Bruce watched the men at the table, finding comfort in their humor. It had been a dangerous mission and rescue, but they were taking it in stride. Bruce caught the eye of Bear across the table and quietly raised his soda. Bear raised his. Before long this group would split up and the two units would go their own ways again. But what had happened would get passed on by word of mouth, and an institution memory among the units would add this one to their shared history.

Bruce got kicked under the table. He looked over at Cougar, surprised, and got an imperceptible nod toward the door. Bruce looked over and felt shock course down to his toes like a hot twinge. "Wolf." His quiet, forceful word got the man's attention. "Gracie's here."

Wolf spun around, the chair legs scraping on the floor.

Grace was crossing the room to the self-serve coolers where the water was kept and hadn't noticed them at the back table. She glanced over at the noise and stopped. Bruce felt like he was going to drown in those blue eyes as her gaze locked with his. Chagrin was an expression he hadn't seen before and he smiled at her. She broke eye contact to glance over the group. The change to her expression when she saw Wolf... Bruce was going to remember that look of joy for a long time.

"Wolf!"

Bruce rose to his feet as did Wolf as she changed course to join them. Her hair was wet, like she'd dunked her head and toweled it dry. The flight suit was rumpled. Wolf lifted her clean off the floor. She gave him a hard hug back. He took his time lowering her back on her feet. "Grace, you are supposed to be on the *GW*. What are you doing at Incirlik?"

She scanned the group and the table. "I'm hungry?"

"Gracie."

"My Hornet ate a hairball of AAA. Interesting flying. Is that sausage pizza?"

Pup pulled over a chair. "Bless you," Grace said. The young SEAL blushed.

"That was you overhead," Wolf said slowly.

"Hi, Dasher, Cougar." She looked pointedly at her cousin as he took a seat beside her. "What do you think you were doing belly flopping in a minefield? Life was boring?"

Wolf looked her over from head to foot to assure himself she was in one piece. "Had I known you were watching, I would have crashed with a little more elegance."

"I was tucked under Thunder's wing having a nice, quiet, routine flight when suddenly I've got SAMs and MiGs messing up my plans."

Wolf laughed. "Nice flying."

"At least I was smart enough to stay out of the sand." Grace glanced around the table again, her gaze stopping on Bruce's hands, and he felt an urge to tuck them in his pockets when her smile flickered. The ropes had burned through his gloves and left raw skin and blisters. She glanced up at him. "I owe you a drink."

There were a lot of ways to answer that—yes, he'd been the one going down the rope, to no, it was not that big a deal. Instead he just smiled. "Yes, you do." She'd acquired a tan since he last saw her, and it looked good on her. Freckles had appeared. Her self-assured confidence hadn't suffered for the tough flight.

"I'll get them, Grace." Wolf pushed back his chair again. "What do you want?"

"Pilot's special. Get Bruce one too."

Wolf groaned. Bruce raised an eyebrow when Wolf headed toward the kitchen. This could be interesting.

She leaned forward to see around Cougar. "Hello, Bear."

"Gracie."

"How's Kelly?"

Bear smiled at the mention of his wife; he'd been married two years. "Loving Virginia life. Not sure what to think of snow. Playing tourist. You've got a headache."

She blinked as she thought of how to answer that. It was the first time Bruce had ever seen her search for words, and he narrowed his eyes as he realized what it was Bear had observed. She was smiling, but it wasn't reaching her eyes. They were dark with pain. Start of a migraine? G's, noise, and adrenaline would do that. "The AAA casing smacked into my canopy," Grace finally replied. She helped herself to leftover pizza.

Bruce shot a look over at Bear. They had both seen a lot of crashes. What she wasn't saying suggested a lot.

Wolf returned with two glasses. "A pilot special. Diet coke, cherry juice, two cherries, and a dash of vanilla. They didn't have hazelnut."

She tasted hers and nodded her approval. Wolf slid a glass over to him. Grace looked at him and winked. Bruce sampled his more cautiously. "Pretty good."

She chuckled.

"Have you already got a room for the night?" Wolf asked.

"Yes. I brought my toothbrush this time. It's a short stop; I'm on the 0800 propeller hop back to the *GW.*"

"I suppose you're going to sleep in rather than join me for an early breakfast."

Grace turned Wolf's arm to look at his watch. "Absolutely."

Bear leaned back and exchanged a silent look with the other SEALs. Dasher rose moments later. "Speaking of the time, we're taking off at 0700. My boss will get annoyed if I'm flying with less than four hours sleep."

Cougar got up and hauled Pup to his feet. "Grace, I'm going to put the child to bed. It's past his bedtime. Next time we get a chance to visit remind me to fix you a SEAL special."

"I'll do that. Night, guys."

Bear leaned over and handed her a blue free calling card. "Make sure Wolf calls Jill before you send him to bed."

"Glad to, Bear." She looked over at Rich who also rose. "Thanks for hauling Wolf home safely rather than leaving him in the sandbox."

"I owed him a few," Rich replied easily. "Good night, Gracie."

The table cleared out and left only the three of them. Wolf started clearing the table, putting the glass bottles in the blue recycling bin, setting them carefully inside, not tossing them.

"You can ask," Grace commented, leaning back and watching Wolf. Bruce got the feeling she had momentarily decided to forget he was here. Her attention was on Wolf, and there was a quiet focus to how she was watching her cousin. If Bruce could have left without disturbing the two of them, he would have.

Wolf stopped moving bottles, turned, and just stared at her. "There's blood on your flight boots."

"Nosebleed, not mine," Grace replied easily. "We had a deck hand get hurt when an oxygen tank cart slid and slammed him into the tower."

"And the flight? How close was it really?"

"Only my own errors. I nearly stalled out. The slotted flaps and aileron got chewed up. She could have sustained a lot more damage and still been airworthy."

"You aren't supposed to be getting yourself shot down."

"Don't pick a fight at 2 A.M."

"What was I supposed to tell your dad?" he bit out.

"Frank, she was doing what she loved?" Grace leaned over and caught his face in her hands. "Relax. I'm going to grow old with you. You're family. You're stuck with me."

"You—" Wolf leaned forward and smacked a kiss on her nose. "Gidget, go to bed."

"Are we okay?"

"When I get my heart out of my toes."

She slipped the blue card Bear had given her into his pocket. "Go call Jill."

Wolf glanced over at Bruce. "I'll see her to the dorm," he promised.

"What time is it there?"

"Nine A.M."

Wolf got to his feet. "I'll go call Jill."

Grace placed her hands on the back of his chair as she watched him leave, then leaned forward to rest her chin on her hands. "Did I handle that right?"

Bruce had no idea. "How close was it really?"

"Minimal flight controls. Ninety degrees and rolling over, crashing altitude. I couldn't eject even if I wanted to."

"You willed the plane to fly."

"Muscled and babied it back."

He slid her one of the remaining water bottles that hadn't been opened yet. "You handled it just fine." Sometime tomorrow he'd try to get over the impact of knowing she'd nearly gotten shot down while providing cover for their exit from Iraq.

"How'd you get the name Striker?"

Figuring out the tangents a woman took was one of the things he had learned long ago not to even try to do. Bruce stretched out in his chair, crossed his ankles, and smiled at her. "August '89, The Game." The memory was a rich one. "The PJs were playing the SEALs for the division playoffs. I struck out on a fastball and I've never been able to redeem myself."

"Over a decade and you still have the handle."

He flexed his fist as he smiled. "I somehow manage to renew it every year."

Her laughter was soft and spontaneous. "I wish I hadn't been tagged with Gracie."

"Why?"

"I don't think I'm particularly graceful."

"It's how others see you. How I see you."

"Jill once said you specialized in being kind. She was right."

Her words surprised him, and he wished she could see what others did. She'd nearly melted her cousin's heart with that promise to be around to grow old. She smiled at him and Bruce felt warmth curl around his heart.

He'd love to keep her up talking but it wouldn't be fair. Her evening had been even longer than his. She would have launched from the *GW* hours before that rescue. "Have you taken something for that headache?"

"Yes." She reached for the water bottle. "I'm sorry about your hand."

"It will heal. Friction tore through the gloves by the end of the drop."

"I wasn't on the channel to hear radio traffic, but I could see you were having an interesting night. Was that a normal mission?"

"The ones involving water are much more scary."

She blinked. He liked her laughter. It bubbled. "You're serious."

"We train for nights like tonight. I'm glad we were able to get in and get them out quickly."

She thought about that, her gaze probing his expression as she rolled that answer around, testing it. "Ecuador was like this, only not as quick."

Ecuador had been much, much worse than this. He'd seen a man he was trying to reach shot in the head. "Yes."

"Do the risks bother you?"

Only the failures. That kind of reassurance she didn't need to hear tonight. "Not really," he replied easily. "I only live once. I long ago decided I wanted to do something that mattered. Hauling guys out of danger is worth the risk."

"I feel that way about flying; that I was born with a love for it."

"Why the Navy?"

"I hate flying level and slow."

She was priceless. "You don't do much of that in the Navy," Bruce agreed, smiling at her and wondering what it would take to someday convince her to take him flying with her. She'd probably try to make him toss his lunch with a few snap rolls.

Grace pushed back her chair. "Come on, help me find the place where I dumped my stuff. This base is so big I get lost getting from point *A* to *B*."

"Have your billeting slip?"

She tugged open the pocket of her flight suit. "Somewhere."

He glanced at the piece of paper she found. "Easy; first building past the fitness center. But quite a hike from here."

"You've stayed on this base before?"

"A few times. It's our hub for deployments in this area. They've got a great bowling alley."

They walked outside. The night had comfortably cooled and the stars were bright. "I don't know if I'm going to be able to sleep on a bed that's not rocking."

"Somehow I think exhaustion will compensate."

They passed the family community center. "This way." Bruce pointed left.

Instead she stopped and turned in a full circle. "You know, if I didn't know better, we could be on a base in the States. It's obvious Americans helped build this side of the Turkish air base. Even the buildings look like those from home."

"Homesick?"

"Some. I miss the small things. My apartment is over a bakery. I miss waking up to the smell of fresh bread in the morning.

Movies with Jill. Sunday comics. What about you?"

"Popcorn."

"That's it?"

"I've already got your company."

"Smooth, Bruce, very smooth."

"I thought so. Things I miss—I'd add evenings at the beach. It's where I spend most of my time. I've got simple tastes."

"There's popcorn and soft ice cream in the *GW*'s dirty-shirt wardrooms."

"The Air Force has better movies."

She graciously nodded. "I'll give you that one." She walked backward, expanding her list. "I miss busy streets and libraries and TV with lots of channels but nothing on, grocery stores with packed shelves, church choir practice, weekend volleyball practice, fast food served in super-size, ice cream shops, ATMs at every corner, daily mail delivery…."

His smile grew as the list went on. "You're homesick."

"More than I thought. Six months is a long time to be away."

"You'll love it even more when you get back."

"True."

They passed the fitness center. "There's your building."

"Where are you?"

"Back the way we came a bit." He walked her to the door. "I suppose I could save a few weeks of mail time by hand delivering a letter." He pulled it from his pocket.

"You were carrying it?"

"I was adding a postscript when we got the call out."

She took it. "Maybe I'll save it for the morning." She laughed at his expression. "I'm kidding. I'm rather a fanatic about mail. I love getting it."

"Good. I enjoyed getting yours."

She looked at the letter, scuffed her foot on the concrete.

"Thank you for what you did tonight. I would have been lost if something had happened to Wolf."

Bruce fully understood. "It was my pleasure, Grace." She looked up, and he smiled at her. It was too early in the relationship to say good night in the way he would prefer. "It was great to see you tonight, even if it was under these circumstances."

She pulled open the glass doors. "Would you do me a favor?"

"Sure."

"Next time Wolf weaves right when he should weave left—find a camera and take me a picture."

He laughed. "I'll do that. Good night, Gracie. Sleep well."

It was a single person dorm room. There was a small refrigerator, dresser, closet space, a combined bookshelf and desk unit, a double bed. The walls had no color and the tile floors had throw rugs, properly placed to square corners with the furniture. After months of slipping into a narrow bunk and pulling a blue curtain to provide privacy, Grace found the space almost too much. She sprawled on the bed. There was a peaceful point where sleep had been denied when her body stopped complaining. She knew as soon as her eyes closed she would be sound asleep. She had to read the letter first.

It was addressed to her but not yet sealed. She pulled out three pages of notebook paper. *Lord, thanks. This is a great way to end the night.* She'd meant it when she said she loved letters. They were glimmers into someone's soul.

Ben had written regularly, but they had been short notes not that different from Wolf's. She'd known Ben very well. For him, saying *I miss you* had been practically putting his heart on the page. She'd saved every one of his letters. She had a feeling she would now be saving Bruce's.

He liked to chat on paper, she realized within the first couple paragraphs as it continued the free style he had shown in his first letter. She laughed as she read about the parachute jumping.

His letter turned serious. *"The military teaches you not to get attached to the place or the thing but the people."* She twisted a corner of the blanket around her finger. She liked his perspective, agreed with it.

"Ben carried your picture."

It caught her by surprise.

"God can fill those holes I'm sure you feel when life gets quiet."

She started fighting tears as she read. Bruce didn't know the half of it. He just had to point to the hole and she felt the emotion. She missed the incredible friendship she'd had with Ben. And she hated the fact she hadn't been able to say good-bye to him.

The letter turned to Ecuador and Wolf, and she turned the pages slowly. *"My partner Rich had been hit in the initial rescue attempt and Wolf became my second. He jokes he loves adrenaline, but when you need him, Grace, Wolf is the steady man who is there to do what needs to be done."* Bruce understood her cousin. She was relieved to find the friendship between the two men was deep and solid from both sides.

John 14:27.

Where was a Bible when she needed one? She leaned over to the desktop where she had put her flight bag. When there was room based on the number of mission documents, she carried her small New Testament. She was intensely curious to see what Bruce had chosen to say. She found the verse.

"Peace I leave with you; my peace I give to you; not as the world gives do I give to you. Let not your hearts be troubled, neither let them be afraid."

She read the verse a second and a third time and was struck

with one immediate realization: If she wanted to write a letter at Bruce's level, she was going to have to step up her letter-writing skills. It had been a casual letter on the surface, but the comments were woven together from casual statement about today, to perspective on the situation, to a point he wanted to make. He was a message person. He was a man who had something to say and knew how to say it in a profound way. And as she read his letter again, part of her heart started to resonate as he touched something deep inside that others had never made an effort to reach.

She saw the postscript and laughed.

"P.S. What do you think is going on with Jill and Wolf?"

She reached for a pen and paper.

THIRTEEN

★ ★ ★

NORFOLK, VIRGINIA

She was in love with the dog. Jill held open the back door and waited for the yellow Labrador to consider the steps. Bruce had gotten himself a dog that had to be a hundred dog years old. "Come on, honey."

Jill had a vet visit scheduled for tomorrow. If arthritis could be ruled out, the dog still occasionally ran acting like a puppy, maybe it was cataracts. Jill had begun to suspect the dog was depending on hearing and smell to find her way around.

Emily preceded her into the kitchen. It was nice to have the company. Jill set down the grocery sacks she carried on the counter. Fitting in a stop to the grocery store had meant a very early morning, but she'd been out of eggs and bread and she wanted an omelet for breakfast.

On her docket this morning was cleaning up Seaman Tyler Jones's apartment. The crime scene technicians had been thorough; there was fingerprint dust everywhere. At the hardware store last night she'd found paint to touch up the walls. She hoped to hear today from the insurance agent with the initial paperwork. She'd go shopping this weekend to start replacing stolen items.

This afternoon the subcontractor was finishing the counter addition to the receptionist area at her newly leased offices. She was finally seeing light at the end of what had been a year-long effort to get offices for herself and Terri closer to their clients. The day's schedule made her tired before it even began.

"Do you want lamb or roast beef?" She offered the two tins. Since Bruce was paying for the upkeep, the dog was eating top of the line food. "Lamb? Lamb it is."

She fed the dog and put away the groceries.

Pausing at the calendar on the wall, she drew a big X through May 11. Only thirty-two days left until Wolf was home, forty-eight days to Bruce. From the fabric-covered box on the counter by the toaster she pulled out a folded slip of paper, then leaned her elbows against the counter as she opened and read it. Her laughter startled the dog. "Sorry, Emily." She held up the piece of paper. "The treat for today is a trip to Grace's to measure the windows for new blinds. Rather a dud, huh?" Emily came over and Jill reached down to stroke her coat. "I agree—not on par with a trip to the park. I wore you out yesterday. Today you can just curl up and sleep while I work." She'd fit in the stop at Grace's on her way to the new offices.

Adding the slip to her day planner, she started fixing an omelet, humming along with the song on the radio.

She'd missed Wolf's call. She was still kicking herself about it. She'd been busy with the police so it hadn't been her choice. She was going to have to find something to send in his next care package as a special apology. She had finally changed message tapes not wanting to erase Wolf's message but not wanting to hear again his voice change from expectation to disappointment when he realized she wasn't home to take the call.

He was doing fine. It was hot. He'd run into Bruce and Bruce was fine. He'd gotten her last package, and had she gotten his last letter? He'd try to call again but didn't know when he'd be somewhere he could. He missed her.

Did he have to add those last three words?

She missed him like crazy. She might as well pack up her social life while a deployment was under way. The important people in her life were overseas and her life had shifted to supporting them. There was a three-month tour party for the stateside families coming up. She would use it to get big greeting cards signed for each squadron, take lots of pictures, and have video tape greetings made that could get passed around the ready rooms. She ate her breakfast while making lists, trying to decide on games for the kids.

A glance at her watch had her pushing back her chair. "Emily, ready to go?" The dog was under the kitchen table, never one to move far afield.

Jill carried out the kitchen trash. The sack tore as she tried to force it into the metal can. The phone rang in the house. She looked with frustration at what had to be picked up, at the distance to the house. She left it and hurried up the stairs hoping the dog wouldn't get curious, eat some of it, and get sick.

"Hello?" She was out of breath and didn't hear a reply; she heard only static. "Hello?"

"Jill?"

There was an echo, but it was Wolf's voice. "Wolf. Hello!" The nearest chairs in reach were full. She sank to the floor leaning against the wall, holding the phone tight. "Where are—"

"Jill, it's Wolf."

There was a delay to the words; they were speaking on top of each other. She bit her lip as she waited for him to take the lead in the conversation.

"I missed you last time. I was worried."

Always be honest, Grace counseled, but this was a lousy time to try and explain there had been three burglaries. She didn't want him worrying about her; even more she didn't want to lose precious moments in a phone call over the issue. "I was late getting back from a client." It wasn't a good answer, but it wasn't a lie either. She hated the fact the answer suggested he hadn't been a high enough priority in her day to make sure she was there for his call.

"Did—see the news?"

"Something's happened." She scrambled to reach the remote on the counter.

"Bruce is fine. Grace is fine. They hit—radar in—"

She was losing him and it wasn't fair. "What happened?" The TV clicked on and she muted it. CNN showed breaking news at the bottom and a Pentagon spokesman on the screen.

"Everybody is fine. B— connection. I miss you."

"I miss you too," she raised her voice to promise.

She was listening to only static again. After a minute she accepted reality and hung up the phone. She waited ten minutes and it didn't ring again. The Pentagon spokesman was talking about strikes over Iraq to suppress antiaircraft artillery sites. She shut it off, finding it distressing to watch. It was after 2 A.M. in Turkey. Wolf had been calling her after the completion of his mission.

Lord, I hate living with the constant uncertainty of what might happen to them. It's making me a stressed-out wreck. She wiped angrily at tears that had formed. Her sense of having today under control was gone. *Thank You for keeping them safe.* She was kidding herself to suggest she could handle this kind of relationship.

A strike in Iraq meant Terri would be swamped at the office today with calls from relatives wanting to send special messages to those on the *GW.* Jill had her own set of messages to send, some of which could go over by e-mail and others by mail, a note to wish them well and let them know how the news was playing at home. Some of the kids in Grace's flying club were so uptight about her being gone that they called Jill every week to see if she had heard anything. She'd need to call them today. Unfortunately she had executed this contingency plan before.

She wanted them home. She so desperately wanted them home. She wished they were civilians.

She picked up her purse and keys. The dog had stretched out on the top step of the porch. There was salsa on her muzzle. Jill sat down beside the dog and buried her face in the warm coat.

I want to be confident and solid. It's not fair that they can handle it and I'm the weak link. I just want some security. I'm tired of getting scared.

She pushed herself to her feet and went to clean up the trash.

INCIRLIK AIR BASE, TURKEY

Bruce stepped back when he realized Wolf was talking with Jill. He walked over to the bench across from the kiosk and sat down to wait. Wolf eventually hung up the phone and walked over.

"How is she?"

"The connection was lousy."

Bruce waited but Wolf didn't say anything more. "Think I could get through?"

"I tried calling back several times and just got dead air. I'd suggest you try in the morning before we leave. Do we go look at Gracie's plane?"

Bruce looked at Wolf, trying to figure out why he was changing the subject. The man was uptight, and it had been his sister at the other end of the phone call. "No, I don't know that I could handle seeing the plane tonight." He didn't think Wolf could handle it.

Wolf sat down beside him. "We should find that dorm room and call it a night. I'm beat."

"Jill okay?"

"She hadn't heard the news about the strike yet."

"Oh."

Wolf stared at his boots and shook his head. "Now she'll worry."

"She'll handle it." It wasn't much of a consolation. She wouldn't have a choice about the matter. Bruce felt for his sister, knowing how difficult this would be for her. CNN would probably stay on this story for the better part of the next couple days, and Stateside Support, Inc. would have to handle a deluge of inquiries.

"She missed my earlier call because she was late getting back from a client."

"It was probably unavoidable."

"*She* suggested the time."

Bruce blinked. Wolf was ticked. Mad at himself, mad at the situation, mad he hadn't been able to talk to Jill before the strike happened. Bruce sighed, understanding entirely. Jill was half a world away, and there was nothing Wolf could do to help reassure her. "Not the conversation you were expecting."

"No."

Something had to be done. Bruce rubbed his sore hand. "Are you going to marry her?" He caught Wolf off guard with the question. He was ready to turn Wolf's life upside down a bit. It was time.

Wolf gave a rueful smile. "I didn't figure you'd be too thrilled about the idea."

"I'm not sure that I am. But limbo isn't working too well for either one of you. She's going to be thirty next week," Bruce pointed out. "It might be easier to handle the separations if she knew you were hers when you were home."

"Her biggest problem isn't the separations, but accepting we would probably be moving every few years. She's got bitter memories from her childhood about all the friends she lost over the years."

"She's snowing you. Everyone moves. She's better equipped now than she ever was before to be able to plug herself into the military communities quickly and to keep friendships strong. She's still just not sure about accepting military life."

"At least she let me take her window shopping for rings."

"Did she?" He wanted to push things along, but he didn't like finding he was out of the loop.

"She's thinking about it." Wolf looked at him. "Tonight obviously shook you up. Anything else?"

"Yes." Bruce stepped out on a limb of his own. "Tell me what happened with Grace and Ben."

The early morning was humid warm. Where was Jill? Bruce stewed about it as he walked down to the flight line, frustrated that he had not been able to get ahold of her. She hadn't been at her office and she hadn't answered her cellular phone. He dumped his gear in the back of the Pave Low helicopter. He was the first crewman to arrive; he'd left the other PJs finishing breakfast.

His helmet and vest were on the side bench. There was an envelope tucked in his helmet. Surprised, he took a seat and pulled it out. Grace's handwriting. She'd gotten someone to deliver it? He had wanted to see her this morning but knew she'd be occupied with the maintenance chief and hustling to make her flight back to the *GW*. Wisdom had said it was better not to interrupt her job.

He opened the letter, curious to know what she had written early this morning. He read and his smile faded. Last night's close call had caused ripples in his own life, in Wolf's. It had also caused ripples in hers.

Bruce ~

You write a wonderful letter.

This will be a short note because I think I may be able to get it to you before you leave in the morning. I want to say at the start that I've learned a lot of things about life from the guys in my life—my dad, Wolf, Ben. I learned something from you tonight.

Ben—he taught me how to handle the danger, to understand it and minimize it, to train for every contingency, and to take a great deal of care so that those chains of failure that lead to a crisis get broken early.

Wolf—he taught me to love being in the military. He taught me to love being part of a bigger whole, to love being part of a team. Thank you for being part of that safety net. He can do his job because you are there to do yours. Thank you for giving me back Wolf.

John 14:27. What a great verse. I needed to hear it tonight. There hasn't been much peace inside over the last couple years.

You mentioned the air show. Ben and I had our first fight on the trip out there. He wanted to get married and I didn't see how it was possible. He worked and trained in Houston, launched from Cape Canaveral, Florida, and was coming up on a nine-month-long tour at the Russian training facility. I was based in Virginia and went to sea for six months at a time. It wouldn't work. It was the only decision I could see at the time. Now it's the one decision I deeply regret.

What's your secret, Bruce? How do you make the pieces work? You have shown in the quiet way you play down Ecuador and the relaxed way you handled tonight that you are at peace. You've shown me it's possible. I have a full life while at sea and an incomplete one stateside. But I don't see how to have both when this job requires everything I feel I have to give. I can't do it all.

Okay, I've whined. Only when I'm really tired…

I think Jill and Wolf are heading to a decision point sooner versus later. They have a good relationship, and the emotions cut both ways and run deep. Wolf has grown up since Ecuador. He's ready for something permanent. Jill's a wise lady. She's thinking about what it means to sign up, for the first time to voluntarily accept the implications of what it means to be the wife of a military man. She'll make the right decision.

God bless, Grace

2 Samuel 22:1–4, 32–33

And David spoke to the LORD the words of this song on the day when the LORD delivered him from the hand of all his enemies, and from the hand of Saul. He said, "The LORD is my rock, and my fortress, and my deliverer, my God, my rock, in whom I take refuge, my shield and the horn of my salvation, my stronghold and my refuge, my savior; thou savest me from violence. I call upon the LORD, who is worthy to be praised, and I am saved from my enemies…. For who is God, but the LORD? And who is a rock, except our God? This God is my strong refuge, and has made my way safe."

Bruce closed his eyes, feeling an overwhelming surge of emotions at the words she wrote. And he finally understood the entrance to that deep reservoir that made up Grace. Jill thought in emotions. Until now he'd missed seeing what fit Grace. She thought in questions. The key to that reservoir was the questions.

She was a pilot—trained as a pilot and she thought like a pilot. Anticipating events, staying ahead of the curve, that was where she felt comfortable. He understood the emotions she felt about her past with Ben. In a way he was pleased she had that burden, for it showed the depth she let relationships touch her life. They mattered and a tragedy tore deep.

He thought about it and tugged out his notebook. He wrote back only one question.

Grace, did you love him?

FOURTEEN

★ ★ ★

MAY 19

USS *GEORGE WASHINGTON* (CVN 73)

MEDITERRANEAN SEA SOUTH OF CRETE

id you get my birthday present?" Grace asked, pressing the phone tight and covering her other ear in order to hear Jill. The bank of satellite phones on the third deck near the post office was a recent addition. They were popular and it was necessary to sign up for ten-minute blocks or else queue up in line and hope someone missed his or her slot.

"It's gorgeous! Thank you." Jill's voice sounded hollow, and there was an echo because it was storming out and it was distorting the transmissions from the ship. "I've already got my figurines moved into the display case. They look great under the lights."

"What did Wolf get you?"

"A gorgeous jewelry box. And he and Bruce stunned me— they went together to get me a new dining room table."

"Yes! I hoped they would be able to get it arranged."

"Terri from the office was in on it. I got home and I had a new table waiting with a huge sheet cake on it and forty people crowding the living room. There was a huge card with hundreds of signatures. Was that your doing at the deployment party?"

"Yes. It was a good day?"

"Excellent," Jill reassured.

"Are either Bruce or Wolf going to be able to call?"

"They just did," Jill said, sounding more excited about that than the gift. "They tag teamed on a satellite phone borrowed from some British unit. I have no idea what that means, but it sounds like something they would arrange."

"Yes, it does." Grace leaned against the metal passageway wall, pleased to hear the guys had been able to call. "Have you sent Wolf that mushy greeting card yet?" She'd been reading between the lines of Wolf's letters and Jill's. Something good was brewing. It was about time.

"Grace, I can't. What if he doesn't like it?"

"Come on; it's got Wolf written all over it."

"What if someone reads over his shoulder? He'll kill me."

"Making guys blush is good for them."

"I'll think about it."

Her time was running out but she didn't want to let Jill go. Grace missed her. She was looking forward to a girls' night catching up on news while they shared nail polish and hair curlers and clothes catalogs. "My time is up; I'm going to have to go. Happy birthday, Jill. And many more."

"Thank you; your birthday present was stupendous. It's great to hear your voice. Fly safe!"

"I'll write," Grace promised, saying good-bye. She hung up and turned the phone over to the next sailor waiting. Everyone on this ship was missing someone at home.

The ship didn't take weekends off but there was a sense of it being Friday. Duty shifts were entering the weekend recovery phase where time was allocated to completing paperwork from the week's training, maintenance teams could catch up on the inevitable list of needed repairs, and supply ships could replenish the stores. The mess was doing a special meal of barbecued ribs tonight, and the morale and welfare officers had arranged new movies.

They were south of Crete, sailing toward the Red Sea and the

Persian Gulf. The storm had limited flight operations, a defensive air protection blanket for the carrier battle group being the only planes sent up. If Operation Northern Watch had been tense, they were heading into trouble. Covering Kuwait meant heavy flight schedules.

Grace began the long trek back to her stateroom. This far down in the bowels of the ship was the home of the sailors who kept the ship running, and there were very few familiar landmarks. She started stepping over the watertight hatches that interrupted every corridor at regular intervals.

Off corridors on this third deck were the ship's laundry, machine shops, the ship's store, and a mess that could seat five hundred sailors for a meal. Another deck below were the nuclear reactors and the turbines. She was very willing to leave this side of the Navy to the men who had sailor in generations of their blood.

The first thing she taught a nugget: Find the squadron ready room, find your stateroom, and find the dirty-shirt wardroom where you could get a meal while still wearing your flight suit. It was possible to work, sleep, and eat for weeks without ever venturing this deep into the bowels of the ship.

There was a huge air-conditioning plant aboard, but it existed first to cool the electronic warfare equipment that was jammed into the heart of the aircraft carrier nerve center, and second to cool the ship for comfort. When they reached the warm waters of the Gulf, these lower levels of the ship would turn into a sauna.

She climbed her first ladder, ascending to the second deck. She took a short corridor jog and climbed again. Now she was starting to see familiar sites. She reached the hangar deck. An expanse over two football fields' long cut into the heart of the ship; it was an area that could hold as many as sixty aircraft inside. About thirty were below at the moment, the rest riding out the rainstorm tied down by chains on the deck.

Murky storm-darkened daylight filtered in from the stern of the ship where the hangar bay was open to the elements. The storm was not severe enough to close the massive blast doors. Crews were busy, planes opened up and showing their guts. This ship sailed with the machinery to fix anything that broke aboard the ship or a plane. The platforms on the fantail even allowed the maintenance crews to test a rebuilt engine at full power.

Thunder ripped the air and rolled through the open hangar, echoing and adding to the noise. Grace looked one last time at the open air and turned to continue to work her way back to her stateroom.

The rain was a mixed blessing. She'd been praying for it, but it was falling at the wrong place. The rain was at sea and was not reaching shore. This storm would actually result in making the drought inland worse as it would exhaust what built-up energy there was in the atmosphere.

She reached her stateroom an hour after she had left to make her phone call to Jill. Since two people being on their feet at the same time was crowded and three was the limit without slowing each other down, Grace skirted the hanging ironed shirts and slid onto her bunk. She had another thirty minutes before she would begin her six-hour shift standing as the squadron duty officer.

She reached for the book she'd tucked in the corner of the bunk. The paperback was beat up and dog-eared, a copy of Mark Twain's *A Connecticut Yankee in King Arthur's Court*. It had arrived in a care package from Bruce over the weekend. There was a library on board ship, but it was a long trek and she rarely went that direction except for Sunday services at the chapel. And nothing in the library could compare to this gift. Bruce had drawn little smiley faces in the margins and laughter notes and underlined sections. It was a fascinating, if unusual, way to say hello. Bruce had found a way into her deployment and was occupying more and more of her thoughts.

"Did you love him?"

She hadn't answered his last letter yet, was still struggling to find the right words. She was glad Bruce wasn't always that intense. She was learning not to open his letters until she had time to sit down and really read them. The man told stories about Wolf to keep her abreast of what was going on, told stories about his own days with a dry sense of humor, and probed into her emotions all in the same letter.

Loneliness on this tour was proving to be a very relative thing. His letters kept arriving to fill what free moments she had. She'd finish her letter to him later tonight.

Lord, this is a fascinating relationship and I wish I knew where it was heading. It's going to be so strange seeing him and talking in person after this deployment. Letters have a way of going into topics and adding details I normally would not mention. You surprised me with this friendship. Thanks.

Bruce –

Your last letter and package arrived and have filled my days with many enjoyable hours. I read in snatches of twenty and thirty minutes. I find myself spending my downtime relaxing with your words. You're good company.

I haven't answered your question before this, not because I don't know the answer but because I do. Yes, I loved Ben. I knew him, understood him, and trusted him. I'm disappointed in myself that I made an assumption that I couldn't handle the complexity of marrying him. A few years ago I quaked at the thought of trying to land aboard the carrier, and now I'm comfortable guiding other pilots to a safe landing. I grew into the role. I should have approached the challenge of marrying Ben in the same way.

Is there anything that God cannot handle? Anything He cannot teach? Anything He cannot inspire? I took my eye off the larger goal and let a short-term obstacle loom larger than it should have.

I have to admit you have pushed me back into studying the Word while on deployment. Normally those intense periods come during the stateside breaks. It is enjoyable and refreshing to be so deep inside God's Word. I've been loving the nuggets of gold I'm finding. Time's tight. I've got to go.

All God's best, Gracie

2 Chronicles 20

Then Jehoshaphat feared, and set himself to seek the LORD.... "O LORD, God of our Fathers, art thou not God in heaven? Dost thou not rule over all the kingdoms of the nations? In thy hand are power and might, so that none is able to withstand thee.... O our God, wilt thou not execute judgment upon them? For we are powerless against this great multitude that is coming against us. We do not know what to do, but our eyes are upon thee."...

"Hearken, all Judah and inhabitants of Jerusalem, and King Jehoshaphat: Thus says the LORD to you, 'Fear not, and be not dismayed at this great multitude; for the battle is not yours but God's.... You will not need to fight in this battle; take your position, stand still, and see the victory of the LORD on your behalf, O Judah and Jerusalem.'...

When Judah came to the watchtower of the wilderness, they looked toward the multitude; and behold, they were dead bodies lying on the ground; none had escaped....

So the realm of Jehoshaphat was quiet, for his God gave him rest round about.

FIFTEEN

★ ★ ★

JUNE 3

TURKEY/SYRIAN BORDER

W hat do you think that defector had to say?"

"I don't think we're watching the Syrian/Turkey border for our good health," Bruce replied, wondering how Wolf could recline on rocks for so long without ever shifting. He was doing his best to match the man's stillness even while stones dug into his belly. They had the high ground, and to their east the Euphrates ran from Turkey into Syria. Through the night-vision-equipped binoculars, the river had a glow to it as the heat absorbed during the day reflected back into the air. It was the only water in a region where the drought had taken a firm hold.

"Terrorist attacks?"

"Maybe. Rebel raids at least."

Syria tended to look the other way as remnants of the Kurdish Workers' Party fighting Turkey's control of the southeast districts retreated into Syria and Iraq as safe havens. Turkey had reacted with military raids in the past, going after the rebels, but the politics of the moment were sensitive. Turkey wanted approval to upgrade its roughly two hundred F-16s, and escalating tensions with Syria didn't help their case.

To keep the tension under control, NATO had extended its ground observations of the Turkish borders with Syria and Iraq. There were too many NATO troops in Turkey not to worry about the constant terrorism threat the rebels represented.

The SEALs were spread out in two-man teams along this particular set of steeps. As Turkey closed off one path, the rebels created another. Locating those new routes was the sole objective of nights like this. Bruce was content to be out with friends; it was a useful exercise to hone his own night navigation skills. They were looking for men and backpacks, the movement of weapons often done by foot soldiers in the rebel cause.

"It's been quiet lately in this sector," Wolf commented. "Too quiet?"

"To have percolated up to the highest level of the Syrian government, whatever that defector had to say, it's going to be something bigger than even a coordinated set of terrorist strikes. I wouldn't be surprised to see the Syrian army realigning itself and shift out of Lebanon, then come north."

"What a happy thought that is," Wolf commented, scanning the terrain.

Bruce watched a flight of planes high overhead go toward Iraq. Routine night flights had also been increased, an unusual action that suggested they were monitoring electronic signal traffic much closer than they had in the past. Stepped up surveillance without obvious cause was an indication the military was acting based on possibilities, probing to find out what had concrete underpinnings.

"Did you hear from Jill?"

"I got a care package with a mushy card," Wolf replied. "Did you hear from Grace?"

"A really nice letter."

Wolf looked over at him and good-naturedly shoved his shoulder. "So what are you going to do about it?"

"Write her back. What are you going to do about Jill?"

"Go home."

Bruce smiled. "Good answer." Wolf would be leaving at the

end of next week. There was nothing that would make Jill happier. Bruce was heading home in a couple weeks too.

"There." Wolf lowered his binoculars and pointed to the east. "1.4 miles, past the knoll. Four men."

TURKEY/IRAQ BORDER

The fighter planes were flying high tonight, mere ghosts passing across the stars. He sat back on his heels when he noticed the formation of three aircraft and tracked them by turning his body as they flew east. He was an old man and he had seen many flights of military planes. There were only three planes tonight instead of the normal four.

One pilot had the misfortune of passing into a thermal temperature gradient, and the jet exhaust left a contrail of ice crystals behind to mark his path across the sky. The moonlight showed the upper winds dispersing it into an ever widening line.

The campfire popped and sparks flew. The gnarled wood sputtered as the small amounts of sap inside sizzled. The warmth the fire reflected was welcome, for the change in temperature from day to night was marked; his bones protested and his joints ached.

He was hungry but he did not reach for the small iron cooking pot. There was enough dinner for only one, and his grandson would need to eat when he returned. The hesitation he had felt about bringing the boy on this reconnaissance trip had faded. His grandson had been useful. The boy could go where the mountain goats ran with an ease he could only envy. Whether the boy's father could be trusted to remain quiet was another matter.

He thought of his family as he stirred the fire and felt a weariness fed from disappointment. He had hoped in his lifetime to pass on to his children something better than what he had been born into, but his time was almost gone. He had been born in a refugee camp, and it looked like he would die still displaced from a homeland. There was no place for his people in a Europe remaking itself.

He knew the fire made his camp visible to the radar sweeping the ground but he let it burn bright. He was on the safe side of the Turkey/Iraq border, and they would merely note his presence. Each month at the full moon he made this journey, and tomorrow he would have to think about such things as hiding the fire. There were still occasionally Navy SEALs prowling the area stopping the most egregious of the weapons trading that happened throughout this area, men much like those he had escorted a decade ago into Iraq during the war, men he still considered friends. They were to be avoided now if only because he was too old to find a new path each month and so would protect the one he now had.

The Kurdish uprising in northern Iraq, the freedom fighters finding safe haven in Albania: His brothers were all around this area, all fighting for that same sense of homeland. And everywhere his brothers went, the Americans came. They came with NATO; they came with the United Nations. The names changed but not the truth. The Americans came.

Within a few hundred miles of his camp there were three divisions of the Turkish army, two divisions of the Iraqi army, nine terrorist training camps in the desert, two no-fly zones that required a U.S. aircraft battle group to support, and over eight thousand United Nation and NATO peacekeepers. There was room here for everyone but the people who had lived on the land for centuries.

He read the U.S. newspapers and followed the debate on how internationalist a posture America should take in the new administration. He read the opinion pieces and the letters and the editorial pages and he found the lack of understanding amazing.

America had not fought a land battle on her own homeland since the eighteen hundreds. No, the Americans fought their wars on the other side of the oceans, far from their own shores, here on *his* homeland. They came and imposed their no-fly zones and strove to block people's dreams for freedom.

He turned the stick and the glowing tip turned bright red. He wished he could turn his quest as hot.

He couldn't bring the war to their homeland; that was the ambition of greater men than himself. But around him the unrest was stirring. It just needed a strong breath to bring the spark to life. He could reach into the sky and pluck down a plane. He could turn their ambition to be everywhere into a liability.

They would leave.

Send a plane, maybe two planes, into the sand or the shimmering sea and the Americans would decide they would move to another place. They would leave the situation on the ground to the Europeans who had long practiced live and let live when it came to territorial compromises. Europeans understood compromise was needed to fix centuries of artificial boundaries in the land. What Russia had done centuries before needed to be rectified, not set in cement lines on a map.

One man, a few missiles. He had no desire to kill a pilot, no desire to see men on the ground sent to hunt for him. But if it would bring peace, maybe it was worth the price. He thought about it as he watched the fire. He would have to disappear as men came on the ground to hunt him. He would need stored provisions, enough for months, left throughout this area.

"Grandfather."

He looked up and he smiled as his grandson returned. "Bring it to the fire and you may open it."

The boy carried a burlap knapsack with him, retrieved from

under the rock ledge where the desert hawks had once nested. From the bag came a parcel wrapped in gray cloth to protect it. The wooden box was hand carved. The wood top slid to one side to reveal a heavy parchment paper.

He accepted the paper from his grandson and read the request by the firelight. The items his brothers prayed he would bring them were few compared to months in the past. It was yet more tangible proof that their numbers were dwindling. The younger men had given up hope of change and did not join as they once had. His own son was one of them. "What does it say, Grandfather?"

He ruffled the boy's hair. "That there is still work for old men to do."

He proposed to take on a nation. It was the work of younger men, but none were here. He still believed he could change things. It was an act of valor to stand for his people. And the history he studied said, at least for a round or two, it was possible that he might even be the victor.

There were other elders to talk to, consensus to be formed. His actions would affect many. He had time. It was the only thing he truly had. The Maker had given it to all men equally. "Eat. And tell me again about your dreams for when you are as old as me."

The boy laughed and eagerly began to talk.

TURKEY/SYRIAN BORDER

"What is that they are carrying?" Wolf asked, dialing in a tighter focus, trying to figure it out.

Bruce could just pick out the detail as the single file line of men moved down a steep incline, following the contours of the land. The men in the middle of the line were carrying something between them on a pole. Whatever it was, it weighed enough to bow the pole it was lashed to. "It looks like a sheep."

"They are heading from Turkey back into Syria. Poaching?" Wolf speculated.

"Food is now something to steal at night from your enemies. It tells you something about the seriousness of the situation within Syria," Bruce agreed.

They watched the line of men disappear.

Bruce had a feeling they were watching the tip of a coming conflict. Wars had been fought for land, for oil. They were on the verge of fighting one for water if the drought continued. The pressure on livestock, on agriculture, on people's basic need for water would be the match that ignited it.

Turkey had agreements linking Syria's antiterrorism efforts to guaranteed amounts of water flow from the Euphrates. But agreements could not dictate drought. Already there were grumbles about the new dam at Birecik, Turkey, and charges of water being unfairly diverted. They could cut off rebel routes and stop weapon sales, but until the tension in the region abated, the odds were better that events would surge toward violence than retreat toward peace.

Bruce lowered his binoculars. "We may be heading stateside, but I've got a feeling we will be back."

SIXTEEN

★ ★ ★

JUNE 12

NORFOLK, VIRGINIA

What time is Wolf's flight getting in?"

"1340—uh, 1:40 P.M. I'm even talking like them now." Jill flung open the door to her closet. "Terri, can I borrow your shoes, the red flats?"

"You're going to wear the dress."

Jill looked with longing at the red-and-white sundress still hanging under plastic. "It's for tonight. The new blouse and jeans. The red flats should match." She'd gone shopping for Wolf's return, and most items coming home had been red. She didn't have shoes to match.

"I'll bring them with me to the office."

"Thanks. I'll stop on the way in and check if Jim's landlord was able to get the water leak fixed. Can you handle the bank deposit today?"

"Sure."

"You're a gem. See you in a few." Jill rushed through getting ready, took the stairs down two at a time, wondering where she had left her purse. "Let's go, Emily!"

She opened the refrigerator and didn't have to count juice bottles. There was only one left. She had ordered in several cases early on so she could count down the days with them. Wolf's flight was coming into Naval Air Station, Oceana. There were several transports arriving with gear and men, and she wasn't sure if the SEAL contingent had their own flight or was part of a larger group. It wasn't a matter of if she would be early, it was a question of how early. She hoped she hadn't overdone the homecoming.

She hadn't been able to get to sleep last night. She was so nervous about today. Twelve weeks. She hoped the reunion lived up to Wolf's expectations. She paused to read again the note on the refrigerator. Her mushy card had gotten her a mushy note in return. Wolf had surprised her.

I miss you. I miss your laughter. your perfume. your smiles. your pretty eyes. your phone calls that wake me up. your shoes left under my couch. your lipstick in my car. your purse left wherever we were just at.

I want your company. a long walk at the park. a day at the beach. a movie watched from the back row. a day picking out mushy cards for each other.

I miss you, Jill.

A line of *X*s and *O*s ran in a heart around the words. The reunion almost made up for the separations. Almost.

"Emily! Come on. It's time to leave, honey."

She was relieved when the dog appeared from the living room, wagging her tail. Jill bent down and kissed her muzzle. "Good morning, beautiful." She was half afraid the dog was going to die of old age before her brother returned. "Let's go."

NAVAL AIR STATION, OCEANA

Jill was glad she had remembered to bring sunscreen. The sun was hot and the breeze nonexistent. Wolf was coming back as part of a much larger contingent of soldiers rotating between Norfolk and Turkey. The southeast end of the parking lot along the runway had been turned into a welcome home area with a large open side tent and tables to give families a place to wait for the flight.

The plane arrived five minutes ahead of schedule to an enthusiastic chorus of cheers. Her first sight of Wolf was in a stream of guys coming off the transport; he was wearing a floppy hat that had a small American flag in the brim. She laughed at that classic Wolf gesture. He looked good, so deeply tanned it merged with his desert cammies. He was with his buddies, Cougar on one side and Bear on the other.

Families streamed through the gate in the fence to meet the men. She edged herself to the left where she could step up on a concrete curb and see better rather than join the queue trying to get through the narrow opening. Jill saw Kelly and Bear find each other, watched as the man swept his wife up to twirl her around.

Wolf spotted her wave and lifted his hand. He leaned over to say something to Cougar, got slapped on the shoulder. He headed her way and slipped off his sunglasses. The closer Wolf got, the better he looked. She stayed where she was rather than rush to the fence. She smiled at him instead, a small smile that grew the closer he got. "You promised to come find me."

"That I did." He vaulted over the fence. "Hi, Jilly."

"Hi." She was not quite eye level as she teetered on the concrete perch. He picked her up and smothered her in a hug. She buried her face in his shoulder, wrapped her arms around him, and hugged him tight.

"It's good to be home."

She leaned back and beamed at him. "I missed you."

He kissed her nose. "That's for the birthday I missed." He leaned down and kissed her until she was out of breath. "That was for the last letter." He looked her over from head to toe. "You got a haircut. You look wonderful in red. The necklace is beautiful. The glasses are new?" She giggled. He was trying. She never wanted to lose this man. "What do you have planned?"

"Candlelight, a special meal. An attempt to cover as many of your 'I miss' list as I can."

He twirled her around. "Laughter, smile, perfume, shoes under my couch, lipstick left in my car?" he offered.

"Covered. What's going on with Bruce and Grace?" She'd been dying to ask ever since his last letter.

"Something pretty wonderful. I'll tell you all about it over dinner."

JUNE 22

USS *GEORGE WASHINGTON* (CVN 73)

PERSIAN GULF

The weight room was squeezed into a corner of the ship in a cleared out storage room just past the chapel. "Grace."

"One minute," Grace told her roommate Heather. She pushed through the last five reps with the barbell. She hated working weights. She did it because it was discipline, because if she didn't she paid a price weeks later when she wanted the benefits of having done it. She'd only had marginal luck squeezing in runs around the flight deck during scheduled downtimes while the flight deck crews conduced their daily FOD walks. She often joined those careful searches of every inch of the flight deck to pick up any foreign objects—screws, pens, paper clips—before they could get sucked into an engine and blow it up.

Grace let the weights settle back and reached for her towel. "Okay."

"The flight schedule for tomorrow is out."

She accepted the single sheet of paper that governed everything happening in the squadron. "Thanks." It was complete flight ops in one comprehensive glance: briefing time, launch time, recovery time, and the formation type and mission details. She was up for a 0500 launch in a four-plane formation. She'd be flying over the oil fields that had been destroyed at the end of the Gulf war. She had picked up two additional assignments, a 1400 launch in a two-plane formation and a short shuttle hop at 1600. At the moment they were two pilots short in the squadron due to medical downs and everyone was having to carry the extra load.

Grace owed Peter a thanks. He'd put himself down for the mission planning and given her a two-hour break in a very long day. She wasn't looking forward to the two tanker refuel stops—winds had been strong at the higher altitudes. "How's your day look?"

"I get to sleep until 0600." They shared a rueful smile.

They had passed the three-month point of the cruise. It was the hard stretch of a deployment, and everyone aboard was showing the wear of the long days and hours. Problems at home were trickling in, and it would be another two months before the anticipation of their homecoming would start to take over.

"I'm heading to the ship store," Heather said. "Need anything?"

"I'll come along," Grace decided. "I need to get something, anything, to send Bruce."

"Nothing is about what you will find. I'm so ready for the port call at Bahrain."

"I figure it will get canceled for security reasons. The one I'm looking forward to is Naples, Italy," Grace said. They were scheduled to be there for six days on their way home, and it would be their best break of this deployment.

"Going to get up to see Rome this year?"

"I'm thinking about trying it. I saw Pompeii last time."

"Let's stop by admin and get signed up for the train tour," Heather said.

"You're on."

Bruce ~

We've started major flight ops over Kuwait. So far we haven't been out to the live fire range but it's coming. I can tell we are entering month four. It's a slugfest to get up every morning and repeat yesterday's routine. I miss the sun when it's not trying to fry what it touches. I miss a lazy day to sleep in.

Iraq is saber rattling again, annoyed with Kuwait's latest OPEC position and still irritated with Saudi Arabia over some mosque decision. Needless to say, Iraq wanting to cause some grief means picking on the Americans. Iraqi Republican Guard troops have been moving recently in what they say is an exercise. I'm glad I'm not one of the Marines on the ground having to figure out what their intentions are.

I know it sounds like I'm down, and I guess I am. Deployments are always a balancing act of emotions, energy, and rest. We're in the heavy work stretch. I'm conserving energy. I mentally get up for the flights and the focus needed and the rest of the time I try to let myself spin down.

I've got my head crammed full of SLAM missile avionics at the moment. We're getting an upgrade for the data-link pod installed next week, and I'm the check-out pilot for the squadron to make sure the maintenance section figures out all the particulars of the upgrade. I spend most of my downtime trying to keep up with the technical reading. There's hasn't been much time to answer your last letters. I'm sorry about that; I don't want it to imply I haven't relished getting them. I have.

I hope this package arrives before I get home. It's not much of a gift but I guarantee you don't have one. Our onboard metals shop was stamping out the marshal star type badges with the unit logo on them as a way to calibrate the fine aligns of the press equipment. You were going to get a hat with the *GW* logo; that tells you how limited the ship store has become. The next major replenishment is due Friday, and what seems like half this ship's crew has been tasked to haul boxes for that six-hour operation. Needless to say, a prior planned transfer of supplies didn't happen as originally scheduled, and this one is much larger than normal.

I hope this letter finds you enjoying your return stateside. Enjoy a movie from beginning to end for me. I'm an expert at the ten-minutes-and-fall-asleep way of watching one.

God bless, Gracie

SEVENTEEN

★ ★ ★

JUNE 26

PENSACOLA, FLORIDA

Bruce was doing his best to enjoy his welcome home party. He wanted to crawl away somewhere and sleep for a month, but Jill had worked hard to put this together. With Wolf's help, she'd somehow managed to arrange a party in Pensacola. She'd invited not only the other PJs and their families, but many of the Coast Guard units he had worked with. The party was great; he just didn't have the lady he wanted around to share it.

"Bruce?"

He smiled at Jill as he took the glass of punch with a quiet thanks. She'd driven down over the weekend to bring back his car, open his house, stock his refrigerator, and leave him several home-cooked meals. She'd transformed the community center with streamers, music, food, and even gifts for the guests. Jill perched on the arm of his chair. Petite, short blond hair with curls, vibrant green eyes, and a love of laughter, she looked more like their mom every year. "You need another few days for your mind to catch up with your body."

"Sorry, I don't mean to be so not here."

Her hand on his shoulder squeezed. "You're allowed. You are home; that's what matters the most. Sunburn and all."

Emily licked his hand and nudged his fingers. Bruce resumed lazily stroking her coat. "I figured she would have forgotten me by now." He didn't try to explain how nice it was to find the dog not only remembered him, but seemed to welcome his company. His dog had given one of the few barks he had ever heard her make and came practically prancing to meet him. Once the party had begun she'd flopped down beside him.

"She's loyal. She likes you. Are you glad to be back?"

"Do you have to ask?"

"Just checking. It sounds like you and Wolf had some fun while you were gone."

He leaned his head back. She didn't know the half of it. "Most of it was pure boredom. They cut back training to essentials for the location. I haven't combat jumped in three months or scuba dived."

"Oh, you." She kissed his forehead. "Wolf, come tell my brother to behave."

"What's this?" Bruce caught her hand.

She broke into peals of laughter. "It's taken you long enough to notice."

"Jill."

"Wolf said it was okay with you."

Bruce shot a look at the SEAL coming toward them who looked decidedly sheepish at the moment. "He's stretching what I said a bit." A tug caused Jill to tumble from the arm of the chair onto his lap. "Are you happy about it? Because otherwise I could make his life miserable for you," he offered, at the moment finding it an interesting suggestion. He was suddenly jealous of his friend; he didn't intend to lose a sister.

"Be happy for me."

"Really?"

"Really. He learned to write mushy letters."

Bruce considered her. "Is that what it took?"

She giggled.

"So," he had no idea how to phrase it, "what are you thinking?"

"I said yes to a ring, and I told him I'd think about the wedding date. I want Grace home."

Bruce was relieved; the idea of her getting married was no longer theoretical, and he wanted some time to figure out what a big brother was supposed to do in such a situation. Pay for the wedding? Make sure Wolf didn't talk her into eloping? He was in over his head. "Sounds smart."

"Let me up."

"Nope. Look what you went and did while I was gone. Had a birthday. Got older. Collected a ring." He loved her giggle. "This is a bit of an Air Force versus Navy quandary too. Just for the principle of the thing—"

"You've got one of your own."

He raised an eyebrow.

"How's Grace doing? Have you heard from her?"

He walked into that one. He patted his jacket pocket. "I've got her last letter right here," he assured, amused.

"Do you?"

"She writes a nice letter."

"Mushy?"

Bruce just smiled at her.

USS *GEORGE WASHINGTON* (CVN 73)
PERSIAN GULF

She needed more gas. Grace scanned the sky for the lights of the tanker. Against the black sky and bright white stars she was searching for the faint lights of a tanker circling in an figure eight horseshoe pattern. Refueling at night was a reality of Gulf deployments. Where was that tanker?

United Arab Emirates was her emergency divert field. She wanted fuel, she wanted a place in the landing stack, she wanted to land on the ship, and she wanted to go to bed. The sequence was full of small crises to avoid. She had launched with 12.3 thousand in fuel, but she'd been burning it at more than a pound per mile. She needed gas.

Her wingman had refueled and taken the last of the JP5 from the flying Texaco in the sky they had first been routed to. She'd been given vectors to a KC-135 tanker on angels 12 as a backup, but there wasn't a bright billboard to tell her where it was in its pattern.

She was flying with Bushman on this hop. The nugget had improved over the tour, but he was still too quick to overreact for her comfort. And flying formation made him skittish. He was holding off her left wing.

There it was. The white lights tracked left to right across the horizon a mile ahead. She'd be able to join up during one of the long lazy legs of its pattern.

She double-checked that her weapons were safe, extended the F/A-18 retractable refueling probe, and called up the air-refueling checklist on the left display screen. She tracked the tanker, matched speed, and then climbed the last thousand feet at a snail's pace to settle in behind the massive plane.

"Eagle 01, astern, nose cold, all switches safe, looking for 5.0."

The tanker extended its drogue, a two-foot wide basket at the end of a long hose. It stabilized below the slipstream behind the tanker. Lights turned orange. "Eagle 01, you're cleared for 5.0."

She nudged up her speed and closed with the tanker at a peaceful three knots. She just had to plug her refueling probe into the center of the basket, fly forward to put an *S* bend in the hose, and gas would flow. Simple.

Wind sent the basket hurtling to the right.

Grace flexed her hand on the throttle and eased back. The basket continued to whip up and down and now she felt it in her controls. Crosswinds. She looked at the fuel she had on board. *Calm winds, Lord. Please. I need help.*

Problems in life had become only one. Getting gas. Bingo fuel levels to United Arab Emirates were coming up fast, and she did not want to leave Bushman to return to the ship alone. The basket stabilized.

She eased forward again. The probe caught the edge of the basket, and in a split second decision to either try it anyway or pull back, she eased her jet back.

The tanker began a slow turn in its figure-eight pattern to avoid running into unfriendly airspace. This was getting complicated. Getting gas while in a turn or even a change in altitude was possible, but it certainly made the flying interesting.

She looked at her fuel on board. This was not a good night to go swimming. Another minute and she diverted to UAE.

She nudged her approach to two knots closure and matched the tanker's turn rate. She pushed the probe into the basket, nudging forward to bend the hose. The tanker's amber light turned green showing flow. She watched the fuel gauge creep up.

For nine minutes she stayed focus. Very focused. She was hugging the belly of a gas tank with fuel flowing at a thousand pounds per minute. She was determined to control the wind, not the other way around.

Fuel reached 9.0. She slowly disengaged from the probe. The drogue relaxed.

"Eagle 01, fuel 5.0. Thanks, tank."

She reduced power to three knots separation.

She had fuel.

One problem down.

She slowly descended and retracted the fuel probe. That had been twenty minutes she would not care to repeat. *Bruce, I miss your not being around to catch me if necessary.* Doing her job halfway around the world late at night when the rest of the air wing had called it a night and it was just her and her nugget wingman preparing to break to the landing pattern was incredibly lonely.

Bushman nearly bumped her. She tossed her plane into a forty-degree bank to avoid the wing clip.

"Sorry, Eagle 01." He broke radio silence to apologize.

EIGHTEEN

★ ★ ★

JULY 1
PENSACOLA, FLORIDA

Bruce was sitting on the beach when he opened the letter from Grace. He'd changed into ragged shorts and slipped on tennis shoes over bare feet and dealt with the sweat of hanging drywall by wading into the surf. It was a good tired that came from the end of a hard day of work. He hollowed out a holder in the sand for his soda.

"Hi, handsome."

He raised a hand in acknowledgment but didn't bother to look. The women running on the beach were universally cute but he had other priorities. Emily rejoined him and vigorously shook her coat to rid herself of salt water. "Really, honey, did you have to do that?" He wiped his face dry on his arm, then reached over and wiped her nose off where sand was clinging. "Admit it, you're a fraud. You're only as old as you want to be."

Emily sank down with a sigh on the towel he had brought out for her and rolled over on her side. Jill was right. The dog was a duchess, an old duchess. Bruce leaned over and retrieved a piece of salt-water taffy. He unwrapped it for Emily. "Enjoy." It would take her twenty minutes. Bruce stretched out on his beach towel and carefully opened the letter he had intentionally saved. This one had set a record, arriving within a week of being sent.

He started reading. And his smile faded; this wasn't good. *Lord, I didn't need this one.*

Bruce ~

I'm okay. My profound conclusion at the end of today—life is about handling one crisis after another and still having enough energy left to be standing to handle the next one. Tonight I nearly ran out of gas, nearly got hit by my wingman, and had to land with an uncertain lock on the left landing gear. It turned out to be a wiring short. I'm wiped. But I'm standing, sort of. I'm leaning against the wall beside the third deck post office mailbox hoping being upright keeps me awake long enough to sign this.

Give Jill a hug for me. She sent me fuzzy slippers. I owe her a big one. I won't mention what happened to my socks last week. (Actually it was pretty funny, but it will need to be told in person to convey its true dimensions. Those who think we Navy brats have boring lives have never seen us play.)

Night, Bruce.

Gracie

Bruce reached for the pad of paper and pen he'd tossed beside his towel.

Grace ~

Thanks for starting that last letter with "I'm okay." I can read between the lines. I hear near swim. It's a sunny day here, 1500 Saturday afternoon. The sand is warm, the surf is calm, the water a clear rich blue. It would still kill you if it could. The Persian Gulf isn't so nice; it would eat a jet or a pilot in a gulp.

When Gulf Air Flight 072 went down with 143 people aboard while trying to land at Bahrain International Airport, I was stationed about ten miles away. The search and rescue went on through the night, and when daylight came, it became clear why no survivors had been found. The water was shallow, five feet in most places. It was strune for miles with wreckage, life vests, clothing, and victims.

It's not the way to die, honey. If it comes down to a choice, take your chances on the broken bones and get out of the plane while you have a chance. You may dread yanking the ejection handle, but I'm confident that if it's the best option, you'll take it. Wolf would be miserable without you, not to mention Jill and me. Tell your nugget wingman to pay better attention next time; there's a SEAL and a PJ watching.

The thing is—I know an accident is as likely to happen on any day while you are deployed; the last trap is just as dangerous as the first. And I know what can happen during training stateside. You're talking to a man who is very much a realist about such things. The military pays me to worry about pilots. I know the risks firsthand. You have a career built on no margin of error. So you handle it like most pilots by simply not thinking about it or that it could be you. That invincible confidence is a wonderful thing that keeps you calm, working problems to the very last item in a checklist. You're in my prayers daily, Grace. I'm grateful you have such a focused intensity to be the best; it keeps you alive when those surprises happen.

How about a mushy letter?

I want to write you one without you misunderstanding why. I think you're a special lady, Grace. And you're coming home to the place you once said felt incomplete.

Why don't you try to close the circle and find that completeness? There are a lot of us around who see you for who you are and who would gladly make room for you in our lives. Me, Cougar—who bugs Wolf for news about you—Rich, who somehow managed to acquire your picture too. (Not that I wouldn't have a few words with those guys if they dared to do more than flirt, but that's another point.)

With Ben you saw the separations as a problem that couldn't be overcome. Grace, being apart is not good or bad, it's just part of the relationship. We've done pretty well at a friendship for six months. Take a risk. Find out what you can have stateside in the next months. On the next sea tour you can find out if it can comfortably coexist with your job. That's the secret of peace; it's not complicated. It's putting together the parts of who you are and letting yourself be complete.

Do you have plans for your Fourth of July? I'll be watching the fireworks here and thinking about you. Next year if we're both stateside you've got a standing invitation to join me. See, I just planned part of your life. Life is about planning events that you would enjoy and keeping all those plans that life lets you hold on to.

I've been trying out that list of things you were homesick for; it had some wonderful items. I'm sending you a big batch of Sunday comics. Enjoy. I've taught Emily to love popcorn. The TV with lots of channels has even less on it than you'll remember.

I've been lazing around the beach the last four days, feeling about as energetic as a baked clam. I'm glad to be home, Grace, but only to you will I admit I already miss the deployment. I was on the front lines. Now, I'm back training to get the privilege to go back to the front lines. Please don't ever let the long days and the distance leave you thinking you made the wrong career decision. You made a valuable one, and I, for one, deeply appreciate what you do. I wish you were sitting on the beach with me today, able to see the civilians walking by. They have no idea what is being done around the world to keep them safe.

The ring Wolf gave Jill is very special. I've never seen her so happy and so nervous at the same time. She's looking forward to seeing you.

I'm looking forward to your return home too. I miss you, Grace. August 26 is less than eight weeks away. Think of me occasionally between now and then.

Bruce

Psalm 34:7–10

The angel of the LORD encamps around those who fear him, and delivers them. O taste and see that the LORD is good! Happy is the man who takes refuge in him! O fear the LORD, you his saints, for those who fear him have no want! The young lions suffer want and hunger; but those who seek the LORD lack no good thing.

JULY 4

USS *GEORGE WASHINGTON* (CVN 73)

ARABIAN SEA OFF THE COAST OF OMAN

From the vantage point of vulture row, the planes on the flight deck were being moved around like cars on a big parking lot. Grace loved to watch the activity. She'd come to the best viewing spot on the ship. Vulture row was a narrow balcony just aft of primary flight control, six stories above the flight deck, one of the few places where a spectator wasn't in the way. Elevator one lowered two planes to the main hangar deck in the heart of the ship. It was a down flight day and a welcome day off.

There were worse places to spend the Fourth of July.

She watched Bushman land and catch the third wire. He was learning.

Lord, all the sacrifices to reach here have been worth it. She was content.

Bruce ~

I have enjoyed your letters. Your last one has put me at a bit of a loss for words. Touched is probably the closest to capturing the emotions.

The deployment is wrapping down, and tomorrow we will officially hand off offensive flight ops to the USS *Truman*. I'm at peace. It's been a good deployment. I told Wolf before I left that when I returned, I'd be ready to move on. The low-grade grief that lingered after Ben's death has begun to fade. Frankly, hard work is a wonderful remedy for what ails.

I've made some fabulous friends on this tour. Living on top of six others does that. I'm going to feel lost those first few weeks home with all the space. Would you do me a favor and bring a handkerchief with you? I have a feeling I'm going to need it when I see Jill. I'm presuming that you will be there, and I don't mean to do so. Already the awkwardness of translating a friendship on letters to one conducted in person has begun—forgive the stumbles as I sort this out. Please know I'm approaching it with no expectations. I'd much rather simply enjoy whatever comes.

I'm sure I'll be riding the ship to the pier rather than getting the privilege of being one of the seventy-five pilots who get to make that final ship to shore flight. I don't have enough seniority yet. It's probably just as well as it's going to take me those last couple days aboard to figure out how to pack my duffel bags to bring everything ashore. I am always astounded by how much I've acquired.

Rome should be excellent. Thanks for the restaurant tips. Heather and I are planning to have a wonderful time. I always have a problem setting aside the work to truly play, but I think I'll manage it for the three days ashore. I know, I know. I'm in the Navy; I should have world tourist in my blood, but in reality I find it overwhelming. The language mix is confusing, the traffic incredible, the prices unexpected, and the history around every corner astounding. I'll go to Rome and accumulate my one shore visit memory for this deployment.

I'm going to do the smart thing and turn in now. Good night, Bruce.

God bless, Gracie

NINETEEN

★ ★ ★

AUGUST 19

NORFOLK, VIRGINIA

Jill pushed open the door to Seaman Jones's apartment with her left foot, struggling not to drop any of the sacks she carried. Her little finger was turning numb as the plastic bag handle cut off circulation. She especially didn't want to tip the carryout containers of food. She made it to the kitchen and carefully lowered the sacks. "How's the wiring coming on the new speakers?"

"I've almost got it figured out," Wolf called from the living room. She walked through to see. He had the stereo cabinet pulled out into the room. Wolf turned on the radio to test it out. "Were you able to find a fifteen-foot cord?"

"Twelve feet was as long as they had."

"It'll do. I wish Detective Reese would find the guy who did this. I'd like to have a few words with him. He ripped apart the back of the unit when he stole the CD player."

"Six weeks without a burglary. He's moved on," Jill replied, relieved at that fact. Scott was still convinced he would eventually catch up with the guy, Wolf was still growling about the fact she hadn't told him what was going on, and Bruce—her brother hadn't been pleased with her. She'd learn. Next time she would handle the situation differently and tell them what was happening stateside.

Jill settled on the couch, seeking a minute with her feet up before she started putting away items she had carried in. She was drowning with welcome home preparations for her clients. Most of it was time sensitive, from groceries to getting them an extra hundred dollars in cash so they could easily get out that first weekend home without worrying about where their ATM card was and what their finances looked like. She was going to make it, maybe, if nothing else went wrong.

"Thanks for helping me out." The last replacement items for Seaman Jones had been delivered yesterday, and she'd been struggling to find time to get them unpacked.

"I wish you'd asked me days ago."

She was feeling guilty enough about the workload as it was; dragging him into it had been admitting defeat. "It's my business; I'm supposed to be able to handle it." Wolf pivoted to look at her and she sighed. "Sorry, I'm still working on the partnership implications of wearing your ring."

"Obviously. You're going to have to reconsider letting me be a business partner. I'm going to meddle; you might as well make it official."

"I'd rather figure out how to shove the business back into a reasonable box so it doesn't keep interrupting the time we have to spend together. It's a business, not the most important thing in my life." He'd shown up at her place this morning with a sack of muffins, coffee, wearing a T-shirt that said Jill's My Sweetheart. She would have loved the freedom to follow up on his hug with an offer to spend the day at the beach. Instead, she'd been forced to suggest she needed to eat in the car on the way to the office. She was tired of this job. Jill reached for the binder that contained her master plan, a sheet for every client, to see what stops were next on her list for the day.

"The job is cyclical in its demands, quit fighting it. You've got this organized. Do I smell lunch?"

"I brought Chinese. I'm organized enough to see I'm behind schedule. Would it be okay if I leave you here and go on to Craig's?"

"You should have asked Bruce if you could keep Emily a few more weeks. I don't like you going to clients' homes alone."

"I'm carrying in grocery sacks to stock refrigerators. Emily would go nuts. And I promise, I'm careful. There are fourteen more stops to make today. What about if I make the three near here and come back for you in an hour?"

Wolf shifted back toward the stereo cabinet. "I'll have the VCR subdued by then."

"Better you than me."

"Eat lunch first or take it with you."

"Yes, sir."

He laughed and tossed her his wallet. "Stop and get us a movie for tonight? When we stop for the day, you'll have a reason to put your feet up for more than a couple minutes."

It was the best offer she'd had all day. "Deal."

AUGUST 26

USS *GEORGE WASHINGTON* (CVN 73)

OFF THE COAST OF VIRGINIA

Grace wrapped the gift she had bought Jill in Rome inside her blue cotton T-shirt and added it to her duffel bag. She'd found the small painting at a gallery and fell in love with it. She had to pack her flight gear, her uniforms, and her casual clothes brought for liberty. Her bunk was covered with piles. She'd already emptied her locker and her cubbyhole in the squadron ready room.

Grace leaned against the bunk and offered a photo to Heather. Her friend was stretched out reading the latest issue of the shipboard newspaper. "Do you remember when we took this one?" It had been taken with one of the Polaroid cameras that floated around the ship.

Her friend took it and chuckled. "My hair coloring had not

yet completely faded to return me to a brunette. Probably six weeks out."

"That's what I was thinking." Grace handed Heather another one taken last night at their stateroom version of a good-bye party. "Did you see this one?"

"It's amazing what six months does."

"I'm now showing gray hair," Grace noted, depressed by the sight. "Bruce is going to notice."

"He's a smart guy; he won't comment. Wear your cover."

Grace hadn't worn her Navy hat since she'd been deployed. "I think I'll have to. Are you standing the rails for the homecoming?" A large contingent of sailors were part of the official homecoming detail.

"Yes. Want to join me?"

"If I get packed, I'll come up." Grace hadn't been assigned but she'd enjoy it. Sailors in dress uniform would man the rails of the aircraft carrier, standing at parade rest, as the *GW* entered port and was guided by tugs against Pier 12. When the loudspeaker on the flight deck called attention on deck, over a thousand men and women would answer with a crisp hand salute.

The mood on the ship had done a 180 in the last few weeks. Smiles were back, cheerful good humor, a smartness to steps. They were ready to get home. Talk around the mess table had turned to family and friends. Bruce was right, the military taught you to value relationships.

Grace turned back to her packing. She folded the pillowcase that had been her one special comfort from home. Books, music tapes, flight schedules, training bulletins—she found niches for them. She looked at the letters carefully arranged on the bunk by date. Bruce had sent her fourteen letters during the course of the deployment. Jill had sent her thirty-six; Wolf had sent nine along with half a dozen boxes. She didn't want to know how many she had written—whatever the number, there had not been enough of them. After some thought, Grace put the letters in her flight bag. They were the items she would treasure the most from this deployment.

She picked up the notebook she had made her temporary diary for this trip. In the first few pages were a jotted list of Scripture passages as she kept track of highlights from her studies. She smiled as she traced her finger over the list. God was gracious. He loved her. And life was good. It wasn't a bad set of facts to go home with. Bruce said test and see how well the pieces could fit together; she was ready to find out.

NORFOLK, VIRGINIA

Norfolk was celebrating the arrival of a carrier group. Bruce appreciated that fact as he took out his wallet for the third time in an hour. It was a military town, and every business was having a homecoming special of one kind or another. Movie theaters, restaurants, clothing stores—everyone hoped to get those fifteen thousand sailors back from six months at sea to spend money with them by providing a special sale. Bruce paid the florist and carefully took the wrapped flowers.

The first of the twenty-six ships in the *George Washington* carrier group had arrived yesterday. Bruce bought a newspaper on the way back to the car so he could check the summary for arrival times and locations. Roughly seven thousand sailors, marines, and air wing personnel were coming home today. The aircraft carrier USS *George Washington* was scheduled to pull into Pier 12, Naval Station Norfolk, at 1000. Knowing the Navy, it would be precisely on time.

Bruce thought about Grace's last letter. She sounded nervous. He smiled. Nervous was good. Anticipation was a wonderful thing. He was about to get a chance to establish a new first impression with her. How this relationship translated to face-to-face would establish the tone for the next months. He didn't want to rush her, but he definitely planned to seize the moment. He had settled on jeans and a black T-shirt, trying to keep it low-key. He wanted her to settle into a relaxed pace of stateside life, wanted to help minimize the inevitable disorientation that came with the transition. Showing up in Air Force blues would just remind her of a hurdle to overcome.

Bruce followed the map Jill had given him and parked in Open Parking Lot QP-6. He passed massive tents set up along the parking lot and large signs directing people with military precision to the New Mother's Tent, Air Wing Tent, Medical, Children's Tent, Hospitality Tent. The Navy was doing what it could to take care of the thousands coming to meet the ships. He crossed the street to join hundreds of others walking down to Pier 12.

The pier was huge, allowing two aircraft carriers to dock, one on either side. Jill had told him she'd be over near the Air Wing tent. He finally spotted her at the refreshments table and made his way to join her. She was putting out giant sized cookies. He helped himself to a chocolate chip one. "Hi."

"Are those flowers for me or Grace?"

He smiled at her.

"I thought so. She'll love them. Did you see Wolf? He was getting me the balloons."

"He's coming with them. He's got a long line of kids tailing him. Need help?"

"I think we're okay. As long as the ship doesn't arrive early."

"Jill, where do you want these?" Terri called, holding up blue platters.

Bruce wisely got out of his sister's way. She was busy now; she'd be swamped once clients began to arrive.

Where did he want to wait? Wolf had warned him that Grace would take her time leaving the ship, not wanting to get caught in that initial press of several thousand people coming down the ramps. After walking around the area to consider options, Bruce took up station at the *T* of the pier, a distance away from where the sailors would disembark, but where he would be able to watch the crowd. He could already see the *George Washington* in the distance.

USS *GEORGE WASHINGTON* (CVN 73)
NORFOLK, VIRGINIA

Grace headed up to the flight deck, a huge open expanse now that the seventy-five planes were absent. They had returned to stateside bases while the carrier was still a hundred miles out to sea. A few planes would be flying today, proudly showing the squadron colors during the arrival ceremonies.

Grace made her way to the LSO platform at the ship's stern where Heather had said she would be. The pier was already in sight and growing ever larger even as she stood stories above it on the back of the ship. There was nothing simple about a homecoming. Jill would be here. Wolf. Was Bruce here?

She searched the gathering crowds, knowing it was unlikely that she would locate him but feeling the pull to try. What was she going to say when she saw him? She had been thinking about it for days, and she still didn't know.

The flight deck loudspeaker called attention on deck, and the sailors' salute was matched by the striking of the band playing on the pier. A roar of jets had her looking up. Tomcats, followed by Prowlers and Hornets. They were greeting the returning ship with crisp formations and just a bit of showing off. She watched them with a smile, wishing she were one of those lucky few pilots.

★ ★ ★

"See her?" Bruce asked. Wolf had solved the problem of trying to see over the crowds by stepping up on the concrete barrier. All around them there were reunions going on, and in the confusion finding Grace was proving to be a challenge. She would be heading in this direction. If they somehow missed each other, the meeting point was at the Air Wing tent.

"We should have told her to wear something other than white," Wolf commented.

Bruce looked over toward the crowd of people flowing into the Air Wing tent. Jill was somewhere in the middle of that commotion near the red balloons, greeting clients.

A hand touched his shoulder and Bruce felt a jolt ripple through his system. "Hi."

Wolf jumped off of the concrete barrier. "Did you have to do that, Gracie?" She'd come up behind them. Wolf picked her up and swung her in a circle. "Welcome home." She buried her head against his shoulder and hugged him back, laughing.

Grace lifted her head and smiled over Wolf's shoulder at him. "Hi, Bruce."

She looked good. Very good. He'd forgotten how blue her eyes were, how much they reflected her laughter. He smiled back. "Hi, Gracie."

She patted her cousin's back. "You can let me down now, Wolf." Her cousin reluctantly did so.

"My welcome home." Bruce offered her the flowers he held.

"I'm going to have to come home more often. Wow." He'd chosen the most fragrant blossoms he could find and it had been worth it. For that brief moment when she lifted the blooms to breathe deeply, she seemed totally and completely relaxed. She looked up and caught his gaze. "Thank you."

"You're welcome, Grace. It's wonderful to see you."

She tilted her head, considering him. "You look different than my last memory of you."

Wolf strangled a cough.

Bruce punched his arm.

"I think it's the black eye. Yep, I think that's it."

"He went left when he should have gone right," Wolf explained.

She looked between the two of them. "Basketball?"

"Gracie, he landed in a tree during a night jump."

"Ouch."

"Crosswinds," Bruce said in his own defense. They'd been up at Fort Bragg, the units rotating back joining up to get in some real jumps to shake off the rust. The CARP jump hadn't gone as planned. The C-130 came in low and fast. They jumped at eight hundred feet using the wind from the plane's forward motion to fill the canopy and were on the ground in twenty seconds. They called it a Controlled Aerial Release Point, but about the only thing controlled was the fact it guaranteed they were going to hit the ground hard with minimal exposure to enemy fire. He'd hit a tree.

Wolf took pity on him and distracted her. "Have you seen Jill yet?"

"No! And I want to see this ring I've been hearing about. Is she at the Air Wing tent?"

"Keeping station under all the red balloons." Wolf led the way, clearing a path for them.

Grace reached back and caught Bruce's hand and tugged. "There is more to this story. Walk with me. Talk."

Bruce fell in step beside her, amused. This spurt of energy and homecoming emotion would wear off. Did she want to just go home and crash? Want to enjoy the freedom of a night out on the town? He'd settle for something in the middle if he could talk her into it.

TWENTY

★ ★ ★

S he was losing her voice. Grace couldn't remember when she'd had such a wonderful welcome home. She'd settled on one of the picnic tables at the east corner of the Air Wing tent and was fighting the desire to visibly wilt. Families of the squadron personnel and kids from the flying club had been coming by to say hi. She was just about smiled and hugged out.

"Grace," Bruce handed her another cold drink.

"Thanks." He settled across from her at the table. She braced her chin against her hand and decided she would be quite content simply to look at him for a while. Bruce was better looking than she remembered, even with the black eye. The man had to scrunch up to fit a picnic table; he was a tall man with broad shoulders and powerful forearms, strong hands. The sun had lightened his short dark hair. She had forgotten the way his eyes added to his smile.

"Did you sleep last night?"

She gave a rueful smile. "Not much."

"You want to get out of here?"

She looked over to where Jill was in the middle of arranging the charter bus for her clients who needed a ride home. Grace had already arranged to meet Jill for breakfast tomorrow; the two of them were going to have a great time catching up on news. "I'd love to get out of here. Did you see where Wolf put my gear?"

"He's already taken it down to my car." Bruce offered her a hand up, and then simply chose not to release hers. She laughed lightly as she tugged and he tugged back. He squeezed her hand.

"Now that you're back, I'm not letting you go."

"Then don't forget my flowers."

He picked up the large glass she'd converted into a temporary vase and handed it to her. "How long can you stay in town?" she asked as he led the way to the parking lot.

"My flight back leaves tomorrow at 0500."

"Too bad."

"Oh, I think I can pack a few days' worth of stuff into the one we have. Assuming you can stay awake."

"That may be a bit of a challenge."

The parking lot had begun to clear out. Bruce released her hand to unlock the car door for her. "My welcome home gift," he offered, as she picked up the package in the passenger seat.

"On top of the flowers?" She settled her makeshift vase between her feet. "But I didn't get you anything."

He chuckled. "Go ahead and open it."

She didn't want to rush it. By the time she finally lifted the box lid, Bruce was pulling out of the base. He'd remembered her words from Incirlik. It was her list of *I Miss* items framed. She loved it. "This is wonderful."

"Just in case you're at a loss of what to do in the next few days."

"It's a perfect gift."

Outside the car window familiar landmarks were passing by. She found it interesting that she didn't have to give him directions to her home. He parked in the lot behind her building and retrieved her bags. The bakery was busy. Grace stuck her head in long enough to share a greeting with the owner and a promise to stop back by later, then headed upstairs to her apartment. She used keys she hadn't used for months and pushed open the door.

The apartment smelled of lemon oil and cinnamon. "Just

drop those in the hall," she murmured, setting off to wander through the rooms, getting reacquainted with her space. There were current magazines on the end table, mail neatly arranged on the desk, and a stack of movies from the local video store on the table. Bruce watched her, leaning against the archway to the living room. There were even homemade cookies in the cookie jar. Her answering machine was filled with friends saying welcome home. And flowers.

She had missed the fresh flowers. She counted six vases as she wandered through the apartment. Jill had outdone herself. Bruce was watching her, not saying anything, just letting her absorb it at her own pace. She smiled at him as she ended her tour. "It's good to be home. I'm going to get changed."

"Take your time. I know how nice it is to have options in clothes again."

She stepped into the bedroom and was confronted with a full closet of clothes. "I didn't think guys reacted that way to clothes."

"It's the principle of the thing, having choices again."

She heard the TV turn on as she pulled out the first blouse. This was not going to be an easy decision. "Should I find something casual or something elegant?"

"Surprise me. I'll adapt my plans to fit."

She finally settled on jeans and a knit top, choosing old favorites. She paused to enjoy the roses by her bedside. "Do I owe you thanks for all these flowers?"

"Wolf sent a few of them too."

Her cousin may have sent the daisies, but the roses—Bruce had gone out of his way to make a statement. She looked at them a few times as she dressed, brushing her hair. She took her time with makeup. "Where's Emily?"

"I left her with my partner Rich for the weekend."

"Is she doing okay?"

"She loves the beach."

Grace thought about socks and shoes, then wandered out to the living room barefoot instead. Bruce was rewinding a video-tape. Her apartment looked small with him here.

"You look gorgeous."

"Bruce."

"You do."

"And you're embarrassing me," she smiled at him even as she said it, pleased that he wasn't commenting on the freckles and the touches of gray hair. She headed to the kitchen; she was craving fresh fruit.

"There's a new restaurant a block over we can check out for a late lunch."

"Sounds wonderful." She wasn't in a hurry to leave. She settled on the chair by the couch holding a pear and the first group of welcome home cards from her kids at the flying club.

"I kept all of your letters."

"Did you?" She opened the first one and didn't dare glance over at Bruce. He sounded incredibly self-satisfied.

"Did you keep mine?"

"What if I said no?"

"That blush tells me you did."

She looked over at him, amused, charmed, and decided it was worth taking the risk. "Just what are you hoping for from this friendship?"

"As much as we can make of it."

She tilted her head, thinking about that. He liked to arrange things too much to leave it that open, but he was playing it safe. "Good answer."

"Find shoes. Let's go take a walk, go shopping, and get some lunch."

"But that's work," she felt obliged to protest.

"Sunshine that is just pleasantly warm, people, exercise…"

She let him pull her to her feet and went to find shoes.

He took her hand as they strolled the streets of her neighborhood, talking about what had been going on with Jill, things she had missed in the news in the last months. The neighborhood had changed.

"You're not listening."

"What?"

He grinned. "Exactly."

"Sorry. I leave for a few months and new businesses appear."

"Lunch, and then we'll wander through a few of them."

He was as good as his word. Bruce bought her lunch, and then they wandered through a new gift shop where he handed her cards, one after the other, from humorous to serious. "When's your birthday?"

She tilted her head and considered that twinkle in his eye. "I'm not telling."

"Gray hair. Must be the big 3-0."

She was past thirty and had a feeling he well knew it. She politely stepped on his toe as she reached for a birthday card that had a black balloon on it. "I know when yours is."

"Only because Jill insisted on having me serenaded last time."

She smiled.

His eyes narrowed. "That was your doing?"

"I'm not telling."

He draped an arm around her shoulders and tugged a lock of hair. "Wise woman; I'd have to retaliate."

She giggled at the threat. "This one's for you." She handed him the card.

"You wound me. Here." He handed her the one he had been looking at.

She glanced down, expecting a birthday card. It wasn't. It was a sweetheart card. And it left her speechless. He hugged her. "Want me to buy you one of those stuffed penguins?"

The question asked with a touch of hopeful expectation broke the serious moment. She looked at the display he indicated and laughed. "Don't you dare. I can't believe Wolf started this crashing penguin joke."

"I think they're cute."

"Emily is cute; stuffed penguins are just stuffed penguins."

"Why do I get the feeling you were a serious child?"

"Wolf needed someone to show some common sense."

"True." He tugged her into a bookstore next. "Whatever you like. I'm buying."

"A dangerous offer. Carrying too?"

"Sure."

She pointed to the left. "Mysteries first."

He left her occasionally to take tangents through side aisles. She got caught up reading the first chapter of one of the books and lost track of time. He draped an arm around her shoulders and laughed softly. "Buy it."

She glanced up, smiled at him, and closed the book. "It's not that good."

"Sure, it's not." Bruce chuckled. She added it to the stack of books he carried. "I've got one for you, Grace. Second book down."

She tugged it from the stack. The book was a collection of letters from the Civil War, soldiers writing back to their families. She flipped through it, found them fascinating. "I didn't know you were interested in history."

"The people stuff of history."

She got caught by a yawn. "I'm fading on you." It had been an 0500 morning and she'd been running at full energy for six months. Fatigue was taking over.

"You're allowed." He turned her toward the counter. "Let's go buy these and you can curl up with a good book."

They wandered back to the apartment at a leisurely pace— Grace reading him some of the Civil War letters aloud, Bruce steering her around obstacles she threatened to run into as she read.

Back at her apartment, she headed toward the couch and kicked off her shoes. It had been a long time since she had enjoyed an afternoon more.

"Take a nap. I'm going to read a book and watch you sleep."

She tilted her head as he settled in the chair across from her, amused. "Are you?"

"Absolutely."

She needed a catnap, and the last thing she wanted to do was toss him out. She snuggled back into the cushions. "I've missed this couch." She made herself comfortable. She was at peace.

"Grace?"

"Hmm?"

"Welcome home."

She smiled as she drifted toward a nap. "I think I've decided to like you."

Bruce ~

You made my first day home so special. I don't have words to say just how much it meant to me.

Thanks for the flowers.

The afternoon letting me nap.

The double feature in movies that had me laughing so hard I could barely breathe.

The hug good-bye.

It's strange to be sending a letter via e-mail, knowing you will get it as soon as I hit send. Please be careful as you train. I teased you about the black eye, but I know it could just as easily have been a broken leg. I laid awake for several hours last night, getting accustomed to the shadows and the sounds and the stillness—home is very different from the carrier—I laid awake and I thought of you. Some friendships are gifts, and yours is in that category. I don't know where this is going, but I find it fascinating to find out.

Grace

Grace –

It's going somewhere interesting, and we'll wisely take it one day at a time. (You're adorable; did I mention that when I saw you?)

Yours, Bruce

TWENTY-ONE

★ ★ ★

SEPTEMBER 2
NORFOLK, VIRGINIA

She was grateful to have her pillow back. Privacy. Quiet. A comfortable bed. Grace wrapped her arms around a massive feather pillow as she stifled a yawn and let herself drift awake. It was absolutely wonderful to be home. A week, and it was still settling in.

She hadn't been able to sleep in and enjoy it nearly enough for her liking. Shore life was incredibly busy. There were two new pilots—nuggets—to get integrated into the squadron. Equipment upgrades. Weapons quals coming up in Nevada. Sea trials with the full fleet prior to the next deployment. Her day planner was already filling up with commitments and dates.

Her apartment was hot and it smelled like yeast. The bakery downstairs started its day at 3 A.M. She had to be the luckiest officer in Norfolk. She had a sprawling affordable apartment over the bakery, a branch library across the street, and a short walk away, Naval Air Station, Oceana, where there was a plane with her name on it. Life was great.

The phone was ringing. Grace finally let herself acknowledge that the real world was trying to intrude. The temptation to let the answering machine take the message was strong. She reached over to answer it. "Lieutenant Yates."

"Good morning, Gracie."

"Bruce." She tucked the phone between the pillow and her

169

cheek, letting the delight she felt at hearing his voice wash over her. "I don't know if I'll get used to this instant communication."

"It's nice to be thinking of you and be able to pick up the phone and tell you that. What are your plans for today?"

"Sleep in. Wander downstairs and eat breakfast at my favorite bakery, maybe even watch some Saturday cartoons while I pretend to be industrious about cleaning house."

"I woke you up."

She wrapped the phone cord around her finger. "I think I won't answer that. What about you?"

"I'm already at the office." Amused. He was definitely amused.

"Something come up?"

"Just the normal rotating weekend shift. The weather is good in the gulf, Cape Canaveral is quiet for a few days, we're getting ready for unit reviews next week, and I'm doing paperwork."

"Sounds like a quiet, boring weekend." She was glad; she knew it could change on a dime with a phone call, but for now he wasn't doing something that might kill him.

"The best kind. I've already run two miles on the beach and done an hour of PT on the quad with the guys."

She shouldn't take the bait but she couldn't resist. He'd been teasing her about the workout routine she had with its cornerstone of forty-five minutes on a treadmill at the base gym. "What's your time?"

"Come run with me sometime and find out."

It wasn't the first time he'd asked, but she gave him the same answer. "We'll see." She wasn't ready yet to cross to his turf. It would inevitably pick up the pace of their relationship, and she wanted a few more days to get accustomed to the idea.

She heard a phone ring. "I've got to go, Grace. Enjoy today. Think of me."

"I probably will," she conceded with a laugh as she said good-bye.

SEPTEMBER 8

Bruce ~

I like getting up and finding an e-mail waiting for me. I think electronic greeting cards are cheating a bit, but I have to admit the crashing penguins are hilarious. I'm just sorry Wolf started this. He did give me one of those stuffed penguins as a welcome home gift, a fact I'm sure you know. Let's see, what else to say...after over a week of phone calls and e-mails I'm finding myself struggling to find a topic.

Church was great. The chapel on the *GW* was just below the flight deck, and we'd have to pause the songs when the catapult began launching planes. It's nice being at church for a service that goes as long as it goes, and people still linger around afterward. There's a new Bible study meeting on Friday night, and I'm going to host this week. Where people will park will be interesting, but at least I don't have to worry about what to serve for refreshments. I'll just stop downstairs on the way home from work.

The first new nugget flights start Monday, getting them accustomed to the squadron formation flying and our briefing focus. We've gained two pilots straight out of Pensacola. Was I ever this young and green? I'm breaking in pilots who have landed on a carrier less than a dozen times. Bushman seems seasoned by comparison.

Thunder has gotten the formal promotion; he'll step up to squadron CO in October. I'm so pleased for him. He's a great boss. That's all my news. I'm heading in to work now. I'll be home late; we're doing a sunset hop tonight.

Thinking of you, Grace

SEPTEMBER 9

Grace ~

How was the sunset hop? I can't imagine anything more

beautiful than being at angels 15 to watch a sunset over the water. I'll be away the start of next week. We've got a live fire exercise at Fort Bragg. I figure we'll be gone Monday through Wednesday; it's a flight up and back.

I'm sorry I missed you. Rather than play phone tag I thought I would drop you a note. I like pen and paper. Emily gave me a scare today; she got into some chicken bones. I keep waiting for her to appear in the doorway, choking, as one of the bones works through her system. I'm enjoying a late night on my new back patio. (The concrete set up nice, despite the fact I had Rich "helping" me.) I've been trying to wade through the book you sent me, but it's a challenge. How can you read murder mysteries? It's scary; there is no other way around it.

And honey, your movie tastes...we're going to have to find a compromise there. *Castaway* might be a wonderful movie, but the last thing I want to do is sit through a realistic look at a plane crash. Spielberg's *Saving Private Ryan* was excellent, but it left me walking away uneasy. I've worked both plane crashes and wars; I see enough reality in life. When we finally do get a night arranged to see each other, how about something innocuous like the *102 Dalmatians?* I've heard it's pretty good from the PJs who took their kids.

How did choir practice go? How was the Friday night Bible study? Did you have a good turnout? I think of you on Sundays. Our choir has dwindled to seven and you know they are in trouble when they're asking if I want to join. Take care. I miss you.

Bruce

TWENTY-TWO

★ ★ ★

Grace found her cousin's car in her spot when she got home Thursday night, so she parked temporarily in her neighbor's spot. Wolf was in the bakery, chatting with the owner and tossing a hot donut hole between his hands to cool. "Have you tried these, Grace? They're wonderful."

"They are personal favorites." She accepted the one he handed her, and he bought a box of them. "I thought you were meeting Jill tonight," she commented as she led the way upstairs.

"I'm meeting her in an hour." Wolf helped himself to a soda once they got inside.

Grace checked her answering machine and couldn't resist; she also checked her e-mail.

"Anything from the man?"

She smiled at Wolf's question but was disappointed when she scanned the list of incoming e-mails. "No."

"We're heading to Florida tomorrow for a long weekend. You promised me you would move on after the last deployment. So move on. Bruce is a great guy. Come with us."

She looked over her shoulder at him. "I can't invite myself to Florida."

"I just invited you. I'm going to be in Pensacola for four weeks of classes; I need to haul my stuff down. Jill wants to see Bruce's house and she needs a vacation. You can room with her at the hotel. All you have to do is throw jeans and a swimsuit in a suitcase and come along."

She leaned back against the desk. She was tempted by the idea. Wolf was big on doing things on the spur of the moment, and getting Jill away for a long weekend to see Bruce was a good idea. "I can't get that kind of time off this quickly."

"You already said maintenance was pulling your plane to do an engine overhaul. I checked with your CO. You can get a few days."

She read what he wasn't saying; for all his spur of the moment actions, Wolf rarely left loose ends around to foil his plans. "What are you thinking?"

"Afternoon flight tomorrow, get in about dinnertime, come back at the crack of dawn Tuesday."

"I'll make a few calls, if you tell Bruce I might be coming."

"Chicken. Pack light if you want me carrying your luggage."

"Did you tell Jill that?" She laughed at the face he made. "Go. I'll call you in the morning if I'm able to come." Seeing Bruce as part of a foursome sounded like a smart plan.

SEPTEMBER 15

PENSACOLA, FLORIDA

He had guests coming for the weekend; Jill and Wolf were coming down to see the house.

Bruce stirred the spaghetti sauce as he held the phone and listened to it ring. *Grace, where are you?* She wasn't answering her phone.

Wolf had called from the hotel and Bruce knew it was right at a fifteen-minute drive. Knowing his sister and her speed when on vacation, he allowed twenty-five. He put the water on to boil. He checked the dining room again to make sure he had remembered to set out the grated cheese. Salad and pasta was a simple meal; he'd dress it up with toasted garlic bread and cheesecake for dessert. Wolf hadn't said, but Bruce had a feeling they were coming down to discuss wedding details.

When he was able to talk to Grace, he would ask for ideas about the wedding gift.

He heard the sound of a car in the drive and turned down the sauce. "Company is here, Emily." If he started her thinking about moving now, she might make it to the door by the time they came back inside. He paused on the steps when he saw the car. Wolf and Jill were here but they had brought a third. Bruce shoved the towel he held into his back pocket, wishing he had taken a minute to change. He walked down to meet them.

"You weren't expecting me."

"No, I wasn't. Doesn't mean I wasn't wishing. Welcome, Grace."

She shot a look at Wolf, who just leaned against the side of the car and smiled back at her. Bruce got the drift pretty quickly. He'd owe the man one later. For now, he just tried to get his friend out of the hot water he was in. "I've been trying to reach you, so it's a good thing you're here." He reached out and caught her hand. "There's something you have got to see. Jill, dinner's on the stove. Would you watch it for me?"

"What?" Grace asked, as she got pulled along.

Bruce took her through the house and into the library he had just begun to work on. The new windows were in, the walls were painted, and he had half the built-in shelving complete. The next four boards were varnished and drying. "It's around here somewhere." He scanned boxes of items he'd packed to protect and made a guess on where to find it. "Hold this." He handed her the small can of putty and rag sitting on a box, then tugged it open.

He'd guessed correctly and pulled out the album. "Sit, the carpet is new."

She laughed but did as he asked, sitting down beside him.

Bruce opened the album to a midpoint and put it in her lap. "I found this and I immediately thought of you."

"Bruce." She traced her hands over the patch of STS-71. It was one of the first shuttle flights he'd stood watch for, and one Ben had flown on. She slowly turned the pages. They had been having a preflight party, and the whole crew had come. There were several photos of Ben. "I was deployed off the Balkans when he flew this mission." She was blinking away tears. Bruce rubbed her back.

"I thought you would like to see them."

She reached over and hugged him. "Thank you."

He kissed her forehead. "You've got twenty minutes while I put the finishing touches on dinner."

She caught his hand as he got up. "The album. Why?"

"Grace, you didn't have a single picture of him out at the apartment. It's time to dig out the pictures." He squeezed her hand. "I hope you like spaghetti."

"Love it."

"Good." His dog showed up in the doorway and wandered toward Grace, her tail wagging slowly. "Em, best behavior. We want her to stay a while."

Grace laughed and reached over to ruffle the animal's fur. "She's still adorable."

"Growing older by the day. Twenty minutes."

Grace nodded and he left her in the library with the photo album and his dog.

"So how are you doing on the house?" Grace asked.

"Renovations are ahead of schedule," Bruce replied easily,

picking up the salad bowls. Grace had insisted on helping him clear the table, and his over-the-head look at Wolf had his friend taking Jill for a walk on the beach after dinner so he could have a few minutes alone with Grace. "I'm finishing the library and going to start on the guest room and bath next."

"Ambitious."

He chuckled. "Plenty of time. If I do it wrong, I'll just rip it out and do it again."

"Patience, I admire that."

"When I want to be. And no one is around to hear my comments at the flub-ups."

"Would you mind if I take a couple pictures from the scrapbook to have copies made? I'll return them."

"Take as many as you like." Bruce poured her a cup of coffee and gestured to the back patio. "Leave the plates in the sink; we'll get them later."

"Patience extends to clutter."

He smiled. "In my own home." He held the door for her. "The white chair doesn't try to pinch your back but it likes to wobble side to side."

She settled into it with care and a soft laugh. "Warning noted."

"A coming project." Emily came to join them and Bruce stroked her head. "I'm glad you came, Grace."

She slouched to move her back farther from the offending split in the metal, rested her neck against the back to watch the stars, and crossed her ankles. "You know why nights like this are gifts?"

He looked over at her, intrigued with the relaxed posture as much as by the question. "Why?"

"I don't feel guilty for stopping to enjoy it."

"A touch of guilt over time off? Now that's no way to live."

"It goes in streaks."

"I was going to suggest we go skydiving this weekend, but that might break your safety streak."

"I'm made to fly the plane, not jump out of it. I saw the pictures in your hall. You've got a few jumps under your belt."

"A few. Rich and I like to go up on our time off."

"What plans did I just interrupt? Were you planning to jump with him this weekend?"

"Grace, standing up Rich is a pleasure. Good buddies are the kind that conveniently disappear when three is a crowd."

"Jill and Wolf just disappeared."

"In this case I think Wolf wanted to kiss Jill without doing it in front of big brother so that I don't have to show my ingrained protective streak."

She chuckled. "Probably true. Your sister is good for my cousin."

"It's mutual." Bruce watched Grace as he finished his coffee. "Incirlik shook Wolf up."

"I know."

He waited, wondering whether she'd add anything else. She didn't.

How many Incirliks were part of her makeup? How many close calls and surviving because she did her job with perfection were part of her history? He'd changed because of Ecuador and other similar nights. Grace had her own set of such places and times.

Bruce heard Wolf and Jill before he saw them, his sister laughing. "They look good together."

"Yes, they do. I'm glad I introduced them." She smiled. "Someone has to watch out for Wolf."

"You don't have to stay by my side all weekend."

Bruce—warm, content, and half thinking about dozing—

opened one eye long enough to glance at Grace. "I'm perfectly content to shadow you for the weekend. I see no reason to let another PJ have your time. They'll just tell you stories about me that aren't entirely true."

She laughed as she settled back in the patio chair with her plate. The gathering that had ebbed and flowed in numbers over the weekend had come to the hotel poolside to enjoy lunch and have some fun. Jill had invited friends, Wolf had put the word out to other SEALs coming down for the training class, and the PJs had gotten the word through Rich—it was a good group, a diverse mix of Navy and Air Force. There was a miniature golf game in progress on the hotel's six-hole course; the water volleyball game was in a temporary lull. Grace swam earlier in the day, then changed into shorts and a white top. Bruce was comfortable keeping station in a chair and letting the others flow around him, in no hurry to join in. He was going to talk Grace into coming down to the beach later.

"I'm amazed at your ability to simply relax in the midst of this. You're not exactly lazy, you just...conserve energy," Grace commented.

"Should I thank you? I think that was a compliment."

"It was."

"I choose where I want to put my attention," Bruce replied.

"You're watching me again."

He smiled. "I enjoy watching you."

A shadow blocked out the sun. "Lunch is over; you ready for that swim?"

Bruce looked up at Wolf, amused. "I thought you learned your lesson last time."

"Come on, Striker. I want a rematch."

Bruce looked over at Grace. She just quirked an eyebrow.

He looked back at his friend. "Okay, Wolf; you've got your rematch." He wasn't above showing off a bit. He got up.

"Rich calls it. The man who swims the farthest before coming up for air wins."

"Fine with me," Bruce agreed.

PJs and SEALs suspended the golf game as word spread, and they began assembling at the deep end of the pool.

"Men, they're nothing but boys at heart," Jill remarked, making Grace laugh. "Go, Wolf!"

Bruce glanced over at his sister and smiled. "I'm sorry, sis. He's going to lose."

"You hate the water," she replied confidently.

Respect was closer to the right word, but that was beside the point. Bruce had no intention of losing. He glanced at Grace, who had moved to sit on the end of the nearby recliner, watching them. She was enjoying this. He turned his attention to the pool and the challenge.

He knew Wolf. This was going to be a race measured not in a lap but in how many laps. The shallow end of the pool would be a big problem. He couldn't kick and keep momentum going through those last five feet, and trying to do so would just cost extra energy. Holding his breath was all about controlling how much energy was needed that would take oxygen. Distance was the bottom line for this race, not speed covering that distance. He'd go with his strength—that push off from the walls. Bruce nodded to himself, deciding that strategy would serve him best.

Wolf was stretching, stationing himself at the edge of the deep end, preparing to dive in. Bruce dropped into the water, choosing not to start from a diving position. He heard the puzzled comments and ignored them.

"Ready, gentlemen?" Rich called. "Get set. Go!"

Wolf dove into the pool.

Bruce dropped below the surface and pushed off from the wall.

Wolf had already lost. Bruce knew it. All he had to do was go farther than Wolf, and since he was following, he wasn't the one spending energy trying to set the pace. Doing just a little bit more than someone else was easy. Out in front, Wolf would have to turn to see where he was.

Wolf made the turn in the shallows as Bruce approached. Under the water, Bruce saw Wolf's foot strike the stairs. Learning from it, Bruce used his hands to provide his momentum and made his own push from the wall as hard as he could so he would propel past the stairs before the momentum dropped.

It set the pattern for the race. By the second lap, Wolf had set out to increase his speed. By the third lap, Wolf had gained a full lap on him. By lap five, Bruce saw Wolf's pace slow. Bruce fought the fact his lungs were burning as he approached the wall in the deep end and made certain he put maximum power in the push-off. He was limiting his actual swimming to only what was necessary to keep him straight.

Wolf finally broke the surface for air.

Bruce had been lapped twice; he did his best to put out of his mind the fact he was now the only one swimming. It had been so much easier to follow Wolf. Four more laps. He decided it even as he had to purse his lips in a fight against the overwhelming pressure to breathe. He wanted air, desperately. He'd get air after he accomplished his goal.

He kept swimming.

Under the water, noises were distorted. He could hear several people yelling his name. He finally let himself drift toward the surface after making the turn for lap four. He had won, but that hadn't been the reason he had determined to stay down for that extra lap. Bruce floated on his back and sucked in oxygen.

"You're a black manatee."

He glanced at Wolf and saw the man holding the edge of the pool, breathing hard.

"Energy and desire. I wanted it more than you did," Bruce replied, timing words for breath.

"You earned it."

Wolf pulled himself from the pool. Bruce eventually swam to the side and accepted Wolf's offer of a hand out.

Grace was waiting with a towel and he took it with a murmured thanks. "You held your breath forever."

He swiped his finger across Grace's nose, smiling at her.

"Why?" she whispered.

He looked at her, then glanced at Wolf. "He needs to know I can rescue him, no matter what the jam," he said. "I have to be able to last longer than him under water if I'm going to be able to help him. Help any of them."

"Another PJ to SEAL silent message."

"We depend on each other, Grace. Testing the man beside you during peace time is how you trust him in war."

"Wolf trusts you."

"I know. Which is why I had to beat him. I plan to keep that trust."

"You swam with your watch on."

He looked down and winced. "Not waterproof either."

"I was afraid it wasn't."

He slid it off and held it up. "My birthday…drop a hint to Wolf to replace it."

She laughed softly as she took it and dropped it into her pocket. "I can probably manage that."

He was a fascinating man. Grace watched Bruce as he maneuvered through the crowded room carrying a pilot's special for her. She'd chosen the place for dinner, a memory from her days training in Pensacola. The music was loud. The seafood restaurant packed. It was hard to hear. She was surrounded by a mass of Air Force personnel and felt a little like she had invaded enemy territory. Not that the Bear Cubs seemed to mind. Wolf and Cougar could make friends anywhere, and they had found Rich, which was all it took to form a tall tale table.

Wolf was telling Jill some tale and being helped along in the storytelling with great delight by Cougar and Rich. Grace smiled, watching. It was wonderful to see the Bear Cubs enjoying a night of fun.

Bruce was going to turn her life upside down. Grace could feel it. And she couldn't say she minded. He fit in here, just like he fit around the group this afternoon at the pool, as he had fit in during Jill's deployment party.

"Are you sure this is your idea of a fun evening out?"

Grace laughed at the hopeful tone under that question as she took the glass Bruce offered her. "It's not so bad. They are all just a bit younger than I remember."

"Seasoned crews normally hang out at the restaurant down on the pier."

"I've been there. Quieter, sedated, not as much fun."

He settled beside her at the small table and tugged over the basket. "Better munchies, sports TV you can hear, thicker menus..."

"Your age is showing."

He smiled. "A little."

She smiled back at him and clicked her glass with his after sampling it. "Not bad. Not exactly on recipe but pretty good."

"Give me enough time to practice." He nodded to the other table. "Think I should go rescue Jill? She's like a little piece of china among that crowd of guys."

"Remove her from the center of attention? You wound me. Wolf is keeping good care of her."

"It's the principle of the thing."

"Sure it is." She rather liked seeing this side of the man; Jill would always be his little sister. "I like you, Bruce."

He winked at her. "It's mutual, Miss Grace."

She blushed at the intensity of being watched again. "We could invite Bear and Kelly over to join us." They were at a table across the way.

Bruce nodded. "We could. And Bear would give me his silent look that suggested I shouldn't. He's trying to talk her out of going windsurfing tomorrow."

"Why? Kelly's good at it."

"He's not."

"Oh."

Bruce smiled. "Exactly. Kelly's good for him. He's just enough of a legend in the SEALs that marriage was perfect. It added a touch of marshmallow."

She caught a swallow going down the wrong direction and laughed. "Marshmallow?"

"Kelly's definition."

"What if I take pity on you and we go look at the sailboats?"

"They're all moored up."

"Walk, Bruce. Simple stuff. Nothing complex."

"So I'm a little slow on the hints."

She got up and picked up the glass. "I'll help you learn. Go tell Wolf where we're going or he'll have to play curious cousin and come find me."

"Why do I get the feeling you're a bit in awe of him?"

"Wolfy? He's just...persistent."

"If we're going to check out sailboats, what if I find someone around here who has one we could take out for a few hours?"

"First weekend here and you'll spoil future ones. Just a walk. Can we pick up Emily later?"

"I knew the real attraction for the weekend was my dog."

They left the restaurant after stopping to say good-byes to new friends and old.

Bruce offered his hand and Grace accepted.

"My ears are still ringing."

Grace laughed and squeezed his hand.

"Do you sail?"

"Some. I'm not very good at it."

"No need to be in order to enjoy it. We could go fishing some weekend, scuba diving."

"I'd enjoy those enormously." She didn't push a conversation, content to simply walk with him, and he didn't rush to fill the silence either. It had been a long time since she let herself enjoy a night like tonight. Work seemed so far away—Norfolk, flying, the race to keep up with schedules and plans. "Could I ask you something?"

"Sure."

"Why did you buy a very old dog?"

He smiled. "There's a story in that."

"Is there?"

"I wanted a dog. I ended up at the pound. Emily was one of those dogs who didn't show much emotion at seeing someone but had that patient gaze and an assumption that I'd come to her."

"Did she?"

"You think I'm making it up?"

"No. Just find it fascinating that you chose an old lady dog instead of an in-his-prime collie or shepherd."

"I wanted a dog that would like sitting on the back patio. Those are rare. Why haven't you ever had a pet?"

"How do you know I haven't?"

"Fish do not count as pets. And I know because I was curious enough to find out."

She found it fascinating that he would admit to something that simple. "Pets take…space and time and remembering to feed them and vet visits and worrying about things like heartworm and fleas."

"Yes. And?"

"Admit it, you were just ready to have a pet."

He hugged her. "I'll work on you. Cat or dog?"

She couldn't figure out an answer to that. She'd never thought about it.

"Oh, we have a problem here. Fuzzy with attitude? Friendly and lazy? Yappy and excited to see you?" he asked, hopeful.

She laughed at his classifications. "Not a terrier. I know that much."

"See? You just moved a step toward a pet."

"Bruce, you're going to change my life."

He rubbed his thumb along her shoulder blade. "Probably."

"Enjoy doing it too."

"Absolutely."

She hugged him back.

"I'm glad you came." The beach was deserted at the early morning hour and Bruce was taking advantage of it, using walking Emily to give him an excuse to have one last moment with Grace before she left with Jill and Wolf.

"So am I."

Bruce tucked a strand of hair behind her ear. "Maybe I could come see you some weekend?"

"I'd like that."

"Maybe kiss you good-bye?" He'd been thinking about it all weekend.

She just smiled at him. At least it wasn't a no. He leaned

down, tipped her chin with his hand, and gently kissed her. "I'm really glad you came."

Her hands slid up to his shoulder. "Could you maybe come visit soon?"

He rested his forehead against hers. "I seem to remember I have a key to my sister's place. I could even bring Emily up with me. Buy you a lunch, another mushy card..."

"I promise to make it a less scary movie."

"That has possibilities. Should we play it safe and make it a double date? I could ask them to join us, and Wolf and I can bat around who's picking up the tab."

"Would you buy me a pilot's special?"

"Better yet, I'll fix you one. I acquired the official recipe."

"Did you?"

"Pricey too. It cost me a nice fishing lure."

"Then by all means, visit and I'll make sure I have all the ingredients."

"Grace! You coming?" A voice from the parking lot hollered.

"I'm getting paged."

"Let him come and find you, then get embarrassed for interrupting."

She chuckled and stepped back. "You're dangerous for my peace of mind."

"Mutual, ma'am. Think about me this week."

"I probably will, if only to wonder how training is going."

"Please, I'm too old to be reminded of the coming 0400 hop."

"Only PJs would think of getting up before dawn to go drop into the sea."

"True. Bravery and smarts don't always go together."

"I've got to go."

"Wolf does seem to be leaning on the car horn."

She walked backward up the path to the stairs going up to the parking lot. "Are you going to say good-bye?"

"Ladies first."

"I don't want to."

"Then we won't," Bruce replied comfortably. He tugged a piece of candy from his pocket. "Catch."

She caught the tumbling piece of candy. "Where did you find it?"

"Early Valentine's Day?" It was a heart-shaped piece of chocolate.

"You mean it was left over from earlier this year."

"Last year more likely," he corrected. "Stored in my freezer just for you."

"Romantic."

"Practical. I need room for the frozen fish."

She laughed and bit off a piece, starting up the stairs from the beach. "Call me."

"Count on it."

"Wolf, I'm coming! I'm not deaf." She glanced back one more time. "Not before your 0400 hop."

"Now would I do that?"

She just smiled and waved and disappeared from view.

Wolf carried her bag upstairs for her. Grace unlocked her apartment and accepted it. "Do I get a hug good-bye?" Wolf asked.

She leaned against him to give him a one-arm hug. "You're learning. You normally try to duck them."

"I'm a changed man since Incirlik," he replied, squeezing her. "Thanks for coming this weekend."

"I enjoyed it."

"You and Bruce seemed to be having a decent time."

She just smiled. Wolf wanted more than that, but she knew

when silence was the better course of action. "You've got to get Jill home and then get back to Pensacola for the start of the class, and I've got to get to work."

"You are an incredible clam at times."

"Working on it."

"I want my chatterbox back who tells me more than I want to know."

"Good-bye, Wolf."

"For now, Gidget. For now." He headed downstairs, whistling, to take Jill home.

Grace tugged the door shut, looked around her apartment, and with a small laugh reached for her bag. And to think on Friday she was convinced she would be coming back to this place wanting to bury her head in the sand after a less than successful visit.

"Did it exceed expectations? Oh yeah," she said as she carried her bag to the bedroom. She opened her closet and retrieved her uniform. She was due on base at 1300 and it would be good to be early.

The doorbell rang as she polished her shoes.

What had she forgotten? Hopefully not her purse, she'd never hear the end of it.

"Lieutenant Yates?"

"Yes." The deliveryman was holding a huge bouquet. She accepted the vase, delighted. "Hold on a sec," she asked and made the tip worth his time.

The flowers were from Bruce, she was certain of that. But to have been able to time the delivery so close…Wolf must have called him after dropping her off.

The card was tucked inside. "Grace, check your e-mail."

She cleared the desktop and made a place for the vase, then pulled up her e-mail.

Grace ~

I started this note to you last night and wanted to time it for your homecoming. Thank you for filling my weekend with joy. Besides Emily's embarrassing me by deciding sawdust was good to eat, there wasn't much I can think of I would have changed. I miss you already.

Bruce

Bruce ~

The flowers are beautiful, and I will think of you often. I wish I had more elegant words to offer to say thanks.

Grace

Grace ~

You just did, beautifully.

Bruce

TWENTY-THREE

★ ★ ★

SEPTEMBER 28

PENSACOLA, FLORIDA

Bruce unlocked the back door and picked up his duffel bag of clothes he would have to wash in the morning. Lackland Air Force Base in Texas had been hot. The television was on in the den. "I'm back, Rich." He walked through to the kitchen in desperate need of a drink as he heard his partner turn off the television and come to meet him. "Emily okay? The roofer and the window guys get out?"

"Emily ate you out of house and home and slept, the roofing estimate is on the table, and the window guy laughed first but gave you a quote. I don't think he was that eager to get selected."

"Can't blame him. Those two attic windows are suicide projects. You want the job?" Bruce asked.

"Not if you're going to get annoyed if they leak."

"Smart man. I know my own limits. Someone will get paid to replace those two."

"How was the meeting?" Rich asked.

"Do you want to be tasked to Argentina?"

"Not particularly."

Bruce studied options in the refrigerator. "Then it was a waste of time. Thanks for staying over and keeping stuff moving for me."

"Free food, cable that works, I've had harder assignments in my life."

Bruce pulled out the orange juice and in the light of the

191

refrigerator caught sight of what was on the table. The kitchen table was stacked, not with newspapers and the occasional bill but two crates of letters. He turned on the overhead light.

"What's this?" He picked up one and found it addressed to him, care of his squadron. The pit of his stomach got a tight feeling.

Rich looked at the crates. "Would you believe the Air Force post office lost a sack of mail?"

"What am I supposed to do with it?"

"Answer it?" Rich laughed at his expression. "Didn't they ever tell you that legends never die?"

"Maybe a bonfire."

"Admit it, mail is nice. Grace called."

Bruce set down the orange juice carton. "When?"

"Last night, about nine. I've got her number written down around here somewhere."

"Did she leave a message?"

"Nope. We chatted for about twenty minutes. I asked, and she just said to mention she'd called. Here it is. She's in Phoenix tonight." Rich handed him the scrap of paper and smiled. "I'll make myself scarce so you can call her back."

"Appreciate it," Bruce replied, already dialing.

Rich laughed and retrieved a soda. "You've got it bad. Can't blame you. Nice lady."

"Scram."

"Scramming."

"Grace. It's Bruce. Did I catch you at a bad time? What are you doing in Phoenix?" He reached for the nearest chair.

PHOENIX, ARIZONA

Grace pulled another soda out of the ice bucket, now more full of water than ice. "The hotel air-conditioning is struggling to keep up. I'd open a window but it's like ninety-nine degrees and muggy out and it's Phoenix of all places. It's supposed to be dry heat." She cracked the tab on the soda and got sprayed. "Hold on, Bruce."

She dropped the phone and scrambled to get a towel. Wonderful. Her white shirt was now going to be forever stained with purple. "So much for the new carbonated grape soda; I just took a bath in it. What a sticky mess." She started gathering papers together spread out around on the floor. The table had been too small.

"Your trip is sounding more and more like mine."

She smiled and wished he wasn't half the country away. "But I get a super-duper plane to make up for the aggravation."

"Have you seen it yet?"

"I got an intro hop two hours ago. Sweet, Bruce. Sweet. I bet it could slam past a Tomcat and make that bird look like it was a prop flight. I'm dying to get more than a ferry job out of it."

"Think the squadron will get the upgrades?"

"Eighteen months, just about the time I get to do sea tour number three. Wouldn't that be excellent timing? New Hornet upgrades and a new job as chief of a shop. I'd even take maintenance chief to get to care for these darlings."

"You're like a guy at a car show."

"Worse. The things I get heart palpitations over will never fit my budget." Grace tugged over the spec manual. "I could read the altitude maneuverability indexes. Incredible stats."

"Better yet, what's the price tag?"

"Sixty-two million a plane. Cheap compared to what you all in the Air Force are wanting to spend."

Bruce laughed. "A bargain. What's your flight schedule?"

She leaned back against the bed and pushed papers threatening to topple back into a stack with her toe. "I ferry it sedately across country to Texas and then to Norfolk. It's going out for the first carrier landing tests and then to load testing. Wish I got that job too."

"How'd you swing the ferry job?"

"Peter got the flu."

"Poor Peter. Did you give it to him?"

"Would have if I'd thought of it," she admitted.

"You are having a good week."

"Yeah. Tell me about yours."

"Let's not. Yours is more interesting."

Grace laughed. "One of *those* meetings."

"They were hoping to snag volunteers for an eight-month TDY in Argentina so they don't have to decide which units to shuffle around. We're all over limits on twelve-month travel, and the Air Force hates the red tape of getting waivers issued," Bruce replied.

"They'll get the waivers and choose a unit."

"I know. I felt just a tad guilty about not volunteering until I decided I'd volunteered for Ecuador, and before that Honduras. Someone else can volunteer this month, hopefully someone un-attached."

"If you did say yes, I'd understand."

"I know, Grace. I just didn't want to go. On occasion that's a good thing."

"Yes, it is. It was nice to talk to your partner Rich."

"I heard you two had a chat."

"Did you two really get lost at sea last week?"

"Only in the sense that we knew where we were, but the recovery planes didn't," Bruce said.

"You hit the emergency squawk."

"And had to spend the rest of the day explaining why we turned an exercise into a real-time recovery. Getting a concussion can wash a PJ out of the job forever, and Rich took a pretty good thump when the raft failed to inflate properly. We had the survival gear doing its best to drown us for a few minutes."

"What a wonderful image."

Bruce chuckled. "It's just water, and I can hold my breath a very long time. I was just petrified of the idea I'd have to give Rich mouth-to-mouth. Now that would have been scary."

"He's fine?"

"My partner is indestructible. He wrestled the raft back into submission, yelled at the sea for slapping him around, and got us turned around and on track to pick up the other PJs, who were by that time almost half a mile away because of the current drift. It was an all-around good training exercise for the problems it threw at us."

"And you were doing this while it was still essentially dark," Grace said.

"The sun was just thinking about coming up," Bruce said. "It's not like there were any sharks around to make it interesting or boats to try and run us over."

"That sounds like both have happened in the past."

"On occasion," Bruce agreed. "How many times has Incirlik happened?"

"Point made. Several, most of them more interesting."

"Thought so. So what are you doing still up at this time of night?"

"Bruce, time zones work to my advantage. It's still early here."

"A momentary aberration in math. Had dinner yet?"

"Room service. But the Navy is cheap on the per diem. I had a salad."

"Wilted lettuce?"

She chuckled. "How did you guess?"

"I've lived in enough hotel rooms. Are we still on for this weekend?"

"Saturday morning, 1100, Jill's. Casual dress."

"Where are you taking me?"

"You'll just have to show up and see."

"A mystery."

"The best kind of weekends. Get some sleep, Bruce. You'll need it."

"Thanks for the warning. Dream about me, or your plane, tonight."

"Probably the plane."

"Probably. Night, Grace."

She hung up the phone, feeling lighthearted, happy. It was nice having him a phone call away. Bruce was an easy man to talk to. He'd let her into his world; she was looking forward to this weekend and a chance to pull him into hers.

SEPTEMBER 30

NORFOLK, VIRGINIA

Bruce pushed open Jill's door. "You said casual. I see you meant it." Grace was wearing a very old sweatshirt with cut off sleeves, traces of white paint, and jeans that were white at the pockets and knees from wear.

"I did. You weren't so sure, I see."

"Casual but being broken in. I didn't think you'd appreciate the jeans that Emily tried to bury."

"That bad?"

"Pretty much." He leaned against the door frame. "You can come in, Grace. I think you've been here a few times and Jill is up now that it's 1100. You're prompt by the way."

"Since I woke Jill up with the phone call at 1000 I figured she might finally be moving. Why don't we just head out and come back later today to bug her? Bring Emily."

"Where are we going?"

"A surprise until you're at least in the car and have no choice but to come along."

Bruce laughed and snapped his fingers. "Emily, come on, honey. She's a duchess. One with her own sense of time."

"I'm learning that."

The dog paused at the door, lingered at the top of the stairs to smell the air, considered for several moments the stairs before taking the first one and then bounding down them in a rush.

Grace opened the car door. "She's welcome to join us in front."

"Got a towel? She can take the backseat and sleep. She's not much for putting her head out the window. She'd do it once or twice until she starts to sneeze, and then her ears go back in annoyance at the wind."

"Better yet, I have a couple blankets." She got one from the trunk.

With a laugh, Bruce picked up Emily to assist her into the car. "I don't know about this."

"Trust me; she's an essential part of the day's plans."

Grace tugged a sheet of paper out of her pocket. She handed it to him as she pulled out of the drive. "Welcome to a day in the life of Grace."

"Where do the tomatoes go?"

Grace sank face down on her couch, kicked off her shoes, and groaned. "I don't care. Anywhere. I'm too tired to think."

Bruce appeared in the doorway. "I've worn you out."

"I think I died somewhere between picking out Wolf's birthday present and the dry cleaner. That visit to the gym about toasted me."

"We've still got the library, the bank, a stop at the greenhouse, and a visit to your dad's. I'm intrigued with that last one."

"Scratch that one. Dad went up to Washington, D.C., to annoy our state senator over the defense appropriations bill. He didn't call, which means his flight was delayed, again. He's getting a reputation for the scathing editorials on airline service."

"Maybe another time. I'd like to meet him."

"I'm sure he'd like to meet you too."

"Don't fall asleep. We're due at Jill's new office at 1600 to help her move file cabinets."

"Okay."

"You're falling asleep."

"Cat nap. It was a very late night getting ready for today."

He joined her in the living room, then lifted her feet to sit on the far end of the couch. He rubbed the sole of her foot. "Want to tell me what happened last night? The answering machine message was cryptic, but even I figured out you were somewhere at 0200."

"Wolf needed some help with a friend. That feels good." She'd been emergency baby-sitting until about 0400. Wolf was helpless with kids.

"I thought it was something like that. Everything okay?"

She shrugged.

"Deployments are stressful on families."

"Yeah. He'll call if he needs me."

"Why didn't he call Jill?"

Grace smiled. Jill was lousy with crying kids.

"Oh."

"Twenty minutes of sleep. Then we'll go again. And add a stop to get gas to that list of errands."

He tugged down the throw on the back of the couch. "Sure."

"Now I know I really like you. Beach tonight. I'll make up for today."

"Don't apologize. I've been enjoying a day in the life of Grace."

★ ★ ★

The moonlight on the water was dancing atop the waves. They had the beach pretty much to themselves. Bruce stirred the fire in the small public fire ring. It was the kind of peaceful night perfect for sitting around, talking. The stars were bright, the wind gentle, the moon a perfect bright circle.

"You like to rescue things, don't you?"

Bruce glanced over to where Grace was brushing Emily's coat with a dog brush she had brought down with them. If he had wanted to script a weekend with her, he couldn't have come up with something better than these last hours. The firelight played over Gracie's hair, adding golden highlights, deepening her blue eyes. "What?"

"You rescued Emily."

"I suppose so."

"When did you decide I needed to be rescued?"

Her question caught him off guard. "Grace."

"When?"

"You looked a little lost last Christmas," he allowed slowly. Was she mad? "I decided it made sense to do something about it."

"You thought this relationship out before you sent that first letter during the deployment."

He was relieved at the mild tone. "You credit me with more than I could accomplish, but yes, I thought about that first letter a great deal. It surprises you that it would matter that much to me?"

"Yes."

Bruce set down the stick he was using to prod the fire to life and stood up. He dusted off his jeans. She tipped her head to look up at him, curious. "Come here." He held out his hands.

"What?"

"I've got a question for you, best asked on more level ground."

She let him pull her to her feet. He slid his hands up to cup her face. "You're beautiful, you know that?"

"You said a question."

He tucked a strand of hair behind her ear. "I know, but it's time you heard a few compliments in words, not just on paper. Miss Grace, would you care to be my girl?"

She leaned her head against his chest. "You do have a way with words, Striker."

He wrapped his arms loosely around her. "I would like nothing better than to share many more weekends like this one with you."

She didn't say anything for a long time, then rubbed her cheek against his shirt. "I'd love to know how to make this work."

He tipped up her chin with his thumb. "You let me figure that out." He leaned forward and gently kissed her.

Bruce ~

You asked about dreams for the future. You ask fascinating questions.

I've got a job I love and I've got peace with my God. Life as it is now is good. What I want most is to have a relationship that can be part of my life but doesn't so strain it that I lose what I have. Does that make sense? It sounds so self-centered. I know you must feel a constant sense of hesitation with me, wondering is she committed to this relationship? I really like you, I enjoy your company, I trust you, and talking to you brightens my day. I will step out as far as you want to with this relationship because I trust you. But it's a friendship that may need to stay a friendship for a few years.

I'm not saying I couldn't walk away from my career if something huge came up that meant it was the best decision to make. I'm more saying I really don't want to step into something that makes those kinds of radical changes necessary. Oh, I'm floundering here. I fear the reality of two military jobs will make this unworkable. Simple geography will kill us. Let me end this letter before I get things more muddled.

Yours, Grace

Grace ~

Relax. We'll figure it out by listening to each other and a lot of honesty. You're worried about geography; I'm worried about more simple things like how to overcome it. We've seen marriages with both in the military that thrived. It's not impossible. Think about a day in the distant future that looks something like this:

Letters, e-mails, and phone calls can shrink the distance so we can keep in touch. Two military careers mean two home bases wherever we happen to be stationed—so our commuting back and forth is the next problem. Getting stationed on the same coast should be possible even with the way the Navy and Air Force like to schedule us.

Two home bases, so double everything. You should be able to walk into the place and feel at home regardless of which city it is. Remember those days in training when home was somewhere other than the base in which you were living? There were benefits in those days. I see more opportunities than I do insurmountable obstacles. We just have to get creative.

What I want is simple. Ecuador decided a lot of things for me, because I finally understood that life will probably be shorter than what I'd like regardless of if it's another year or fifty. I want to fill it with the things I treasure. Remodeling a house because I love to build something that as long as it survives will reflect part of my time and effort; a dog because it's the one dream of a childhood unfulfilled; and making people more of a priority because this life was meant to be shared.

I like sharing it with you. How many people can understand my job? You understand it in the best way. To a pilot, PJs are the knights in shining armor coming to the rescue, and I have to admit, it's nice to be with someone who sees my job that way. You understand my priorities, and I understand yours. God, the military, family. They can coexist.

Do I miss you? Horribly. Do I think of you all the time? Absolutely. Do I wish you were here? More than I can put into words. But still I am content. Nothing thrills me more than knowing I'll get to come up and watch you fly some weekend soon.

Thinking about you, Bruce
Matthew 7:7–11

Ask, and it will be given you; seek, and you will find; knock, and it will be opened to you. For every one who asks receives, and he who seeks finds, and to him who knocks it will be opened. Or what man of you, if his son asks him for bread, will give him a stone? Or if he asks for a fish, will give him a serpent? If you then, who are evil, know how to give good gifts to your children, how much more will your Father who is in heaven give good things to those who ask him!

TWENTY-FOUR

★ ★ ★

OCTOBER 21

NORFOLK, VIRGINIA

How's the weather there?"

"Windy, just beginning to rain," Grace told Bruce, pushing back the window drapes to watch it coming down. "The planes have been tucked down for the night, and flight ops to the USS *Harry Truman* have been canceled while the storm front moves through. Are you going out?"

She was falling in love. It was scary and wonderful and overwhelming. She worried about Bruce on nights like this. The storm that was just touching them had been buffeting the Florida panhandle for hours. It was wonderful just to hear his voice.

"If the storm stays this intense, I wouldn't be surprised. I'm going back to the office to wait it out there. No use sitting at home and trying to drive later into the brunt of the frontline winds. The worst is still to come ashore."

"Is Wolf still there?"

"The storm delayed their flight out; he's still at the base housing." Grace heard thunder behind him. "Shh, it's okay, girl. Emily is afraid of the thunder."

"Poor girl."

"She's quivering under the table at the moment, not wanting to leave the room I'm in even as she tries to hide. I haven't left yet, just because of how she's acting."

"What about taking her downstairs to the basement workroom, turning on that old stereo, and giving her a bone and a small place where she's comfortable?"

"I'll try it. I need to figure out something."

"Would you call me occasionally if you get a chance?"

"I will," Bruce promised. "Hang tough, Grace. I'll be careful."

She appreciated the reassurance he offered without her asking. She knew he meant it. But weather could be vicious, and it was easier to confront a man than it was to confront nature's fury.

Grace hung up the phone and rested her head against the kitchen wall. There was always a surprise waiting around the corner. Bruce had been planning to be here this weekend; instead he was standing watch for trouble, ready to go out if called upon.

Ready to go out and possibly not come back.

I should have sent Bruce the card. I'm a coward at times, Lord. It's a perfect card that comes close to finding words for what I feel. Remind me of tonight next time I have a chance to do something nice and wimp out at the last moment. It was an opportunity lost.

Grace returned to her studies brought home from work, using the technical reading to force her focus. Bruce would get that call; there were too many people likely to ignore the danger in this weather. And Wolf, bored, would probably volunteer to help out if he could. She kept the weather channel on, watching the radar tracks, paying special attention to the winds and the height of the storm clouds. She didn't know how they could fly helicopters in this. She always wanted to be above storms, not below them flying low to try to see the ground or the water.

She gave up on the studies and picked up the top newspaper in the stack of overseas papers she routinely read. Turkey was getting tense; there had been another SCUD test fired within Syria, and in retaliation Turkey had moved troops down to the border. They bickered over border raids, over water levels, over diplomatic visits and who would visit whom. It was posturing but being done with an intent to rile.

Lord, they need rain. It wasn't the first time she had prayed it, but it was becoming more urgent every day.

A growing problem across the ocean—it was probably going to be her problem again soon. She was now reasonably certain that their deployment to the Gulf would in fact become another deployment focused on Turkey.

The phone rang at 8 P.M.

"Grace, it's Jill. Is your power still on?"

"Yes."

"Mine went out about ten minutes ago; it looks like the neighborhood is out."

"Grab your stuff and come over." She'd love the company.

"Actually, I was wondering if you would like to come this way. I was just finishing up making cookies and I've still got the stove since it's gas."

"Sure. Expect me in twenty minutes."

Grace dressed for the weather, pulled on her flight boots with her jeans, and retrieved the plastic poncho that was a practical part of her Navy life. Knowing how power outages could linger longer than expected, she took Jill extra candles and a torch style light.

When she stepped outside and tried to tug the door closed, the rain lashed her full in the face and blew back her hood. She raced through the standing water to her car. To think Bruce trained to work in conditions like this. *Lord, have mercy on brave men.*

She started her car, relieved when it turned over immediately. Even inside the car the sound was deafening.

Jill's neighborhood was indeed dark. Grace had to slow to five miles an hour to find the right driveway. She had her key out to Jill's front door and used it even as she rang the doorbell.

"You're wet."

She smiled as she stripped off the poncho. "I'm Navy. We're supposed to like being wet. But it's down my collar and it's annoying." She used the towels Jill brought her. "What have you been baking? It smells wonderful."

"A cherry pie came out just before the power died."

Grace took the flashlight Jill handed her and trailed her friend into the kitchen.

"I was planning on a welcome home dinner for Wolf. If you're hungry, there are great options already fixed."

"Maybe later." Grace settled down at the kitchen table. "Did you two figure out a wedding date?"

Jill beamed. "Next fall. September would be nice. Wolf will have his reenlistment paperwork through by then, and we'll have an idea of where he's going to be stationed. He's trying for another rotation here."

"Have you told Bruce yet?"

"Next time he can get here."

Grace nodded, understanding the desire to talk in person. "He'll be pleased."

"I think so. He and Wolf have become good friends. It helps."

"Ecuador, Turkey—they have had some interesting days together. Have you thought about what you'd like for a wedding present? Bruce is sounding me out on ideas."

"Is he?" Jill smiled at that idea. "I'll think about it. Something for the house would be nice." She gestured to the weather. "Bruce will be fine tonight."

"I know." It did no good to assume otherwise.

The power flickered back on. Lights came on, appliances began to hum, a radio and the TV came back on. Grace waved Jill to the cookies. "I'll get them." Grace followed sounds, reset-ting clocks that were chirping, turning off and back on the TV, which had come back on to fuzz.

She found the weather station and watched the radar tracks that showed a swirling cloud wall stretched along the East Coast. The Florida panhandle was getting the back side of the massive storm, but it looked to have weakened in the last hour. She turned to CNN for the news.

"Jill, did I tell you I got a slot in the NATO headquarters next month? It's only a six-week rotation but it's a plum assignment. My first planning sessions with the British squadrons. It's going to be great."

CNN interrupted with "breaking news" tones. Grace turned in the doorway to look back. A reporter standing under bright lights with pounding rain behind him came on. There was a C-130 cargo plane down in the Atlantic. Behind him a Coast Guard helicopter was lifting off.

"I wish the phone would ring."

Grace dealt out her seventy-third hand of solitaire, having picked up the habit from Rich. "It will," she promised Jill. The question was whether it would be good news or bad. Worry couldn't change anything and Grace had learned to refuse to let it enter in. God was keeping Bruce and Wolf safe. She was trusting that absolutely because there was nothing else that could be done.

The first reports had been wrong. It was almost always the case in a breaking story. A C-130 had picked up a distress call from a plane inbound for Savannah. Coast Guard and now PJ units had gone out, searching for a plane that was lost in the storm clouds, hoping to find it before it ran out of gas and slammed into the sea. Radar contacts were intermittent.

"Bruce hates water," Jill commented.

"Why?"

"Something from when we were kids. He couldn't float when he was learning to swim for the longest time."

"Really? He hides it well. He outswam Wolf."

Jill pulled out an old photo album. "It's called want-to. Did you ever see the old family album?"

"No, but I'd love to."

Jill slid it over.

ATLANTIC OCEAN, OFF THE COAST OF GEORGIA

"The edge of the search box is coming up in twenty seconds. We're turning back into the wind," Dasher called over the internal comm circuit.

"Roger." Bruce lowered his binoculars and rubbed his eyes.

"It would have run out of gas by now. It's down in the sea," Rich said quietly from the other side of the interior, darkened to make easier their ability to see into the night.

"Yes." But they would keep looking. There were four teams searching the area of last contact and a faint radar blip captured by the USS *Harry Truman* keeping station a hundred miles east outside of the storm front. Bruce raised the binoculars again. "It was a woman's voice."

The intermittent radio contacts had been power boosted and relayed to the search aircraft to provide them with as much information as possible. A small private jet with smoke in the cockpit forced a descent in altitude below oxygen pressurization levels to prevent a flash fire. Navigation instrumentation was intermittent. The pilot had reported one soul on board, given fuel, and static had covered her next words. She'd been calm, flying as best she could to determine her original vector into Savannah, but she'd simply run out of time.

They had been too late. Bruce felt an incredible sense of failure over it.

"Another ten minutes and we'll be called back for fuel."

"Roger, Dasher." Bruce wasn't surprised that the controllers managing this search were going to send them back to shore rather than ask them to midair refuel in this weather. The plane was already in the sea. No one could change the reality of the limited fuel the jet had on board: The clock said she had run out of gas several minutes ago. A ditch at sea took calm waters to have a chance of success. In these seas, the impact would destroy the plane, and the pilot would not have a chance.

The odds were good the wreckage would never be found.

Tonight was a failure.

COAST GUARD STATION
St. Petersburg, Florida

"Are you sure you're okay?"

Bruce drank more coffee and did his best to ignore his headache. "Just tired, Grace."

"What happened?"

"We never got close to her."

Silence met his words.

"Her. I'm sorry, Bruce."

He took a deep breath and shook off the disquiet. "So am I. We're going to be heading back to Pensacola; the Coast Guard now has this search. Our weekend plans are shot."

"Call me after you get some sleep; we'll sort it out."

"Thanks, Grace." He meant it more than he could put into words.

"Tell Emily hi."

He gave his first glimmer of a smile since going out. "She's probably chewed up my tools as a way to say she missed me. I'll call in twelve hours, Grace."

"I'll be around," she promised. "Here's Jill."

Grace ~

Have you ever seen the movie *McLintock* with John Wayne? Now there was a movie. I'm lying here unable to sleep, flipping channels, and I caught the end of it. Emily is on the bed, having no problem sleeping whatsoever. I swore I would never do it, let her on the bed, but she met me with the saddest eyes when I got home. I'm a goner for mush. Anyway, back to the movie. John Wayne has a line, "all show and no stay."

It resonated. It meant a lot for me to be able to call you when I got to shore and could catch a moment. Knowing you were a phone call away made it easier tonight. It was the hardest kind of night—someone died and I wasn't able to help. It's part of this job, just like being a hero, but it's the hardest part.

I don't want an easy relationship, Grace. I want a deep one. I don't need a marriage that shows well but doesn't have the stay. So think about making this serious, and let's talk about it.

I know we can work around the separations. It is a strength to know I have you there behind me, and I want you to have the same assurance. Flying is a gift—do you have any idea how rare your temperament and skills are, how perfect they are for the job you have? I met another pilot tonight whom I admire having never met her. Whatever happened to cause the chain of events that eventually cost her everything, she was handling those moments professionally. And had it been anything other than the added hit of extreme weather, I'm confident she would have brought the plane in safely.

Tonight was as profound as Ecuador for me. It can cost us to wait until the ideal moment. There are no perfect moments in our lives, just opportunities to seize.

Good night, Grace. God bless.

Bruce ~

I made the same decision tonight, as I played game after game of solitaire. I want to be there for you, no matter what happens, and I don't want to wait for ideal circumstances before we move forward. You're right. There will be no ideal circumstances. There will be a right moment when God arranges the timing. A two military career couple—we'll make it work. I commit that to you. Let's sort out schedules for a weekend together either here or there so we can talk.

Grace

TWENTY-FIVE

★ ★ ★

NOVEMBER 8

PENSACOLA, FLORIDA

I don't think this was what I had in mind when I said I wanted to be there for you." Grace checked the parachute rigging Bruce wore, looking for problems. "Wolf, back me up over here." The day was sunny, clear, and the guys wanted to go jumping.

"You're doing fine, Grace. Check that none of the straps have turned," Bruce instructed.

Wolf crossed over from his partner Cougar to join them. "You need to start jumping for fun, Grace."

She finished checking the straps. "I fly the planes; I don't jump out of them."

Bruce reached over and adjusted the pilot scarf she wore above her jacket. "You look cute doing it too."

She loved the scarf. It got cold at altitudes with the plane door open. She was taking up three PJs and two SEALs today, flying with the man who owned the plane and ran the parachute jumping school. He would act as her copilot and then as jump master. She would fly straight and level and he'd clear the guys out of the plane. Simple, but hardly easy. Not with these backseat drivers.

Wolf took over the safety checks on Bruce's gear and cleared him ready to jump. Bruce checked out Wolf's gear.

"Ready to go?" Grace had already done her preflight of the plane.

"Let's do it."

The guys piled into the back of the plane and took their seats.

Grace ran the checklists and cleared with the controller the right to taxi. It was a small airport that had one runway, and the controller answered her by first name. She was the only plane preparing to fly. She used the full length of the runway to bring the small plane into the air. She was after smooth and pedestrian. She'd show off by doing her part of this jump flawlessly.

The PJs and SEALs were men who took jumping seriously, but on this Saturday afternoon they were jumping purely for the fun of it.

It wasn't demanding flying. She climbed to altitude, reversed course, and returned on a vector over the jump school.

"Straight and level from here."

She nodded to the copilot. He got up to become the jump master.

The guys stepped out of the airplane one after the other.

She heard the call for last jumper. Waiting thirty seconds to make sure she was clear, Grace banked the plane and counted chutes. Five open colorful canopies. The guys had formed up in a straight line. They were trying to hit the huge *X* they had painted on the grass one right after the other. "I've got to think a bit about the company I've been keeping."

Her copilot buckled himself back in and laughed. "Head on down; they'll want to jump again."

"I was afraid you would say that."

She saw the first man touch down with a flare right on the target and his chute begin collapsing around him.

"Admit it, you had fun." Bruce reached around Grace to open the movie theater door.

She smiled at him. "You looked cute getting sat on by Wolf."

"Buttering me up is not going to get me to see a mushy movie." On the last jump of the day the landing had not gone as planned. He had become a pancake under his friend.

"So what are we seeing?"

Bruce read the marquee. He sighed. "A mushy movie." He bought the tickets. They had been alternating weekends—Grace coming to Pensacola and him traveling to Norfolk. They had seen enough movies at this theater they had fallen into a pattern of where to sit. They were a few minutes late, and the opening credits were finishing as he held the theater door for her. She followed the small lights on the aisle.

"Grace?" Bruce leaned over to whisper to her as she settled in. "What did you tell Wolf before that last jump?"

"Did I mention Jill had her camera with her when she came out to meet Wolf?"

"I don't believe you did."

"She promised to make a copy for you."

"It's dangerous to let you two drive down here together."

"You're just now realizing that?"

He leaned over and kissed her for that giggle. She was fitting in with his friends and family just fine.

TWENTY-SIX

★ ★ ★

MARCH 10

PENSACOLA, FLORIDA

Somewhere out in the world on one of the blue oceans an aircraft carrier launched warplanes; in the deep cold waters a nuclear powered submarine hunted. Civilians on the beach had no idea what the military was doing at this minute to defend their shores. It was just as well. They wouldn't understand what the military knew.... There was no such thing as playing defense on the enormous oceans, just many shades of offense.

"Gracie, you're dripping on me."

"You need to wake up."

Bruce cracked open one eye. In silhouette, the bright sun behind her, Gracie was all tan, curves, and— He closed his eyes again, content with the impression. She was beautiful. And he was going to marry her.

"I'm resting." He was wise enough to know she didn't want to be asked just yet. She needed to know that what they had built during the last few months was going to stay strong through a deployment. He was about to get a chance to prove it. She was leaving for another six-month deployment in three days. He was already depressed.

If his assumptions were entirely wrong about how they could make it work out, he had a fallback plan in mind. If he had to quit his job and trail her around from base to base he could adjust. He'd had his career. The guys were beginning to call him

Old Lucky. He wasn't going to push the odds. He could get a good civilian job as a paramedic when he eventually left the military.

Grace nudged him with her toe. She was going to stand there until he agreed to wake up. They had had these silent standoffs before. They amused him, and she started them because he figured they also amused her.

He had more patience than she did. "Sit down while you wait," he suggested with a comfortable sigh. The sun was warm, the beach all theirs, and unless his sense of time was off, they had over an hour before they were due to meet Jill and Wolf for dinner.

She sank down on the sand beside him. "It's not like you to be so tired. What's wrong?"

She was leaving in three days—that's what was wrong. And he hadn't slept well last night as he pondered that reality. He reached over and intertwined his hands with hers and squeezed. "I'm going to miss you."

"Thanks. I'll miss you too."

He opened his eyes and squinted against the sun's glare to see her face. "That had real emotion in it." He sat up, brushing sand off. "I promise I won't find another favorite lady while you're gone."

She shoved his arm. It got the smile he had hoped for but it faded quickly. He rested his hands on her shoulders and waited until she met his gaze. "I love you, Grace. This deployment is not a threat to that." His thumb gently rubbed her shoulders. "What do you need to hear so that sticks?"

She held his gaze, offered a soft smile. "That's what I needed to hear."

"You're sure you don't want more words?" He was going to miss that smile. He leaned down and kissed her, storing up another memory for when she would be gone. "We'll make this work, honey. However it is necessary."

"Are you forward deploying?"

"I haven't heard anything yet. We might be. The Balkan flights are growing and they could use another team of PJs on the ground; the upcoming NATO exercises will need coverage."

"It would help if you were able to do TDYs while I was gone so you'd be home when I get back."

She was already thinking like they were a permanent couple. There was comfort in that. "I'll see what I can do."

She got quiet again. Bruce wrapped his arms more firmly around her. He wished he could reassure her better on how it was going to work out. They would make it up as they went along.

"In the future there will be more days like this one," Bruce said. "I promise you that."

"I know."

He rubbed her arm. "Come on, let's go back up to the house. I'll change and we'll head over to the hotel." There was no use getting sad about what they couldn't change. They still had a couple days before she deployed.

She pushed to her feet.

Bruce took her hand as they walked back.

The phone was ringing as they entered the house. Bruce picked it up in the kitchen. "Where, Rich?" He caught Grace's attention. "CNN."

He joined her in the living room. A major earthquake had just hit Turkey. Bruce watched the reports: a magnitude 7.4 and an epicenter in the southern region. "One hour. I'll be there." He hung up the phone. "Get your things; let's get you back to the hotel to pack. I'll find you a flight back to Norfolk, ASAP."

Grace simply nodded. Bruce knew the *GW* deployment would be moved up. The last earthquake in the southern region had caused over a hundred million dollars of damage at Incirlik Air Base. The Air Force had patched together the runways and turned the base into the hub of relief flights for the country. Operation Northern Watch would be moved entirely to carrier operations. And there wasn't a carrier available...but there was one that could be sent with dispatch.

TWENTY-SEVEN

★ ★ ★

MARCH 22

USS *GEORGE WASHINGTON* (CVN 73)

ATLANTIC OCEAN

The carrier was preparing itself for going into harm's way. An expedited transit across the Atlantic, rough seas, the weather uniformly choppy—it was pressuring the flight deck crews, the pilots, and the sailors alike. Safety drills for fire and water, incoming missile drills, battle group drills—they were ringing out glitches in every procedure in preparation of the task ahead.

Grace was too busy to miss Bruce for eighteen-some hours a day. The other moments when she shut her eyes to sleep, he was at the front of her thoughts and he stayed there.

The earthquake had destroyed three of twenty-one dams on the Euphrates, not disrupting the huge gravel dams themselves, but damaging the sluice gates that allowed water to flow and power to be generated. The Euphrates' water level was dropping daily, Syria was accusing Turkey of not dedicating resources to the critical problem of the dams, and there were now daily satellite shots showing Syria moving troops north. On top of the twenty-three thousand reported dead within Turkey, the two countries wanted to go to war. It was senseless, but the match had been tossed. Somehow NATO and the United Nations would have to figure out a way to put the lid back on.

In the midst of training nuggets, getting her own flight hours in to requalify for carrier landings, and assuming the new mission

planning load that came with this deployment, Grace was struggling to keep ahead of the demands.

They were tasking with orders to assume Operation Northern
Watch flights over Iraq. On the surface the orders were similar to
what they had done on the last deployment. They were enforcing
a no-fly zone, providing reconnaissance, watching borders. But
the situation on the ground was very different.

They would be flying over a Turkey now in the midst of a
national crisis. They would be flying within miles of a growing
Syrian military presence. And Iraq was taking advantage of the
chaos to move troops.

Peace was far away.

Bruce -

How are you doing on the ground? Do they have the refinery
fire under control? How are the rolling blackouts? News comes
in, but anything over an hour old is pretty dated. I heard about
the terrorist bombing at the cafe. Rescue workers getting hurt—
senseless violence, and so sad.

I'm glad you are currently based in the relatively safe haven at
Incirlik. Did I really need to know they had just put in Mylar
sheeting on the base housing windows in order to handle a bomb
blast? I'm glad it had the corollary effect of helping to minimize
damage during the earthquake, but I wish the terrorist threat level
wasn't so high it was needed.

We will be in range to begin flights for Operation Northern
Watch in four days. You can feel the tension around the
squadron. My biggest headache in the planning is the lack of
emergency divert fields. So many airports are either still repairing
damage or are heavily involved in relief flights. Since this earthquake, Iraq has twice flown MiGs into the no-fly zone. Peter's

assessment to the squadron is not if there will eventually be a confrontation, but when. I'm worried about nuggets. Nothing new there.

Life has changed. The responsibility is heavier. The needs more pressing. The awareness of the risks higher. Without being morbid about it—Bruce, there is a letter for you left with Jill. I wanted to say a few things, just in case. I want a hug next time I see you. A long one. A tight one. And I may let you fix me a pilot's special.

I pray this finds you well.

Grace

Grace ~

I have confidence you'll watch the details and have safe flights. We need you overhead. Your job right now is as vital as any on the ground. If there weren't overflights right now, I have no doubt there would be war.

It's tense here, for the base is home to thousands of Turkish military as well as numerous civilian contractors, and all of them have stories filled with grief. The concrete apartment buildings that pancaked— The destruction is so incredibly complete. The major way of getting supplies and people around are helicopter flights. The PJs have unfortunately been busy. We've had two helicopters go down in the last day due to being overloaded.

I take this day by day. We will be moving forward soon. Communication is going to get very hard after that, for not much is moving that is not emergency related. Know you are in my thoughts and prayers.

Catch the third wire.

All my love, Bruce

TWENTY-EIGHT

★ ★ ★

MARCH 28

USS *GEORGE WASHINGTON* (CVN 73)

MEDITERRANEAN SEA OFF THE COAST OF TURKEY

There was not much time to relax around the VFA-83 squadron ready room—for flight operations were going on twenty hours a day and one briefing cycle was backing up against another. Grace called the mission briefing to order precisely at 0800. There were six pilots taking notes, including Peter, her new CO.

"From 1000 to 1530 our mission on this flight is to control Iraqi airspace east of the Tigris down to the thirty-sixth parallel. Our secondary objective is to take reconnaissance photos to evaluate present water levels in the Tigris River," Grace opened, setting the stage for the information to come. Flights didn't happen, they were scripted.

There was nothing in the briefing—its order or content—that she had not thought through in detail. She brought down the white board listing mission assignments. "I will be leading the four-plane Panthers flight; Peter will be leading the four-man Torry flight providing aircap."

She talked through the mission flight. Rendezvous points, the altitudes and formations they would fly, speed, navigation markers, routes of ingress and egress.

She turned to safety. She reminded pilots of the facts they had to live by—bingo fuel levels, minimum distances between planes, the code words for task saturation and vertigo. Both conditions could threaten the safety of a formation flight, and by using the code words it was possible to alert other pilots to what was going on even though it meant acute embarrassment to admit you were flying below par. The best pilots were honest early; the nuggets sometimes got in real trouble before they spoke up.

She went into detail on the emergency divert fields, search-and-rescue codes, emergency procedures over water and land, and location of tankers and order of refueling. She discussed geography and weather, clicking on a tape to show the latest weather radar clips for the flight area.

"No shooting at friendlies." She tugged down a poster of a MiG. "This one is not friendly."

Peter smiled. She'd borrowed it from Intel to make her point. There were enemies close by during this flight, and if flying at Mach 1 directly toward them, twenty miles of distance could blink by in a minute.

Satisfied her point had been made, she nevertheless spent two minutes on the flight characteristics of the MiG—how fast it could fly, turn, climb, the type of weapons it could be configured to carry. She went on to talk about known SAM batteries and AAA sites in the areas of the flight profile.

The pilots listened carefully and took notes. They were depending on her to give the details necessary to successfully accomplish the mission and to get home alive afterward. There was nothing casual about a mission briefing.

"We trap back on the carrier beginning at 1650. Remember to watch the crosswinds, fly the meatball, and grab the third wire. I'm open to questions." There were few. "We're concluded."

"Good brief, Gracie."

"Thanks, Thunder."

In thirty-five minutes she would be on the flight deck settling into her Hornet, prepared to lead the mission she had just briefed. And tonight, ten minutes after the last plane landed back aboard the carrier, she would be leading the debrief of the mission. Every deviation from the mission briefing would be discussed in detail. Pilots learned early to check their ego and pride at the door. Debriefings were unanimously more difficult than briefings.

Her objective was simple: Survive today and tomorrow she would get a chance to do it all again.

TURKEY

Grace ~

Mail hasn't arrived yet so I'm sure I'm at least a few letters behind. Dasher set down the helicopter in a parking lot of what used to be a school. The roof collapsed, the walls— At least school was not in session at the time. It's 1300 and it's already been a very long day. Rebels planted land mines on one of the roads through the mountains. A UN vehicle ran over one. One dead, three injured. We handled the evacuation.

We're now sitting in the parking lot waiting for word that our assigned tanker is overhead. We've been midair refueling the chopper ever since we came in-country. It's an interesting way to handle getting around. When gas will arrive is not always predictable; I've learned to seize these quiet moments.

I've been watching the flights overhead. Honey, if those formations are your squadrons, you've been having long days too. Before we all go different directions for the day, we've been getting an 0500 gaggle briefing for the hundred of us based at Incirlik so that any one of us can respond should trouble be reported. It's not a great solution to the lack of manpower, but so far it's been workable. Yesterday we flew over the location where we were stationed last year. The plateau has a gash through it where the land tore open. Despite what I've seen around here, I was still surprised to see it.

I miss you, Grace.

"The tanker is inbound," Rich called.

Bruce folded the letter in progress and slid it into his flight suit pocket.

OPERATION NORTHERN WATCH
IRAQ/TURKEY BORDER

The land below looked so quiet and peaceful. Grace checked the pilots in formation with her and then descended to twelve thousand feet. A smooth mission. The stress of the day had faded as she settled into the mental zone of peak performance. She had done a good job anticipating the details. She was ahead of the flight mentally, anticipating steps rather than having to fight a sensation of being rushed and having to keep up. She began taking pictures of the Tigris.

Below her, dark red swirls of sand burst up in eddies. When the summer winds blew at their maximum and became sand-bearing winds, the sky would turn red under the onslaught. She'd be willing to land on the carrier at night in the rain if only it would break the drought. She saw her first Iraqi tank north of Dahuk.

Bruce ~

I wish I could talk to you on the phone, in person, if only for a moment. I saw the first sight of what I'm sure has caught everyone's attention: Iraq moving forces north, just as Syria has done.

We're stacking coverage, EA-6B Prowler and Hornets in dual formations with F-14 Tomcats holding in race car patterns above us. Everyone goes out with a full weapons load.

There is no sense of optimism aboard ship, only a growing reality that something is going to pull us into this growing conflict. I listen with intense interest for news of the world, but no one seems to have good answers about what is happening.

We will soon start flying coverage of eastern Turkey and the mountain passes that have been rebel routes in the past. If something breaks, the skirmish line will be on the ground simultaneous with one in the air. We are ready. With God's help, I pray being prepared to fight will be enough to continue to deter that fight.

This note is to say I love you. The pressure of events has overtaken what I hoped to be able to write, to find words to capture the depth of that emotion. The change between the last deployment where I was one of the seasoned pilots to this deployment where I am now one of the flight leads is major. It's what I wanted, and now that I have it I find it incredibly intense. "God is my helper" has become very real to me. I'm leaning hard against Him. Overwhelmed, pressured, I am leaning hard against the verse in 2 Corinthians 12:9 that says, "My grace is sufficient for you, for my power is made perfect in weakness." It's become my verse. God is bigger than this burden.

I'm sleeping well. Flying better than I ever have in my career. I can feel my plane around me, if that makes sense. A year ago I had to think about flying as well as think about the mission. Now it's only the mission. The flying has now become instinctive.

I've circled around the same topic several times now and it's obvious I'm tired. I'm calling it a night.

I love you. Gracie

Grace ~

Three letters arrived today. A sweet, fragrant treasure. Please don't worry about me or our relationship. I know you, your days, your life, and I love you too. Knowing you are busy and working hard just makes me more eager to give you that long hug when I see you next. You are my sweetheart forever.

Bruce

Ephesians 1:17, my new favorite verse for you.

I do not cease to give thanks for you, remembering you in my prayers, *that the God of our Lord Jesus Christ, the Father of glory, may give you a spirit of wisdom and of revelation in the knowledge of him,* having the eyes of your hearts enlightened, that you may know what is the hope to which he has called you, what are the riches of his glorious inheritance in the saints, and what is the immeasurable greatness of his power in us who believe, according to the working of his great might which he accomplished in Christ when he raised him from the dead and made him sit at his right hand in the heavenly places. Ephesians 1:16–20

TWENTY-NINE

★ ★ ★

APRIL 4

BIRECIK DAM, TURKEY

Diving in a rock dam—Bruce looked down at the water and wished he were somewhere else. Birecik Dam was the fourth largest gravel dam in the world, a huge curving pile of rocks that had taken six years to construct. It stopped the mighty Euphrates. Water behind the dam stretched for miles. It had taken five minutes of walking just to climb up to the observation platform from within the hydroelectric power station. The dam itself had been built to withstand an 8.3 earthquake shock. And it had. The power plant, however, had not. And Turkey desperately needed the power back on.

NATO, the U.S. Corp of Engineers, the Army Third Division—anyone with expertise had been brought in to help. Now the Navy SEALs and PJs were asked to lend a hand, and it was becoming obvious why. This was diving at its most dangerous.

"They are getting high sulfur readings in the water at this end of the reservoir," the Army engineer said.

Sulfur. As in magma gas? Earthquakes shattered slabs of rock underground, breaking up rock formations that trapped oil and natural gas and water in large naturally occurring underground aquifers. And when magma flowed it found those new openings to the surface. "You think the earthquake opened a fissure?"

"It's possible," the engineer replied. "We've found few other explanations for the water readings. We can do a lot with water samples, but we can't determine how big the problem is or how to stop it without someone finding the source of that sulfur."

"And if you don't solve it before you get water flowing again, you risk concentrations in the Euphrates sufficient to kill fish and make the water unfit to drink."

"Not to mention damaging the hydroelectric generation equipment we are working to bring back online. Can you handle the dive?"

"We can do the dive." It made sense now, why the PJs had been asked in addition to the SEALs. The SEALs did more combat diving, but the PJs trained to stand watch during shuttle flights. One of the worst-case scenarios was a shuttle encountering trouble just as it cleared the tower and having it come down in the shallow water right off the Cape Canaveral launch site. The PJs trained to work around hazardous fuels, to get into a partially submerged shuttle and get the astronauts out. "We're going to need specialized equipment flown over." Among other unique items, they had acid-proof, vulcanized rubber dry suits.

Bruce had no idea what was down in the water. If they had sulfur, he was willing to bet they had even more nasty things at the source of the contamination. "We need to see the last sonar soundings taken of the lake bed and a full briefing on what has been observed at the dam since the earthquake hit."

"We're trying to come online in the next couple weeks."

"We can get equipment here by day after tomorrow."

USS GEORGE WASHINGTON (CVN 73)
MEDITERRANEAN SEA OFF THE COAST OF TURKEY

"Did you see this latest out of Intel?" Peter asked, coming into the squadron ready room carrying a large photo.

"Something on tonight's mission?" Grace closed the four-inch-thick flight manual for the F-14 Tomcat. To eventually lead a landing signal officer team, she had to know the flight characteristics of every plane in the air wing. Helping a pilot in trouble during twenty seconds of a landing meant she had better be instinctive and dead-on in her answers.

Peter laid down a LANDSAT satellite image of Lake al-Assad in Syria. From the high altitude, the lake looked like a lizard with a long tail and a big head with its tongue stuck out. She'd seen it last night during the regional security briefing given to all the flight squadrons. The lake had shrunk compared to the six-month-ago photo; the drought was now obvious even from the satellite shots.

"And this?" Peter set down a newspaper; the photo looked to be taken from the observation platform at the massive dam.

The water was filled with floating dead fish.

She checked the newspaper source to see if it was a smuggled photo printed in one of the opposition newspapers. She stilled. Syria had let this run in the official newspaper on the front page. They were conveying information but also making a political statement to the region. "Maybe a runoff problem from the Euphrates?"

"Something in Turkey is flowing downstream. I don't like it. You're talking about the primary water supply for a third of Syria. If it becomes contaminated—"

"An earthquake, now this. The ecology disasters are growing," Grace said.

"I wouldn't be surprised to find they are related."

"There have been rumors of buried biological weapons within Syria."

Peter nodded. "An underground contamination; something is killing the fish—it's going to be an interesting day flying."

They were flying today over eastern Turkey and the mountain passages, down into Iraq, and then patrolling the Syrian border on the flight back. A complex flight trying to cover many objectives. "Agreed. Any changes?" Peter was leading the flight today, had briefed it an hour ago.

"For now, no. What really bothers me is the fact the newspaper is five days old. Has the problem abated? Grown worse? Syria isn't going to let experts come in to check unless it's to their political advantage."

"What we understand about Syria could be sketched on a napkin." Not for the first time she wondered what Wolf and the SEALs had been doing in Syria last year. Something was brewing in there, and it looked more and more likely it would be her problem before it was over.

THIRTY

★ ★ ★

EASTERN TURKEY

The mountain range that sliced through eastern Turkey and northern Iraq was jagged peaks and deep ravines, the echoes on radar making Gracie cautious if not nervous. It was the type of terrain where a shoulder-fired surface-to-air missile could leap toward her with no warning. Her thumb moved on the stick to rest on the weapons select switch.

She kept her eyes scanning the terrain as they crossed through the mountain pass at eighteen thousand feet and felt relief as the ground ahead flattened. She hated mountains. They hid dangers, made the weather unpredictable, and gave no place to execute an emergency landing.

The navigation markers lit, and she changed course south, following the markers she had preset, staying tucked in tight beside Thunder. They would be out of the mountains of eastern Turkey and over the deserts of Iraq in minutes.

On the radar she could see the distinctive *V* of three blips and the return codes of the interrogating IFF transponders. Two Pave Hawks and a Pave Low III helicopter flew close to the ground. They were heading across the valley to the southwest. A rescue mission. "Go, boys, go," Gracie whispered, watching the blips. "I wish you every success."

She wondered briefly what had happened, for there had been no emergency calls over the radio channels she monitored, and the absence of Turkish fighter cover in the area suggested it was not a pilot in trouble. Rebels were active in these districts of Turkey—maybe another bombing.

Gracie followed the helicopters on radar until they disappeared back into the ground clutter. She toggled radar back to the look-down feed she was receiving from the high altitude AWACs. The best defense was to see trouble coming a long time before it arrived.

OPERATION NORTHERN WATCH
IRAQ

Grace preferred the desert. It was sand and heat and visibility for miles. Within one flight the geography changed from mountains in Turkey to desert in western Iraq back to mountains in northeast Iraq. Her back was sore from the long flight and she flexed her hands often to deal with the stiffness. Hours of flying had gone according to plan.

"Viper 02, bandits bluebird plus 10, angels 2," Peter called.

"Viper 01, contact," Grace confirmed. Two MiG-29s from an airfield west of Baghdad were heading north toward the no-fly zone. With a flick of her finger on the stick she switched weapons to air-to-air missiles. It was the first time MiG-29s had come up to challenge in fourteen days. The number of skirmishes had so far been games of chicken, but there was always the day it changed.

"Viper 01, illuminate?" she asked. They had already worked out their game plan for this situation.

"Viper 02. Roger."

Gracie wouldn't like to be in the seat of the MiG pilots at the instant she hit the switch on her long tactical radar; the cockpits would be a symphony of warning alarms and red lights as their threat radar suddenly screamed missile lock. In her own helmet she could hear the low-pitched buzz that was the missile under the Hornet's wing quivering to be released so it could go after the radar beam it now had locked into its guidance system.

The MiGs had been warned.

Gracie's hands grew sweaty as the MiGs kept coming toward the demarcation line for the no-fly zone. *Come on, turn.*

At literally the last second, the MiGs turned sharply to fly the line rather than cross over.

Gracie felt the tense muscles in her back unlock and the moisture in her palms disappear. Playing chicken with live missiles was an interesting way to spend the day.

She hated the tactical situation she and Thunder were in. They were now less than a mile from the apex of their flight plan, but looping around to return back to Turkey would put their backs to the MiGs and the heat seeking missiles they carried—not a good idea.

She switched the sweep area of the radar and saw the flight of four Tomcats over the mountains in northern Iraq changing course. They were coming to assist. "Viper 01, aircap."

"Viper 02. Roger."

As soon as help arrived, she and Thunder would be free to break off and cross back into Turkey.

Two more images appeared on the scope. Gracie grimaced. "Viper 01, bandits bluebird plus 20, angels 3." Two more MiGs were launching. Its ability to use rough field airstrips was one of the things she both admired and hated about the Russian plane. What were they doing?

"Viper flight. Snap zero eight zero!"

The trigger word from the AWACs controller had her slamming her F/A-18 Hornet into a crushing g-force turn. A streak of white raced by. What *was* that? The AWACs controller had just saved her life.

She groaned against the g's as she climbed at the performance edge of what the plane could do. She got altitude, put the sun behind her, then leveled out to seek a look-down shot if it came to that.

The Tomcats vectoring to join them were still a minute away from being able to help.

Thunder came alongside. "Viper 02, angels 28."

"Viper 01. Roger."

She leveled out at 28,000 feet. The second set of MiGs were climbing to match them and were closing in on the no-fly zone with no indication they were going to turn as the others had. The rules of engagement were simple: Don't fire first. A horrible rule when the first rule of air combat was he who fired first won. A shoulder-fired SAM from the ground should count.

Gracie heard the tension in the voices of the AWACs controllers as they started calling in more assets. Since there was nothing Gracie could tell them that they didn't already see on their own powerful look-down radar, she ignored the radio traffic. She was busy at the moment.

Getting out of the fight was the plan. But it wasn't going to be easy.

The MiG-29s now racing for the no-fly zone were coming straight toward them. This was going to be a free-for-all. And there was no way to safely disengage without getting a missile in their backs.

Were they really going to restart this shooting war today over a piece of sky? She had no choice but to wait it out as the MiGs closed to the thirty-sixth parallel. A sense of calm settled deep inside. It wasn't her decision. If they started the fight, she and Thunder would end it.

The lead MiG broke the line in the air and immediately fired. She saw a white streak leap from under its wing and the MiG jerk as the weight of his craft shifted. The incoming missile had locked on to Thunder and he dove to evade, firing chaff to confuse the missile lock.

Gracie fired back. Thunder was no more than diving away when she flipped her finger to select the humming AMRAAM, locked on the crosshairs, and pulled the trigger. The missile leapt from the rail directly beside the fuselage under her left wing heading for the lead MiG. As soon as she had tone that the missile was clear, she focused on the second closing MiG, maneuvered to get a lock, and immediately fired her second AMRAAM.

"Viper 02. Fox one. Fox one," she tersely told the controlling AWACs indicating which missiles she had fired.

The MiGs blacked out radar emissions and dove to avoid her missiles. The missile tracking in on Thunder lost its direction lock and spiraled away.

It was a temporary reprieve. The other MiGs were joining. Four on two. Gracie grimaced at the odds and rolled her Hornet to dive and rejoin Thunder. They were running out of airspace to work with, and this was not a dogfight to have over Iran.

Her neck began to ache at the constant pivoting to see the world around her. Below her, sand was turning to rocks. The fight was spilling north toward the mountains of eastern Turkey, and it was an uncomfortable place to fly, let alone have a dogfight.

A powerful sense of dread hit. A MiG had turned in behind her. She jinked the Hornet around the air to keep breaking the missile lock, her body taking a pounding with every maneuver.

"Viper 02, snap zero six zero."

She immediately did so and could almost read the markings on the missile Thunder shot at the MiG closing on her.

The MiG exploded.

The shock wave buffeted her plane, and for a moment it

threatened to snuff out one of her engines. She fought back for control, got it, and swiveled around to reorient the world. A MiG was screaming up from below to angle a shot at Thunder. "Viper 01, snap roll!"

His Hornet went from level flight to a steep roll in an instant. There was nothing she could do. The missile the MiG fired at him was there, and the chaff Thunder fired didn't have time to disperse. The missile hit the left wing of his Hornet. She saw the ejection charges fire and propel him away as his plane engulfed in flames.

Thunder. Oh, God, keep him alive.

"Birddog, Viper 01, White water!" She radioed to the AWACs controller, hoping like crazy those PJs were still close by. Thunder needed help—fast.

The pressure on her body made it hard to breathe as she slammed the F/A-18 Hornet into a twenty-degree-per-second turn, reversing course. Afterburners pushed up her speed. She was going to hold this airspace at any cost until help arrived for Thunder.

"Viper 02, Cowboy 01. Inbound." The flight of four Tomcats made their presence felt. Her radar warning system suddenly went white. The MiGs were going to get their electronics fried if they stayed to fight.

"Viper 02, Cowboy 01. Break vector 20."

Gracie didn't want to leave Thunder, but her presence would only complicate the aircap. She was down to one air-to-air missile. Before replying, she adjusted her radar to scan low to the ground, sorted out the clutter, and saw with relief a *V* far to the west but coming in their direction. Thunder had help coming. She wished she could get a secure emergency radio transmission with him to confirm he was okay, but she couldn't risk the contact.

"Cowboy 01, Viper 02, vectoring camel plus 20." With a hard left on the stick and a forward move on the throttle, she broke away from the fight and turned toward the mountains of eastern Turkey. The Tomcats closed to provide a wall of protection behind her to prevent the MiGs from taking advantage of the situ-ation.

Her first fight, and she'd lost it. She would take time to feel the anger later.

For the first time since the firefight had begun, she took a moment to scan all the red warnings on her panels. Her plane was flying but it was protesting. The shock wave and shrapnel that had threatened to snuff out an engine had done lasting dam-age. As the adrenaline faded, she forced her hand to unlock its white-knuckle grip on the stick so she could reach forward to the right DDI panel and start troubleshooting the problems. "Birddog, Viper 02, declaring snowbird," she radioed the control-ling AWACs, warning she was flying a crippled bird.

Between her and safety were thirty nautical miles of airspace of very unpleasant terrain. The fight had pushed her far into northern Iraq. She was determined not to have to bail out. Bruce would say don't push it, get out of the plane, but she couldn't yet, not unless there was no other choice. She was not going to have on her record for eternity—first woman pilot shot down behind enemy lines.

BIRECIK DAM, TURKEY

"Where did he go down?" Bruce shouted to be heard above the noise as Dasher spun up the Pave Hawk helicopter. There were missile exchanges going on in Iraq while they were sitting around a conference table talking water depths and temperature. What a mess in priorities. He leaned back to let Victor and Frank take the bench seats.

"Ten kilometers in, north of the bend in what used to be the Zab River. The Twenty-seventh is already inbound," Rich yelled back as he whirled his finger and Dasher nodded, lifting off. "The fight is spilling north; we've got four Tomcats and three MiGs still tangling. One Hornet is coming north with shrapnel damage."

"Where do they want us?"

"For now, heading to the border. This skirmish is going to be over soon one way or the other. The question is, will the fighting spread? Syria and Turkey are both sending up planes."

"Oh, joy."

THIRTY-ONE

★ ★ ★

"Striker. Radio traffic."

The grim tone in Dasher's voice and the fact the pilot turned to look back warned him. Bruce reached over and flipped the switch so he could listen to the same radio traffic his friend was.

"Viper 02, Birddog. Say your state."

"Viper 02, angels 9, 3.8."

It was Gracie's voice.

Lord, not this. Not Grace.

"She's flying the Hornet that took the shrapnel damage," Dasher said quietly over the radio traffic.

"Is she hurt?"

"Unknown. She's got stabilizer damage and hydraulic problems."

"Where is she?"

Rich unfolded a terrain map. He'd been computing coordinates from the radio traffic. "About here."

Bruce winced. "Can she make it through the mountain passes?" he asked Dasher.

"She sounds determined to try. She's got maybe ten minutes at the rate the plane is dying around her before controls become totally unresponsive. That's enough time to clear the pass and make an emergency landing at Colemerik."

"Tight."

"Very. Anything else goes wrong, she won't have the resources left to react."

Bruce looked toward Rich.

"Ammo is loaded, medical supplies have been replenished. We're ready," his partner replied.

"Dasher, get us cut free to go meet her flight."

"The request is already in. They're checking who is nearest to reach her."

"Birddog, Viper 02, requesting vector home base under 10." Grace was calm, working the problems. Bruce grimaced. She was fighting to keep altitude but didn't feel confident she could climb above 10,000 feet.

"Viper 02, Birddog, vector blue plus 30, angels blue plus 4."

"Viper 02. Roger."

Hang on, honey. Stay with it.

Dasher would get them clearance to go after her. Bruce reached for his medical kits. "She's O-Negative. Where's the nearest trauma unit?" He couldn't lose Grace this way, not like this.

IRAQ/TURKEY BORDER

Gracie felt chilled, the sweat soaking her flight suit cooling against her skin. She wished she could move her legs to ease the cramp in her right calve but had to settle for tugging against the ankle restraints and flexing the muscle. The aches were becoming more pronounced. A bruise on her right shoulder was making her grip on the stick come at a painful cost.

Time felt like it had slowed down to a painful degree. Safety was ahead. She had to get through the mountain passes and figure out a glide path into Colemerik that needed minimal maneuvering.

Warning alarms lit across her console and sounded around her. Details registered immediately: an incoming shoulder-fired SAM, fired from the ridgeline to the north, under half a mile away. Seconds until impact.

Gracie slammed the throttle forward and the stick hard left. She took the punishment because there was no option and dove her plane away. She didn't have the altitude to be playing the game, and she could feel the control surfaces fighting her as the failing hydraulics worked against her. The SAM never acquired lock as she shifted altitude; it raced by above her.

When the second SAM came up from the other ridgeline, she would have closed her eyes and swore at the unfairness of it had there been time. Combination attacks against a crippled bird. It was the tactic of a predator, moving in for a kill.

She wasn't going to give them the pleasure.

The plane fought her as she brought the nose up, forcing it into a steep turning climb. She was giving the SAM what it wanted, the bursting bright heat of her jet engines. The warning noise in the cockpit intensified as the missile closed in on her plane.

It was a heart-wrenching move, popping chaff and then tipping the F/A-18 nose first to the ground. Gravity pulled her down with heart-stopping speed.

She was going to make it. She heard the whistle as the surface-to-air missile shaved through the air feet away from the belly of her plane.

And then it hit the chaff decoy.

The explosion flung her plane inverted into a flat spin, the world going crazy around her. She couldn't eject while facing the earth.

Both engines snuffed out.

The ground spun toward her at a sickening pace. Wonderful. She was going to die with a broken nose. *I'm sorry, Bruce. I am so sorry.*

THIRTY-TWO

★ ★ ★

She's off the scope," Dasher warned. The tension in the chopper leapt in magnitude. "We've got SAM signatures."

Bruce clenched one hand around the other so hard he about broke his own knuckles. "Transponder codes?" The ejection seat would have its own emergency signature, as would the plane.

Dasher was running the frequencies. "None," he replied grimly. "Her electronics were a mess but that shouldn't have affected the ejection seat."

"What was her last altitude?"

"Angels 7.4. And in those ravines…"

Striker knew exactly what Dasher wasn't saying. They would be dealing with a search area where radar would be of little help. "Head to the last coordinates. And get firepower to cover us."

"Where are you, Gracie?" Striker whispered, scanning the terrain from the open door of the chopper. The wind buffeted his face. His flight suit wasn't as much protection as he would have liked. The emergency radio frequencies she had been given remained stubbornly silent.

The nausea in his stomach grew with the jerking of the Pave Hawk as they flew the terrain at twenty feet above the rocks. He ignored it as best he could.

Rich's hand tightened on his shoulder. "There."

Striker's heart sank as he saw the wreckage. The F/A-18 had pancaked, cut a deep swatch into a ravine, and come to rest at a forty-degree down angle. Rocks and loose debris were still avalanching around the wreckage. One wing had sheered off and folded back over the fuselage; the rest of the plane was in fragments.

"Rich, you're with me. Victor, Frank, keep a sharp eye out. We don't need unwanted company."

They had to rappel down from the chopper to the top of the ravine as there was no place for Dasher to set down. The rising smell of jet fuel was overpowering. Striker dug his boots in to get traction on the loose shale as the swinging rope threatened to push him off balance.

"Think we can get down there without bringing this on top of us?" Rich asked as a small river of stones and dirt slid into the ravine.

Striker uncoiled the rope he had brought with him. "Tie off, go down far to the sides of the wreckage, then swing back in toward it?"

Rich nodded and undid his own rope, then moved across the rocks to one of the pines. Striker moved to the other side of the wreckage to tie off his own. The descent was slippery. He kept his eyes pealed for the one thing he most feared seeing: a body.

Bracing his back against the rope, he walked in toward the fuselage wreckage, watching every step he took to make sure jagged metal didn't slice his rope or cut open the bottom of his boots.

The top of the left wing had peeled back like a can lid and now rested over the fuselage. Striker put his shoulder into moving the heavy wing flap away. He found the front section of the canopy had been sheared away. *Gracie.* Striker nearly threw up. The cockpit, one of the smallest for a fighter plane, had crumpled around her. The front of her flight suit was covered in blood.

The visor on her helmet was down. He carefully pushed it up.

Her eyes were wide open and unseeing. She'd snapped her neck? She had the glassy look of someone who was dead.

"Gracie?"

He pulled off his gloves and struggled to get his hand between her helmet and flight suit. He found a pulse. For a moment he thought it was his own, pounding through his cold fingertips. He moved his hand over her face and felt faint breath against his palm. "Rich, we're going to need the heavy extraction equipment down here. Rush it."

"I'm on it."

Bruce struggled to find secure footing on the loose ground to tie off his rope so he could get to work. He got his medical pack wedged into the debris and opened it.

Her nose had bled heavily. He eased her crash helmet off, afraid of what he might find. Had the g-forces been vicious enough, they would have ruptured not only the blood vessels of her nose but also her ears.

Honey brown hair tangled around his hands. He was relieved to find no additional blood. He carefully checked her eyes with his flashlight, looking for the hallmarks of oxygen deprivation that came at high altitudes if the pressure mask failed. He was relieved to get normal pupil reaction to the light. No catastrophic head injury; that was a miracle.

He started working the trauma list: breathing, blood, bones.

He ran his hands carefully down her arm. He didn't find the obvious compound fractures he had expected. If she hadn't broken her back...there was no good way to know until she awoke enough to move her limbs. There was a gash on her left arm, but all the blood on her flight suit appeared to be from the nosebleed. Her legs were likely going to be another matter, given the way this plane had crumpled.

How was she pinned? He moved his flashlight to get a look

around the crumpled metal. The better question, how was she not pinned? It looked a lot like the aftereffects of a race car crash, only with the chassis cage left intact. The electronics of the cockpit had folded back on her. He pulled on his gloves. Some of the components he was able to push back, others driven practically into her lap he couldn't budge.

He strained to reach down and check her legs, free them from the restraint straps. He cut his hand as ragged metal sliced through his glove, and he bit back a curse at the pain. Resting his weight on the side of the plane, he angled the light farther in and strained to see the problem. Part of the seat-locking mechanism had twisted and sheared.

He froze. Whatever had hit her plane had driven a sidewinder back into the undercarriage of the fuselage. The release mechanism was missing; the round was live. And she was practically sitting on it.

He heard the falling gravel as his partner rejoined him.

"Rich." Very slowly Striker moved and redirected his light, illuminating the live round. If the plane shifted, that round was going to explode. And at the moment he was leaning on the fuselage.

His partner's eyes widened but he said nothing, only set down the equipment he had retrieved, reached for his knife, and started moving dirt. In another situation they would have sandbagged the round. For now a ridge of dirt and a fulcrum to brace the plane would have to do.

Striker held still for three minutes until Rich had the brace in place. He eased back, able to breathe again. "Thanks."

"Don't mention it."

Getting Gracie out would mean being creative. He could forget moving the ejection seat. "See what you can do to get these display panels pulled back. I think we can get the chains and power winch around at least one of them."

Bruce checked her pulse again and found it holding steady. Her breathing was good, and given it was twenty-four minutes since her plane had disappeared from the scope, she was surviving the initial shock. At least it didn't appear that she was bleeding to death. He eased a neck brace in place and secured it.

Retrieving his own knife, he began cutting through the restraints holding her to the wreckage. A low shuddering groan broke from her when he freed the right shoulder harness restraint. He carefully ran his hand over her arm. Her shoulder didn't appear dislocated but she had clearly done some damage here. That she was coming conscious was a relief but she had very bad timing. "Gracie, stay still."

The voice drifted through the deep fog she was in.

It hurt.

She wanted to scream but found that took breath she didn't have.

"Easy, Gracie. We're here. Don't move."

The deep voice echoed in her mind as she tried to attach a meaning to the words. Who was here? The plane, missiles, earth... She flinched as it registered. She'd crashed.

She forced her mind to clarity amid pain that was excruciating. Her right shoulder was screaming at her. The man's voice was calm. She wasn't in a hospital. Doctors fussed about pain.

He'd called her Gracie and it sounded like second nature. Stay still, he said. An order. Thinking was so hard.

"Gracie?"

She knew she had to answer but the words wouldn't connect.

"Let's get this finished while she is still out of it. We could try to cut the panel away."

"Not until the jet fuel dissipates more; we can't risk hitting a pocket of it with a spark."

Two voices. *Where am I?*

She had to move to relieve the pain. Her weight was leaning back against her injured shoulder and it was killing her. The realization she was sitting up startled her. She was still in the plane?

"How much clearance do we need to free her legs?"

"Two inches."

"Call Boeing and complain. They used reinforced ribbing—two inches might as well be a foot." Something heavy pressed against her right leg. "Give me the metal cutters. And remind me to lift weights more often."

Her eyes didn't want to open but she forced them.

She was looking at trees, the ground? It was a confusing mix of brown, green, and tan. She jumped as it moved. Woodland cammies. If she had been able to, she would have laughed.

His head jerked around.

"Hey there, Gracie."

She liked the voice. It was a warm cascade of sound. She couldn't move her gaze away from the blue eyes looking back at her even if she wanted to. Even blinking hurt, and it felt like her head was going to explode with the brightness of the sky behind him. She tried but had a hard time sorting out his features from the confusing face paint.

He angled his body around to face her, leaning at an awkward angle so she didn't have to move to see his face. "I know you're hurting; I can see it in your eyes." He spoke quietly, in no hurry, giving her time to sort out his words.

"Bruce…"

"We're going to get you out of here. Rich is here too."

Her white knights. She tried to smile at him. In survival

school they had forgotten to tell her how nice it would be to have someone rescue her.

"Can you move your hands for me, Grace?"

The very thought was agonizing. She felt tears slip down her face. *No. It hurts.*

"Try, Gracie."

He was holding her left hand. She flexed her fingers against his, exploring, experimenting, testing the strength and seeing if it was real.

"Good." He moved his hand away, hurting her with its loss, taking away what she wanted to cling to. "Now this hand."

She wanted to scream when he touched her right hand. She closed her eyes as the world washed away in white and her breathing shallowed against the intense radiating pain.

"Hold on," he ordered. The pain seared as he moved her in the seat, and then it eased into a dreadful ache. "Better?" The sickness inside was intense, and she nodded slightly but didn't try to open her eyes. Let them work. She wanted out of here. Something rough brushed her cheek. "Okay, Gracie. Just hold on. You're going to hear metal pop."

The weight against her legs pressed heavy and she heard his breathing turn harsh as he strained. Then she heard the awful sound of metal giving. "Pull it, Rich," he gasped.

"I've got it. Watch your footing!"

Not knowing what they were doing was worse than knowing. She forced her eyes open. It sounded like an explosion around her as the mangled display was pulled over the edge of the cockpit and dropped away, triggering a small avalanche of rocks, dirt, and debris.

"Let's get her legs free."

"What about..." His partner didn't finish the sentence.

"Gracie, look at me."

There was nothing gentle about Bruce's order. Her eyes left the tangled metal and angled to see his face.

"I don't want you to move when your legs come free. Do you understand? I want you to stay absolutely still."

She didn't understand why he was worried, but she forced herself to nod.

"I'm going to cut your boot laces and the top of the your boots so I can slip your feet free." He quirked a grin at her. "I hope you're wearing clean socks."

He leaned down before his unexpected comment registered and she could try to return the smile.

His hand slid down her left leg and she felt the tug as he started to work. Laces snapped and she felt the heavy leather rip. His fingers wrapped around the back of her ankle and pulled her foot free. Her knee struck something sharp and she gasped at the pain. Her leg had been stationary so long the small movement felt like a dagger.

She'd broken her leg? Nausea curled inside. She had to be able to fly again. Her shoulder was hurt, her legs…her career was over if the injuries were serious enough. And that was assuming they would ever let her fly again after crashing.

She had to fly again. It was her life.

How long had she been on the ground? She could taste the blood in her mouth and the headache was pounding with her heartbeat. She had been on the wrong side of the pass when she went down. It would have taken them time to reach her. She shivered as the wind picked up and swirling debris was driven against her face.

Get me out of here, Bruce.

She heard gunshots in the distance. The sound spooked her.

Bruce ignored them.

She struggled to move her hand to touch his shoulder. "How long—"

He didn't look up. "Relax, Gracie. We're not leaving without you." He started working on her right boot. "Rich, tell Dasher to send down the basket."

When he leaned back, her feet finally free, he was breathing hard. "Now it gets tricky. Hold on, Gracie." He disappeared from her line of sight.

The plane shifted. She screamed. Bruce grabbed the back of her flight suit at the neck as she slid. "Freeze!"

The wreckage settled again. With painful slowness he reached across to her good shoulder and brought her toward him. "Rich, get the cable and come around behind me." Now it was Bruce who sounded spooked.

Wind whipped up as a Pave Hawk circled lower. Seen from below, it looked like a big black deadly bird. A steel cable was lowering. The gunfire was getting closer. *Hurry, guys. Please hurry.*

"This is going to hurt like crazy, but there's no other way to get you out. The vest will protect your shoulder from the worst of the shocks. You'll feel the pressure as it inflates," Bruce said, slipping something gray around her.

She closed her eyes as his shirt brushed across her face.

"I don't want you to try to help me. Just stay relaxed and limp. I'm going to be lifting you out from behind."

The fear at that idea was intense.

He leaned around to see her face, and his eyes burned with intensity as he studied her. "I won't hurt your shoulder. Trust me."

She believed he would try but everything hurt.

The vest inflated, the pressure tightened to the point of pain. His hands slid behind her back. "On three." She cried out at the movement, unable to prevent it, every bone and muscle in her body coiling away from the pain.

For a moment she swung in the air with only the strength of his arms keeping her from tumbling. Then his partner grasped her legs and she was lowered down. The relief to be lying down was enormous.

Bruce knelt beside her, rapidly securing straps. He looked dangerous kneeling there, very much the soldier he was. Blood from his hand dripped on her face; he grimaced and wiped it away. "Sorry."

"'s okay."

He locked the cable onto the stretcher. "Take her up, Rich. I'm going to destroy what's left of this plane."

Rich leaned over and attached Bruce's cable instead. "I've already got the charges planted. Get out of here."

Bruce shared a look with his partner, then looked down at her. "Close your eyes. We're going up."

He looked up and touched his radio. "Raise us, Dasher." Before she could get ready for it, the stretcher was lifting from the ground. The sky circled above her as the stretcher spun.

Bruce covered her face as they approached the helicopter, protecting her from the intense wind. He was dangling from a cable beside the stretcher being hoisted to a chopper with gunfire going on below them. He did this for a living. The assumptions she'd had about PJs had changed. It took something more than bravery to do this job.

"Grab her."

She felt hands grasp the stretcher at her feet and it stopped spinning. Metal scraped against metal as she was pulled inside.

The relief was overwhelming. *Thank You, Lord. Thank You.*

Her stretcher was lifted a foot and clamps locked it down. Striker swung in beside her and rapidly unlocked the cable. "Get Rich out of there." The cable was swung out and lowered again. "What do we have?"

"A reinforced squad of rebels trying to work down the pass. They won't get past."

"I never thought they would."

Watching a guy smile in face paint was interesting, as was watching him while lying flat on her back.

The soldier beside her winked at her then looked at Striker. "What took you so long?"

"She was sitting on a live sidewinder."

Her eyes flew to Bruce's at that comment.

"I figured you didn't need to know."

She swallowed hard just thinking about what could have happened. No wonder he had been so insistent she not try to move.

He ripped open a package from his bag. He drenched a sterile bandage in water and carefully wiped away the worst of the blood on her face. "How's the headache?"

"Horrible."

"Any double vision?"

"Hard to tell. You did a good job with the face paint."

"Feeling better I see."

She winced when he touched her nose. It felt broken. "Is Thunder okay?"

"Peter?"

"Down in Iraq," she whispered.

"The Twenty-seventh went after him." Striker looked forward to Dasher. "Did you hear anything?"

"A broken arm. He's fine."

She supposed it was relative. In their business, being alive was the yardstick by which success or failure was judged.

Rich was pulled aboard.

"Dasher, get us out of here," Rich yelled forward. "I rigged them for four minutes."

The chopper tipped nose down and headed east. It was nothing like flying a plane; she was glad the stretcher was latched down.

"Wiggle your toes, Gracie."

She did, despite the hurt.

"Good. Any numbness?"

"No."

"How about your ribs?"

"Sore. It's just my shoulder."

"Twenty minutes and we'll have a doctor looking at it."

She had to know if she would fly again. It was her whole life. "How bad?"

"You're alive," Bruce replied softly.

She closed her eyes. He was right. She was alive. "I owe you two dinner."

For the first time his hand shook as he brushed her cheek. "And your dog tags." He tucked a survival blanket around her, designed to trap in the warmth. "Close your eyes and rest."

She accepted his advice and sank back into the darkness, letting herself relax.

THIRTY-THREE

★ ★ ★

NAPLES, ITALY

The hospital corridor was too narrow and too short, making it hard to pace, and the overhead lights had an annoying flicker in them. Bruce found his boots echoing in the corridor matched his headache. The other PJs had stepped downstairs to try and find out what they could about the strikes now going on within Iraq. The retaliation for a shot down pilot had been swift.

Jesus, please. There weren't words for the prayer, only emotions. He wiped at the blood on his hands, finding them shaking as he tried to focus. He'd held it together for the last hour, but it was hitting him now. Someone had shot down her plane. The reality kept bumping into the disbelief that it happened. He was grateful he had the moment to himself because he was ready to admit he never again wanted to deal with such a night. The image of her in the cockpit, the unseeing gaze— Ecuador had been nothing compared to this.

One of the swinging doors at the end of the corridor burst open. Bruce turned, braced for another reporter having gotten past the security. "Wolf! Wolf, she's going to be okay." He stepped in front of the SEAL and nearly got trampled. "Easy."

"Where—"

Bruce stopped the man and squeezed his shoulder tight. "Surgery."

Wolf went pale. Bruce pushed him up against the wall, knowing exactly how he felt.

"I was working on a collapsed bridge outside Incirlik, trying to shore it up so relief convoys could use it, when Bear found me. You brought her to Naples. What, why—?"

"She made a mess of her shoulder. They want to stabilize the pain and send her stateside as soon as they can, possibly tonight. It's a bit like operating on a pianist's fingers; they don't want to do the detailed work here."

"The press—"

Bruce nodded. "I saw them outside. They're swarming. Another reason to get her stateside."

"She's going to hate the attention."

Bruce would have smiled; he knew a bit of what it was like after getting the deluge of mail from his own recent encounter with the press, but his heart was too heavy. "Not as much as she's going to hate being grounded."

"She'll fly again?"

Bruce looked at his friend, just looked. And felt like his heart was breaking.

"Bruce—"

He shook his head.

"No. It will kill her not to fly," Wolf whispered.

"I know."

Bruce could only hope she remembered God still loved her and he still loved her, when she heard the news. Grief was going to hit Grace hard, and his own personal nightmare was beginning. She was going stateside tonight…and he was returning to Turkey.

Wolf punched the wall.

Grace gagged at the taste in her mouth and felt heat like she was baking in the desert sand. She fought through the incredible thirst and the pressure in her chest, the sensation she was fighting g-pressures that would crush her.

"Easy. It's just a dream."

"Wolf?"

"Right here, Gidget."

"Where were you when I needed you?" she whispered.

"Gracie —" The pain in Wolf's voice was incredible.

From the other side of the bed a hand reached for hers and tightened. "Honey, he's been here," Bruce said, coming to the defense of his friend.

She kept looking at Wolf. "Fourth grade. Carrie."

Her cousin blinked, then laughed. "Still aggravated with me over that one, are you?"

"Same blasted shoulder." She fought to lick her lips. "Hurts worse this time."

"I know it does," Wolf said gently.

Bruce rubbed his thumb across the back of her hand. Grace interlaced her fingers with his. "Surgery...over."

"You came through it just fine," Bruce said.

She wiggled her toes. "All my fingers, all my toes..." She smiled against the old rhyme and closed her eyes. "Where am I?"

Bruce slipped her an ice chip. "Naples."

"That's not good."

"Turkey didn't have a standing hospital that had room for you."

"Okay."

"Or the press," Wolf added.

"Famous, huh?"

"Your picture has already made CNN. Your friends are doing a good job talking about you—so far saying only nice things. I got to see Jill on TV tonight."

"Really?" She attempted a smile at that news. She was fighting to stay with them. "I'm tired, guys."

"We'll let you sleep." Bruce leaned over and kissed her cheek, then moved to release her hand. She held on. "Pray for me before you go," she whispered. She saw tears come into his eyes. "Pray Ephesians 1:17."

His hand tightened around hers. "Jesus, I pray that Grace will know You better and better and better...." He leaned over and kissed her. "I love you, Grace."

"Ditto." She looked over at her cousin. "No penguins."

He laughed so hard he had to wipe his eyes. "Gracie, you're priceless."

Bruce sat down on the bench near Wolf. Dawn was breaking. They would be transporting Grace soon, returning her to the States. Wolf was turning an envelope in his hands, letting it slip to one end and tap against his finger, turn, and slide to the other corner. "What do you have?" Bruce asked.

"Grace wrote me a 'just in case' letter before she deployed last year. I put it in my Bible. I wanted to be reminded that something could be worst than what happened tonight, so I opened it." He turned the letter and offered it. "Read it."

Because of the pain in his friend's eyes, Bruce accepted the letter. "You're sure?"

"Yes."

Bruce slipped out the page of paper and read.

Wolf ~

Grace. This is a letter that I know you are going to hate reading. It's okay to be mad at me. I promised not to die on you and if you're reading this, I broke my word. I'm sorry. Whatever I did or didn't do, I messed up. I should have been more careful.

Okay, apologies over. Now tough it out while I embarrass you. You know how I like to have the last word. ☺

Tom, you've been my best friend since childhood. No one could wish for a better cousin. I know all about the broken dates with Shelly when you came to spend Friday nights with me after I busted my arm. You refused to let me whimper at a disaster that nearly ended my career before it began. It's nice being special.

Over the years I've tried not to embarrass you too often with my mushy words, but I can't resist this last opportunity. I love you. I've been blessed to have you as family. No one taught me more about seizing life and living my dreams than you.

I forgive you for scaring the daylights out of me more times than I can count. I think the Lord must have assigned a special guardian angel to watch out for you. You have defied gravity, dodged bullets, and accomplished impossible missions, most of which I know exist only because you frequently disappeared for a few months. I am so PROUD of you.

There has been no better career than flying a Hornet. For helping me reach that dream—thank you doesn't cut it. And I still owe you for the lessons. (I know for a fact you helped pay for those initial lessons. Dad told me you were the source of that special savings account that magically appeared when I was seventeen. Nice, Wolf. Very nice.)

Would you do me a favor and get married, have kids, and be a special dad in their lives? You keep putting it off. The one regret I have is that Ben and I always said there was plenty of time. He died and I lost an opportunity to seize part of my dream. I chose to let the obstacles of combining military and civilian life push back a decision to get married. Be smarter than I was about that decision.

Life has been good. Very good. I'm sorry for the years when I gave you cause to worry about me. You know me, buddy. I grieve slowly and have to think everything through many times before I move on. Your prodding was comforting because I knew you cared. Thanks for that.

If I can't have life, heaven's an even better option.

All my love, Grace

P.S. If my car is still running, it's now yours. Think about me every time you argue with the carburetor.

Bruce read the letter twice, then slowly folded and handed it back. "She loves you."

Wolf was fighting to keep his composure. He got up to pace.

Bruce watched him and didn't say anything else. Those three words said it all.

THIRTY-FOUR

★ ★ ★

APRIL 6

NORFOLK, VIRGINIA

"Can I get you anything?"

The intense pain had changed to a dull ache. Grace tried to fight off the anesthetic to be able to coherently answer Jill. "You're the best friend in the whole wide world."

"And you're still a little foggy with painkillers."

Grace tried to smile, well aware she felt like she was floating. "Probably." She was aware in a detached way that the surgery she had been dreading ever since the doctors had begun taking pictures was over. "Day or night?"

"Day. Bruce called."

She forced open her eyes. Her friend swam into focus. "Bruce called…"

Jill tucked the blanket across her chest. "You talked to him."

Her brow furrowed. "I did?"

"I translated for him at the end of it."

Bruce had called and she hadn't been coherent. "Wonderful."

"It's okay." Jill smiled. "He just needed to hear your voice."

"Did I sing old nursery rhymes?"

"You tried. You don't sing very well."

"Suppose he still likes me?"

"Oh yeah."

Quiet stretched in the recovery room. Bruce had been a tower of strength even long distance; his calm words the one source of confidence as her life spiraled out of control. Some of his notes even came by telegram as he tried to be what she needed. *"When the cares of my heart are many, Thy steadfast love, O Lord, help me up."* She'd memorized the last telegram from him.

"It's hard when they are far away," Jill whispered.

Grace nudged a finger against her friend's hand. "I've got you here to stand in for them."

"You're going to be okay."

"I'm going to be okay," Gracie agreed. She was alive. She could work on it from there. "Are Mom and Dad here?"

"Out in the hall."

"Wipe my tears before they come in."

"Sure." Jill carefully did so.

"Do I look awful?"

"You look like you're a little older, a little wiser." Jill reassured. "What do you want to tell the press?"

"Go away?"

Jill chuckled. "You're a little more famous than that."

"Be my spokesman for a few more days. Give Dad an exclusive."

"Sounds like a plan." Jill offered the water glass. "I'm glad you're home."

"So am I. Wish Bruce were here."

"I wish Wolf were here."

"We've got good taste in guys." Grace groaned as she tried to move. "It's bad."

"It will get better."

Grace sighed. "Get Mom and Dad. I'll smile a while."

Bruce ~

I am printing this with my own left hand. I'm alive. Surgery

over. I love you. GET ME OUT OF HERE.
Gracie

Grace ~

Oh, honey…left or right handed—it is so nice to get your notes. Wolf volunteered to help me with the hospital break.… I love you too.
Bruce

THIRTY-FIVE

★ ★ ★

APRIL 14

NORFOLK, VIRGINIA

"May I come in?" Peter paused in the doorway to her hospital room.

Grace folded the *International Herald* one handed. The sun was shining, her headache had finally disappeared for good, and the newspaper just frustrated her with news about the situation overseas. Her friends were getting shot at and there was nothing she could do. There had been another game of chicken in Iraq yesterday. "I'd enjoy the company."

"I don't remember the pink fuzzy feet."

Grace smiled at her CO and wiggled the bunny feet. "A gift from Jill. They released you to wander the hall."

"About time. The doctors are driving me crazy." She could agree with him there. Peter looked better than the last time she had briefly seen him—the bruises fading, the cast on his arm beginning to lose its bright wet whiteness. Peter had had an interesting thirty minutes on the ground in Iraq. She would rather have her landing than his. He pulled over a chair.

"The penguin jokes are for real." She tugged out a cartoon from her scrapbook; it had arrived this morning from the guys in the squadron. "I think this one is my favorite." A big line of penguins had strapped on the obligatory pilot scarf and goggles and were getting ready to launch from the top of a cliff.

"They sent me a shovel and pail for a sandbox."

She laughed at the image. "You have to give the guys credit; they believe in squadron unity." She'd heard that penguin patches with bandaged wings were beginning to appear on flight jackets.

"Can I get you anything?"

"The right to stay here another two months? I'm going to be disappointed when they kick me out of the hospital to get back their room. The service is first rate." Her shoulder ached, but the sharp pain had disappeared after the second surgery. "The physical therapist is by three times a day, and I got lobster for dinner last night."

He smiled but it faded. "Grace—"

"I know what they're saying, Peter. I don't believe them." She'd never taken a no that she couldn't fly as final before, and she wasn't about to accept one offered by a doctor who could in reality only give her averages and percentages of those able to come back after an injury like hers. "How's your arm?" It was strange to realize broken bones were easier for a pilot to come back from than soft tissue injuries.

He rapped the hard cast. "Desk bound for a while."

"I'm sorry I wasn't able to prevent it."

"I've watched the tapes. Our tactics were good. Two against four and restrictions on who could fire first was a tragedy like this waiting to happen."

She'd been replaying it in her mind numerous times, but it was reassuring to hear him say it.

Grace pointed to the papers. "I've been reading about what is going on, watching CNN. We're missing out on the action." The U.S. had launched a massive raid into Iraq in retaliation, pounding the military airports and radar network, making last year's strike look small.

"I know what you mean about being on the sidelines. But at least one good benefit came out of our skirmish. It reminded everyone there really was a big kid on the block it would be best not to provoke. Syria has started pulling back military units, if not back to prior positions, at least back from the border with Turkey."

"Is it true the *GW* deployment is being extended?"

"Another two months."

The physical therapist knocked on the door. "Ready, Lieutenant?"

Grace glanced at her boss as she struggled to her feet. "If they ever try to get you on the pulley machine, shoot the thing and put yourself out of misery before you begin."

Peter handed her a water bottle. "I've heard you are killing the stationary bike."

She grinned. "Practice. I plan to be able to beat Striker at a bike race some day."

Bruce ~

Four miles on the bike, pulse 72 resting, bp 115 / 70, temp 98.4. I squeezed the tennis ball 602 times today. I would have reached the goal of four digits but my doctor interrupted, spoiling my count. It will be another few days before they let me start working on mobility in my shoulder. Right now the arm is strapped against my chest to prevent any movement.

I'm pecking this note out one letter at a time on a borrowed laptop. Do you have any idea how hard it is to use a mouse left-handed? This letter will probably disappear somewhere unrecoverable before it can get printed.

I can't believe the first plane I crashed came with a multimillion-dollar price tag. A good thing they don't threaten to take it out of my paycheck—I'd be in debt for the rest of my life. I miss my plane: every bell, switch, and button of it. It was a good lady that didn't deserve that kind of ending. At least my one horrible landing in life has now happened.

I am convinced your note on Ephesians 1:17 and your prayer for me were God's preparations for what was coming. That single prayer, that I may know God better, has transformed how I am able to handle this. That first night stateside, when the painkillers weren't taking effect, I flipped through pages in my Bible. I found again the verse written by Paul: "He said to me, 'My grace is sufficient for you, for my power is made perfect in weakness.' I will all the more gladly boast of my weaknesses, that the power of Christ may rest upon me."

I'm getting a good chance to live it. The moments of being overwhelmed come often, and I'm finding the verse something to cling to. God is sufficient for even this.

If it sounds like I am together about this tragedy…the reality is I'm too scared to even think about it not working out. So I am refusing to let doubt have even a glimmer of my thoughts. I don't know what awaits me when the therapist says I've made all the progress she thinks I can make. I desperately want to fly again.

I am working hard to get that recovery off to a good start. No one says the weakness in my shoulder will be permanent or that the mobility won't come back. They just give odds against it happening. Needless to say, it's not what I want to hear.

I'm so disappointed I was out of it during your last call. I admit I cried a bit when the meds finally wore off enough for me to realize what had happened. Jill was able to tell me what you said. Bruce, next time you are able to call, I promise I'll be talking at least coherently.

I know it's not a good thing to suggest you are replacing Ben in my life, but there is one way I want to say a special note of thanks. The one thing Ben always had was a long horizon perspective. In your notes, I hear that same sense of calm about life and events and the passage of time. I appreciate it. When the days seem incredibly long, your letters are a great comfort. I've reread them many times.

I am glad you are at the end of this letter. Please be careful and stay safe. I love you more and more with every passing day. Jill says I can borrow Emily when I get home and I'm looking forward to that. I never had a pet and she's priceless.

All my love, Grace

Grace –

You are the best thing that ever came into my life. I'm dripping water on this pad of paper (don't ask), and the mail guy is standing here waiting to take my reply. I know you're hurting. It's killing me that I'm not there to be with you and that a phone is so far away. Lean hard against God and trust Him. Don't give the doctors too much grief. Spoil Emily for me.

All my love, Bruce

APRIL 18
NORFOLK, VIRGINIA

"How many miles are you planning to ride?"

Grace wiped sweat off her face, feeling like it had already been a marathon distance. "How many have I done?"

Jill leaned over to see the bike counter. "Four."

"Make it six."

"You're stubborn."

"Bored." And growing more convinced each day it was going to take a miracle to get back in shape.

"Do you want to see the latest clippings? You made a couple more newspapers and your second magazine."

"How much mail?"

"You're going to be answering get well cards for a year."

"I owe Bruce an apology. I laughed when he told me about his mail."

"Do you want me to bring any particular movie over tonight?"

"Nothing even remotely like realism; find a cartoon."

"Bruce is converting you."

"Circumstances are," Grace admitted. "Tell Emily hi for me."

"Will do."

The bike mileage finally passed six miles. Grace slowed her pace and began to cool down.

There was a letter from Bruce on her bed when Grace got back to the room. She read it as she squeezed the tennis ball trying to build up the strength in her hand. The paper had curled in spots where water drops had dried. Curious, she smoothed it out. The letter smelled like rotten eggs. *Bruce, what are you into now?* He hadn't been able to call and she knew him—if he was anywhere near where he could get an overseas line he would have.

Jesus, please keep him safe. I worry about him, even more so because I know his thoughts are with me and not totally on the job at hand. Keep him safe and focused.

She could not imagine going through this without him. The day they made this relationship permanent would be the best day of her life. The reality of his job—she'd encountered it firsthand and she was so proud of him. *Please bring him home safe and sound.*

APRIL 24

BIRECIK DAM, TURKEY

Water was finally flowing. Bruce stood on the observation deck of the dam, watching the water flow through the sluice gates. He had stripped down to blue shorts and a cotton T-shirt, was on his fifth water bottle, and felt like he was still baking inside the rubber dry suit. He'd lost at least fifteen pounds during the last week of diving.

The earth had hiccupped; there was no other way to describe what they found. The vent had created a layer of acidic water so toxic, it had spread like a blanket and turned the area around the vent into a white graveyard. It had hovered there like a bubble within the water.

It was a good thing the dam's power plant had not been able to come back online. It would have created a current and spread the destruction throughout the reservoir. Instead, the toxic bubble of death had stayed pretty well defined. They spent ten days creating a pipe network able to withstand the acid, working in wet suits to get the tubing down to the floor of the reservoir, vacuuming and sucking the pocket of acidic water out and into a hazardous chemical tanker.

There was a lot more treatment of the water still to be done, and they had been forced to build a network of intake valves out a half-mile farther into the reservoir, but water was finally flowing. Getting power generation online would take several more days.

"Bruce."

He turned and found Wolf leaning against the stair railing one level down.

"Bear has got a flight coming in to get us to Incirlik. Twenty minutes."

"I'll be there."

Wolf paused. "You okay?"

It was too complex to try and answer that. He simply nodded. "Tired. Tell Bear thanks." Grace was coping without his being there. He was spending his days without her. And there were days he didn't want to live with that sacrifice any longer.

THIRTY-SIX

★ ★ ★

MAY 4

NORFOLK, VIRGINIA

Pull it," the therapist encouraged.

Grace strained against the pulley, using her injured arm to try to lift the weight behind her. She slowly straightened her right arm, fighting the quivering muscles to keep the pull steady and smooth.

"Hold."

Grace clenched her teeth and held it.

"Good. Lower it slowly."

Grace focused on a spot on the far wall and slowly let the weight down, lifting her arm the most painful of the movements in the exercise.

"Relax."

Grace reached with her left hand for the water bottle. Twenty reps with a five-pound weight and her injured muscles felt like jelly. The hospital rehab room was becoming her second home. She had to give them credit: They knew how to work someone right to the edge of exhaustion and stop before injury would happen from the workout.

"Muscle tone is coming back."

"Some," Grace agreed. "Mobility isn't."

"You'll be lifting weights over your head in a month."

Since she could barely lift her right arm level with her shoulder at the moment, Grace had to take the therapist's words on faith. "I hope so."

"I'll see you again in three hours. You want to spend some time on the bike?"

Grace got up from the bench and scooped up her towel. "It sure beats walking the halls."

Overall she was getting back in shape, but her shoulder was taking its own time to heal. She picked up the tennis ball and started squeezing it. Her shoulder might be weak, but some of that she could compensate for by better conditioning her arm muscles and hand strength.

She got on the bike and started a steady ride. They were letting her go home Monday. The doctors were pleased with their work. But they were being noncommittal about her coming back far enough to get cleared to fly. She'd impressed them, but not enough for them to change their odds.

She did not want to go home, was afraid that meant out of sight, out of mind, in a nice kind of way. The press was following her progress—the first female pilot to get shot down. If there was any question on her recovery, she was sure the Navy would prefer her not to fly again. If they let her fly and something happened...

She had to fly again. She just had to. She picked up the pace on the bike.

Grace ~

How's my special lady doing? I miss you, honey. I'm thrilled with the news they are letting you go home. Jill has been sending me updates too, so I admit to knowing all about the mail, and the change in movie tastes, and the fact you tend to pace when you are frustrated. On my behalf, please enjoy a sunset, an ice cream cone, and watch at least one baseball game first pitch to last. (I know you can't sit still that long, but we have to work on it.)

I caught a clip of CNN and got to see you LIVE and

STANDING and joking around with the reporters. That was so much fun. I've threatened to have Jill show up with a video camera to tape one of these workouts I hear about, but I haven't been able to find a VCR while I'm stuck out here in nowhere land.

I'll calling Monday night if at all possible. I've been pulling strings to be able to get to a phone. Honey, joking aside, I know recovery is slower than you would like. One day at a time, Grace. Wherever this goes, God loves you, I love you, and the answer hasn't been written yet. I am praying for you.

Love, Bruce
Psalm 18:35

Thou hast given me the shield of thy salvation, and thy right hand supported me, and thy help made me great.

MAY 7
NORFOLK, VIRGINIA

She was home. And she was desperately afraid this was what her life had become. Grace tossed her socks toward the clothes hamper. It was so atrociously quiet in her apartment. She missed the noise of the aircraft carrier.

She curled up on her bed with her big pillow, fighting the blue mood. Emily jumped up beside her and flopped over on her side. Grace would have normally nudged her back down, but instead just reached over and stroked the dog's head.

Emily was old, peaceful, and content. Good company. Grace looked at the clock. Bruce had said he would call tonight if possible. She translated the seven-hour time difference and watched the clock tick away the minutes.

Jesus, I can't imagine being a civilian. The word sounds foreign to me. I can be involved in the Navy even if I'm not flying, but it would be like salt in this aching loss. What do I do? The last thing Bruce needs is to marry someone who isn't grounded and comfortable with life. I want to fly. It's the one thing I have always wanted to do. What do I do if I can't?

She rubbed her shoulder, feeling a burning sense of heat deep in the shoulder. In the quiet of the apartment the reality of what was probably coming was impossible to avoid. She looked at the pictures on the wall, her history at a glance. The Cessna she had soloed in at seventeen, her first days in uniform. The wall ended with a picture of the jet with her name on it, a jet that was no more. Just looking at the pictures made her sad.

I'm having a pity party. This is awful.

She punched the pillows and nestled down and got comfortable. She was alive, and there had been moments during the crash she hadn't thought she would be. When she got over the fact she'd crashed her plane, maybe it wouldn't feel so awful.

The phone rang as she was dozing.

"Hi, honey." The connection was good; Bruce sounded near.

"It's so good to hear your voice." She snuggled the phone close. She had thought he would never be able to get through. And on the night she was hurting… There was no rush to find words. Just hearing his voice was wonderful.

"You're home."

She smiled. "I'm home. It's nice to have my own pillow. And your flowers are beautiful, all of them. Jill had the apartment ready for me. Fresh flowers, fruit, books, movies… I could see a few of your suggestions in the items she brought. She's been taking great care of me, even though it has put her behind in her own work."

"You're her best friend, Grace. She wants to be able to help however she can. How's the press and the mail?"

She tried to laugh. "Increasing in volume by the day. How in the world I became a hero by getting shot down is beyond me."

"I know what the media is like when it swarms. Physical therapy is coming along? You said they were transferring you?"

"I'm working out in the pool now. They eventually want to get me to rotate my arm through a full stroke when I swim."

"It will come. Give it time."

"I want to be able to fly," she whispered, so afraid she would not be able to.

"I know you do. I know. I love you, honey."

Hearing it in words made her tremble. "I love you too."

"Grace, what is it?"

"I feel like I'm making you a consolation prize."

Silence stretched between them.

"I'm okay with that. *Console* is a huge word, a healing word. Lean against what we have, Grace. It will help. You haven't lost everything."

She twisted the phone cord around her fingers. "Are you coming home?"

"I'm sorry, Grace. Five more weeks, maybe seven."

Her disappointment was acute. "I'll be waiting for you."

"I'm going to hug you for a very long time."

"Promise?"

He choked back emotion. "I promise," he whispered.

She dashed away tears, knowing this wasn't fair to him. "I'll be okay, Bruce. Really."

"Take it a day at a time, honey. A day at a time."

She struggled to change the subject. "Are you sleeping, eating, taking care of yourself?"

He chuckled. "I've got Wolf acting like a mother hen. What did you say to him?"

"I asked him to make sure you got home safely."

"He doesn't believe in doing something in moderation."

She smiled. "No. He doesn't."

"Don't worry about me, Grace. I'm coming home just so I can enjoy your company in person, for a long time to come."

"I'll meet your flight if I can."

"Deal. Spoil Emily for me."

"Not a problem. She's been a real joy already."

"I've got to go." He sounded disappointed; she felt disappointed.

"Okay."

"I love you."

"I love you too."

She hung up the phone and watched it, already wishing it would ring again. Emily nuzzled her hand. Grace hugged her. "If you want to get up, I'll fix us a late night snack and we can watch a stupid movie."

The dog jumped down from the bed. Grace got up. She didn't want to go to sleep sad. *Jesus, help lift my spirits. I don't like this sadness.*

She curled up on the couch with a bowl of ice cream and flipped channels. "What about John Wayne? It's that movie Bruce mentioned ages ago." She settled down to watch the movie, wishing Bruce were here to share it. Being alone was the pits.

The phone rang as the movie was concluding at 2 A.M.

INCIRLIK AIR BASE, TURKEY

Bruce tossed small rocks at the big rocks, watching them bounce off. Wolf found him down at the flight line shortly after midnight. "You okay?"

"What's that supposed to mean—okay? No, I'm not okay." Bruce got to his feet to pace, still stewing hours after the call to Grace because he couldn't figure out a letter to send her that would help the problem rather than make it worse. "She's hurting, she's at home, and I'm not there to encourage her."

It was 0700 in Virginia; Grace was probably just getting breakfast. He hoped she had gone downstairs to the bakery where they would fuss over her. She needed someone to fuss over her, and having his sister and his dog stand in for him was a lousy set of alternatives. Grace would get through it without him. That was the problem. She shouldn't have to get through this without him.

Wolf stopped in front of him, crowding his space. "Jill walked in on a burglary last night."

Bruce felt like Wolf had just punched him. "What! Is she hurt?"

"She twisted her knee when she got pushed down the porch steps."

Jill. The blood left his face. "Where's the nearest phone?" A burglar. And he'd let her get away with dismissing the problem last year after the burglaries stopped.

Wolf stopped him. "Grace is at the hospital with her. I told her we'd call at the top of the hour."

Bruce clamped his hand down on Wolf's shoulder. "What exactly did she say?"

Wolf loosed his bruising grip. "It was Grace on the phone, calling from the hospital; Scott was with her. It's not too bad. Jill was on the way to have a scan done of her knee. If nothing is torn, she may get off with crutches and ice to deal with the swelling."

"Did they catch the guy? Tell me Scott caught the guy."

"Not yet. He stole Jill's car—she'd parked it out front so she could unload sacks. Grace says Jill's fighting mad about that fact, but Scott is confident they will be able to catch the guy because of it."

Bruce couldn't believe it. "Her car."

Wolf looked at him, and his attempt to be calm and steady about it gave way to the emotion he was feeling too. "They are both hurt," Wolf said, fury in his voice. "What are we doing over here?"

"I know." Bruce shoved his hands through his hair. "We can't get home."

"I can swim the Atlantic if you can."

"Tonight I'm tempted to try."

THIRTY-SEVEN

★ ★ ★

MAY 8

NORFOLK, VIRGINIA

She couldn't just leave her here. Grace watched Jill struggle to balance on crutches and open the refrigerator. Her friend needed a helping hand.

"No, you can't stay on the couch."

"Did I ask?"

"I know that expression." Jill balanced the carton of orange juice on top of the open refrigerator door as she looked back at her. "I wrenched my knee. I'm home now. I don't need a nurse. You've been up all night and you look worse than I do."

"Jilly—"

"Just let me enjoy being mad and in a snarly mood for a while, okay? The man stole and wrecked my car."

"We can buy you a new one."

"I hope they throw the book at him."

"Nine burglaries—it was probably his last joy ride for a very long time."

"I wish I'd had my pepper spray out and had a chance to give him a face full of it."

"I'm staying. Bad moods are no fun if there's no one around to agree with you," Grace replied. She'd been having a pity party watching a movie and eating ice cream while her friend was lying hurt. That reality made her miserable.

"Please—this isn't your fault. I should have listened to Scott

and learned my lesson about visiting clients' homes after dark."
Jill awkwardly maneuvered into the other room. "Besides needing
a nap, you've got therapy at one. You're not missing it because of
me."

"I can skip a day without it killing me."

"Grace, no. You're not giving up. Skip one day and you'll let
yourself mentally decide it was no big deal. It is."

"Maybe it would be best."

"Do you really believe that?"

Grace finally shook her head.

"Then go to therapy and swim your heart out. As a therapist
told me this morning, pain is good." The phone rang. "Get that
for me?"

Grace stepped back in the kitchen. "Hello?"

"I found someone who might have a lead on a used car," Peter
said.

Grace pulled free a notepad piece of paper. She had known
her boss would come through. Jill would give her fits if she knew
she was doing this, but her friend needed a car and it was one
hassle Grace could handle for her. Bruce had asked for her help.
He was worse than miserable at hearing what had happened, and
this was the least she could do. "Okay, shoot."

"Tom Dantello, retired Navy. The car belongs to his sister or
his cousin, something like that. It's a six-year-old Honda Civic,
seventy-two thousand miles. He's handling the sale for her, and
she needs to sell the car before she moves so it's got a reasonable
price. He lives out on Terrace Drive."

"I know the area." And she knew the name.

"How's Jill doing?"

Grace smiled. "Throwing me out. I'm not a very good nurse. I
appreciate the lead on the car."

"Glad I could help."

Jill had settled on the couch and turned on the television. "You're on the news."

Grace glanced over and winced. "Shut it off."

"You look cute. All wet and irritated with the reporter's microphone in your face. What did he ask you?"

"What reporters always ask. Inane questions. He caught me just outside physical therapy Friday and wanted to know how I was doing."

"You have to admit, you're news."

"When I fly again, it will be news. You've got the pain pills and the muscle relaxants?"

"And the ice pack, the phone, and a bag of M&Ms."

"I'm heading out, but I'm coming back at six with a stack of movies."

"Deal. And thanks for letting me borrow Emily for the day."

Grace looked at the dog stretched out on the rug and smiled. "Watching her sleep is a fascinating way to spend your time. She snores. And when she hiccups she scares herself."

That had to be the car. It was still dripping from a recent washing, and the way the water beaded it had a good wax job. The For Sale sign in the back window was sagging. The license plates would expire in another two months. There was a slight touch of rust on the back left fender. Grace knew Jill would like the dark blue color. She probably wouldn't like the fact the car was up on blocks and somebody was under it, tinkering, a toolbox open on the driveway.

It presented an interesting dilemma. Grace scanned the car as she leisurely strolled up the drive to see what was going on. An extension cord had been run out for the tape deck. She touched a rocking tennis shoe with her shoe and the whistling stopped. The shoes were size eleven Reeboks, long ago white. A thick gnarly hand appeared on the car bumper. The board rolled out from under the car. He was wearing a black T-shirt to go with the jeans, near white hair tucked under a blue bandanna, and his tan looked baked in.

"I'm here about the car?"

An interesting play of emotions crossed his face. "Life got a rewind?"

"Sure. Want me to come back up the drive?"

"Only if you whistle louder than me this time." He rolled the rest of the way out from under the car and got to his feet. He wiped off his hands. "It's not what you think. I thought the car was going into storage for the next few months. I was changing the oil."

"Change your mind about selling it?"

"You still interested?"

"Depends on whether you're as good a mechanic as you were a pilot," she replied, now confident she had indeed placed the name. "It's a pleasure to meet the legend of the green board. No one is ever going to eclipse your third wire landing streak." She offered her hand. "Lieutenant Yates, VFA-83."

He took it. "Now that brings back memories. You'd be the Grace I've seen on TV."

"Guilty." She nodded toward the car. "What are you asking for it?"

"Twelve hundred."

"Throw in the Sweetwater Trio tape and you've got yourself a deal."

"You don't want to at least drive it?"

"I fly better than I drive, or at least I used to."

"Smacking into the ground?" He winked at her. "That wasn't so much of a crash. I put one into the sea, one into enemy head-quarters, and let's not forget the one into the side of the airport tower."

She chuckled. "They show the tapes to every nugget in the squadron."

"I heard I had been immortalized. That's what I get for growing up to be a test pilot."

"Could I ask you something?"

"Sure."

"Did they ever tell you you wouldn't fly again?"

"More times than I could count. Want some lemonade? For the purchase of the car, I'll even throw in a few war stories."

"I'd love it."

NAVAL AIR STATION
OCEANA, VIRGINIA

The fighter planes were taking off in pairs from the runway at Naval Air Station, Oceana. Grace followed the flight with her hand lifted to block the sun.

Peter joined her at the fence. "I thought I would find you here."

She glanced at him. "You sent me to see Tom Dantello intentionally."

Her boss smiled. "Now what gave you that idea?"

"You're arranging an attempt for me to try and fly again," she said slowly.

He simply nodded. She would have hugged him, but she was too incredibly scared that breathing would hurt her chances. "When?"

"There's a class coming in from Nevada at the end of next month. They've got a two-week window to do carrier qualifications with the USS *Harry Truman*. I can get your name on the list if you want it."

She bit her lip. "Six weeks. I don't know if I can get medically cleared by then."

"Try."

Such a simple word. The Navy didn't want the black eye of a female pilot getting killed, and sending her back in the air would be a hard call, one that Peter could help push through the system.

Jesus, do I have it in me to do this? She wanted to try. And yet if she reached too soon and wasn't ready, if she reached and failed, it would be over. She slowly nodded. She'd never know if she didn't risk it. "Thank you, Peter."

"Grace, I've been flying with you a long time. You'll catch the third wire."

THIRTY-EIGHT

★ ★ ★

MAY 28

NORFOLK, VIRGINIA

W hat do you think about this wedding dress?"
Grace leaned over to see the magazine Jill held out. "Really
nice." And perfect for Jill. It would make her look tiny
beside Wolf.

"I think so. Think Tom will like it?"

"Oh, I know so."

"I wish they'd get home sooner, versus later."

"Tell me about it." This was the kind of Saturday Grace loved.
Lazy. Peaceful. Talking about guys. Jill got up to change the
music. "You sure you should have ditched the crutches?"

"They made my armpits sore."

"That's because you are not supposed to lean on them."

"My knee is better."

"Which is why you are limping."

"Obviously. What are we doing for dinner?"

Jill did not want to talk about the burglary. Grace understood
that. Jill was impatiently waiting for him to be caught, but other
than that, she was trying to get on with her life. "I vote for order-
ing in."

"Absolutely."

The phone rang. Grace waved her friend back to the couch.
"I'll get it." She picked up her empty glass and headed to the
kitchen. It was Scott.

"They caught him."

Grace whooped for joy and leaned around the doorway to beam at her friend. "Jill, they caught him." She pressed the phone tight wanting the details. "Where?"

"North Carolina. He tried to rob a house and got caught by an angry dog."

"About time."

"Does this mean I'm out of the doghouse?"

Scott had been hanging around Jill lately, helping her when he was off duty. The man was miserable that it had happened. "Bring us over dinner tonight and maybe. It depends on what stories you have to tell on Bruce."

The cop laughed. "I see Jill has been talking. Ever hear about the tackle box?"

"No, I haven't. It sounds interesting."

"It is. I'll bring over pizza in an hour."

Bruce ~

Jill loves the car. She's even named it her blue bomb. She was able to put away the crutches this weekend, and other than having to take stairs slowly she's doing okay. The guy was arrested in North Carolina last night. You could see Scott's relief. He brought over pizza last night when he got off work. I heard a fascinating story about a tackle box.... You've got a good friend in him.

Tell Wolf that Jill found her wedding dress. It's gorgeous. We've been debating various wedding cakes. Come home; I can't wait to see Jill and Wolf married. You'll have a fun time giving her away while also being Wolf's best man. We're talking about music now.

I'm almost afraid to write this as I don't want to jinx it. The doctors cleared me to fly again. Mobility is not great; it's only back 80 percent, but I passed the strength tests and that was the mandatory part. If I survive four days of flying in the simulator, they'll cut the flight orders for the USS *Harry Truman*.

I get one shot at carrier quals along with a class of nuggets. If I miss the grade, I'm out. I'm at peace with that reality. I'm as ready as I'm going to be. Tom Dantello was right: Flying is more mental than physical. I wish you were here to watch. I'm nervous, incredibly nervous.

Grace

Grace –

I'm so glad you have been there to help out Jill. I've been feeling a bit helpless as a big brother lately; there is so little I can do from here. CONGRATULATIONS on getting the medical release. I've been praying fervently that it would happen. A dream has kept you moving forward all your life. Fly the meatball, the glide path, and watch the wind. You can do it, honey. I'm so proud of you just for being willing to try. I do wish I could be there. Know you are in my thoughts.

I love you.

Bruce

THIRTY-NINE

★ ★ ★

JUNE 14

AIRCRAFT CARRIER USS *HARRY TRUMAN*

ATLANTIC OCEAN OFF THE COAST OF VIRGINIA

She would love to catch the third wire, but she'd settle for the first or even the fourth if she could just find the ship. Grace descended through the clouds. Five miles ahead, somewhere, was the USS *Harry Truman.* The Atlantic Ocean was an incredibly big place at night.

Grace fought the sensation of being task saturated as she kept up the scan of sky and instruments. Flying that had been instinctive months before, she was now consciously doing. It wasn't a good sign, and the more she tried to change it, the more she got herself further behind in the mental game. One poor landing and her flying career was over. She came out of the clouds. Where was the ship?

She spotted a yellow line of lights far ahead. She half smiled to herself as she saw it and felt the fear that was always there in a night landing cause her hands to sweat. She really was going to land on that strip of lights.

Entrance into carrier landing pattern was at a point in the sky three miles behind the carrier at eight hundred feet.

She had made four day traps aboard the *Harry Truman* and knew what she should expect in those last seconds of landing. The LSO working tonight was excellent at his job. She was glad the man was there to help get her safely onto the ship.

She scanned outside the cockpit, across the heads-up displays, feeling out the plane. She started the break for the deck and hit the entrance point to the landing pattern high and increased her rate of decent. Her timing was off. At 250 knots she lowered the landing gear and the tailhook.

"624, three quarters of a mile, call the ball," the air controller said.

"624, Hornet ball, 4.5," she replied. The massive meatball yellow light glowed in the night, the bulbs actually dimmed so they didn't shimmer in the night air. The meatball was above the line of green datum lights. She was still high.

She edged down.

So many people were pulling for her to make this—Bruce. Wolf. Jill. Her squadron. The press had been all over her since news she was going to fly again. She just wanted to land safely and get the entire incident behind her. She'd overcorrected and the yellow light notched below the green lights. She increased power.

She was overflying, trying too hard to fly the plane. She could do this, but it felt like she'd never done it before.

The LSO had yet to give her a single correction, either he was comfortable she was on top of the needed corrections or the radio was dead. She preferred to think positively.

Do not be low. She was not going to fly a ramp strike.

She got the light centered, had the centerline, was on the glide slope. Eight seconds to go. She had this landing. She could feel it. If not a perfect approach, it was still going to put her into the third wire.

The bank of lights went flashing red. "Wave off. Foul deck!"

She shoved open full power on afterburners and pulled back hard, putting the Hornet in a rapid climb, knowing she would be shaking the tower windows with the close abort. Adrenaline surged.

"624, Paddles. Digbat problem here. Good approach. We'll give you a clear deck on the next round."

"Paddles, 624. Roger." She breathed deep to relax. She knew all about digbats, a polite word that covered everything from birds on the deck to a caution light on an arresting wire. There was no margin in a landing, and the LSO waving her off had just saved her life. Maybe she shouldn't be doing this. She wanted to marry Bruce, not have him attending her funeral.

She reached angels 10 and turned, flying the downward leg to come back around for another landing approach.

What am I doing wrong?

The mental zone of perfection she normally had when flying was far, far away. *God, I need clarity. Help me.* She had walked nuggets through this mental moment of crisis. She'd been here before.

She wasn't trusting her shoulder and hand to be there; she wasn't comfortable that weakness wouldn't catch her by surprise. The realization came in the moment before she broke again for the landing approach. The crash had been a fluke. She accepted it. She was going to prove it.

She hit the entrance point to the pattern, was lined up, and on a good approach.

"624, three quarters of a mile, call the ball," the air controller said.

"624, Hornet ball, 4.1," she replied.

"624, Paddles. Wind at twenty-nine knots, slightly pitching keel."

"Paddles, 624. Roger."

The finesse started coming back. The meatball hung like a heavy weight right in the center of the green lights, never clicking up or down. The ship grew larger and larger. She crossed the fantail.

She hit hard and slammed open afterburners just in case she had to bolter. The tailhook caught and the Hornet was jerked to a full stop in two seconds. Grace sucked in her breath at the pain that rippled as the restraint harness tightened, stopping what otherwise would have been her forward crash through the windshield.

She'd give herself an okay pass for that landing. Just a touch right in the lineup, maybe a fraction high in the middle, right into the third wire.

Yellow wands were waving at her. She blinked clear her vision and powered back her jet to idle, raised the landing hook. She followed the waving wands not to a parking place but across to catapult 2. She was going to launch and do it all again. Welcome to carrier quals, she thought to herself with a smile, and wondered if she'd have the energy to climb out of the cockpit when the night was over. It had just begun.

FORWARD OPERATING LOCATION

TURKEY/SYRIAN BORDER

"Have you heard anything?"

Bruce stretched out on his bunk, glanced to the door of the tent, and shook his head. "She should be in the middle of quals about now."

"Grace will be able to make it."

"And if she fails?" Bruce couldn't imagine what that would do to her. Failure wasn't a word in Grace's vocabulary. He didn't want her feeling again the sadness that had swamped her after Ben's death. And he knew not being able to fly would cut that deep. She didn't like to fly slow and level; she needed to be flying for the Navy. As much as he wanted her safely being a civilian, he wanted her doing what she loved even more.

"If something happens, she'll brush herself off and try again."

Bruce smiled at Wolf's confidence. "Any word on the mission?"

"We're on standby."

It was just the two of them. Bruce could afford to be honest. "I hope they don't execute this one. It's stupid."

Wolf took a seat on Rich's bunk. "It would be...interesting." That was one way of putting it. There were rumors that Syria was converting a deep oil well complex at Aleppo to go after water, were attempting to drill under Turkey's border and literally into the reservoir complex. Stealing water—it was a fairly creative solution to Syria's problem. One that would toss a match back on a tinderbox they had just got calmed down.

Bruce shook his head at the idea. "They've got to find a diplomatic solution. I wonder how the military brass learned about the Aleppo project?"

"Our defector?" Wolf speculated.

"Then he's doing a lousy job at stopping a war."

"The diplomats talk; the military waits."

"We need rain."

Wolf nodded. "This mission isn't going to get the go-ahead. Calmer minds will step in. Any mail come today?"

"No."

"I got a letter from Jill."

"Did you?"

"A mushy one."

Bruce smiled. "My sister likes being engaged."

"She's going to like being married more."

He laughed. "Probably. She'll change your life."

"She'll try." Wolf opened a can of peanuts. "When are you going to get around to asking Grace?"

Bruce turned his head to look at his friend. "She's got rather a lot on her mind at the moment."

"True. We could have a double wedding."

Bruce sat up. "Interesting idea."

Wolf shrugged. "Otherwise we end up having two weddings a few months apart. You know they'll want to be each other's maid-of-honor. You're my best man, and assuming no ugly stuff happens, I'll probably stand up at yours."

"It has to be their idea."

Wolf smiled. "Since when has that been a problem to make happen?"

Bruce punched his pillow and laid back down, trying to get comfortable on the cot. "We've got too much time on our hands if we're planning wedding details." He thought about it for a minute. "When?"

Wolf laughed.

USS *HARRY TRUMAN*
ATLANTIC OCEAN OFF THE COAST OF VIRGINIA

She had been assigned a temporary bunk aboard ship. Grace would have gone to the dirty-shirt wardroom to unwind with the other pilots renewing their carrier qualifications tonight, but she didn't want to talk about her crash, and among pilots it was a natural question. They'd want to congratulate her for coming back to flight status.

She set down her gloves and her kneepad, the neat cards and the maps showing her hours of preparation for tonight's flights. Takeoffs and landings that she had prepared for with the intensity of a live missile strike. She'd been prepared, overprepared maybe.

Two fairs and an okay. She'd flown better but she'd survived the grade cut. That was the most important fact. Exhausted, she nevertheless stepped out of the flight suit and pulled on a sweat suit. The physical therapist had given her a set of exercises to help stretch out her shoulder muscles after a flight and make sure they didn't stiffen up.

She started stretching her arm and her shoulder, lifting and slowly rotating it to recover from three hours flying where mobility was limited. *Lord, was all this worth it?* She had her wings back, and she was so tired she wondered if it had been the right goal to go after. She'd flown, she'd been shot down, now she was back preparing to fly again. She could have a calm life with Bruce, be there whenever he was able to be home. Instead she was going after the right to continue a job where she would be gone for long stretches of time.

She could tell she was tired. She was doubting decisions she had made. The exercises complete, she changed again and got ready to turn in. She slid back the curtain on the lower bunk to slip in. A letter and a big bouquet of roses were on her bunk. Tears came to her eyes as she carefully lifted the bouquet. The roses were gorgeous.

Grace ~

Consider this the first of what will hopefully be many long love letters. I am so proud of you. Congratulations. I knew you could do it! Nothing gives me more pleasure than to know you are flying and staying true to a dream that goes all the way back to your youth. Wolf figured out the channels to get this letter to you tonight and got the flowers smuggled aboard. I'm glad it was this letter left for you with the flowers, and not the other I also wrote. It's much easier to be happy for you long distance than sad. I would have been as miserable as you, had tonight run into problems.

I'm sitting watching the stars, pleased to know that wherever you are you can share the same view. My life has become so much richer since you entered it. Never doubt that this is worth it, Grace. As much as I want to be there in person to tell you how proud I am of you, know this letter carries my full heart with it. You have pretty eyes, a laugh that makes me smile, and you write wonderful letters. Your picture is wearing out, it gets pulled from my pocket so often. Thinking of you tonight.

Yours, with an ocean of love, Bruce

P.S. You still owe me your dog tags.

Bruce –

I'm so wiped I don't know if I can write a letter that is readable. I FLEW GREAT! The clouds were so white, and the ocean was so huge, and the ship was soooo small. It was everything I remembered from those first flights as a nugget. Pure terror and overflying, and I got a wave off seconds before landing from a digbat problem—I wish I could bottle tonight and share some of this emotion. Adrenaline returns just thinking about it.

I did not think about the crash tonight; something I feared might happen. Frankly, I was too busy remembering everything that used to be second nature. On the whole, I'm very pleased with tonight. I think the roses are incredible. And your letter stupendous. I want to hug you with ink and paper. I'm now crashing, big time, and will probably sleep through my alarm.

I can't put into words why it is so nice to be back aboard a ship floating in the middle of the ocean with planes landing overhead, what makes this place more special than my apartment stateside. Here there is a sense of…it's a corny word…but of destiny, of dreams and hopes and efforts combining to meet at one place.

That said, Bruce, I am reaching the point where I could see walking away from this and being okay with that. I've got the memories and the experience, and while the second time around is stupendous and I'm so thankful to have the opportunity, I can now feel the difference in perspective. If asked to walk away from this, I could probably handle it with that grace you say I have to reflect my name. Just in case we ever need to talk about that option, don't feel like it's taboo to bring up. I'm going to bed and I'm planning to dream about you.

All my love, Gracie

P.S. About the dog tags, come home and you can collect.☺

FORTY

JUNE 23
NORFOLK, VIRGINIA

CNN was showing the weather forecast for the U.S. Grace listened to it as she worked in her closet, trying to rearrange clothes even as she set aside a few items to pack. She would be out at Nellis for three days at the end of next week. Emily settled across her sweater. "Honey, I'm not going to be gone that long. You don't need to look so sad."

The dog just looked at her, her head resting on her front paws. Bruce was right; Emily knew how to say a lot with her eyes. Grace offered a pair of tube socks. "Want to play?" The dog didn't move. Grace ruffled her ears. "Jill is going to be disappointed that you don't want to stay with her."

The top of the hour news came on. The trucker strike in the European Union led the news. The UN water rights debate had slipped to the fourth story. Grace listened but heard nothing new in the report. Turkey and Syria were still talking about a compromise that would increase the water in the Euphrates by suspending agricultural irrigation currently being done north of the Ataturk Dam. It would be a major concession if Turkey made it. At least as long as they were talking, they weren't fighting.

The *GW* had been conducting aggressive flight operations over Iraq, over the Turkey/Syrian borders. She wanted to be back flying with her squadron, but it didn't look like the assignment would come through before the USS *Harry Truman* replaced the

GW. Grace felt guilty about being stateside, knowing her squadron buddies were flying two or three hops a day and by this point in the tour would be deep in the exhausting phase of the deployment. With her missing, they would all have to cover extra duties.

Grace carried the clothes to the duffel bag on her bed, reached for the phone and dialed. "Jill, I found your shoes. Two-tone blue with a half-inch heel?"

"That's them. Where?"

"Inside a box with snow boots."

"The skiing trip."

"I think so. Are you going to be home? I'll bring them by."

"Sure. I'm rearranging the furniture in the living room."

"I wondered how long it would be before you did your deployment redecoration."

"I'm going stir crazy waiting."

"So am I," Grace admitted. "You want to watch planes at the airport instead?"

"Let's go to the beach. I can work on my tan."

"I'll come pick you up," Grace offered.

"Bring Emily."

"Sure. Maybe it will perk her up."

Bruce ~

I'm stretched out on the beach soaking in the sun, well covered in sunscreen and wishing I had brought my sunglasses. Jill and Emily are building a sand house, or rather Jill is building and Emily is digging. You're right, she's a duchess. I'd share this sunny day with you, but I know you've already had plenty of sun.

I had too-ripe bananas and a mix of Cheerios and Wheaties for breakfast and so far two cookies and popcorn for lunch. I'm sure you were eager to know that. Boredom is setting in as I forgot a book to read. I'm not much for lying in the sun for the pleasure of it. How's Wolf treating you? Keeping you nice and healthy? Of course, I know you most often get into trouble because you have to get him out of trouble.

I know from Wolf how hard it is to deploy and just be told to sit on your hands and kill time. Wolf wants to be able to do something, not just sit between two tense parties and basically be there to get in the way if someone wants to start trouble.

It is my hope that you are so bored you are making your version of sand castles to kill time and that you will eventually get the orders to pack and come home without ever having to act. There is a growing chorus here among civilians about intervening in the Middle East, intervening in the Sudan, and intervening in the dispute Turkey is having with Syria. They don't have people on the front lines. I hope you come home without ever being asked to do anything but be a presence and watch.

At the end of next week I'm heading to Nellis for a few days to get some real flight time in on the bombing range, see if I can get back my timing and shake out any lingering trouble with handling g's. They call it a refresher course; I'm looking at it more from the perspective—been there, done that, now how do I do it better the next time? I never want to lose my flight buddy again, or see the earth spinning toward me. One crash in my lifetime was enough.

Seagulls are diving the beach at the moment, creating an enormous racket. I'm afraid Emily is going to have a coronary she's so excited. Wish I had a camera to catch this moment for you. Love you. Thinking about you.

Missing you.

Grace

FORTY-ONE

★ ★ ★

JUNE 27
TURKEY/SYRIAN BORDER

Wolf spat dirt and sand out of his mouth. "I hate sand."

"Keep your voice down," Bruce whispered as he hauled his friend up.

"Where's Bear? Cougar? They're late. I don't like it."

"I'm sure they're having as much fun as we are. Our guide is waiting."

Wolf cleared his weapon and stepped back up onto the path. "I still hate the sand. And trip wires. Even fake ones."

"I was admiring your reflexes," Bruce replied, trying not to smile.

"This is a place for snakes, not people. Now since I'm here to protect your backside, get moving."

Bruce grinned and resumed the hike. They'd been walking up the faint mountainside trails for an hour, the path grade increasing the entire time. Bruce had been in this area before, only from the air last time. Gracie's plane had gone down a kilometer to the south. Their guide was a Turkish army officer, and along for the hike were two men from the embassy, both former army officers, a lingering reality of the Gulf War when diplomacy and war had been intertwined.

Bruce shifted his heavy backpack, hoping he had packed the right medical supplies. It was hard to prepare when the patient and the problem were left as need to know, and they told him the medic didn't need to know. The fact SEALs had been assigned to come along for security was a pretty good indication this was not a safe place for tourists to visit.

At the turn of the trail the Turkish officer who was their guide stopped. "We wait here."

"For what?"

He didn't answer, simply sat down with his back to a big rock where he could watch the other side of the trail. The two embassy officers slid off the communication equipment they carried and sat down too. Wolf shook his head and started climbing up on the rocks beside the trail to get to higher ground. Bruce followed him.

"I'm betting it's a PKK officer."

"Maybe," Bruce replied. "The earthquake was severe in this region, and yet few casualties were reported. Doesn't that strike you as odd?"

"Not many people risk living in this territory. It effectively changes hands every few years." Wolf scanned the trail ahead with night binoculars. Bruce set aside his pack, glad in a small way to have something to do tonight rather than sit at the forward operating location looking at canvas tent walls. It was a beautiful night out, the stars incredibly bright this far from the nearest town.

"There comes Bear and Cougar. Finally."

"Getting tired of baby-sitting?"

"Only the embassy spooks."

They dropped back to the path to meet them. The two SEALs arrived in the company of a third man. He was an old man; that was Bruce's first impression. An old man with incredible sadness in his eyes.

The man looked around the group, sighed at the sight of the Turkish officer, nodded to the two embassy officers, and stopped when he saw Wolf. "You are Navy SEAL also?"

"Yes."

"Long ago, I walked with SEALs into Iraq."

"You were a guide?"

The old man nodded. "Yes. Guide." Bruce found himself being assessed. "My grandson. You will help him?"

A child. The kind of patient that invariably haunted him. "I'll do everything I can," Bruce replied, wondering what he had just been dropped into.

"Call me Jim. Come."

Wolf waited until the man was some distance ahead, then joined up with Bear. "Jim?"

"Could be. He's about the right age and build."

"What?" Bruce asked.

"During Desert Storm, there was a guide who helped SEAL Team 5 blow up a number of hidden Iraqi chemical weapon storage sites. Jim was the name he went by."

"Where are we going?"

"No idea. But he's definitely our safe passage in and out."

It was a thirty-minute walk into the mountains. Bruce was surprised when the man led them to a small plateau that had been built up as a homestead. There was a fence to keep a few sheep, chickens. Three large tents were built up on a wooden floor. Bruce was willing to bet there were normally many rebels staying here, but tonight the place looked deserted. He was still surprised that the man would give away the location of where he had obviously lived for many years.

Jim gestured for the others to stay here and he pointed at Bruce. "You and one other." Bruce nodded to Wolf. The old man led the way to the largest of the tents.

It was lit by three lanterns but was still dim. The lady of the house, a woman probably in her sixties, rose from the side of the bed as they entered. Bruce nodded a greeting and offered a smile. "Ma'am."

She was exhausted and worried; he saw that as he met her anxious gaze. He lowered his medical pack as he watched Jim have a whispered conference with her.

She nodded and waved them over. "My wife," Jim said simply. "My grandson."

The boy was maybe twelve years old with raven black hair. He was asleep but the fever was apparent, as was the pain. Bruce wasn't a doctor, but it wasn't the first time he had been asked to act as one. Twelve years of medical training had taught him enough to know when he could help and what was beyond him. The boy must have been ill for several days if the grandfather had taken the extraordinary steps to arrange this visit. Asking what was wrong was a rather stupid way to gain the grandparents' trust. "His name?"

His grandmother smiled. "Jamael."

"I will go see the others are comfortable," Jim said and Bruce nodded, grateful the man trusted him enough to let him work. He accepted the chair he was offered. The grandmother carefully moved the blanket, and Bruce saw she had it draped as a tent not to touch the boy's leg.

"Whew," Wolf got caught by surprise and waved his hand to disperse the smell of rotten eggs.

Bruce carefully opened the loose bandage on the boy's leg. Festering blisters and black skin. "Burns." And not the kind he often saw. The last time he'd seen this kind of injury was at an evacuation for an erupting volcano in Japan.

Wolf set up the torchlights they had brought to give Bruce better lighting. "We should have brought more water with us," he said. "Go ask the other guys to hand over their canteens."

The lady squeezed his shoulder. "Water? I get."

Bruce nodded. It was a scarce commodity. He'd use what she brought but make sure they offered what they had as a gift before they left. "Smell the sulfur?" he asked Wolf.

"Oh yeah."

"These are recent burns. He's been near an open fissure that had magma or hot gaseous mud popping in it. How do we find out where he was?" Bruce carefully moved aside the bedding to check and see if the boy was burned anywhere else.

"They aren't going to be volunteering the information."

"Others are going to get hurt if it's still active. People, animals, not to mention the chemical contamination to the surrounding area."

"Couldn't satellites spot the heat?"

"We're talking about somewhere a child would play. A ravine, something small. And if the boy found one, there are probably more of them. Syria had a bubble hit Lake al-Assad, there was one at Birecik Dam, and this countryside probably has several of the sulfur and methane pocket fissures. The earthquake must have ruptured a rock plate that stretches the length of this region and opened it close to the ground."

The boy's left hand and arm had a couple small serious burns as well. He tried to brush off whatever had hit him. Bruce carefully lifted the boy's arm to rest on a pillow. "Did you see Jim's hands? He's probably also dealing with a few burns from trying to rescue his grandson."

"Not that I saw. We can ask him, but I don't think he will say."

The grandmother brought him back water. Bruce accepted the pail, stunned to find she had enough fresh water to half fill it. The water was even cool. "Thank you." She nodded. Jim was resourceful to have provided so well for his family.

Bruce touched her hand and caught her gaze. Her grandson had a very bad burn, but the wound showed no sign of infection. "You did a good job helping Jamael."

She smiled again and moved to sit at the head of the bed where she stroked the boy's hair. Bruce took Jamael's temperature and his blood pressure, knowing it was the length of time since the injury that was the most difficult risk to assess.

Not quite 103 degrees; he'd been afraid it was higher. At some point the boy became so worn down and weak his body could not rally to recover. Jamael needed to be in a hospital where there was someone to provide twenty-four-hour care, but Bruce could read reality. Jim would never take him to a Turkish hospital even if they could find one that had a bed among the other earthquake victims.

His language skills were decent, but they didn't stretch to what the boy was murmuring. Bruce pulled two peppermints from his pocket and unwrapped them. "Jamael?" The boy opened his eyes. They were brown, pain filled, and glazed. Bruce brushed his hand along his hot cheek. "Candy." Bruce said softly, offering one to his grandmother and then to the boy. Jamael smiled when he tasted it. "Suck it." The sugar would help the boy start having a taste for something to eat and drink.

Bruce nodded to Wolf to open the medical kit. The tough decisions were coming. Had the boy even seen a needle, let alone been given a shot? Bruce tried to balance the painkiller against the boy's size and what pain his trying to help was likely to cause.

He'd been in enough situations like this around the world. He could work as a doctor among kids trapped in war zones for the rest of his life and barely scratch the surface of the need. Wolf distracted the boy with a flight patch while Bruce carefully gave him two shots, a painkiller and a strong antibiotic. The grandmother had a harder time with it than the boy did.

Bruce patted her hand. "All done," he reassured with a smile.

Wolf opened the sterile packs. "Your bedside manner is improving."

Bruce slid a large sterile square under Jamael's leg. "I hope your nursing skills have." He carefully cleaned the boy's leg around the wound while he waited for the painkiller to take effect before he started taking care of the burn. He had to remove the dead patches of skin, remove places where skin had tried to heal but had actually curled on itself into the burn. It took almost an hour of careful work. There was good pink skin below the burn that was a great relief to see. The boy wouldn't lose his leg as long as infection was kept out. The boy's grandmother sat quietly watching the entire time.

Bruce carefully applied a thick layer of burn cream to keep the skin soft and infection out, and lightly laid gauze across it. "If I leave supplies, can you do this twice a day for Jamael? Morning and night?"

His grandmother nodded. "Yes."

Bruce took a look at the blisters on the boy's hand and arm. "Wolf, find the bottle of painkillers and cut the pills in half. I assumed the patient was an adult." His friend looked relieved to be able to step away from being nurse. The man did look a little green around the edges.

Bruce decided it was best to leave the boy's hand open to the air. It had to be very painful but it was healing.

"We'll leave all the supplies we brought with us, the antibodies, the painkillers. Give Jamael one white pill and one pink one every morning until they are gone. It's important he take them all."

His grandmother leaned over to make sure she understood which pills, then nodded. "Okay. One and one, each morning," she repeated, touching them to make certain.

Bruce offered her the thermometer he had used. "If it goes up to the red area, have your husband come find us."

"Yes."

Bruce patted her hand again, seeing the fear on her face. "By the full moon, Jamael will be walking again and playing."

She gave a small smile. "He's a good boy."

Bruce began cleaning up the supplies he had used, putting them in the black biohazard bag. "Wolf, find the Gatorade packets."

"Right here."

Bruce dumped one packet into his water bottle and filled it with water. The boy was waking up. Bruce helped him raise his head to drink, then helped his grandmother change the large cotton T-shirt the boy wore. His temperature was down to 100.5. "Do we have any of those baseball cards left in one of the packs?"

Wolf smiled. "Be right back." Bruce hadn't met a boy yet who didn't like to collect things, even a sport he didn't necessarily play.

The boy laughed when he was given the cards, and turned to show the top one to his grandmother. Bruce carefully draped the blanket over the bedposts to keep it from touching the boy's leg. "One more favor, Wolf. Cut loose my sleeping bag."

"A step ahead of you. I'm leaving two, and my dried snacks." The last thing the boy needed was his grandmother getting sick because she was now sleeping on the floor.

"Thanks." Bruce leaned forward one last time and smiled at the boy. "It was nice to meet you, Jamael."

It was a shy smile in return, but a smile, and it about broke Bruce's heart.

"Ma'am." He offered her the chair he had used.

"Thank you." She was close to crying.

"You're very welcome."

Bruce followed Wolf outside. He stopped across the threshold and took a very deep breath, then let it out slowly, feeling exhaustion curl all the way to his toes. "I wish Rich had been available instead of me. He's better with kids."

"I'd say you did just fine," Wolf replied. "Now comes the fun part."

"Kids and politics should not be mixed."

"Agreed."

The men were sitting together in front of the middle tent, a small fire burning, and the smell of tobacco drifted on the wind. It was a silent group, Cougar standing farther away by one of the few trees on the plateau. Bruce walked with Wolf to join them. "The animals look surprisingly healthy considering the drought."

"I saw signs of a couple horses too, probably moved somewhere else for the night. Jim has found a water supply for his family, and it's kept these folks going."

Jim rose and came to meet them.

"Your grandson should get better," Bruce said. "You were right to ask us to come. I left supplies with your wife. If his fever rises, please come get us. They were bad burns—I would really like to see where it was your grandson was playing when he got hurt."

The Turkish officer interrupted them. "We've done our part of the deal."

One of the embassy men intervened, cutting off the Turkish officer, apologizing for him. "Jim, we were honored to help." The Turkish officer tossed a frustrated look at him and walked back to the fire.

"If you can help us too, it would be appreciated but there is no deal, and never was one. When you honor us with a request for help, we will be glad to assist you."

"I know this, Samuel, which is why I sent the message to you. A favor for a favor is fair." The old man knelt down, smoothed the dirt, and picked up a stick. He drew a sketch on the ground. "Where the trails divide, go north. There is a solitary gypsum tree along part of the trail that drops off sharply. Descend the face of it to the bottom of the ravine. There's a new fissure that cuts into the ravine; follow it east. You'll see the mouth of a cave down low to the ground. The weapons are there."

"The stingers?" Samuel asked.

The man tossed down the stick. "The weapons are there."

Bruce shot a glance at Wolf. Stingers? As in what brought down Grace's plane?

"Thank you, Jim." Samuel replied, extending his hand.

"Jamael is worth it."

"And if you need us to come back, we will come quickly."

With a doctor this time, Bruce noted to himself, wondering why one had not been found for this trip. Probably the Turkish officer's influence there, and the fact so little was known before they came.

The old man looked at Bruce. "The planes that go overhead?"

"Yes."

"I watch them. One went down. The pilot is okay?"

Bruce tugged a worn picture from his pocket and offered it. "The pilot."

"There were rumors."

"She's home and will be fine."

"Good. That is very good."

Jim handed back the picture with a sigh and looked at the embassy officer. "This land needs peace, Samuel. And if what is in the cave can bring it…"

"You have my word, Jim. The gesture will go far with my government."

"I will see."

"If you are comfortable we can leave the boy; it would be best if we were in and out by dawn," Bear commented, joining them.

"I've done what I can." Bruce slipped his pack back on.

Polite good-byes were extended to their host.

"Let's get moving," Bear said. "Cougar, take point."

They headed back to the trail.

It took trial and error and a few mistakes as to what consti-
tuted the solitary gypsum tree before they found the ravine.

"Incredible," Wolf voiced for all of them. The ground had
been opened in a gash, one side lifted a foot higher than the
other, and the two sides slid in opposite directions. Bear, Wolf,
and Bruce rappelled down in pairs while the others stood guard.

"Where did he say the cave entrance was?"

"Down there somewhere," Wolf pointed.

"An old cave or a new one just opened?"

"If it's being used as a weapon storage, you would think old."

They found it among the base of the ravine, a twisted squat
tree trying to grow just above the four-feet-long by two-feet-high
opening. It was more a fracture in the wall than an entrance, and
it appeared to open up farther inside.

"You smell that?"

Wolf winced. "Sulfur."

"A cave is also a natural place for methane gas to build up,"
Bruce pointed out.

"You want to wait for a geologist to get here?" Bear asked,
shining his light around the area to see how much of the rockslide
looked new.

"When we're in the area under the watchful eyes of rebels with
essentially a one-time pass to come and go without being shot at?
I vote we get in, get the stingers, and get out," Wolf replied.

"If the cave preexisted the earthquake, there are probably several branches and caverns. I doubt the weapons were stored in the
first few feet of the entrance," Bear replied.

"Wolf and I can do it," Bruce offered. "We stay low, go slow;
it shouldn't be more complex than other cave jaunts we've made."

Bear nodded. "Try it. I'll leave Cougar to pull you out if you
get into trouble, and the rest of us will spread out and set up a
screen. Stay in close touch."

Wolf slid on his gloves, picked up his coiled rope, and glanced at Bruce. "You just don't want to be standing around out here when someone realizes we're stealing what they stole."

Bruce smiled. "Now what made you think that?"

"You know how I love caves. You first?"

"I'd hate to rob you of the honor."

Wolf got down on his belly and slid into the cave. "Spiders. Wonderful."

Bruce nudged Wolf's foot and the man slid the rest of the way in. "It's big and it does open up."

Bruce followed his friend into the cave. There was a breeze through the entrance of the cave, which suggested a much larger cavern ahead where the temperature difference of air underground and that outside was creating a natural eddy.

Bruce squeezed through an area barely large enough for his body. "I like caves."

"You would."

"Something has been pulled through here; the rocks are scraped."

"Ouch."

"What?" Bruce asked.

"Nothing."

Bruce bit back a laugh and kept crawling, following Wolf's boots.

"Finally. Watch the drop." Wolf disappeared from view. Bruce followed him and nearly tumbled when the floor disappeared.

"I'd say that was an effective trap door," Wolf commented, sliding over to prevent Bruce from landing in his lap. They had abruptly entered a long hollow cavern.

It was dry, cool, and what looked liked leaves had blown in from what had to be the solitary bush at the cave entrance. "Smell anything off?"

"No. And the spiders are still alive," Wolf pointed out.

"We're in, Cougar. How's reception?"

"You're clear, power levels are good."

"Roger."

Wolf shown his light around. "Would you like door one or door two?" Two passageways disappeared.

"Two. Those rocks look scraped."

"Two it is." Wolf, half crouched, led the way.

"I'm getting a whiff of rotten eggs."

"Stay low."

Wolf slowed his walk forward. "It's opening up again." Metal rapped against stone. "Watch your head."

Another smaller passageway opened up.

"Paydirt. Hand grenades, a couple mines, ammo, side arms, rifles, even some M-16s." It was a neat inventory, resting upright along the wall with boxes at either end. Wolf started exploring boxes. "Here's a tally sheet in a language I can't read." He handed it back.

"Stingers?" Bruce asked.

"There they are. Still in their Made in the USA cases. The Army investigators will appreciate getting those shipping manifest labels back."

"We can't carry all this out of here and we can't leave it."

"We take the stingers, destroy the rest." Wolf suggested.

"Let's think about that a bit more. Jim didn't come out and say it, but I bet Jamael was hurt somewhere around here. And we were smelling sulfur outside the cave."

"Meaning if we toss one of those hand grenades, no telling what we might accidentally set off."

Bruce nodded. "Exactly. Let's see if we can find where the boy was hurt. Five minutes, and if we have to, we destroy the rifles, take the stingers, and leave the rest behind."

"Sounds like a plan." Wolf looked around. "Back to door number one or do we take one of these three options?"

"How about number four? That rockslide looks new."

"And that opening looks too small for a man of my size," Wolf noted.

"Suck in your gut."

"Thanks for the suggestion," Wolf replied ruefully. He slipped through by turning sidewise. "Instant thin machine." His light cast shadows through the opening. "This cavern is about the size of the one on that side, and it is open above. I'm standing at the base of a huge rockslide, like one of those sink holes you sometimes see appear at ground level. Watch those first few steps."

Bruce followed him.

"Does that look like a boy-sized hat?" Wolf shone his torch on the rocks.

Bruce retrieved it. "Jamael was here."

"Yes. And I'm faintly smelling rotten eggs." Wolf knelt and looked into the one opening present. It curved down and to the right.

"What's that noise?" Bruce asked.

"It sounds like water."

Bruce nodded. "I was going to suggest that, but I figured it would sound crazy."

"Let's check it out."

"You just have to be curious."

Wolf laughed. "I was born that way."

"It could be the fissure that got Jamael in trouble."

"We'll never know unless we go see."

"The way he was burned, he slipped and found himself touching something he didn't realize was so close. Go easy, Wolf."

"Slow and easy," Wolf promised and led the way. "This is the place," he muttered a few moments later. "I can reach out and touch rocks that still feel warm. I don't know what magma looks liked hardened, but the sulfur smell lingers."

"Air okay?"

"Breathable, and, Bruce, it's damp and humid."

"Be careful where you touch. There could be an acid pocket."

"I remember. There are still spiders and what looks like fungus growing. There's an opening ahead." He disappeared. "Oh, my."

Bruce had rarely heard Wolf at a loss for words. He pushed through the opening to join his friend.

"They are never going to believe us," Wolf said, shining his light across the discovery.

It was an underground river, fast running water that sparkled so clear their lights could peer through it to the rock bottom.

They could literally lay pipe right into the spring and have fresh water running for probably years to come, pumped by the earth itself. "We've been praying for water, and it's been sitting here open and reasonably accessible, just waiting to be found."

"Let's see where it's going," Wolf said, following the water. Bruce followed him, wondering the same thing. Did it disappear back into the ground? "Here's part of the fault line where the rock slab cracked." The water was shooting out like a geyser and striking the ceiling a few feet above. The sound of rushing water increased.

"Wow." There was a waterfall flowing down into a deep fissure, so deep their lights could not probe to the bottom. The walls were wet, the roof, water dripping on them. "It's enclosed, so it can't evaporate."

Bruce reached out to touch the rock wall. "This rock face hasn't pitted yet. I bet the earthquake just opened up this passage. The water has been here for a long time, but I doubt anyone has ever known about it. The boy and his grandfather were probably the first."

"And Jim knew what he was really giving away when he revealed the location of this cave."

Bruce nodded. "The man wants peace for his people. Offering water accessible to both Turkey and Syria is a pretty good card to lay down if you want to foster goodwill. No wonder he insisted on the embassy personnel coming along. Water rights in this part of the world become part of every formal peace treaty." Bruce shone his light around one more time. "Let's get them using that communication equipment they lugged in to do some good."

"We still need rain."

"It will come," Bruce replied, confident that it eventually would. "The embassy guys need something fun to do for a change. We lug the stingers out, and we don't talk about this with anyone but the embassy guys. Let's give them time to get their ducks in a row before the Turkish government hears there's another fresh water supply available that dwarfs what anyone thought was in the area."

"Water. It's almost better than finding gold."

Bruce laughed. "Tonight, I agree."

Grace -

I had an incredible night. I'll be able to tell you about it one of these days. I met a brave young man who loves baseball cards. It feels so wonderful to be able to help someone. It sure makes up for all those hours of medical training and missions where I came back having to shake my head and say I wasn't in time or in the right place.

Did you ever save anyone's life? I know you've had a couple close calls as LSO where your quick action averted disaster. I was thinking about you in the moments while I was walking with Wolf. Rich should have been along, but he was delayed coming back from Incirlik when the call came in. It was one of those call-and-go type missions. I'm wound up. Sorry for the wandering letter. Oh, I hope tonight brings a glimmer of peace and not just spirals down into another point of tension.

How's the arm pain? Your mobility? Have you been extra careful? What about the flying? Still loving it? Your last letter was wonderful to receive.

Grace, I miss you. I would love to be sitting with you tonight rather than sitting on a packing box writing this by the faint light of the coming dawn. Sometimes the emotion overwhelms. I so look forward to the day I see you next and just have the freedom to sit and talk.

Much love, Bruce

JUNE 28

Bruce ~

I'm at Nellis at the moment, curled up on my bunk enjoying a few quiet moments before I turn in, catching up on the tail end of the national news. I'll be watching the news this week with you in mind. I've never been able to save a life, unless you count fifth grade as a crossing guard when I managed to stop Charlene from meeting a car face first. It was the most exciting moment in my entire year because I came close to flunking chemistry. Fifth grade was awful otherwise.

I think you were created by God to be exactly what you are, a medic who goes wherever you are most needed. Even your letters come alive when you talk about getting to help someone. Hopefully no one was shooting at you this time. I have a vague memory from the crash of gunshots while you were pulling me out. (You still owe me the details of what really happened.) I hope the boy is in good shape. Baseball cards should be standard issue military equipment; they prove helpful in so many situations.

I'm looking forward to walking the beach with you, (we can pretend to follow Emily which will make it a slow ambling walk), holding hands, and just enjoying listening about your deployment. Save up lots of stories to tell about Wolf and Rich.

I'll be going home tomorrow night, and planning to have a wonderful cross-country flight.

Commercial break—there's this tiny mutt of a dog in a pet food commercial, white and fuzzy with a high bark. I like Emily better, but this one is cute. Anyway, sorry, I've got pets on my mind because Emily started to bring home dogs she thinks are strays. We went walking in the park, I took a seat on the bench with a book, and I thought Emily was asleep. Next thing I know here she comes with this small dog that can literally walk under her, leading her over like she's a sheep dog or something. While I tried to find tags to figure out who the owner was, Emily tipped over my lunch sack and offered her new friend half my lunch. It was so hard not to laugh. I didn't have the heart to scold her.

Life is good, Bruce. The distance between us is a pain, but I've grown to shape my life around letters. And I've gotten in the habit of noting things in my day that I want to make a point of telling you. I enjoy having my life revolve around yours. That's the most profound point I wanted to share tonight. You're part of my life, a comfortable part. It's late; I've got to turn in.

All my love, Grace

JULY 9

Grace ~

I am determined to bring Wolf home safe and sound, but just to give you a head's up, the man's sense of humor is killing me. I found a lizard in my bunk last night. A real one. And Rich is all prepared with a camera to capture the moment for the PJ memorial wall of practical jokes. When Wolf is talking my partner into this foolishness, we are all reaching our limits.

We had a party tonight to celebrate the water rights "memorandum of understanding" that Turkey and Syria just signed. A fancy name for a piece of paper that means we probably won't have someone shooting at us any time soon. Being in-country is the absolute pits when there are men with guns on either side of you just looking for a reason to get justifiably mad at the other guy. So for tonight at least, peace reigns, until the next problem shows up.

The earthquake recovery continues at a slower pace now that rubble has been cleared off roads, bridges have been jerry-rigged, and large massive tent cities have been created for those displaced from their homes.

The logistics of getting aid where it needs to go is incredible. We've been helping out whenever we can, combining relief convoys with military convoys to help expedite getting shipments around. So I'm keeping myself busy while I watch the planes overhead and wait for word I can come home.

You mentioned the rescue. Grace, I died a little that day when I saw you. Your plane was in pieces, your flight suit was covered in blood, and your eyes were glassy. I thought you were dead, honey. I really thought you were dead. And it haunted me that I'd been late in telling you so many important things.

Like how much the fact you love to sing even though you're not very good makes me smile and think, that's my Grace standing out in the choir. And how much I love you for making Wolf feel special. Instead of getting on him for the trouble he gets himself into, you love him for who he is. And when I talk to Jill, she always has a new piece of news to share about something the two of you did together. You make time for Jill, you make time to be a best friend, and I love you for it.

And most of all I wanted to tell you what it means to me that you let me be part of your life. You didn't have to. You could have played it safe and said I already lost somebody I loved with Ben and I don't want to risk loving someone else. Instead, you let me have a huge part of your heart and your affections. There aren't enough words or years to show you how much I love you—but I look forward to trying.

I was afraid after the accident that you would not recover to the point you could fly, and I admit I was racking my brains for ideas of what you might like to do as a civilian. Just to let you know, the option at the top of my list was that I'd retire too and we'd take up giving scuba diving lessons, exploring old wrecks off the Florida coast, and become treasure hunters in our spare time. (Not sure where that idea came from, but it sounds a lot like a Wolf-originated suggestion to me.) When it's time to retire, I'm sure both of us will figure out how to do it with grace, but that hopefully is a long time away.

Mail me a book next time you think about it. Rich just got this series of *X-Files* tapes he ordered some four months ago, and the videos are all the scary kind. I could use something along the nature of a cartoon about now.

With all my love, Bruce

Bruce ~

Sunday comics, a month's worth, coming in this rather interesting care package (Jill helped me, you can tell) and just the thing to bring some laughs. I thought Snoopy and the Red Baron were priceless.

Love, Grace

FORTY-TWO

★ ★ ★

W hat happened?" Bruce shouted to Rich to be heard over the noise. He'd been asleep and suddenly the air was filled with helicopters landing practically outside the tent door. The tent swayed against the changing air pressure.

"A tanker exploded while planes were refueling."

Bruce grabbed his gear. "Where?"

"Just off the coast; early word is survivors have been spotted in the water. *GW* is launching everything they have."

Bruce pushed open the tent flap and understood why he felt like he had been jerked awake when he saw the sky and realized it was still the middle of the night. The emergency gear was already prepared to grab and go. It was a swift change to water gear, grabbing extra scuba equipment. Bruce sprinted to the waiting helicopter with Rich. Vincent and Frank were already buckling in. Search-and-rescue flights were about speed, and unfortunately they had practiced for this kind of accident many times in the past. Dasher headed out to sea. Bruce plugged into the comm to listen in.

The message traffic was terse, directing search-and-rescue assets to cover the territory.

"Who's got the water?"

"The battle group has dispatched four ships to corner the

debris field with lights; small craft are launching into the grids. There were some surface assets in port also heading out. There's a victor class sub out there too."

It was dark. Bruce was expecting the sight of burning fuel on the water but it was still horrifying to see. It was an enormous patch of water already over two miles long with different crash and burn points apparent from more than one aircraft going down. The sky was crowded with search helicopters and spotlights sweeping the surface looking for survivors.

"Eagle 01, Birddog, contact Thunder 01, 127.4."

"Eagle 01. Roger," Dasher replied. "Thunder 01, Eagle 01. Where do you need us?"

"We just dropped smoke and a flare on what looks like two souls in the water just south of grid four. We're bingo fuel."

"Copy red smoke and flare. We're inbound from the east."

"Texaco flight had emergency frequency china two."

"Eagle 01. Roger." The emergency frequency for the tanker crew was about the only frequency silent at the moment.

"How many jets involved?" Bruce asked Dasher.

"I'm hearing it was a full stack. Coming up on the smoke."

Dasher dropped to a hover. They could see the smoke canister bobbing on the water shooting off a continuing stream of red smoke to mark position. The flare was still burning. "Ten o'clock, Dasher! Soul in the water," Bruce hollered, picking out the bobbing yellow stripe of a life vest. The man was drifting close to a slick of burning fuel.

Spotlights illuminated the man and they saw him try to wave. "He's holding onto a second man," Rich called out.

"Take us in for a drop, Dasher," Bruce said, weighing options and going for the speed of putting PJs in the water.

Rich moved out onto the rails as Dasher hovered. He stepped off, crossing his arms to drop straight down. Bruce took a deep breath as he stepped out on the rails, wished this wasn't another ocean adventure, and stepped off to follow his partner. The impact with the water was enough to take his breath. Bruce surged back to the surface and set out at a crawl with Rich toward the survivors. The sea was going to kill men tonight if they didn't intervene to prevent it.

"We're going to burn up here."

"Hold on, man, we've got help overhead to the south. PJs are dropping, so we're not the only ones in the water." Wolf lifted the man higher from the water, wishing he could see where the navigator for the Prowler was. He'd seen the man twice somewhere to the south. Bear had gone after him in the rubber craft; speed was of the essence as the flames were cutting him off.

"Someone clipped me, the hose sliced, and we had fuel streaming over us like rain. No one could get out of the way."

Wolf kicked hard to propel them away from an approaching slick of burning fuel. The secondhand smoke was enough to kill them, it was so thick. The SEALs had been conducting a very quiet training exercise with the sub when suddenly the sky had begun raining fire. "How many chutes did you see?"

"At least six."

"Here comes our ride. The craft has rubber sides; just remember to roll up and over."

"Give me a shove and I'm in," the man replied.

"Find him, Bear?"

"Cougar did." The fact Bear said nothing more warned Wolf there was probably a sealed body bag now aboard the other boat. Bear leaned over the side to help pull them aboard.

"Where do you need me?"

"On the radio. See if you can get directions to the next sighting."

"Do those guys need help?" Wolf pointed to the hovering helicopter.

"I heard they just picked up another two."

"How many pulled out so far?"

"Seven. There's more."

Rescues this big and complex were enough to task not only training, skills, and experience but also emotions. Intermixed with the survivors were the burn victims. Bruce deflated the navigator's life vest so he could maneuver the man he had dropped into the sea to recover onto the body bag laid out in the basket. It was the safest way to lift the body from the water. At least this man appeared to have died from a broken neck before the fire reached him.

"Need a hand?"

The Zodiac rubber craft came from the smoke to the south. "There's an empty vest floating at about six o'clock. Recover it so we don't try to tag it from the air," Bruce called, finishing tightening the straps. He had crossed paths with both sailors and SEALs in the last three hours. He wasn't that surprised to see Cougar back in this grid.

Cougar returned as the basket was lifted from the water to the hovering helicopter. Bruce hooked his arm around the side of the craft and took a breather before he prepared to be lifted from the water.

"What's the latest you've heard?" Cougar asked, offering a canteen of fresh water.

"Twelve survivors, three deceased, and eight missing. Have you seen Wolf or Bear lately?"

"The fishing trawler thought it had a sighting. They diverted to check it out."

"When this is over, why don't you guys come join us for a sailor's toast?"

"I'll pass the word around."

The night was going to haunt him, and Bruce wanted a chance to let it go with guys who understood what this was like. The rope was coming down. Bruce swam to grab it, slipped it around his chest, and signaled for a lift.

INCIRLIK AIR BASE, TURKEY

"Have you called Grace?"

Bruce looked up from his study of the bubbles climbing the side of his glass, trying to decide if carbonated soda went flat because the bubbles popped or because the bubbles dissolved. Wolf was watching him, his expression grave. "No. Have you?"

"She's going to be watching this on the news."

"I know. So is Jill." Bruce sighed and pushed back his glass. "Too many people died tonight because of an accident. It's not the way to end a tour."

"If they were alive when they hit the water, we gave them a good chance of getting home," Wolf replied. "It's going to be a month of picking up debris from the beach. I heard one of Gracie's past nuggets got caught in it."

"Who?" Bruce asked.

"Bushman. He managed to pull off a dead stick landing into the net aboard the *GW.*"

Bruce raised his glass, finding the first reason to smile. "Way to go, Bushman. The man deserves a slap on the back for that landing."

"Grace will be pleased to hear it," Wolf agreed. "Why aren't we calling her?"

Bruce studied him and weighed his answer. "Do you want to

tell her about the guys who didn't make it?"

Wolf shook his head. "Pilots tank every day. I really don't want to tell her I pulled pilots out of the drink who burned to death."

"Let's not tell her."

Wolf studied him quietly. "Are you okay marrying her, knowing this is part of her life?"

Bruce set aside the glass. "It's not the marrying part that bothers me—it's the idea of having to bury. I want old age for her, and tonight shakes that up a bit." He pushed back his chair. "I'm out of it. I'm going to catch a few minutes of sleep."

"Don't dream."

Bruce nodded his agreement. "Glad you were out there, man."

"I wouldn't want your job every day."

"It's mutual. Tell Bear and Cougar to raise a toast to Rich later. As usual, the man saved my hide twice tonight."

"I'll do that. And, Bruce—"

He glanced back at his friend.

Wolf smiled. "Tell Gracie I said hi."

The man knew him. Bruce lifted a hand in a salute.

NORFOLK, VIRGINIA

"How do you handle being a civilian? This is awful."

Grace tucked her cellular phone tight against her shoulder as she added another name to her working list of confirmed okays. Other than Bushman's dramatic landing it looked like her squadron had been lucky. They had refueled just before the incident occurred. "Gina said she heard from Mark Kells, and I just got an e-mail from Nancy saying she had heard from Craig Frances."

"Anything on Frank Carter?"

"The Prowler flight?" Grace ran her list of names. "Nothing

yet. It's awful that our informal network is probably as close to complete as the guys on site trying to figure it out." It was the names they had not heard about that worried her. The dead and missing were figured out because they didn't show up on the lists of the living.

"I'll post an update to the Stateside Support Web site with these names."

Grace pulled e-mail again.

She had lost two friends. She knew two of the electronic surveillance officers from the backseats of the Prowler, and reports of their deaths were sketchy but had that ring of truth that came when crewmen relayed first and secondhand accounts of the recoveries. Sea Stallion helicopters had been lifting off the *GW* deck, and another clip on CNN showed more then six rescue helicopters hovering over locations in the debris field. She knew there would be even more casualties. A refueling accident was one of the things pilots feared most.

The phone rang. "I'll call you back, Jill. I've got a call on the house line."

She hoped it was Peter with the latest names he had heard. "Yes, hello."

"Grace."

"Bruce…" She scrambled to mute the TV. "Oh, it's good to hear from you."

"A long few hours."

She bit her lip and forced herself to hold back the tears that came immediately to the surface. She'd been worried, so worried about him. The last thing he needed was to get hit with a long burst of questions. He sounded down, really down. "Yes." She said gently, wincing as CNN began to replay the tapes of the crash site and the floating wreckage. She turned away from the image.

"Teams responded fast. I'm sorry for the friends you lost, Grace."

"Are you hearing numbers?"

"Most of the missing are being found alive. We may have lost five."

"Five."

"Breathe, honey."

"So many."

"Grace, do me a favor? When you see me next, give me a really long hug."

Her eyes watered. "A really long hug. Gotcha."

"I saw Wolf, Bear, and the other SEALs. They were okay, only minor sprains and singe marks from the work."

Wolf was fine. She closed her eyes, admitting the relief. "Thank you."

"Without shutting you out—Grace, I don't want to talk about it. I can't for now."

She squeezed the bridge of her nose, suppressing the emotions, understanding better than he could realize exactly what he was feeling. When the images were too alive to talk about, when the memories were best forgotten. "Then let's not." She stretched out on the floor and pulled over a cushion from the couch.

"Sometimes I wonder how I keep doing this job."

"The children, Bruce. And all the pilots you are able to help. Did you hear anything about the boy who liked baseball cards?"

"I got a note through one of the embassy guys that he was fairing well."

"I'm glad. When you can tell me that story, I'll enjoy hearing it."

"Wolf ate some sand."

She smiled. "Did he?"

"I'm going to like having him for a brother-in-law."

"He admires you, Bruce." She searched hard to find any subject that would be a distraction for him. She wanted so badly to be with him to give him that hug. "I hear you are going to get yet another chance to renew your handle. I saw the baseball team postings."

"Did they rig the teams again?"

"PJs versus SEALs for game number four."

"Remind me to steal Wolf's shoes. The man loves to slide." She was relieved to hear a glimmer of a smile in that answer.

Silence settled between them.

"God is merciful," Bruce said quietly.

"Very merciful. He'll help you sleep, Bruce. You did what you could."

"I am tired."

"Thank you for calling me."

"I almost didn't."

She understood that too. "Even if you hadn't, I would still give you that very long hug."

"I love you, Grace. If only because you're gracious with calls like this one."

"I love you more. When you come home I'll be waiting."

"God bless, honey."

She returned the phone to its cradle. Five dead. How many of those men would Bruce see when he shut his eyes? *Jesus, bless this man whom I love so much with Your comfort, Your incredible comfort. He needs it, Lord.*

JULY 10

ANTAKYA, TURKEY

In the front of his Bible, Bruce found the first letter Grace had written him on this deployment. He read it while he lay on the bunk, unable to find the sleep he needed. A year that had changed his life. With the letter was a homemade Valentine's card she had sent him. He opened the red construction paper and smiled at the *X*s and *O*s. Her poetry was about as bad as her singing.

There was a more fragile letter in his Bible, one he had forgotten. He slipped out the page of stationery that had come long ago with the box of candy that had melted.

Dear Major Stanton,
I'm writing to talk about my nephew Scott. He was shot down outside of Al-Kut during the Gulf War. He died. But the comfort of knowing the PJs went in to try and help him has been a daily comfort.

Bruce refolded the letter, finding it difficult to read to the end. It was a nice letter, but it was a reminder that memories of loss lasted for a decade.

Jesus, men died tonight because they were here to keep the peace. If there is any comfort available to those stateside hearing the sad news, please provide it. I need to see Grace. Please let this settle down so I can go home soon. Tonight I'm at the limits of my strength.

He loved Grace. He loved her so much. Did he want to ask her to pull back from being a pilot? He was so tempted tonight to do so. He rubbed his eyes where emotions welled. He'd seen too many men die in the line of duty and too many times had been late to help.

If she didn't fly, the part of Grace he loved the most would slowly wither and die. She would be willing and content to make the decision if he asked her, would do it and would probably never look back.

He didn't want to ask it of her. Life was good. God was gracious. It had been a long journey since Ecuador, and he could feel decisions he had made then being tested.

One day at a time, Lord. I will enjoy every day I have, for life will never be long enough. Please, I'd really like to go home.

Grace ~

It's RAINING here. A nice, heavy, wonderful rain. I'm coming home. I hope this is the toughest separation we ever endure. God is gracious. I love you.

Bruce

FORTY-THREE

★ ★ ★

JULY 19

PENSACOLA, FLORIDA

Where are they?" Grace stepped up on the bottom row of the bleachers, looking down the flight line. So many planes coming in, huge cargo planes, some of them hauling helicopters inside. Men coming off carrying gear. Bruce and Wolf's arrival information had been frustratingly vague.

"Try these." Jill handed her binoculars.

"Thanks."

Grace couldn't wait to see Bruce, to offer him that long hug. Five men returned stateside in flag-draped caskets. Pensacola and Norfolk had both spent their weeks in grief, the desire to replace it with a homecoming of joy was incredible.

She was so proud of Bushman. The more information that came out about the accident, the more it became clear Bushman had shown he had indeed stepped up to the excellence needed in a fighter pilot.

She'd been flying, working daily in the gym, and praying for this day. "There they are!" She waved frantically and fell off the bench. Jill caught her, laughing. Grace stepped back, landed on Emily's tail, and the animal yelped. "Sorry, Emily. The C-141B Starlifter."

"Which?"

"The gray giant five planes down. They came out of the back carrying their gear."

"Can we go out there?"

"Watch me. Come on, Emily," Grace led the way to the break in the fence that went out to the flight line. "There's Rich."

"Wolf! Over here," Jill hollered, jumping up to wave. "Left, Grace, they're to the left."

Grace felt like her emotions would burst when she saw Bruce. He picked her up. Picked her up and swung her around and hugged her tight. "I love you," he whispered. "I love you bunches."

She was laughing and crying, holding on tight. "I love you too."

"And I am so sorry I missed the last three months of your life. Shoulder okay?" he asked, worried.

"Fine." She wrapped her arms around his neck, in no hurry to be put down. His eyes were incredibly blue. She held his gaze and leaned forward to kiss him. "Welcome home."

"The best words I've heard in ages."

"I think Wolf missed Jill." Grace smiled at her friend who was similarly defying gravity at the moment.

"We've got a bet on who carries his girl the longest," Bruce said.

Grace laughed and rested her head against his shoulder. It was a bit awkward talking to him with her feet still off the ground, but it was rather special too. She kissed his ear because it was close. "Are you going to ask me?" She held up her left hand and rubbed the very bare third finger.

He kissed her so long it took away her breath. "Thought I might."

"You're forgiven for being gone. Bleachers." She pointed. "That way."

He swung her fully up in his arms to her delight. "Grab my bag."

He leaned down and she tried, finally snagging the duffel bag. "It's heavy."

"Laundry," he confessed.

She giggled over that.

"Did I mention I like the shirt?" Bruce asked.

"You said Hawaiian."

"That I did. Where's your dog tags?"

"You're determined to get them."

"Yep."

"They're in my pocket. I may hand them over later."

"I'll remind you of that."

"I'm glad you're home."

He smiled down at her. "I think you said that already."

"I'm really, really glad you're home."

"What did you do? Wreck your car? Burn down your apartment?"

She laughed. He lowered her to stand on the bottom step of the bleachers and leisurely kissed her again. "What?"

"I got you a cat."

He blinked. She laughed so hard she had to wrap her arms around his neck to remain standing on the bleachers. "Oh, if you could see your expression." She smoothed down the collar of his cammies. "Emily brought her home from the park. Carrying her by the scruff of the neck, the kitten just opening her eyes. We found the mom; it must have been hit by a car." She risked a look at his face. "I couldn't just give away Emily's kitten."

"Of course not."

"Jill and I have been feeding her every hour." She pointed to the box under the bleachers where their stuff was still sitting. Emily had wandered back under there to stand guard over the box.

Bruce sighed, kissed her nose, and stepped over to rescue the box.

He sat down on the bleachers with the box in his lap, and

Grace settled beside him. "The milk bottle is in the cooler."

The kitten was awake, making small noises, and Emily started whining and pacing. "Easy, Em. What's her name?" Bruce carefully lifted the towel and the kitten from the box.

Grace rested her chin against his shoulder as she watched him. "Francis Emily Hogess Burnett."

"Francis will do. Ten minutes home and I'm feeding a baby. Is this a harbinger of things to come?"

"What a nice visual."

He leaned over and kissed her again. "You look good, Grace. Better than your picture."

"I colored the gray hair."

He smiled. "I noticed."

"Wolf, he's calling me old."

Her cousin reached over and ruffled her hair. "You gave me plenty of gray this trip."

Jill sat down on the other side of Bruce and wrapped her brother in a hug. Bruce returned it. "Welcome home."

"What do you have planned for tonight?" Bruce asked Jill.

"Nothing elaborate. We've got dinner waiting at your place."

"A nice start."

"I thought I'd make Wolf take me to a movie."

"Back row, popcorn, and some of those squishy rubber fish?" Wolf asked.

Jill leaned against his knee. "You're never going to grow up."

"Don't plan to."

Grace glanced at Bruce. "Do we dare join them?"

Bruce smiled. "We'll stay home and take care of the baby."

"Fine with me and Emily."

"I was afraid the duchess was going to die of old age while I was gone."

Grace looked down. Emily had stretched out across Bruce's

feet with a comfortable sigh. "She's glad you're home."

"I can tell."

"Really. That's her content expression."

"Come here."

She leaned over and he kissed her softly. "I've got a few months to make up for," he said, smiling. "Dog tags."

With a laugh Grace tugged them from her pocket. "I put them on a longer chain since the one I wore would have strangled you. Duck." She slipped the dog tags on him. "There you go."

"They're pink," he said, shocked.

She giggled. "I would hate to be thought of as just one of the guys."

He stared at them.

"Okay, I did have them specially made."

Wolf started laughing.

"You think this is funny?" Bruce asked, doing his best to keep a straight face.

"Yes."

Bruce carefully handed Grace the kitten. "Hold Francis for a minute."

"He's my cousin."

"It's a Navy and Air Force thing," Bruce replied.

"Oh."

Bruce stepped back, and with an abrupt move caught Wolf in a headlock. "Where's the baby bottle?"

Grace laughed and reached for the camera instead.

"Come on, guys, let's get out of here," Jill said. "This deployment is over."

Bruce took Grace to the beach after dinner. All the letters, phone calls, and pictures in the world would never make up for this.

He'd missed her face, her smile, the sound of her laugh.

She tilted her head and smiled, aware of the inspection. "What?"

"Just enjoying the scenery."

She dropped her eyes but her smile blossomed. He rubbed his thumb across the back of her hand. "This deployment was rough."

"We survived it."

"Can you handle more of them?"

Her hand tightened on his.

He'd been waiting months to ask her, and the timing would get no better than the present. He stopped and settled his arms around her. "Will you marry me?"

She didn't answer. He rested his chin against her hair.

"Yes." Her voice had choked.

"I love you, Grace. I've been thinking about you ever since Ecuador."

"A dog, a house, a wife. It was a good list."

"I wondered if those two words made the letter."

She leaned back. "They did."

"So what do you want to add to that list?"

"We'll start with a kitten. And a long honeymoon."

"I like that second suggestion." Emily barked and Bruce smiled. "And the duchess approves of the plan. When?"

Grace laughed. "Soon."

From the top of the steps to the beach someone whistled. Wolf stood there with Jill. He gave a salute.

"Grace, I was meaning to ask you," Bruce commented as Wolf and Jill headed down the beach toward them. "Wolf had this suggestion of a double wedding...."

Dear Reader,

Thank you for reading this book. The military is a demanding world that forges wonderful heroes: friendships go deep, loyalties are strong, jobs are tough, families are close. I couldn't ask for a better background for a love story. I hope I was able to take you into Bruce's and Gracie's lives to show what it is like to take on one of the toughest jobs in the world.

I wrote this book to remind us our God is sufficient no matter what the circumstances. Relationships matter—the military teaches it like no other profession. And in Bruce and Gracie I got to explore a love story unlike any other I have written.

There are real men like Bruce "Striker" Stanton wearing the uniform today. This is my tribute and thanks to them. They are indeed heroes.

As always, I love to hear from my readers. Feel free to write me at:

Dee Henderson

c/o Multnomah Fiction

P.O. Box 1720

Sisters, Oregon 97759

E-mail: dee@deehenderson.com

Stop by on-line at: http://www.deehenderson.com

Thanks again for letting me share Bruce and Gracie's story.

Sincerely,

Multnomah Publishers

The publisher and author would love to hear your comments about this book. *Please contact us at:*

www.multnomah.net/deehenderson

TRUE DEVOTION

Uncommon Heroes Series, Book One, *by Dee Henderson*

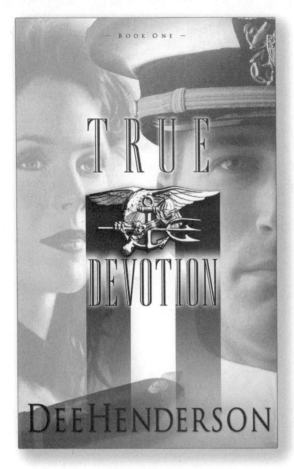

Kelly Jacobs has already paid the ultimate price of loving a warrior: She has the folded flag and the grateful thanks of a nation to prove it. Navy SEAL Joe "Bear" Baker can't ask her to accept that risk again—even though he loves her. But the man responsible for her husband's death is back, closer than either of them realize. Kelly's in danger, and Joe may not get there in time....

ISBN 1-57673-886-8

True Devotion

Kelly slipped her hand into Joe's as they strolled down to the water's edge then turned north to follow the beach toward the Hotel del Coronado where their evening had begun. Music from the Ocean Terrace restaurant at the hotel drifted toward them, the colorful lanterns lit around the Terrace reflecting on the water. It was a festive mood.

"One of the last memories I had in the water before you rescued me was from the last time we walked this beach."

"Really?"

She nodded. "Friday night after dinner. You indulged me with a walk down to the Terrace to buy a frozen fruit smoothy. Remember?"

"I remember the smoothy—it gave me an ice cream headache."

"I had forgotten that."

"I haven't."

"What I remember is holding your hand while we walked, deciding how nice it was not to be walking alone."

He squeezed her hand gently. "Thank you. You're welcome to hold my hand anytime you like."

Kelly returned the pressure, communicating without words her pleasure, and they walked in silence along the shore. This was the best memory maker of the evening. The restaurant, the movie, roses, and the bear—of all the images of the evening, this was the one she treasured most. She had walked this beach with Joe before, but this time it was different. This time in a new way she belonged beside him and it felt that way: special.

The evening was going to end eventually, and she didn't want that to happen. Would he kiss her good night? There were already stars in her eyes; that would certainly cap this evening with the best ending possible.

The moonlight flickered as clouds skimmed over the sky.

Joe stopped.

She looked at him, puzzled, and saw his eyes narrow as he gazed ahead.

There was only the dark shadow of the surf and the resulting white breakers. The sound clued her in, an odd interruption in the withdrawing surf as it pulled back to sea.

They both began to run.

A limp body was rolling in the surf, being thrown by the sea to the shore.

THE O'MALLEY SERIES

The Negotiator—**Book One:** FBI agent Dave Richman from *Danger in the Shadows* is back. He's about to meet Kate O'Malley, and his life will never be the same. She's a hostage negotiator. He protects people. Dave's about to find out that falling in love with a hostage negotiator is one thing, but keeping her safe is another!

ISBN 1-57673-819-1

The Guardian—**Book Two:** A federal judge has been murdered. There is only one witness. And an assassin wants her dead. U.S. Marshal Marcus O'Malley thought he knew the risks of the assignment...he was wrong.

ISBN 1-57673-642-3

The Truth Seeker—**Book Three:** Women are turning up dead. Lisa O'Malley is a forensic pathologist and mysteries are her domain. When she's investigating a crime it means trouble is soon to follow. U.S. Marshal Quinn Diamond has found loving her is easier than keeping her out of danger. Lisa's found the killer, and now she's missing too....

ISBN 1-57673-753-5

The Protector—**Book Four:** Jack O'Malley is a fireman. He's fearless when it comes to facing an inferno. But when an arsonist begins targeting his district, his shift, his friends, Jack faces the ultimate challenge: protecting the lady who saw the arsonist before she pays an even higher price....

ISBN 1-57673-846-9

"Dee Henderson is an extraordinary author whose writing connects with your heart and soul. The O'Malley series is a classic meant for your 'keeper' shelf."

—The Belles and Beaux of Romance

The Negotiator

Dave waited until Kate's brother Stephen disappeared up the stairs. "Why didn't you tell me yesterday? Trust me?"

"Tell you what? That I might have someone in my past who may be a murderer?" Kate swung away from him into the living room. "I've never even met this guy. Until twenty-four hours ago, I didn't even have a suspicion that he existed."

"Kate, he's targeting you."

"Then let him find me."

"You don't mean that."

"There is no reason for him to have blown up a plane just to get at me, to get at some banker. We're never going to know the truth unless someone can grab him. And if he gets cornered by a bunch of cops, he'll either kill himself or be killed in a shoot-out. It would be easier all around if he did come after me."

"Stop thinking with your emotions and use your head," Dave shot back. "What we need to do is to solve this case. That's how we'll find out the answers and ultimately find him."

"Then you go tear through the piles of data. I don't want to have anything to do with it. Don't you understand that? I don't want to be the one who puts the pieces together. Yesterday was like getting stuck in the gut with a hot poker."

He understood it, could feel the pain flowing from her. "Fine. Stay here for a day, get your feet back under you. Then get back in the game and stop acting like you're the only one this is hurting. Or have you forgotten all the people who died?" He saw the sharp pain flash in her eyes before they went cold and regretted his words.

"That was a low blow and you know it."

"Kate."

"I can't offer anything to the investigation; don't you understand that? I don't know anything. I don't know him."

"Well, he knows you. And if you walk away from this now, you're going to feel like a coward. Just what are you so afraid of?"

He could see it in her, a fear so deep it shimmered in her eyes and pooled them black, and he remembered his coworker's comment that he probably didn't want to read the court record. His eyes narrowed and his voice softened. "Are you sure you don't remember this guy?"

She broke eye contact, and it felt like a blow because he knew that at this moment he was the one hurting her. "If you need to get away for twenty-four hours, do it. Just don't run because you're afraid. You'll never forgive yourself."

"Marcus wouldn't let me go check out the data because he was afraid I would kill the guy if I found him."

Her words rocked him back on his heels. "What?" He closed the distance between them, and for the first time since this morning began, actually felt something like relief. He rested his hands calmly on her shoulders. "No you wouldn't. You're too good a cop."

She blinked.

"I almost died with you, remember?" He smiled. "I've seen you under pressure." His thumb rubbed along her jaw. "Come on, Kate. Come back with me to the house, and let's get back to work. The media wouldn't get near you, I promise."

Marcus and Stephen came back down the stairs, but Kate didn't look around; she just kept studying Dave. She finally turned and looked at her brother. "Marcus, I'm going back to Dave's."

Dave gave in to a small surge of relief. It was a start. Tenuous. And risky. But a start, all the same.

The Guardian

It was a good night for a sniper, Marcus realized as he checked with the men securing the perimeter of the church property. They were running behind schedule and Marcus could feel the danger of that. Twilight was descending. In the dusk settling in the open areas around the church across the clusters of towering oak trees, the shadows themselves spoke of hidden dangers.

It was time to move.

Marcus raised Luke on the security net. "I'm changing the travel plans. We're going to take the family out the back entrance. Cue us up to leave in five minutes."

"Roger."

He reentered the church.

Marcus had been too occupied during the last hour to really look at Shari, an unfortunate reality that went with the job. It was everyone else who was the threat. He looked now and what he saw concerned him. She was folding; he could see it in the glazed expression, the lack of color in her face, the betraying fact her brother had noticed and now had his hand under her arm.

Definitely time to leave.

Marcus moved to join them and relieve Craig.

Shari saw him coming and broke off her conversation to join him. "Marcus, could—"

The window behind her exploded.

Shari heard someone gasp in pain and the next second Marcus swept out his left arm, caught her across the front of her chest at her collarbone, and took her feet right out from under her.

She felt herself falling backward and it was a petrifying sensation. She couldn't get her hands back in time to break her fall and she hit hard, slamming against the floor, her back and neck taking the brunt of the impact. His arm had her pinned to the ground, his hand gripping her shoulder. He wasn't letting her move even if she could.

"Shari—"

She couldn't respond; her head was ringing so badly.

That had been a bullet.

She wheezed at that realization, her lungs feeling like they would explode. Around her, people were screaming.

Another window shattered.

Marcus forcibly pulled her across the floor with him out of the way. "South. Shooter to the south!"

She could hear him hollering on the security net, and it was like listening down a tunnel. Who was bleeding? Someone was bleeding; she could see it on his hand.

It was coming home to her now, very much home. Someone was trying to kill her…again.

The Truth Seeker

Lisa O'Malley was sitting on the side step of the fire engine, silent, one tennis shoe off as she'd stepped on a hot ember and burned the sole, her stockinged foot moving slowly back and forth in the soot-blackened water rushing down the street toward the nearest storm drain. Her gaze never leaving the dying fire. Her brother Stephen had wrapped a fire coat around her, and she had it gripped with both hands, pulled tight.

Quinn Diamond kept a close watch on her as he stood leaning against the driver's door of a squad car, waiting for a callback from the dispatcher. She was alone in her grief, her emotions hidden, her eyes dry. She'd lost what she'd valued, and Quinn hated to realize how much it had to resonate with her past.

Kate sat down beside her.

Quinn watched as the two sisters sat in silence, and he prayed for Kate, that she would have the right words to say.

Instead, she remained silent.

And Lisa leaned her head against Kate's shoulder and continued to watch the fire burn, the silence unbroken.

Friends. Deep, lifelong friends.

Quinn had to turn away from the sight. He had so much emotion inside it was going to rupture into tears or fury.

He found himself facing a grim Marcus O'Malley.

"Quinn, get her out of here."

"Stephen has already tried; she won't budge."

"No. I mean out of here. Out of town," Marcus replied grimly. "The killer goes from notes and phone calls to fire. He's not going to stop there."

Marcus was right. Lisa had to come first. "The ranch. She's going to need the space."

"Thank you."

"I'll keep her safe, now that it's too late."

"Quinn—we'll find him."

That wasn't even in question. He was going to hunt the guy down and rip out his heart.

"I highly recommend this book to anyone who likes suspense."

Don't miss the prequel to the O'Malley series!

Sara's terrified. She's doing the one thing she cannot afford to do: fall in love with former pro football player Adam Black, a man everyone knows. Sara's been hidden away in the witness protection program, her safety dependent on being invisible—and loving Adam could get her killed.

ISBN 1-57673-577-X

Danger in the Shadows

The summer storm lit up the night sky in a jagged display of energy, lightning bouncing, streaking, fragmenting between towering thunderheads. Sara Walsh ignored the storm as best she could, determined not to let it interrupt her train of thought. The desk lamp as well as the overhead light were on in her office as she tried to prevent any shadows from forming. What she was writing was disturbing enough.

The six-year-old boy had been found. Dead.

Despite the dark specificity of the scene, the flow of words never faltered. The child had died within hours of his abduction. His family, the Oklahoma law enforcement community, even his kidnapper, didn't realize it. Sara did not pull back from writing the scene even though she knew it would leave a bitter taste of defeat in the mind of the reader. The impact was necessary for the rest of the book.

Thunder cracked directly overhead. Sara flinched. Her office suite on the thirty-fourth floor put her close enough to the storm she could hear the air sizzle in the split second before the boom. She would like to be in the basement parking garage right now instead of her office.

She had been writing since eight that morning. A glance at the clock on her desk showed it was almost eight in the evening. The push to finish a story always took over as she reached the final chapters. This tenth book was no exception.

Twelve hours. No wonder her back muscles were stiff. She arched her back and rubbed at the knot.

This was the most difficult chapter in the book to write. It was better to get it done in one long, sustained effort. Death always squeezed her heart.

Had Dave been in town, he would have insisted she wrap it up and come home. Her life was restricted enough as it was. Her brother refused to let her spend all her time at the office. He would come lean against the doorjamb of her office and give her that look along with his predictable lecture telling her all she should be doing: Puttering around the house, cooking, messing with the roses, something other than sitting behind that desk.

Sara smiled. She did so enjoy taking advantage of Dave's occasional absences.

His flight back to Chicago from the FBI academy at Quantico had been delayed due to the storm front. When he had called her from the airport, he had cautioned her he might not be home until eleven.

It wasn't a problem, she had assured him, everything was fine. Code words. Spoken every day. So much a part of their language now that she spoke them instinctively. "Everything is fine"—all clear; "I'm fine"—I've got company; "I'm doing fine"—I'm in danger. She had lived the dance a long time. The tight security around her life was necessary. It was overpowering, obnoxious, annoying… and comforting.

With every book, another fact, another detail, another intense emotion broke through from her own past. She could literally feel the dry dirt under her hand, feel the oppressive darkness. Reliving what had happened to her twenty-five years ago was terrifying. Necessary, but terrifying.

She sat lost in thought for several minutes, idly walking her pen through her fingers. Her adversary was out there somewhere, still alive, still hunting her. Had he made the association to Chicago yet? After all these years, she was still constantly moving, still working to stay one step ahead of the threat. Her family knew only too well his threat was real.

The man would kill her. Had long ago killed her sister. The threat didn't get more basic than that. She had to trust others and ultimately God for her security. There were days her faith wavered under the intense weight of simply enduring that stress. She was learning, slowly, by necessity, how to roll with events, to trust God's ultimate sovereignty.

The notepad beside her was filled with doodled sketches of faces. One of these days her mind was finally going to stop blocking the one image she longed to sketch. She knew she had seen the man. Whatever the cost, whatever the consequences of trying to remember, they were worth paying in order to try to bring justice for her and her sister.

Sara let out a frustrated sigh. She couldn't force the image to appear no matter how much she longed to do so. She was the only one who still believed it was possible for her to remember it. The police, the FBI, the doctors had given up hope years ago.

She fingered a worn photo of her sister Kim that sat by a white rose on her desk. She didn't care what the others thought. Until the killer was caught, she would never give up hope.

God was just. She held on to that knowledge and the hope that the day of justice would eventually arrive. Until it did, she carried a guilt inside that remained wrapped around her heart. In losing her twin she had literally lost part of herself.

Turning her attention back to her desk, she debated for a moment if she wanted to do any more work that night. She didn't.

As she put her folder away, the framed picture on the corner of her desk caught her attention; it evoked a smile. Her best friend was getting married. Sara was happy for her, but also envious. The need to break free of the security blanket rose and fell with time. She could feel the sense of rebellion rising again. Ellen had freedom and a life. She was getting married to a wonderful man. Sara longed to one day have that same choice. Without freedom, it wasn't possible, and that reality hurt. A dream was being sacrificed with every passing day.

As she stepped into the outer office, the room lights automatically turned on. Sara reached back and turned off the interior office lights.

Her suite was in the east tower of the business complex. Rising forty-five stories, the two recently built towers added to the already impressive downtown skyline. She struggled with the elevator ride to the thirty-fourth floor each day, for she did not like closed-in spaces, but she considered the view worth the price.

The elevator that responded tonight came from two floors below. There were two connecting walkways between the east and west towers, one on the sixth floor and another in the lobby. She chose the sixth floor concourse tonight, walking through it to the west tower with a confident but fast pace.

She was alone in the wide corridor. Travis sometimes accompanied her, but she had waved off his company tonight and told him to go get dinner. If she needed him, she would page him.

The click of her heels echoed off the marble floor. There was parking under each tower, but if she parked under the tower where she worked, she would be forced to pull out onto a one-way street no matter which exit she took. It was a pattern someone could observe and predict. Changing her route and time of day across one of the two corridors was a better compromise. She could hopefully see the danger coming.

Sara decided to take the elevator down to the west tower parking garage rather than walk the six flights. She would have preferred the stairs, but she could grit her teeth for a few flights to save time. She pushed the button to go down and watched the four elevators to see which would respond first. The one to her left, coming down from the tenth floor.

When it stopped, she reached inside, pushed the garage-floor parking button, but did not step inside. Tonight she would take the second elevator.

Sara shifted her raincoat over her arm and moved her briefcase to her other hand. The elevator stopped and the doors slid open.

A man was in the elevator.

She froze.

He was leaning against the back of the elevator, looking like he had put in a long day at work, a briefcase in one hand and a sports magazine in the other, his blue eyes gazing back at her. She saw a brief look of admiration in his eyes.

Get in and take a risk, step back and take a risk.

She knew him. Adam Black. His face was as familiar as any sports figure in the country, even if he'd been out of the game of football for three years. His commercial endorsements and charity work had continued without pause.

Adam Black worked in this building? This was a nightmare come true. She saw photographs of him constantly in magazines, local newspapers, and occasionally on television. The last thing she needed was to be near someone who attracted media attention.

She hesitated, then stepped in, her hand tightening her hold on the briefcase handle. A glance at the board of lights showed he had already selected the parking garage.

"Working late tonight?" His voice was low, a trace of a north-eastern accent still present, his smile a pleasant one.

Her answer was a noncommital nod.

The elevator began to silently descend.

She had spent too much time in European finishing schools to slouch. Her posture was straight, her spine relaxed, even if she was nervous. She hated elevators. She should have taken the stairs.

"Quite a storm out there tonight."

The heels of her patent leather shoes sank into the jade carpet as she shifted her weight from one foot to the other. "Yes."

Three more floors to go.

There was a slight flicker to the lights and then the elevator jolted to a halt.

"What?" Sara felt adrenaline flicker in her system like the lights.

He pushed away from the back wall. "A lightning hit must have blown a circuit."

The next second, the elevator went black.